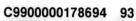

RACHEL

Also by Renée Huggett

Sarah

RACHEL

Renée Huggett

Hodder & Stoughton
LONDON SYDNEY AUCKLAND

First published in Great Britain by
Hodder & Stoughton Ltd 1994

10 9 8 7 6 5 4 3 2 1

British Library Cataloguing in Publication Data

Huggett, Renée
Rachel
I. Title
823.914 [F]

ISBN 0-340-59249-4

Typeset by Keyboard Services, Luton

Printed and bound in Great Britain by
Mackays of Chatham PLC, Chatham, Kent

Published by Hodder and Stoughton Ltd
a division of Hodder Headline PLC
338 Euston Road
London NW1 3BH

ACKNOWLEDGMENT

I would like to thank Julian Luke, Librarian of Minehead Library, and his staff for the generous help they have given me in my research and for their unfailing courtesy.

Chapter 1

The explosion occurred at eleven o'clock on 15 November 1869. It began as a distant rumbling, followed by the violent crash of falling masonry and broken glass. As its thunder echoed across the desert, huge flames shot into the sky and the whole port momentarily appeared to be enveloped in fire; the waters of the Mediterranean seemed to cascade waves of blood.

Charles Cavendish rushed to the open windows of his office in the centre of Port Said. Looking towards the harbour he could see a huge pall of smoke and flames rising to the sky. Another explosion was followed by a series of smaller ones, as though the whole town were being demolished.

He dashed from his office and along the corridor to the stairs. Other bank officials were running down before him, they all turned into the sandy road and hurried towards the blazing harbour.

'What else can happen?' a colleague gasped breathlessly to Charles. 'That Canal's never going to be opened.'

Charles grinned. 'Don't worry. Isma'il won't let anything stop it. He thinks his whole reputation rests on it.'

Crowds of fellahin, walking or on donkeys, chattering and gesticulating hysterically, mingled with the foreigners as they made their way towards the harbour. None of the new European buildings in the business quarter or the modern developments being carried out by the Egyptian government had been damaged, but as they approached the fire they came upon the ruins of old houses and bazaars nearer the water which had crumbled in the blast. Then word spread through the crowd that the fireworks dump had blown up.

As Charles approached, he could see a mass of long-robed fellahin carrying buckets of water from the sea to cast on to the flames. He

1

shuddered, imagining the fate of those who would be held responsible for the disaster. Then he looked further up the coast towards the three pavilions; fortunately, and incredibly, they appeared to have survived. The gold-painted structures glittered in the morning sun and he could see labourers hanging the final brightly-coloured draperies, armed guards standing over them.

At least, the escape of these new buildings, which had been constructed for the great ceremonial opening of the Canal, might limit Isma'il's wrath; more gunpowder could always be brought in for the fireworks display. Not a disaster, after all; more or less a normal event in Egyptian terms.

Charles thought of the lines of forced labourers who had been ranged for years along the Canal banks. In the decade it had taken to build the Canal, the death toll from typhoid and dysentery had been catastrophic, making it ever more difficult for Isma'il to recruit workers for the project. It was a miracle the Canal had ever been completed.

He watched the robed figures struggling backwards and forwards up the beach, swaying precariously under the weight of the water-filled buckets. Their dark eyes stared out from lined, brown faces; Charles could not decide whether it was rebellion that smouldered there or simply the agony of survival. Even in November, the sun shone relentlessly over Egypt, but their guards had no patience with malingerers, waving the kharboush over them menacingly.

Charles had forgotten to pick up his hat when he left the office and even at this time of the year, the sun was beating down on him as they watched another group of fellahin trying to put out the burning houses near the dump. He turned away. The sand was warm even through his leather soles as he walked back down the streets, passing the handsome, blue-robed women with their naked children, and white turbanned men hurrying into the bazaars. Occasionally a fat pasha drove past in his barouche, leaning back ostentatiously on his velvet cushions.

Charles was struck again by the incongruity of the mud houses lining the narrow streets, contrasted with the new villas and houses which had been built by the Europeans and wealthy Arabs on the outskirts of the town. Yet in spite of the drabness of the labourers' existence there was a certain flamboyance surrounding their lives –

2

the vivid red, yellows and orange of clothes, flowers, flags, bunting, the waving green of palm trees, the glistening bronze skin of the children, the blue waters of the Mediterranean lapping up the muddy beach.

When his bank in England had offered him the opportunity of working in Egypt six years earlier, Charles had been hesitant. The increase in salary had been attractive but he knew nothing about Egypt beyond the frequent newspaper reports he read about explorers like Speke and Baker and Burton. Apart from that, he had had the standard English picture of missionaries being eaten by cannibals, harems on the corner of every street, a sub-human race of brown-skinned people, corrupt and ignorant.

To a certain extent, he reflected, it was true – the corruption and exploitation were endemic. Yet when Charles stepped from the ship in Alexandria and saw the new buildings and noted the growing number of European businessmen, he realised that Egypt was no longer a barren desert. For one thing, it was benefiting from the cotton boom, occasioned by the American Civil War. The cotton mills of Lancashire could obtain no raw cotton from the Americas and Egypt had seized its opportunity. Their production of cotton had quadrupled. It was one of the reasons why his own bank had been formed by forward-looking businessmen, who could see the potential for supplying credit to such an expanding economy.

When Charles reached Cairo, Isma'il had just taken over as the head of state – Pasha as he was called – on the death of his uncle, Mohammed Said. Now he had manipulated the Turks into allowing him the title of khedive, or viceroy. To the Europeans, Isma'il was Egypt. Cruel and ruthless he might be, beneath his charm, but he was no ignorant Arab. He was committed to changing Egypt into a modern, prosperous State, intent on playing the Europeans at their own game and, for the moment, appeared to hold the trump cards. He would lose in the end, his dreams were too extravagant, but while it lasted, good luck to him, Charles thought.

As he stepped into the cooler air of the bank – it was never really cool even inside – he was greeted anxiously by Jackson, his deputy.

'There's been a telegraph.'

'From Isma'il Pasha?' Charles interposed, smiling.

The man nodded. 'This disaster. He must have instant credit.'

'How much?'

'Only five million, he says.'

'What's wrong with the French?'

'They want eight per cent.'

'Seems reasonable.'

The official hesitated. 'As you know, he resents their influence. He'd rather pay us a higher percentage with no strings attached.'

Charles frowned. Although these loans were supposed to be guaranteed by the Egyptian government, it was never clear to what extent they were actually intended for Isma'il himself. Isma'il's loan capital was vast; his debts seemed to be increasing by the hour. If he went, would the government honour the debts? Currently, of course, there seemed to be no likelihood of his departure.

'Ten per cent.'

'What period?'

'Just add it to the last loan.'

Jackson looked doubtful.

'It's all right,' Charles said. 'There's still plenty of potential in Egypt. Give him a chance.' Then he added, 'Telegraph London. Tell them my recommendation.'

Charles went to his room, put on his white jacket and left the deserted offices. Everyone had gone to see the explosion. The flames from the dump were now shooting up only intermittently. He walked in the opposite direction, away from the centre towards the new European-style villas on the edge of the port.

Ursula greeted him cheerfully as he strolled up the garden path. He put an arm round her shoulders, running a hand through her short, curly auburn hair. She had had it cut when she came to Egypt, something she would never have contemplated in England.

'You look nice,' he said, glancing at her light blue cotton dress.

'Well, I did get it in the bazaar. Do you find it acceptable?'

'It is in this climate,' Charles said, smiling. 'But what would they say in England?'

'Naturally, I wouldn't wear it in England. What on earth was that explosion?'

'Only the fireworks display gone up in smoke.'

'Oh, no! What will he do?' Ursula always spoke of Isma'il as 'he'.

4

There was, after all, no one else. They walked into the house.

'Oh, he's just taking out another loan. Where's Rachel?'

'Fatima's taken her to the bazaar. They should be back soon.'

Charles walked on through the house to the nursery. Charlotte was sitting on a rug playing with a doll, sent by her grandmother from England.

'Hallo, Charlotte.' The child laughed and kissed him and Charles picked her up in his arms and carried her into the dining-room.

'What have you been doing this morning?'

'We went out in the barouche and mama bought a necklace.'

Ursula poured him a glass of Marsala. 'Yes, from that old scoundrel, Nazim. Took me half an hour to knock him down to 2,000 piasters.' She picked up a carved ivory box from the sideboard. 'Look.'

Charles examined the gold necklace, an ornately coiled rope with a snake's-head pendant. He smiled. 'It's similar to the one you bought last week.'

'Oh, it's not,' Ursula protested, laughing. 'The design is quite different.'

'Oh, well, as long as you like it.'

Charles looked at her affectionately. He often wondered how he could have hesitated about marrying her. His parents were both dead before he reached his teens and he had been brought up in Devon by an aunt and uncle. They had been remote and formal, virtually treating him as a temporary guest. At school he had formed no deep relationships, and when his uncle had found him a position in a London bank, Charles knew that his relatives felt their responsibilities towards him were over.

In London, he had lived a solitary bachelor existence, enlivened only by an interest in music. He had first been introduced to Ursula at a concert, by a bank colleague. He was instantly captivated by her vivacious, warm personality, her laughing grey eyes and her coils of auburn hair. Through the auspices of the bank colleague, he had obtained permission to call on her and eventually to take her alone to other concerts. Ursula had not overtly encouraged his advances; he would not have expected her to. Equally, he had sensed that his presence was more eagerly sought than that of her other suitors. He fell in love.

Then Charles had hesitated. It was the first real relationship he had ever had and, suddenly, he had doubted his ability to cope with intimacy. Women, to Charles, were distant horizons, something seen through a telescope, forever remote and unapproachable. Prior to meeting Ursula, he had never been with a woman, had scarcely been in the presence of one, in any personal sense. To his own surprise, Charles had found himself discussing his feelings and even his doubts with Ursula – although he imagined that this was not quite the correct thing to do.

Ursula had understood it all. It was she who had said, 'Let's get married. I am sure we would be happy together.'

Charles had been shocked and bewildered at her forthrightness. He knew that the pattern for proposals was first to make a diffident and humble approach to the father, to state one's intentions and to establish the size of one's bank balance and future prospects. He feared that because he had spoken to Ursula before receiving permission from her father, she had misinterpreted his diffidence as some kind of indifference to the demands of social correctness, a kind of rebellion. At the time, he had felt flattered by the thought. However, he knew that it was not revolutionary ideas about women or society that had made him act as he had done. The loneliness of his childhood and youth and his solitary life in London had made him uncommitted to any religious or social mores. Even now, Charles still felt a certain remoteness from his fellow-men which, in his professional life at least, was interpreted as silent confidence.

Ursula had liberated him, changed his life. She might be amusing and vivacious in company, on occasion even provocative, but she had also proved to be a competent and supportive wife. It was only in the privacy of their home that she expounded her more controversial views about topics such as equality for women and the iniquitous British exploitation of the lower races. Charles felt that she was doing this more for his entertainment than from belief.

Rachel bounced in as Audi was serving the lunch.

'Come on, Rachel. You nearly missed it,' Charlotte said.

'We were watching the fire,' Rachel laughed. 'Fatima said it was brighter than the lightning.' She sat down beside Charles.

'You'll see a better display on Wednesday,' he said. 'Great

fireworks in the sky. And ships and boats going up the Canal.'

'And we'll be on one, won't we?'

'If they don't sink,' Ursula laughed.

'Will they, Papa?' Rachel looked anxious.

'No, dear. I'll see they don't. Now, let's eat our lunch and then you and Charlotte can go to the park with Fatima.'

'Mama, can I have my hair cut like yours?'

Charles looked at Rachel thoughtfully. She had the same grey eyes and curly auburn hair as Ursula and the same ebullient personality. Ursula must have looked just like her when she was nine years old.

'It's so hot, having it long.'

'Yes,' Ursula said. 'It is. Perhaps we'll have it cut for the celebrations.'

Charles felt a momentary pang of doubt. Was it suitable for Ursula to have the child's hair cut? In Kingsbridge, he remembered as a boy, only the urchins had been treated in such a fashion. Was it suitable, come to that, that Ursula should have cut her own long, auburn hair until it was almost as short as a man's? It was sensible, she said, and yet none of the other English wives had done so. He frowned. Somehow this fact seemed to carry more significance than the act itself.

When Fatima took the children off to play in the park, Charles removed his jacket.

'Are you going out this afternoon?'

'Well, not just yet.'

Ursula looked at him. 'Are you going back to the bank?'

Charles smiled. 'Not just yet.'

He took her hand and led her into the bedroom. She made no protest. The blinds were drawn; it was almost cool in there. He smiled, feeling as he always did a sense of satisfaction that his wishes could be fulfilled so simply. He knew that Ursula could not feel as he did, for women had little interest in the intimacies of married life.

When they had first married, Charles had secretly looked through the volumes of advice she had been given by female relatives – to a large extent because he was desirous of absorbing that advice himself. They were all phrased in general terms, as was suitable for the female mind, concentrating on the behaviour required of nice young women towards their husbands: tolerance, obedience, passivity. This was a concept with which Charles was familiar enough but, uncertain even of the precise qualities of the female form, reading it had given him confidence.

It was clear that women were biologically different, lacking the desires and urges of men, yet Ursula had never seemed to find his embraces unwelcome. In fact, after they came to Egypt she had become, sometimes bewilderingly, responsive. Charles attributed this to the hot climate and the fact that they were no longer within the confines of English conventions.

'What would I do without you, Ursula?' he said as they lay beneath the sheets.

'Why should you do anything? I'm here.'

'Yes. I know.'

'I don't know what we'd do in England, though. Can you imagine going back?'

'No,' he admitted. 'Life there certainly seems less colourful.'

'Well, we don't have to go back for a couple of years. If it weren't for my parents, I don't think I'd wish to return at all.'

'You won't have seen them for four years. They must be looking forward to seeing you. And they're getting on, you know.'

'Yes. If only they would come out here.'

'Well, they're not likely to do that. They've heard too many tales of horror from the other English.'

Ursula laughed. 'Mother's always asking me if the servants are to be trusted. And do the natives all carry swords?'

Charles took a clean shirt and trousers from the wardrobe. 'I must get back. Don't forget we're going to the dinner tonight and the show afterwards.'

Charles knew that Ursula loved the displays of stylised dancing performed by the Ghawazi, and she would often stand in the bedroom trying to imitate their raised arms and the delicate positioning of their fingers.

Charles walked back through the streets in the afternoon sun. The buildings cast dark shadows across the sand; there was the usual afternoon air of desertion. He would be glad to get back to head office on Thursday. They were only here because of the Canal opening and Port Said lacked the beauty and interest of the capital. Admittedly, this villa was probably better than the one they lived in in Cairo, because it was newer and more modern, but he liked the large house which was their permanent home.

In return for Charles's efforts with the bank on his behalf, Isma'il had presented the villa in Port Said to Charles 'for his perpetual use'. Isma'il might be a rogue, but he was as generous as he was grasping. Ironically, part of what Isma'il borrowed from the bank was frequently returned to Charles, who was its source, in gifts.

The other bank employees were beginning to wend their way back to their offices. A number of them were English; the remainder were Greeks, Armenians, Prussians, a couple of Frenchmen. Even that was a pleasure to Charles; he felt more at ease with the casual attitudes of the foreigners than with his own colleagues.

He asked for the Egyptian government ledgers to be brought and contemplated them thoughtfully. A loan in 1864 of £3,500,000 issued at 92. Interest eight per cent for fifteen years. Another one in 1867 for £2,500,000 – the borrower Da'ira Sanieh, Isma'il's personal estates. £2,000,000 at seven per cent for twenty-five years. Another one this year for £8,000,000 – the borrower once again Da'ira, interest seven per cent at 80, period thirty years. Charles reflected on his bank's position. The terms for repayment were gradually increasing; but by the time they fell due, Isma'il knew he would probably be gone, it wouldn't be his problem. He had vast estates and had achieved his acquisitions by maintaining the mystery of what funds were attributable to his personal credit, and what were the debt of the Egyptian government. There was an even further doubt about whether, as the head of a subject State, he was permitted to contract debts at all, without the permission of the Ottoman authorities.

Charles shrugged. At the moment, Isma'il was safe enough. The Europeans had invested too much in him to make life difficult.

The following day, Jackson came into Charles's office with the news that a ship had become stuck at the other end of the Canal. 'Evidently it's embedded, broadside on across the entrance to the Canal. Nothing will move it.'

Charles shook his head in disbelief. 'But how did it get there? What was it doing? Sightseeing? The French will be going mad.'

'They'll probably suspect the English of sabotage. Trying to foil their great achievement.'

Charles smiled. 'Well, with their technical skill, they should be able to think of some solution.'

Rumours poured in during the day that the ship was being dismantled, that it would be taken apart piece by piece, that thousands of fellahin were trying to move it with ropes. Then news came that de Lesseps had rushed to the scene. He surveyed the situation, ordered gunpowder and the ship was unceremoniously blown up.

Charles sighed with relief. He knew that the English had never supported the Canal project, suspicious as ever of the expansion of the French into Egyptian affairs. Yet now that it was almost completed, the British government was quietly assessing how it could benefit from the event.

He left the office early. Yet as he walked up the garden path Charles still felt a sense of unease. In return for his support, Isma'il had given him not only the houses in Port Said and Cairo; he had also transferred sums of money to Charles's personal accounts. It was all pretty normal procedure and a number of the senior officials of other banks benefited in the same way. To Isma'il, it was as natural as night following day. To the Greeks, the Poles, even the French, it was standard business practice. Still, Charles could never remove the nagging doubts. Isma'il had even made presents of jewellery and furnishings to Ursula. She accepted them as perfectly normal, but he never discussed bank matters with her and he wondered whether she understood the implications. What were the implications? If his bank knew, they would probably be quite happy about it. After all, he was bringing them enormous business, millions of pounds in potential profit.

The next morning, when Rachel danced into the room, Charles put all doubts and anxieties out of his mind. 'Come, Papa. We have to go.'

'Rachel,' Ursula said sleepily, 'it's too early. Go and play until we're ready.'

'I have to get dressed,' the child persisted.

'Yes. But not yet.'

Fatima came and took the child's hand, saying, 'Come, Rachel. Let's go and play until Mama and Papa are ready.'

Through the windows they could hear the babble of voices, drivers shouting to make way for their barouches, donkeys clopping along the road, horns blowing and, in the distance, a ship's siren.

'Sounds as though they've started already.'

'Oh, he's just making it seem as though the whole of Egypt is celebrating,' Ursula said.

'One day they probably will. Think how it will increase their trade. They'll have control of the shortest sea-route to India.'

That day, Ursula dressed formally for the Canal opening. She wore a violet-coloured silk and lace gown, sent from England, with wide, pear-shaped frills and a bustle at the back with gold silk underskirts. A wide ribbon on her hair hung down at the back and she carried a parasol.

Then she looked at her new white kid boots, snug around her calves. 'I can't wear these,' she said. 'I shall die of heat.' She pulled them off and snatched up her gold sandals. 'These look better, in any case.'

Charles wore a long black jacket, a stiff white shirt and grey trousers.

Ateibi, one of the servants, was to take a valise down to the port so that, when they embarked, they could make a change of clothing.

Then Rachel appeared in a white silk dress, gold combs in her now short curly hair. She twirled round to show them her dress, her eyes sparkling with excitement.

'Now,' Ursula said. 'You must be very good today. Remember, there are very few children permitted to attend. It's only thanks to Papa's good offices.'

'I know how to behave,' Rachel said primly. 'Fatima has taught me how to bow and curtsey.'

'Well, I don't know if that will be necessary,' Ursula laughed. 'Now, let's take Charlotte along to Mrs Montgomery's.' As the celebrations were to last for three or four days, it had been arranged that four-year-old Charlotte should stay in Port Said with Mrs Montgomery who was to look after other English children. She was the widowed mother of one of the bank officials and she took it as her

11

duty to ensure that English standards of propriety and behaviour were maintained in this alien culture.

Her front door was opened by a fellahin, followed by three or four young children who greeted Charlotte eagerly. She forgot her petulance at not being allowed to accompany her mother and father and disappeared with them along the hall. Mrs Montgomery walked imperiously towards them, her hand outstretched. She continued to wear the gowns she wore in England – high-necked, laced-fronted bodices, wide skirts, bustles – as though she had never noticed the change of climate. She was even wearing her elbow-length silk gloves.

'Charles, Ursula. Do come in.'

They followed her into the drawing-room. The curtains were partly shut, casting light shadows across the furniture which she had had imported from England. Great settees, damask covers, deep arm chairs, even a piano. 'You have to maintain standards,' was her often-quoted remark.

'Are you sure you can manage with all these little ones?' Charles asked doubtfully.

'I should hope so, dear boy. Remember, I brought up ten children of my own. These little souls are not likely to cause me much trouble.'

'And Fatima is here to help you.'

Mrs Montgomery smiled indulgently. 'I shall probably have more trouble with the servants than with the little English creatures.' Then she added, 'You look charming today, dear Ursula.'

She lightly emphasised 'today'. Charles knew that Mrs Montgomery disapproved of what she considered to be the casual way in which Ursula normally dressed. She had frequently felt it incumbent upon herself, in view of her matriarchal role in the English community, to remind Ursula of her duties as the wife of an important bank official. 'We must all set an example,' she would say. 'It is important for our children and also to show the natives how to behave.'

'And can you manage the arrangements for having the children sent up to Cairo on Saturday?'

'As a matter of fact, Charles, I am travelling there myself. So have no worries. I will accompany them with the servants.'

'Perhaps we should say goodbye to Charlotte?'

'No,' Mrs Montgomery said decisively. 'If she sees you again she may be upset. Leave it to me. She will be perfectly happy. And you, dear Rachel. You are most fortunate to attend such a celebration.'

Rachel had been standing quietly in the background, holding her mother's hand. Mrs Montgomery silenced even Rachel.

'Yes,' she said quietly.

'You'll soon be going to school in England, I suppose.'

'No,' Rachel said firmly.

'She's not ten yet,' Ursula said defensively. 'We thought not for another couple of years.'

'Yes. Probably. As she's a girl.' Mrs Montgomery looked thoughtful. 'Though personally, I think it can never be too soon. This isn't a good environment, I mean spiritually speaking, for a child. And there are so few English children here. Well, enjoy yourselves, my dears. And give my regards to the Pasha,' she added laughing.

As they walked through the garden in the sunshine, Rachel said anxiously, 'I don't want to go to England. I want to stay with you.'

'Don't worry, Rachel. It's a long time yet.'

'But I don't ever want to go.'

Charles looked at the tense face raised to his. They had only been back to England once on leave since coming to Egypt, when Rachel was just eight. They had stayed with Ursula's parents, who had been kind and indulgent to Rachel. She couldn't have unhappy memories of it, Charles thought. It was simply that she didn't want to be separated from them. She would settle down soon enough.

'Well, we'll see,' Ursula said.

But Rachel continued to argue belligerently, stamping her feet and saying that she hated England and how horrid they were to think of sending her there. Ursula talked to her quietly, assuring her that it was a long time away, but when Charles threatened to return her to the hotel, she fell silent.

When they alighted from their barouche at the three pavilions, specially constructed for the opening ceremony to house Christians, Muslims and Copts, her face brightened and she pointed excitedly. Wide flights of steps led from a central base to the pavilions, each crowned by a giant, oblong canopy of painted gold wood, each canopy hung with heavy silken drapes, one red, one white, one green.

The area was already thronged with people and there was confusion as guests tried to distinguish which pavilion was which.

Charles led Ursula and Rachel to the pavilion which was to accommodate the Christians. The Englishmen were all, like Charles, in grey trousers and black jackets; the ladies in their long silk and frilled crinolines, each of them carrying a parasol. Isma'il occupied the centre seat on a dais above, reserved for the hierarchy. His frock-coat was elaborately decorated with medals, his neat auburn-coloured beard and moustache encompassed a smooth-skinned face, his eyes looked impassively from beneath his red fez.

By his side sat the Empress Eugenie of France, the Emperor of Austria in scarlet pantaloons and a white tunic, members of the royal families of Holland and Prussia and officials and military personnel. Behind them stood a line of Isma'il's bearded bodyguard dressed up, Charles reflected, to look like English guardsmen. Across the floor on the other side was the pavilion reserved for the Muslims. Their coloured robes and white turbans, the white robed Arabs on camels at the back, formed a sharp contrast to the soberly dressed Englishmen.

There were assemblies of Roman Catholic, Coptic, Moslem and Greek Orthodox priests, all of whom solemnly blessed the Canal in turn and then the celebratory sound of guns rent the air, and martial music echoed round the pavilions. Rachel looked around with delight. There seemed to be bands in every corner, all playing a different tune.

For a moment, Charles looked up at the pavilions, imagining the whole edifice crashing in on them. Nothing could be certain in Egypt. He and Ursula smiled at each other. Isma'il had been determined that this should be the display that would finally put Egypt on the international map. And in his six years of power he had certainly been effective. He had played the Sultan off, his legal master, against the Europeans, he had established an impressive life style and behaved like an emperor. His private wealth was equalled only by his audacity in acquiring it. Before the opening of the Canal, he had made journeys to the capitals of Europe, issuing personal invitations to the Heads of State, promising them free passage and accommodation in sumptuous apartments.

Charles looked down to speak to Rachel and realised that her seat was empty. Absorbed in watching the display, he had not noticed her disappear. He turned to Ursula. 'Where's Rachel?'

'I don't know, Charles. Where is she? How did you let her go?'

'I didn't let her do anything. She must have sneaked off,' Charles replied in irritation.

'Sneaked? What do you mean?'

'She should have said where she was going.'

'Well, find her, Charles.' There was a note of anxiety in Ursula's voice.

'All right. Stay here. She can't be far away.'

Charles stood up, glancing around him and then towards the dais where Isma'il looked down from his painted throne. He saw with horror that Rachel was slowly mounting the steps in front of the royal guests. Charles blushed with embarrassment. What was the child doing? He began to push through the rows of English spectators. Rachel had reached the top step and he saw her raise her skirts in a sweeping gesture and make an exaggerated curtsey. Isma'il smiled and bowed to her and the Empress of France held out her hand and beckoned Rachel towards her. The Empress was speaking to her and Rachel was smiling and replying, then she turned and jumped down the steps and walked back towards the English pavilion – whose occupants were watching her in silence.

Charles glanced back at Ursula. To his annoyance she was smiling and waving to Rachel to indicate where they were sitting. He went back along the rows.

'Ursula,' he said in a low voice, controlling the fury he was feeling. 'It is not a smiling matter.'

'Oh, Charles, it was a harmless gesture.'

As Rachel reached them, Charles grabbed her arm and pushed her into the seat beside him. 'What were you doing, drawing attention to yourself in such as fashion?'

Rachel looked surprised at his stern expression. 'I just wanted to curtsey like Fatima taught me.'

'It is reprehensible behaviour. Everyone was looking at you, Rachel.'

'I didn't—'

'Don't dare to leave my side again. This will be the last time you attend an adult function.'

Charles realised with embarrassment that he had raised his voice but the attention of the spectators had returned to the dais.

'Charles,' Ursula whispered. 'She did not mean—'

'We will discuss it later,' Charles replied curtly.

The long ceremony over, the huge assembly trailed out from the pavilions, headed by Isma'il and the Empress, towards the waiting ships.

The Empress went in her imperial yacht, Isma'il stood at the helm of his *Mahrousa*, and the English guests boarded one of the British ironclads which would take them all to Ismailia, the new town which had been built in celebration of the Canal. A great fleet of ships followed them along the Canal which was lined on either side by the labourers who had built it.

On the Christian ships, wine flowed freely and a band played at each end of the deck. Ursula and Rachel had lunch with the ladies in a specially fitted saloon, while Charles and the other men went to a separate apartment and then stood on deck, cynically discussing the absurdities and extravagance of Isma'il.

The sun was approaching the horizon before they saw the outline of the great new palace which had been built at Ismailia, surrounded by modern hotels and bazaars. It was here that they would meet the other fleet of ships coming up from Suez. With further ceremony, Isma'il declared the Canal open and the waters flowing down from the Mediterranean met the still waters of the Red Sea.

Charles and Ursula were taken by barouche to their hotel. Rachel had been placed in an adjacent room, but Ursula demanded that she sleep in their apartment. Amid more confusion, furniture was moved and beds remade.

'You must go to bed now, dear,' Ursula said. 'It's already dark.'

'Why can't I go to the banquet?'

'It's only for adults,' Charles said. 'You were lucky to come today. No one else of your age was permitted.'

'When you're in bed, you'll be able to see the fireworks through the window. It will be a great display,' Ursula added, moving off to change her gown.

Charles took his new white suit into the dressing-room, then he came back to say goodnight to Rachel. He had refrained from remarking upon her poor behaviour until now.

16

'Now, let us have no more misbehaviour, Rachel. I hope your actions at the ceremony were simply the result of your excitement but I want no repetition of it. Should you require anything, there are two English ladies in the next room who aren't going to the banquet.'

Rachel peered at him belligerently as Ursula kissed her goodnight.

'Papa, I'm not going to England.'

Ursula said impatiently, 'Rachel, you're being a silly girl. We'll talk about it when we get back to Cairo.'

'Well, I'm not.'

Charles said sharply, 'Goodnight, Rachel,' and closed the door behind them.

'Charles,' Ursula said, as they walked along the corridor. 'I wonder if it would be possible—'

Charles put an arm around her shoulders and said, 'Ursula, do not start that discussion again. As you know, I wanted to leave the children in England in the first place. There are no suitable schools here for older girls. And you have to remember, she won't live in Egypt for ever. When she's grown up she'll be in England. She must learn to live there, mustn't she?'

'She could have a governess, Charles.'

'Ursula, we have been through this before. I want her to live in a proper English environment. We may find it agreeable here, but it is not suitable for young people. We shan't be here for ever, either.'

'No. I know.' Ursula sighed.

'Now,' Charles said, 'come on. Let us enjoy the banquet.'

'I don't know if I can face another,' Ursula made a face. They had already attended one the night before in Port Said.

The palace was bright with thousands of lights, and after the banquet they danced in the huge ballroom, designed to emulate Versailles. Isma'il sat on a throne, watching his guests with the quiet assurance of a man who believes he is unassailable. Charles wondered whether he felt a secret anxiety about the enormity of the task he had set himself.

It was almost dawn when they stepped from their barouche and climbed the hotel steps. A streak of blue light spread across the eastern sky and Ursula yawned, muttering, 'I hope Rachel won't wake too soon.'

As they went into the apartment, Ursula crept across the room to look at her. 'Charles,' she said sharply. 'She's not here.'

Charles walked quickly to the bathroom. It was empty. They cast a hasty glance round the room, behind the chairs, beneath their bed.

'Charles, perhaps she's in with the English ladies.'

Charles replied with conflicting feelings of anxiety and anger, 'We can't wake them. It's only five o'clock.'

'But supposing – she isn't there? We must find out.'

'Yes,' Charles crept down the corridor and lightly knocked on the door.

There was no answer. He knocked louder. A muffled voice came from inside.

'I'm sorry, Madam,' he said. 'It's Charles Cavendish. Rachel is not in her room. Is she with you?'

After a few moments, a night-capped head came round the door. 'Come in, dear boy. What has happened?'

'Rachel is not in her room. I hoped she would be with you,' Charles said quickly.

'No, she's not with us. I visited her before I retired. She was fast asleep then.'

Charles turned to the door.

'You must raise the alarm instantly,' the lady said. 'Anything could have happened to her in a place like this.'

Charles hurried back to Ursula who was still dressed in her ballgown. 'We must summon help,' he said.

Within five minutes, there was turmoil in the hotel. Bells were ringing, doors were flung open in consternation, there was hectic activity as the proprietor and his staff dashed up and down the corridors. An English child was missing: the repercussions could be too horrendous to contemplate. The police and local militia were called, the order was given to search every house in the vicinity. Charles dispatched a party to the Canal; perhaps she had gone to look at the flotilla of ships still anchored along the banks? Another group went to the palace; Rachel had known that was where she would find her parents.

The few older English children were questioned. They had all been safely tucked up in their beds, although one of them said petulantly,

'She doesn't like playing with us; she only likes the Arab children.'

When Charles returned to the hotel, the sun was rising in the sky. Ursula was walking slowly up the stairs to their room where she sat down nervously on the edge of the bed.

'Charles, it's our fault.'

'Whatever do you mean?'

'We shouldn't have talked about going to school.'

'What has that got to do with her disappearance?' he said impatiently.

'Perhaps she feels we don't want her. That we're sending her away.'

'What nonsense. We're doing it for her own welfare. And after the events of today, the need appears to be even more urgent.'

'It must be something we've done.'

Charles shook his head in exasperation. Then he said more quietly, 'You're upset, dear. It's got nothing to do with school. We must just concentrate on finding her.'

He had begun to harbour awful fears of kidnapping, or of some terrible disaster, that she might have fallen into the Canal. 'You'd better wait here, dear,' he added. 'I'll go down to the town.'

The hotel was still being searched as Charles went down the steps. How would you find a child in this teeming mass of humanity? A barouche took him through the narrow streets to the fringes of the desert. He got out, looking across the grey-gold sand to the distant misty hills. For a moment he was aware, as he always was, of the strange power of the desert. He knew that most foreigners saw it as a barren wasteland, infested with mosquitoes, vultures, a merciless sun and uncivilised bedouin. But there were also a few people like himself, on whom it cast a kind of spell.

He saw a camel in the distance, moving slowly towards where he stood, plodding along as though, at any moment, it might trip over its own feet. As he began to turn away, he looked at the rider again and stopped. Could it possibly be? It was preposterous. He called to the driver of the barouche.

'There,' he pointed. 'Over there.'

The man looked. 'It is the child,' he said in astonishment. The barouche hurtled over the sand towards the approaching camel.

Charles jumped out and grabbed at the reins. 'Rachel,' his voice trembled with anxiety and controlled fury. 'Where have you been?'

Rachel slid down and stood beside him, laughing.

'I went for a ride. I watched it getting light and the sun coming up.'

Charles almost struck her, but he picked her up abruptly and placed her in the barouche.

'How did you get here?'

'I walked through the streets. This bedouin let me ride a camel with him.'

Charles looked disdainfully at the robed figure following her.

The man jumped down from his camel and bowed. 'The young lady wished for a ride,' he said obsequiously.

Charles waved at him dismissively. 'Take it,' he said abruptly and turned back to Rachel. 'Do you realise the confusion you've created? You will be in serious trouble over this.' He took her by the shoulders and shook her, looking into her defiant little face.

'Why shouldn't I?' she said, but her question was defensive rather than provocative.

'Why?' Charles shouted, but he controlled his anger and said roughly, 'Are you all right?'

'Yes.'

The barouche was driven hastily back to the hotel and Charles ordered Rachel upstairs to their apartment.

Afterwards, he realised that there had not been a single word of criticism or reprimand from Ursula. She had flung her arms round Rachel, who had burst into tears over Charles's treatment of her, and had said soothingly, 'Papa didn't mean anything, love. He was just concerned about you.'

The three of them returned to Cairo in silence. For the first time Charles felt a barrier between himself and Ursula; he saw that Rachel was getting out of hand; he even felt himself in sympathy with Mrs Montgomery and the other matrons. Egypt was no place for a child; she had been given too much freedom. He began to think that she should return to England earlier than they had planned. He knew that Ursula would oppose the idea. Of course, he could override her objections; he was the master of the household. Yet their relationship had never been like that; could he suddenly demand such subjection? They had always discussed their plans together. Nevertheless, it was up to him to make the decisions. It was he who was responsible for providing a home and income and for deciding the direction of their lives, the education of their children, the standards to which they should conform.

When he left the office the next day, Charles walked through the old town back to the house. Cairo seemed so civilised after Port Said, he was glad to be back. He walked through the crowded bazaar area, with the delicately-carved wooden structures of the houses jutting out above the sandy street, and looked with satisfaction at the elegant proportions of the red and white El Mooristan Mosque. Turbanned Egyptians sat on the ground in front of the buildings on each side of the street, donkeys laden with bags were jerked forward by shouting fellahin, a corpulent pasha, accompanied by his veiled wife, stepped aside for him.

As he passed through the bazaar, he hesitated at the entrance to one of the illegal gambling kiosks. He had decided not to visit them any more; he realised that they held a curious attraction for him. Well, just one more visit, perhaps.

An hour later, he came home.

'Been gambling,' Ursula asked cheerfully. She thought it was quite normal, why should he not gamble if he wished? Of course, Ursula was unaware of the sums of money involved, of the risks as well as the benefits.

'Where's Rachel?' Charles queried, avoiding the question.

'Oh, she's just out playing. You don't need to worry about her, Charles. It was just a thoughtless thing she did.'

'I am worried, Ursula. Not because of that, exactly. But because I think she needs more discipline.'

'But she behaves correctly. She is polite, obedient.'

'She has a great deal of freedom, though. It can't be a good idea for her to mix with the servants' children so much. She seems to find them more compatible than the other English children.'

'She'll have to settle down and be serious soon enough,' Ursula replied dismissively.

Charles cleared his throat. 'Well, I am considering sending her to England this year, rather than waiting for another two years.'

Ursula turned on him angrily. 'No,' she said. 'She won't go.'

'Ursula, I think it has to be my decision,' Charles said.

'She would be unhappy. Perhaps by the time she's twelve, she'll find it more acceptable.'

'Ursula, it is not for Rachel to find it acceptable or otherwise. It's what we think is correct for her.'

'Well, we don't. I am absolutely opposed to her going now.'

'Then I am afraid I must make the decision alone.'

Ursula pursed her lips. 'Very well,' she said. 'If Rachel is to return, I shall also go. I shall live in England with the children until they are older.'

Charles felt a cold anxiety grip him. Would she really leave him, just like that?

Ursula changed her tone. 'Dear Charles. Let us come to an agreement. I will ensure that Rachel behaves with more restraint. She is such a child, I could not abandon her in England just yet.' Her tone of voice made England appear to be the undesirable place – rather than Egypt. 'I will pay more attention to her behaviour. She is a good girl, you know.'

Charles hesitated. He knew that any other man in his position would have insisted, dismissed her womanly qualms, demanded her obedience and sent the child packing.

'Well, we'll leave it for the moment, as we're all going to England in two years' time. But I shall pay attention to her behaviour.' Charles said curtly.

The matter was not raised again and after the celebrations were over, life returned to normal. But Charles began to feel that Ursula's carefree and independent behaviour, which had attracted him to her in the first place, was perhaps too frivolous. He remembered remarks she had made, books she had mentioned when he first met her; a ridiculous document she had got hold of about the emancipation of women, some notion that women were at present degraded by society.

He had paid little attention to her chatter at the time and she had naturally forgotten these preoccupations when they married. It occurred to Charles that it was probably why her father had been so instantly agreeable to his proposal of marriage. He must have felt Ursula needed the restraining influence of a husband. Perhaps Mrs Montgomery was right, and Egypt was an unsuitable place for Europeans.

He wondered if he had been fulfilling his masculine role with sufficient dedication. In future, he would ensure that Ursula and Rachel made no mistake about who was in charge.

Chapter 2

They arrived at Southampton Water early on a February morning in 1872. One pale ray of sunshine glinted across the bows of the ship as they entered the docks and then disappeared behind dense clouds. Charles raised his Astrakhan collar higher around his neck and pulled on his gloves. The rails around the deck were cold and damp.

He looked down at the mass of boats, ships and funnels, and upwards at the armada of masts and sails through which their tall ship was being piloted, his ears assaulted by horns, hooters and blasts from other vessels. Great clouds of smoke rose into the air; eventually, he reflected, all the sails would be gone, only the smoke from engines would remain. Already it was being said that the days of sail were numbered. He looked across at the huge warehouses and customs houses along the quayside; a great new area of docks had been built since they were last in England.

Further along the coast, he could see a large ship-building yard and huge vessels being repaired in the dry dock. He was struck, as he always was when he returned to England, by the sense of a striving activity that seemed to emanate from every individual. Everywhere he looked, men were lifting, pulling, running, heaving, shouting. He thought of the contrast between the spectacle before him and the fellahin, forced-labouring incoherently in the fields and on the building projects in Cairo, coerced, enslaved, ignorant. The civilisation that this country was spreading to the rest of the world was something he felt proud to be a part of.

Ursula and Rachel were sitting on deck seats with Charlotte between them, a blanket draped across their knees. When he waved, they stood up and walked towards him. They looked strange in the long, bustled dresses and coats which had been sent from England.

The furs Ursula wore around her neck virtually concealed her face. Rachel, who was almost as tall now as her mother, wore a wide-brimmed velvet hat to match her purple gown and dark grey coat. At first Rachel had protested at the restrictions of the voluminous skirts and long sleeves, but during the last few days as they sailed into the cold northern air, she had been only too willing to abandon her light Egyptian dresses and sandals. She had folded them all neatly and packed them in a box.

'I'll keep them all ready for when I come back to Egypt,' she had said to her mother.

Ursula had laughed. 'By that time, they won't fit you. You shall have lovely new dresses when you return.'

Charles had listened anxiously to the conversation, hoping Rachel was not going to make another scene about her return to England. There had been many months of arguments on the subject, but Ursula had deflected Rachel's anger, and cleverly pointed out all the attractions of life in England. She had painted a picture of a great, expanding country, the greatest country in the world, filled with promise and opportunity.

'You will have an education which would be denied you in Egypt. You will acquire many accomplishments, you will meet interesting people. As you get older, you will enjoy a social life which can only be provided by cultured people. There is no culture here. There are so few English people.'

Gradually, Rachel's protests had changed to reluctant curiosity and finally even to enthusiasm.

Charles walked towards them. 'How are you feeling, dear?' he said to Ursula.

Ursula had been confined to her cabin with sea-sickness for most of the journey and Rachel and Charlotte had spent much of their time with the captain's wife and children. The captain and his family had seen Egypt only from the deck of the ship and Rachel entertained them with flamboyant stories of her travels into the desert, of their visits to mosques and temples, of shopping in the bazaars.

Ursula smiled uncertainly. 'I feel better now that we are approaching land.'

'We shall soon be on the train to London. I am sure that will be a smoother journey.'

26

Charles supervised the unloading of their leather trunks and travel chests while Ursula and Rachel said farewell to the captain. The children said goodbye in the Arabic words which Rachel had taught them, promising that they would meet her again in Egypt.

Then they were treading carefully down the gangway, buffeted by a cold north wind.

Charles marched before them along the dock, past the building yards. The forges were belching out dense smoke and the noise of the steam hammers almost deafened them.

Amidst a great deal of shouting and passengers crowding along the platforms, and porters wheeling trunks and valises to the luggage vans, they boarded the train and the porter showed them to their private compartment.

Rachel wiped her gloves across the windows so that she could look out.

'Rachel, the windows are covered with grime. Look at your gloves now.'

Rachel sighed, her lips beginning to tremble. 'Mama, I thought it was going to be nice. Everything seems horrid.'

Ursula sprang up and sat beside her. 'Oh, darling, it will be all right. I don't mean to criticise you. It's just—' She stopped as though she were suddenly aware of the great chasm that separated life here from the world they had known in Egypt.

'You see here, in England, everything is different. You're not a little girl any more, are you?' she continued cajolingly. 'You'll be treated as a lady. You'll like that, won't you?'

Rachel shook her head doubtfully.

'I wish I were a lady like Rachel,' Charlotte interposed. She clutched Rachel's hand. 'Then I could stay in England with you.'

Rachel smiled. 'Well, you will when you're old enough,' she said.

'Rachel is going to a lovely school in the country,' Ursula said cheerfully. 'She'll write and tell you all about it. And you'll have nice holidays with the Damarells, Rachel, and sometimes you'll come up to London to visit your grandparents.'

Rachel nodded.

Charles began to feel a certain boredom with Ursula's preoccupation with Rachel's happiness. Ursula had always assumed that Rachel would go to a school in London and live with her grandparents, but a few weeks ago, Charles had decided that Rachel should go to a boarding establishment in the country. He felt that Ursula's mother was too indulgent for a wayward and rebellious child like Rachel, who needed discipline and firm direction. He had chosen Kingsbridge because that was where his childhood had been spent. It was also convenient in that Ursula's distant relative, Maria, had recently married a widower, Arthur Damarell, and taken up residence there. Charles knew the Damarell family; they were solid Church-going people. Rachel would stay with them during the vacations and he believed they would have a restraining influence on his daughter. There had been protests from Ursula but Charles had been adamant. She finally accepted his decision and now even gave the impression that she recognised its wisdom. Perhaps she had begun to recognise Rachel's waywardness.

It was dark when they reached London and Charles hired a Hansom cab to take them to Ursula's parents in Suffolk Square, off Hyde Park. He pointed out the city's great buildings as they went along and they watched a lamplighter turning on the street lights with a long pole.

'That's Westminster Abbey and there is the House of Commons where the parliament makes laws. And that's the River Thames, the most famous river in the world.'

'More famous than the Nile?'

Charles laughed. 'The Nile is just long,' he said. 'The Thames has an important history.'

The cab rumbled round the park and finally turned up a cobbled drive, past lawns and flowerbeds to a large house surrounded by trees.

Suddenly Ursula's parents were running out to greet them and soon they were being led through the large, gas-lit hall filled with flowers and aspidistras to the drawing-room. A great log fire blazed in the marble fireplace and Rachel rushed towards it.

'Oh, it's lovely,' she said. 'It's so cold in that barouche.'

'You must feel the cold here after that hot climate in Egypt,' her grandmother said sympathetically. 'But you'll soon get used to it. It's so much healthier here, you know. It's not natural for English people to live in that sort of weather.'

Rachel and Charlotte were made a great fuss of by their grandmother and Ursula's father promised to take them next day to see the Tower of London.

A fire burned in the bedroom allocated to the girls and Ursula protested laughingly that they were being spoilt.

'Nonsense,' her mother said. 'I don't see enough of my grandchildren. When they're here, I shall treat them as I see fit.'

When the children had gone to bed, she reverted to the topic which recurred in all her letters.

'When are you and Charles coming back permanently?'

Charles and Ursula looked at each other meaningfully.

'Mother dear,' Charles replied, 'my career has taken me there. It provides a great deal for Ursula and the children.'

'But there are excellent opportunities in this country. Surely you do not need to go to the other side of the earth?'

'Millicent,' Ursula's father interposed firmly. 'It is not for you to question Charles's decision. It is for him to decide what is suitable for himself and his family.'

Ursula's mother sighed. 'Yes, I know. But it is a great sadness to me that I might not live to see them grow into adulthood.'

'Mama, do not speak so. Now that Rachel is to live in England, you will see her for part of her vacations. It would be too much for you to have her with you all the time.'

'Yes. But why must she be in Kingsbridge? There are plenty of establishments in London for the education of young persons.'

'I feel the country is more suitable for Rachel,' Charles said defensively. 'I grew up in that area and my aunt and uncle lived there until their deaths. It was they who recommended the establishment to which she is to be sent.'

'Such matters are for Charles to decide, Millicent,' Ursula's father interrupted firmly. 'Come, Charles. Have a port in the smoking-room. Tell me all about this Isma'il who seems to be dominating world politics at the moment.' He turned to Ursula. 'Delighted to have you back, Ursula. You look very well.'

'Oh, I am, Papa.' Ursula laughed. 'Life in Egypt is very agreeable, although I know mama worries about me.'

'As I frequently tell her, she has no cause for concern while you're

29

in your husband's capable hands. But naturally she has no understanding of larger issues.'

The topic was dropped but, in the privacy of their bedroom, Ursula began to voice her anxieties.

'Mama is much frailer than when we saw her last, Charles. I feel much concern for her health.'

'Yes, dear,' Charles agreed. 'But we have to accept that she is no longer young, and her recent illness must have left her weak. She will have the vacations to look forward to, when Rachel may visit her.'

Ursula frowned. Charles knew that her real anxiety centred around Rachel. He felt a certain irritation; he did not want a replay of her doubts.

'I fear that Rachel will not take kindly to life here,' Ursula continued. 'It will be all very well while we are with mama and papa, but I know little of these relatives in Kingsbridge. Will they treat her with the same forbearance?'

'Ursula, I have realised even today that it is as well that Rachel has come home. She has gained a false impression from life in Egypt of the behaviour required of an English person. In years to come she will be grateful that we brought her back to her native land. Remember, it is here that she will find her future husband.'

Charles turned away and went into his dressing-room to indicate that the conversation was closed. Even now, he felt a certain inadequacy in dealing with Ursula, fearing that she might persuade him to change his mind by using feminine guile. Privately, Charles recognised that it was really his own inexperience which had created the problem. It was obvious that the world of men and women was strictly divided, and although his own marriage had never appeared like that, he saw now such separation was inevitable.

In the end everything had worked out as he basically wished, he reflected, because of his own decisiveness. At the time, he had felt almost betrayed by Ursula; he remembered her opposition two years earlier when he had considered bringing Rachel home. In the event, it had not proved a problem. He had known he could not take leave from the bank at that time to escort Rachel back to England and his job and career had to come first.

Charles had discussed the situation obliquely with Mrs Montgomery, who just as obliquely observed that women relied on men to make decisions; men were the providers, the protectors, the decision-makers. Women, although influential in the domestic realm and responsible for the correct running of a household, tended to be over-zealous in the protection of children. It was natural and desirable, but it was for men to measure their interests against that wider social background of which women had less experience.

'It is so important for girls to be educated in the womanly accomplishments,' Mrs Montgomery had said. 'And that can only be achieved in England. But it is for the husband and provider to decide at what time such a course is to be embarked upon.'

'It is my opinion,' Charles had said, 'that Rachel should go to England now. But I find it impossible to arrange such a proceeding with the bank. And I would be reluctant for Ursula to go with her alone.'

'Ah, no. I think that would be most unsuitable. I am sure dear Rachel will not suffer from a longer sojourn in Egypt. She is a dear child, and so like her beautiful mother.' Then she had added sagely, 'Dear Charles, I am old enough to be presumptuous. In my experience, there is much innocence in feminine protestations. The desire of women to make their own choices and decisions is strictly limited and cannot be taken seriously.'

Over the next month, Charles experienced all those pleasures of middle-class life which he seemed to have missed in his own childhood. He accompanied his father-in-law to his Club in Pall Mall, where they discussed the affairs of the nation with other members. They met Henry Ponsonby, the Queen's private secretary who, although a Liberal himself, was finding it difficult to soothe the nerves of those Liberal politicians who were becoming increasingly disenchanted with the conservative views of the Queen. Charles realised that there was a great desire for reform in the country, that the growing poverty in the cities was causing more and more concern in informed circles. He visited his bank headquarters in Holborn to report on developments in Egypt and discuss the desirability of the bank acquiring interests in the Suez Canal and the expansion taking place in Port Said. The family took long walks across Hyde Park and St James's in the afternoons, and in the evenings he and Ursula enjoyed the musical concerts and soirées given at her parents' home and at the homes of their friends.

Ursula spent the days with her mother, calling upon friends, holding At Homes. But it was Rachel and Charlotte who were the centre of attraction. Ursula's mother arranged for her dress-maker to measure Rachel for new gowns and it seemed that every afternoon when he returned, Charles was confronted by a laughing Rachel, showing him her latest acquisition: velvet gowns, woollen skirts, white muslin blouses, silk petticoats, capes and robes, until even Ursula protested that she was being spoilt.

'Mama, Rachel will not require such a wealth of clothes. Kingsbridge is only a quiet country place, there cannot be the social activities which we find in London.'

'Of course there will be,' her mother replied. 'The Damarells are an important family in that neighbourhood, are they not, Charles? You are acquainted with them through your own aunt and uncle. And remember, Maria is my second cousin. She would only marry into a socially desirable family. Charles, do you not think your daughter looks charming?'

Charles looked at Rachel thoughtfully. Her wavy auburn hair was growing longer and her grey eyes looked at him expectantly. Yes, she had a beautiful face.

Charles smiled. 'Yes, of course she does. But she will be carried away by vanity if you keep telling her so. And she is only twelve, mother.'

'Young ladies cannot learn too early how to dress,' Ursula's mother replied.

'We're going to St Paul's tomorrow,' Rachel said. 'It's to celebrate the Prince of Wales's recovery,' she added knowledgeably.

'Really?' Charles laughed. 'And what is he recovering from?'

'You know quite well,' Rachel said. 'He had typhoid and poor Queen Victoria thought he would die.'

They went in a carriage to the cathedral, through streets filled with a million people cheering the Queen and her son, and stood at the back of the cathedral watching Queen Victoria as she walked slowly down the aisle on the Prince's arm.

'She's so small,' Rachel whispered. 'Is she the Queen?'

'Yes.' Charles smiled. He had a picture of the great gold statues of

Rameses that Rachel had wondered at when they were at Thebes. Her idea of royalty was far removed from this plump little lady in her black gown.

Charles thought of their last visit to Siwa. Long ago, Ursula had told Rachel the legend of Siwa, of how centuries before Christ was born, Alexander the Great had visited the Temple of Amun at Aghurmi, a village near Siwa, and there he had been told that he was a god.

Rachel had been entranced by the tale and had constantly requested to hear it again, so Ursula embellished it as she went along, telling her of Alexander's exploits and of his god-like attributes.

Charles realised that the ancient history of Egypt had taken the place of the fairy stories Rachel would have listened to in England. How would Little Red Riding Hood and Cinderella or even that new story, Alice in Wonderland, which her grandmother had given her the other day, seem to her after the incredible lives of the Pharaohs?

As though sensing his thoughts, Rachel said softly, 'She isn't a God, is she?'

'No,' Charles smiled.

But when they emerged into the street and watched the Queen and Prince drive away in their open landau, to the cheers and waves of the crowds, Charles wondered whether the nation didn't see her as such. There had been so much criticism of her since the death of Prince Albert, of the fact that she never appeared in public and continued to behave as a disconsolate widow although Albert had been dead for eleven years. Yet here they were, apparently carried away with joy and enthusiasm.

As their carriage passed through Cheapside and they made their way towards Pentonville, he observed too the great derelict areas of slums, the poverty and degradation. Beggars, children with bare feet, cripples, lunatics, drunks, tenements and decaying houses filled with people, young painted women standing in alleys, and so much filth that the carriage constantly swayed from side to side as the driver led the horses around the piles of rubbish.

Yet these were the very people who had been cheering the Queen . . . He wondered whether the agitation for reform of which his father-in-law and the other Liberals spoke was a preoccupation of the upper classes, for there was no evidence of it here. In some ways, he felt little patience with these people. The Liberal reformers had not seen life in countries like Egypt. There, the poor and the slaves had no chance of improving their lot; here, in this free country, the poor could drag themselves out of their penury by hard work and diligence, and make decent lives for themselves.

Ursula's parents accompanied them to Paddington Station for their departure to the West Country. They were to stay with the Damarells for a month, to settle Rachel with her relatives and introduce her to her new school. Then they would return to London before their departure to Egypt.

Ursula's mother looked with satisfaction at Rachel's new blue velvet gown and dark-blue cloak. 'You look most elegant,' she said. 'Your relatives in Kingsbridge will be impressed with their new charge. And take care of those lovely kid boots.'

Rachel smiled. 'Thank you for all your lovely presents. And I shall come to spend some of my vacation with you in the summer, won't I?'

'Of course you will, dear girl.'

She embraced Charlotte who was clutching the baby doll which her grandmother had given her, saying, 'And I'll see you in a month's time, dear child.'

Ursula put her arms round her mother. 'Goodbye, dear Mama. You have been of such assistance. You have convinced Rachel that England is a happy place to be. Has she not, Rachel?'

Rachel laughed. 'Oh, so much better than I imagined.'

Charles looked at his smiling daughter with relief. She seemed to have forgotten all her antipathies towards England. Once again, he thought, just a feminine foible. Of course, the final parting would be difficult but he told himself that she would soon recover.

The train sped through the fields and rolling countryside of the West Country and eventually pulled in to Exeter Station.

'Now we are in Devon,' Charles said. 'The climate is warmer in these parts. Look, already there are spring flowers in the gardens.'

Then they were in Plymouth and Charles told the girls about Sir Francis Drake and Plymouth Hoe and the great adventurers and seamen of Devon who had explored the world, discovered new countries, and began to establish the British Empire. At the station,

Hansom cabs awaited passengers for the outlying towns and villages. Their luggage was piled up in front with the driver, who asked Rachel jovially if she would like to ride in front with him.

Rachel's face lit up with delight, but Charles said quietly, 'No, Rachel. You will ride inside with us.'

The cab made slow progress through the hilly countryside, but at last they reached the little town of Kingsbridge where their luggage was piled into a carriage to take them the final part of the journey, along Duke Street and Church Street and beyond Waterloo Place to an imposing residence on a hill. The carriage went up the short drive and they alighted before the flight of steps to the front door.

It was flung open by a servant in a starched white apron and cap. Behind her stood a tall, well-built elderly man with white hair and a tall statuesque woman in a grey gown with a large bustle.

Ursula went towards them. 'You must be Aunt Maria.'

Aunt Maria smiled, waiting while Ursula mounted the steps. 'Ursula. It is a pleasure to meet you. We were but children when I last saw you. Younger even than this,' and she pointed to Charlotte.

Ursula kissed her politely on the cheek. 'Yes, I have but a dim recollection of the event. I think we were visiting your parents in Dorset. Mother has spoken much of you. I believe you are second cousins? Though I think you have not seen her for some long time.'

Aunt Maria extended a hand to Charles, saying, 'Pray, introduce us.'

'This is Charles,' Ursula said. 'And this, of course, is Rachel. And young Charlotte.'

'Rachel is more . . . grown-up . . . than I anticipated.'

'She is only twelve,' Ursula said.

'Mmm. In these parts, twelve-year-olds do not usually dress with such . . . extravagance.'

Rachel said cheerfully, 'Oh, my grandmother has bought me many fine clothes. It is most fortunate.'

Aunt Maria raised her eyebrows slightly but did not reply.

Ursula turned towards the elderly man, saying, 'You must be Mr Damarell.'

Mr Damarell had been contemplating them quietly.

Charles shook his hand. 'It is most kind of you to receive us. I have a happy memory of visiting you and your parents when I lived here as a boy with my aunt and uncle. You were working at the mill, I remember.'

Mr Damarell inclined his head in acknowledgment. 'Ah, that is many years ago. My parents have long since passed on. I took over the mill some twenty years ago. Your aunt and uncle are much missed in the neighbourhood. Sadly, your aunt's death followed very closely upon that of your uncle.'

'Yes. It was upon their information that I chose to bring Rachel to Devon to attend the school they had recommended. My childhood memories of the Devonshire countryside also persuaded me that this would be a good environment for her.'

'Certainly,' Aunt Maria said firmly. 'And more suitable than the undesirable influences of the city.'

'London is exciting,' Rachel said instantly. 'I feared it would be dreary after Cairo.'

'Oh, indeed?'

Then Rachel saw the cautioning expression on her father's face. 'But I know Kingsbridge will be even more exciting,' she added.

'I doubt if the epithet "exciting" could be applied to this neighbourhood,' Mr Damarell said quietly. 'It is not something we would find desirable.'

'Come, Arthur,' Aunt Maria said, 'let us take our guests into the drawing-room.'

They passed through the geranium-scented conservatory and along the hall. A dark oak grandfather clock was striking its slow, booming chimes as they passed. Charles remembered the same kind of clock in his uncle's house, listening to that identical sound as he lay in bed. There was also the same smell of polish, and an airlessness that seemed to emanate from the furnishings, anti-macassars, velvets, old furniture. Charlotte grabbed Rachel's hand as they stood at the door of the drawing-room and hesitated, waiting to be invited in.

'Come, girls. Lizzie will take your cloaks.' A servant girl who looked younger than Rachel took them and Aunt Maria bade them sit down on the chaise longue.

They looked round at the heavily-furnished room, a piano, large

36

leather arm chairs, another padded settee on which Charles and Ursula sat, thick dark red damask curtains, side tables covered with linen cloths with embroidered edges which reached to the floor.

Rachel stood up again and began to walk around the room. 'This room is a bit like Mrs Montgomery's in Cairo,' she said. 'She's an old lady we know. And all these ornaments!'

Aunt Maria frowned slightly. 'You are a very self-possessed young woman. No doubt customs in foreign parts are different from those pertaining in the old country.'

'It has been a very easy-going life,' Ursula said lightly.

'Oh, I am sure Rachel will soon adapt,' Aunt Maria replied. 'She will realise that her behaviour might be considered rather forward for a young person.'

She turned as another young white-aproned girl entered the room. 'Ah, Gertie, place the tray on that table. Give a plate to our guests. I'll pour the tea myself. You can't rely on these servants to do anything, can you?' she remarked to Ursula.

Ursula half-smiled as she took the plate from the girl.

Charles stood up to help her but Mr Damarell said, 'Leave it to the ladies, Charles. Maria likes to manage household matters herself.'

Charles sat down again.

'What beautiful flowers you have everywhere.' Ursula smiled encouragingly at Charlotte and Rachel as her glance swept round the room.

Aunt Maria beamed. She looked suddenly almost coy as she said, 'Yes. They are the bouquets which still remain from the wedding.'

'Oh, yes, of course!' Charles exclaimed. 'It was very recent, wasn't it?'

'Only two weeks ago. Two weeks today, in fact.'

'May I rather belatedly wish you both joy and happiness.'

'Have you only just got married?' Rachel sounded incredulous.

'Yes, young woman. Marriage is not reserved only for the young and immature.'

'Oh, I'm sure—' Charles began when he was interrupted by the entrance of another young girl, wearing a long brown serge coat and close-fitting hat.

Mr Damarell stood up to make the introductions.

'This is my daughter, Bertha. Bertha, Mr and Mrs Cavendish and their daughters, Rachel and Charlotte.'

Bertha walked awkwardly over to Charles and Ursula, and hesitantly extended a hand, saying, 'How do you do?'

Charles smiled. She was probably a few years older than Rachel but she had none of the confidence and ebullience of his own daughter. Her sombre clothes emphasised her plain features and her rather shapeless figure, yet as her dark brown eyes looked into his, there was a mixture of rebellion and amusement in her expression. He began to feel that he was in a household of strange undercurrents. Their conversation sounded like something which had already been rehearsed, as though they were speaking from a pre-determined text while their true thoughts and feelings remained unexpressed. Memories of his own childhood came back to him. His aunt and uncle had spoken like this, as though words were intended to conceal reality rather than promote it. Although it had made his aunt and uncle appear remote, it had given a kind of security to his childhood, a certainty that all was right in the world. When Rachel became accustomed to them, no doubt she would feel the same way.

Bertha shook hands with Ursula and then went over to Rachel and Charlotte.

Rachel smiled. 'Come and sit here.'

'There will be more room for you, Bertha, on the other settee,' Aunt Maria said firmly.

Bertha looked at Rachel's gown and her grey kid boots. 'You've just come from London, haven't you?'

'Well, we shan't be introducing those fashions to Kingsbridge,' Aunt Maria said.

Bertha removed her coat and hat, passed them to Lizzie, who stood silently in the corner awaiting orders, and went over and sat on the settee. Rachel stood up and went and sat beside her.

'Yes. But I used to live in Egypt.'

'Oh, did you? What is it—?'

Then Bertha looked up and caught her father's eye. He was looking at her reprovingly and she was silent.

Mr Damarell stood up, saying, 'Perhaps Lizzie could take the girls to their room.'

Aunt Maria looked irritated. 'I was about to suggest it,' she said sharply. 'And come, Ursula and Charles. I will show you to your bedroom. Supper will be served promptly at seven. The gong will alert you. Betsy will attend to your toiletry while you are here, Ursula. I have found her the only satisfactory domestic in this household.'

She nodded towards the door where another older girl had appeared and now followed them up the wide staircase.

Mr Damarell nodded to Charles. 'The rest of the family will all be returning from business shortly. When you have refreshed yourself, come down to the smoking-room.'

At supper they were introduced to Mr Damarell's three sons who were all employed in and around Kingsbridge. It was made clear that Charlotte and Rachel were being allowed to eat with them as a special concession while their parents were staying. Normally, they would eat in a children's dining-room. It was also made clear that conversation at table was confined to adults; children were seen and not heard.

When Charles closed the bedroom door that night, he prepared himself for a long argument with Ursula about the impossibility of Rachel finding happiness in this household. He had even begun to doubt his own decision. Had his desire to give her a proper English upbringing been mistaken? Would it have been better for her to have remained in Egypt with them? He reminded himself that he was doing this for Rachel's own welfare. No. He would not listen to Ursula's objections.

Ursula yawned as Betsy unhooked her tight-bodiced dress before she crept from the room.

'That poor girl looks exhausted.' She took the pins from her hair.

Charles waited.

'Do you know, Maria is only four years older than I?'

Charles raised his eyebrows. 'She looks and behaves old enough to be your mother.'

'How old is Mr Damarell?'

'Arthur? He must be about ten years older than I am. Fifty-four, I suppose.'

'My parents are a lot older, and I suppose they look more frail, but they don't seem—' Her voice trailed into silence.

Charles put his hands on her shoulders, saying reassuringly, 'Rachel will only be here during the holidays and she will be visiting your parents. Perhaps—'

'Oh, I think Rachel will be all right. Maria isn't as fierce as she pretends. She is only establishing her authority. It must be difficult for her with four grown-up sons and a daughter who has been accustomed to ordering the affairs of the house. Bertha is only seventeen, but evidently she was running the household with the help of the many aunts in the neighbourhood.'

Charles nodded, concealing his surprise. After all her concern about Rachel, how could Ursula now be so sanguine? Women's behaviour was even more enigmatic than he had supposed. Then he remembered Mrs Montgomery's words, 'Women's desire to make decisions is very limited.'

'I am glad you see it so, Ursula. We shall also have to persuade Rachel that it is in her own interests.'

'Oh, I think Rachel will raise no objections.'

Charles raised his eyebrows in astonishment. How could she suppose that Rachel would accept the restrictions of this household?

For the next few days, he prepared himself for the inevitable battle. Nothing happened. Rachel spent her time with Bertha, arranging flowers, learning how to do tapestry, visiting in the afternoons with Aunt Maria and Ursula. Quiet, serious, fifteen-year-old Richard, who had just begun work in his father's mill, was permitted to take her for walks around Dodbrooke and Kingsbridge. Aunt Maria made no overt criticisms of Rachel's behaviour, but her expectations and attitudes were implicit in all her remarks. Rachel behaved as though she were unaware of any friction, smiling pleasantly at Aunt Maria's comments on her extensive wardrobe or on her determination to join in adult conversations.

Perhaps, Charles thought, Ursula had been more successful than he had realised in convincing Rachel of the advantages of English life. He decided with relief that no further action on his part was necessary but he delayed taking Rachel to visit her school until a week before their departure.

He knew that the school would affect Rachel more immediately than the holidays she would spend with the Damarell's. He glanced anxiously at Rachel as their carriage went up the long drive towards the large house on the outskirts of Kingsbridge – the Devonshire Establishment for Young Ladies. Looking over at the house, he saw some young girls of Rachel's age, standing before long french windows, watching them. They were all dressed in long black skirts and white blouses with wide sleeves.

They were shown in to Miss Gordon's large office. Miss Gordon was small and neat, with hair tied severely back in a bun, but she smiled sweetly at Charles. 'Ah, this is the dear child we shall be receiving.' She nodded to Rachel, 'Sit down, my dear. What a pleasure it will be to have you.'

'As I explained in my correspondence,' Charles said, 'we have only recently come from foreign parts. Rachel has not lived in England since she was an infant.'

'Ah, it will be strange for her, but we shall soon make her familiar with our little ways. We are very concerned to give our young ladies all those accomplishments so important for a happy feminine life.'

She discussed briefly with Charles the many activities in which Rachel would be involved, the fees which would be paid termly in advance and the exact requirements of the school uniform. Rachel suggested that she might bring her own clothes for any formal events, to which Miss Gordon readily agreed.

'You can keep them in your room,' she said. 'They will then be there should you need them. In this establishment, we only have two young ladies to a bedroom.'

They were taken around the house to inspect the bedrooms, the dining hall, the school room, the music room, the gardens where each young lady had a plot for growing flowers.

'What a strange thing,' Rachel said. 'Are there no gardeners?'

Miss Gordon smiled indulgently.

'Ah, of course. But exercise is important for growing girls. And if you have no interest in a little gentle gardening, there will be other talents you can develop.'

They did not meet any of the other students; Miss Gordon explained that they had gone for their afternoon walk.

As they left, Miss Gordon put an arm around Rachel. 'Goodbye, dear child. I look forward to your residence here when your parents depart.'

As they were driven back to Kingsbridge, Charles said, 'It is a commodious place. And Miss Gordon appears to have the interests of her pupils at heart.'

'Every time she speaks, she says "Ah".'

Charles smiled. 'Yes.'

He looked at Rachel. Her auburn hair had now grown to her shoulders; she was wearing a pale blue cloche hat and a dark blue coat with a fur collar. All the clothes her grandmother had bought her made her look so much older, so self-possessed. Yet she was still such a child.

'I hope you will be happy there,' Charles felt that he must make some statement. He must know her feelings.

'Papa, I know that you are doing this for my happiness.'

'I simply wish you to have the opportunities of any other young English girl.'

She smiled at him, a cool, distant smile; he felt as though he were the child, being reassured by her. He sighed. Men were so much easier to understand.

It was arranged that Aunt Maria should accompany Rachel to Plymouth to see her parents and Charlotte off on the train to London. This was the moment that Charles dreaded. Both Ursula and Rachel had seemed so sensible, so agreeable, but how would they behave when faced with that final parting? It had been agreed that Ursula should come to England to visit half-way through Charles's next term of service, but that would be two years away. Did Rachel realise how long that was?

It was a cold April day as they journeyed through the countryside to Plymouth. Only Charlotte seemed to be aware of the impending departure, clutching her sister's hand in silence. Rachel and Ursula talked about clothes and the pretty gardens and of how they would see each other quite soon. Then they were at the station, the train was waiting at the platform and Rachel stood with Aunt Maria beside her, suddenly looking pale and unsmiling.

Charlotte began to cry, Ursula leaned from the window, tears pouring down her face as the train began to move slowly along the platform and she called helplessly, 'Oh, Rachel. Rachel!'

Charles looked through the window at the pale girl, standing stiffly beside Aunt Maria, a distant expression on her face, one arm raised in farewell. Next time he saw her she would no longer be a child, she would be sixteen by then.

He felt a cold, terrible anxiety as he turned to comfort the two weeping females beside him.

Chapter 3

Rachel walked briskly along the platform towards the exit. They were gone. She felt a deep pain inside that she had never known before, a sense of panic that almost overwhelmed her. Suddenly she was alone.

She turned at the barrier and waited for Aunt Maria, walking haughtily along the platform, taking small, careful steps because of the straight, tight cut of her rustling and frilled grey silk skirt. The looped-up bustle at the back trailed along the ground in a great mass of material. She drew her purple cashmere woollen cloak around her and adjusted her small, flat hat with its veil dangling at the back. Aunt Maria was very conscious of the fact that she had come from Dorset and before that she had lived in Exeter. She intended to be the leader of subdued, decent, matronly fashion in Kingsbridge. She looked reflectively at Rachel.

'It's good to get that over. These farewells are always tiresome.'

Rachel sensed that it was her aunt's way of offering sympathy. But she didn't want sympathy. That would only make it harder to bear. She wouldn't think about it. She just wouldn't think about her mother or Charlotte, shut them out of her mind until she felt safe to let them back in. She turned away sharply and shrugged her shoulders.

'Yes.'

'Come, girl. We have an hour or so to wait before the horse-bus to Kingsbridge. We shall go to the Hoe and have a cup of tea in the tearooms there.'

The Hansom trundled up the steep hill and they alighted on the green slopes at the top. The pale May sunshine lay across the smooth waters of the Sound and Aunt Maria decided they would take a short walk along the pier before tea.

'Observe the fort over there,' she said, pointing to an island in the sea. 'Behind the breakwater. That's Shovel Rock. They built forts all round Plymouth abut ten years ago.'

Rachel looked at two ships sailing majestically beneath them, then gloomily to the open sea beyond, to oceans that took ships far away.

'What for?'

'I don't know,' Aunt Maria looked irritated at the question. 'For protection. Against the French, I suppose. Come, it's breezy up here.'

Rachel sighed, looking back across the grey water. It had seemed an adventure, coming to England. She and Charlotte had stood on the deck, looking at flying fish and dolphins and the sea red with the setting sun. But now the sea meant only a long journey; she could never reach them if she needed them. Conversations she had heard in the Damarell household told her what the sea was really like. Many of their relations were connected with the sea, fishermen, masters of vessels, pilots, and they all told another story. They saw the sea as an enemy, something to be feared, a great uncontrollable power.

Aunt Maria walked sedately into the tearoom. Tea was served to them in a silver pot by a waitress in a black crinoline and a white, frilled apron.

'There's a stain on your apron,' Aunt Maria observed. 'Spoils the appearance.'

The girl blushed.

'And wipe round the cups before you pour the tea.' The girl did so. 'You can't be too careful in this sort of place,' she said to Rachel, 'these common people aren't particular.'

It was dusk when they reached Kingsbridge but no one had returned yet from work. Rachel followed Aunt Maria into the silent hall and gave her cloak to Lizzie. 'Pray, take it to my room.'

If she went upstairs, she knew she would be drawn into the room her parents had occupied, she would have to look at their absence. If she waited until everyone was home, there would be no opportunity. She went into the drawing-room where Aunt Maria had just finished questioning the housekeeper about the day's activities.

'I shall go up and dress for dinner, Rachel. Perhaps you would prefer to remain in what you are wearing,' Aunt Maria suggested in a kind tone, as though she had felt Rachel's reluctance to go upstairs.

Rachel watched her climb the stairs and then wandered into the conservatory. The pale geraniums reminded her of the lush green foliage along the banks of the Nile, their heavy scent was reminiscent of the strange perfumes she had known in the bazaars. Her lips began to tremble but she shook her head and went back into the drawing-room. How could she bear these slow, lonely days? Then she had an idea. She would make out a long calendar of days and as each day passed, she would cross it off. She would pretend she was taking a long journey and at the end, there she would be in Egypt again.

Mr Damarell was the first to return. He was always up at daybreak and prided himself on the fact that none of his employees had ever arrived at the mill before him. It also ensured that there were no late-comers. Now that Richard was employed in the mill, Mr Damarell had taken to returning earlier in the evenings, leaving Richard to see that his employees did not leave before time.

'Come along, Lizzie,' Aunt Maria said sharply as he entered the hall. 'Take the master's coat.'

'I can hang up my own coat,' her husband said mildly.

'It is not your place,' Aunt Maria smiled firmly. 'You have done these things far too long. You have forgotten what it's like to have a properly-run household.'

He smiled briefly, asking, 'Did you have a satisfactory journey?'

'They departed in good spirits, I believe. And Rachel behaved very sensibly.'

Mr Damarell glanced at Rachel. 'Good girl,' he said. 'The time will soon pass. And you've got your schooling to attend to.'

Rachel nodded briefly. 'That was papa's view.'

'Very sensible. These foreign parts aren't good for women.'

'Mama is there.'

'Rachel, that is quite different,' Aunt Maria interposed. 'She is a married lady. It is for your father to decide what is suitable for her.' She turned as James came into the room.

'Good evening, Papa – and Mama.'

Rachel had a sense of comfort as she looked at his kindly face.

James was a thatcher in Kingsbridge and on one occasion he had taken her to collect the hazel and willow sticks he used and shown her how to bend them like hairpins to secure the thatch in place. She had watched him as he carried the long straw up to the roof with a forked branch that he called a yack. James wasn't much taller than she was and her mother had told Rachel that he was delicate.

James turned to Rachel. 'I'll take you to the lantern lecture this evening, if your aunt agrees.'

'Oh, yes.'

'Is it a suitable topic?' Aunt Maria looked doubtful.

'It's a talk by a missionary, recently returned from Africa. A topic in which Rachel may be interested.'

'Very well. I know you'll keep an eye on her. Now that her parents have departed, your father and I must feel responsible for her welfare.'

James smiled at Rachel and went to dress for dinner. Dressing for dinner meant that the men changed from their working clothes into black suits and the ladies into different dresses; not like the evening dress the men wore in Cairo and the brilliant gowns that the ladies and her mother had worn.

Bertha and Thomas arrived at the same time.

Twenty-year old Thomas was an apprentice foundryman in Dates Dockyard in Kingsbridge. He was even taller than his father, with a round face and a ruddy complexion.

He looked cheerfully at Rachel. 'My, you look fine in that blue gown, Rachel. You must have turned the boys' eyes in Plymouth.'

'I hope not,' Aunt Maria said severely. 'Rachel is only a child.' She frowned. 'I think the clothes her parents have provided her with are rather advanced. But, at school, she will wear more normal attire for her age.'

'I'm nearly thirteen.' Aunt Maria seemed to introduce the question of her age every day. It was as though she divided life up into neat boxes, your age deciding which box you should be placed in. Children, young ladies, young married persons, mature women, she had them all firmly sorted out.

Thomas winked at Rachel as he left the room.

They were halfway through supper before Richard returned from the mill.

'One of the machines needed attention. John Boscomb and Jack Hill stayed behind with me.'

Richard sat down opposite Rachel. Rachel liked his face. He had nice soft brown eyes and curly brown hair which was always combed neatly in place. But he was very serious; he hardly ever seemed to smile.

Rachel grinned at him and he nodded briefly.

'James and I are going to a lantern show tonight. You could come, Richard.'

'Why can't I go?' Bertha looked indignant. 'I'm older than Rachel.'

Mr Damarell looked at the two girls but did not speak.

Aunt Maria interposed.

'Would you both stop talking and eat your food. This is not a ladies' tea-party. And James has kindly invited Rachel this evening to take her mind off her parents' departure. There is no call for you to accompany them, Bertha.'

Rachel frowned into her plate. Was it true? Did James just feel sorry for her? She looked at him but he was discussing Mr Disraeli with his father and Thomas.

'I don't agree with all these liberal views of Gladstone,' Mr Damarell was saying, 'but that Disraeli is a charlatan.'

'The lads in the Dockyard are all for Gladstone,' Thomas said. 'They think he's interested in their welfare, sir.'

'They probably do,' Mr Damarell looked critical. 'Pandering to all their demands. Unions and welfare for the poor. Higher wages. If he's not careful, he'll have them wanting to run things. And look at all this freedom he's giving to the Irish.'

'There's a lot of poverty, Papa. It can't be right for people to go hungry.'

'Hh. What they need is to work a bit harder. Practice thrift like I did as a youth.'

Mr Damarell stood up and they all rose as he said Grace. Rachel closed her eyes. When he had thanked God for the meal, Mr Damarell always added a bit more. Rachel thought he wished he were a preacher.

'Let us remember that only God can see into our souls. We may hide the designs and intentions of our minds, we may conceal our secret thoughts from those around us, but God sees all.'

Every time he mentioned God she had a picture in her mind of the great statues at Luxor and the god who had come to Alexander in Siwa. Momentarily, she felt the panic she had felt at the station, but she breathed hard and followed Bertha from the room. It would be all right. Mama had said that England was a nice place. Everything would be all right when she went to school. It would be fun with all those girls. And James was kind and Richard told her all sorts of interesting things about the countryside.

It was only when she was alone at last and climbed into bed between the cold linen sheets that grief overcame her. She blew out her candle and longed for Charlotte and her mother's arms around her and the golden sunshine of Egypt. She thought of her last trip through the desert with her father to the monastery at Wadi El Natrun, riding a camel with her mother to the Siwa oasis with the ruins of old earth houses rising up the hillside. She saw the sun glittering on the water as she and Charlotte walked along the banks of the Nile.

It was so long, they were so far away, she could never survive. The feeling of panic seized her again. When she wrote she would tell papa that he must come and get her, that her schooling didn't matter. Papa had said that it was important, that one day she would marry an Englishman and must know how to conduct herself and run a proper household. Well, she wouldn't marry. She would live with mama and papa in Egypt. Her tears subsided and at last she fell asleep with exhaustion.

Yet in the morning, it seemed different. The sun was shining through the casement; perhaps something nice would happen today. Bertha crept into her room as the breakfast gong sounded.

'Are you ready?' she whispered. Bertha wasn't supposed to be there.

Rachel nodded as she finished coiling her hair into a short plait.

'Why did you have your hair all cut off?'

'It's hot in Egypt,' Rachel said. 'But I've decided not to speak of Egypt any more.'

Bertha looked mystified. 'Why?'

'Because I said so. Come along. We'd better go.'

'I like that gown.' Bertha looked enviously at the pale blue silk, with its tiny bustle at the back.

'It's not as nice as the dresses I had in—'

Rachel stopped. She was going to forget. She blinked. 'Come on.'

Rachel found that life in the Damarell household was so filled with activity that she had little opportunity during the day to think about anything but the immediate demands of living. There seemed to be a constant stream of relatives visiting them, all of whom lived in Dodbrooke or Kingsbridge.

There was Uncle Jonathon, the tailor and his wife Alice, Uncle James the carpenter, Aunt Martha who was a straw-bonnet maker and who came to visit them from Dartmouth, and Uncle John who was the captain of a ship in Brixham.

Every afternoon was occupied with At Homes or visiting the houses of other ladies in the neighbourhood with Aunt Maria and Bertha, and sometimes they took parcels of food round to the poor people who lived in the ancient cottages.

The conversation of the ladies was different from that which took place when men were present. They talked about the latest fashions in Plymouth and Exeter, about the newest styles in furnishings, the suitability of brightly-coloured velvets and cretonnes for bedrooms. But they also discussed marriage and the unsuitable behaviour of various unmarried maidens in the vicinity.

When Rachel asked Bertha what they meant, Bertha explained that one young lady had been seen, unaccompanied, sharing an umbrella with a young man whom she scarcely knew. Another one had danced three times with a gentleman to whom she had only just been introduced.

'But why not?'

'Because it's forward,' Bertha said. 'It's not considered correct behaviour. But mama will ensure that you behave properly when you get older.'

'Aunt Maria is not your mama, is she?'

'She is now, Rachel. Papa wishes me to call her that.' Bertha frowned. 'She's not like my real mama was, though.'

Rachel looked at Bertha's pale face. It was really sad. 'Never mind,' she said. 'We won't talk about it, like I won't talk about Egypt.'

'No. I'm glad you've come, Rachel. It will be nice to have you in the holidays. It's lonely with all those brothers. You can't talk to boys.'

They were sitting in the conservatory of Aunt Julie's house in Kingsbridge. Aunt Maria appeared from the drawing-room, saying, 'Come, girls. It is time to depart.'

A clock struck four-thirty as they went through the front door.

'Pray, ensure that Rose does not over-tax herself now that she's in a certain state,' Aunt Maria added as she kissed Aunt Julie lightly on the cheek.

'What does that mean?' Rachel asked as they climbed into their carriage.

Aunt Maria frowned. 'We do not mention that kind of thing in company, or in front of gentlemen, Rachel,' she said. 'Dear Rose is to have a child. But she would be very immodest even in discussing it with her husband.'

'Doesn't her husband know, then?'

'Rachel, that's quite enough. We don't want all these questions. Wait until you're older. You'll know soon enough.'

Rachel decided that she would ask James later, for James didn't seem to mind her questions. Yet even James told her that young ladies did not discuss such matters and she should be mindful of the advice given to her by Aunt Maria.

At the end of the summer, on the day before Rachel departed for school, she and Bertha were invited to a young person's birthday party. Aunt Maria had been uncertain about accepting the invitation, since it came from a farmer's daughter at Loddiswell, whose social position she viewed with some doubt.

But Mr Damarell said that he, and his father before him, had known the family for years and it was appropriate that they should go. Bertha protested that she had no suitable garment of her own, so she was permitted to wear one of Rachel's. For one afternoon, Rachel forgot her parents and Charlotte. They played games, ran in the fields and watched the cows being milked in the yard. There was no Grace before they had their tea and the children's plump, laughing mother had made jellies and junkets and, for each of them, a special little cake with their name on it in icing sugar.

She told Rachel how pretty she was and how she liked her lovely silk dress and hair ribbons and when the carriage came to collect them, she kissed Rachel goodbye.

'It was such a lovely party,' Rachel told Aunt Maria when they reached home. Aunt Maria still looked doubtful. Since her marriage to Mr Damarell she had taken control of a household which she felt had been run inadequately since the first Mrs Damarell's death and was now devoting herself to improving the family's social standing. Of course, Mr Damarell was respected, he was wealthy and influential in community affairs, but it was important that they should associate with the higher echelons of society, the gentleman farmers and the rising number of solicitors and doctors.

'This is a small community, my dear Maria,' Mr Damarell said good-humouredly. 'They are respectable, God-fearing people.'

The next day, Rachel went to school. She was accompanied on this occasion by Mr Damarell.

'Why won't you come, Aunt Maria?'

Aunt Maria shook her head.

'It is for men to conduct these arrangements,' she said. 'It concerns financial matters which Mr Damarell will manage on behalf of your papa.'

The carriage turned into the school entrance. A large white notice board announced, in black letters surrounded by a delicate green tracery of leaves and blue flowers, The Devon Educational Establishment for Young Ladies. As they drove up the gravel drive which swept in a semi-circle to the wide entrance steps, Rachel looked with anticipation at the long, red brick, two-storey house. Some of the bricks were a paler colour, as though they had faded over the years. The stone pillar balustrades around the balconies on the first floor had gaps here and there where masonry had been damaged and never repaired.

They entered the large entrance hall, from which open doors led into high-ceilinged rooms. The hall was clean and white, as though it had been recently painted.

They were shown into a drawing-room to await Miss Gordon's summons. Rachel stood by the window. The settees looked as though they were not meant to be sat on. They were upholstered in heavy damask, patterned with large red roses and bright green leaves, and the cushions seemed to stand erect and untouchable. She glanced up at the high ceilings, which were cracked across in places and wavy cracks curved here and there down the walls. A brass gas lamp stood on either side of the white marble fireplace which looked as though there had been no fire in the grate for many years. It was as if no one lived here really.

Mr Damarell sat down on a high-backed wooden chair and placed his arms on the long leather-surfaced mahogany table. He looked around at the small black wooden tables and the pink upright arm chairs with embroidered anti-macassars, commenting, 'Seems a substantial sort of place. I hope you'll be a credit to your parents, Miss, sending you here.'

'Yes.' Rachel suddenly realised she had never actually talked with Mr Damarell. In fact, he didn't talk to Bertha or Aunt Maria, either, in the way he talked to James and Thomas.

They were led into Miss Gordon's room and she greeted them with her sweet, amiable smile.

'Pray be seated, Mr Damarell. Miss Cavendish, you are to share a room with Miss Sophia Curzon,' she smiled at Rachel. 'I shall summon her so that she may conduct you there and see to the delivery of your luggage. When I have discussed matters with Mr Damarell, you will be brought back here so that I can acquaint you with all the necessary procedures.'

Mr Damarell stood up and kissed Rachel formally on the cheek. 'We shall look forward to hearing of your satisfactory progress.' He smiled at her kindly.

'Ah, Miss Sophia. Here is your new room-mate, Miss Rachel Cavendish. Pray take her to her room. Her luggage is being conveyed there. I will ring the bell when I wish you to return here.'

Miss Sophia was tall, with blue eyes and fair hair which was coiled round her head in a wide plait.

'Yes, ma'am.'

She looked demurely at Rachel as she followed her into the hall but as soon as the door was closed, Sophia turned to Rachel eagerly, asking, 'How long are you going to be here?'

'Well . . . I don't know.' Rachel sounded surprised.

'It's horrible,' Sophia made a face.

'What is?'

54

'Everything. You might as well know.'

Rachel frowned as they climbed the stairs to her room. 'Miss Gordon was very nice, Miss Sophia.'

'Heavens, don't call me that. That's only for when she's around. Just Sophie. And you'll soon find out whether she's nice or not.'

They entered a small room, which contained two beds, a dressing-table and a small wardrobe.

'Is this it?' Rachel looked astonished. 'The rooms Miss Gordon showed my papa were much larger.'

Sophie laughed. 'Yes. She always does that. Those rooms aren't really occupied at all, except by the Gorgon's guests. It's no good complaining, though. "I find your behaviour insolent and ungrateful".' Sophie mimicked Miss Gordon's voice. ' "Sadly, I shall have to report this to your parents if I hear any more of it." '

Rachel smiled uncertainly.

Sophie touched Rachel's pale green taffeta gown, commenting, 'It's so long since I wore anything like that. In fact, I've never really had such a dress. Only sort of children's clothes. I was only ten when I came here.'

'Don't you go home in the holidays?'

'My father's abroad. My mama died when I was little so I'm in the charge of my grandmother. I stay with her in the holidays. She thinks I can make do with my school clothes. How old are you?'

'Nearly thirteen.'

'I'm thirteen and three-quarters. Papa comes home next year and I'm going to get ill.'

Rachel looked puzzled. 'How do you mean?'

'Well, if I'm ill he'll have to take me away. Miss Gordon doesn't like sickness on the Establishment premises. Anyhow, you'd better change. The Gorgon doesn't like to be kept waiting.'

'What do you mean, the Gorgon?'

Sophie grinned. 'Don't you know the story? She was a woman with snakes for hair and anyone who looked at her was turned to stone.'

'Oh.'

Rachel removed her taffeta gown and silk petticoats and put on the black skirt, white cambric petticoat and white blouse. The hem of her skirt only reached above her ankles. Her mother had been told that full-length skirts were not permitted until you were sixteen. She pulled on the regulation short black boots and glanced in the small looking-glass which was only large enough to reflect her face.

'Look. You can see yourself in the window.'

Rachel peered at herself, exclaiming, 'Oh, it's awful. I look like a tweeney,' then jumped as a shrill bell peeled above her head.

Sophie laughed. 'Bells ring all the time, in every room, for everything. Come on. I'll take you down.'

She knocked on Miss Gordon's door. There was no reply. 'We have to wait here until the Gorgon calls,' Sophie whispered. They waited in silence for five minutes.

'Come in, girls.'

Miss Gordon was alone. Her soft smile embraced them both. 'Come and stand here, Miss Rachel. You may go now, Miss Sophia.'

Rachel sat down on the wooden chair which faced Miss Gordon. Miss Gordon smiled as she said, 'Young ladies do not sit down unless bidden by their elders, do they, Miss Rachel?'

'Oh.' Rachel stood up again.

'Now, let us just run through the regulations.' She handed a piece of paper to Rachel. 'Perhaps you would read it to me. Then we shall know that you have understood it all.'

Rachel looked at the sheet of copper-plate handwriting and then glanced at Miss Gordon.

'Come on then, girl. Let us not waste valuable time.' Her gentle voice was rather sharp.

Rachel read aloud:

Young ladies will conduct themselves with decorum at all times.
The time-tables must be strictly adhered to and punctuality is required.
There will be no conversation in halls or corridors.
Silence will be maintained at meals unless you are addressed by a member of staff.
Time-table – Monday to Saturday

Breakfast	7 am
Prayers in chapel	8 am
School room	9 am
Lunch	12 noon

Resting in bedroom and inspection, after which suitable reading may be undertaken	1 pm
Embroidery and needlework	2 pm
Household management	3 pm
Exercise and deportment	4 pm
Musical instruments	5 pm
Supper	6 pm
Prayers	7 pm
Lights out: girls up to 14 years	8 pm
all others	9 pm

Anyone arriving late in the dining-room will forego the meal. A repetition of the misdemeanour will result in the loss of privileges. Sunday is a day of rest and prayer. Reading and activities of an uplifting nature will be permitted. Attendance at church is required morning, afternoon and evening.

Rachel came to the end of the document. She looked at Miss Gordon and asked, 'What are privileges?'

Miss Gordon smiled. 'Ah, that will not apply to you. The older girls are granted certain privileges for good behaviour. Now, Miss Rachel, your father explained that your rather unbecoming hairdress is attributable to the hot weather of the tropics. Until it has grown to a suitable length, pray ensure that it is held neatly in place with combs.'

'Miss Gordon, can I wear my own clothes on Sundays?'

Miss Gordon's smile disappeared.

'Miss Rachel, all personal clothes are assigned to the attics to be collected when you depart for holidays. Also, Miss Rachel, please understand that normally I do not encourage questions from young ladies. Now that we have had our little introductory talk, you will find you have no further need for queries.' Miss Gordon glanced at the black marble clock on the mantelpiece. 'As it is now past five, you may go to your room until the 6 o'clock bell rings for supper. Ensure that you are prompt.'

Rachel sat disconsolately on her bed and looked through the window at the lawns below. The flowerbeds were still vivid with gladioli and red and pink and yellow roses climbed delicately over the trellises that adorned the paths. Two girls, much older than herself, were walking slowly arm in arm along the path. Was that a privilege they were having? From somewhere in the house she could hear the sound of a piano and violins. A feeling of loneliness began to overcome her and then she jumped again as a bell pealed through the house. She hurried down the stairs to the refectory but by the time she arrived it was already full. For the first time, she saw her fellow students, what seemed to be hundreds of girls, all in white blouses and black skirts, laughing, giggling, talking. The noise seemed to echo against the high ceiling. She saw Sophie waving at her to come and sit by her on the long bench.

Rachel smiled with relief. Were Miss Gordon's regulations just something on a piece of paper that didn't mean anything? Suddenly there was total silence, as though some invisible sign had been given. At the same moment, the door was opened by a servant and Miss Gordon entered the room and walked slowly to her chair at the top of the table, followed by her staff.

She looked on with satisfaction as the girls around her silently ate their meal of boiled potatoes and stewed meat. When the plates were removed, Rachel waited for the next course. But Miss Gordon stood up, said Grace and led the girls to the chapel.

'Is that all? Rachel whispered. 'I'm hungry.'

'You wouldn't survive on that. We buy things from the grocery and fruit boys when they deliver.'

'But Miss Gordon administers our allowances.'

'Oh, she won't enquire where it goes. She's happy enough if you spend it on victuals.'

That night, Rachel did not think much about her parents. Her mind was filled with conflicting impressions of the day that had just ended. All those girls around her had seemed like the sea rushing in, overwhelming her, submerging her in confusion. What were they all here for? Why was she here? Why had mama and papa thought it important for her to come to a place like this? And Miss Gordon. Why didn't she want anyone to speak? She knew from life at the Damarells that there were all sorts of things in England that you didn't do. Young people didn't speak at the table and you didn't go into the toilets on the ground floor which were reserved for gentlemen. The servants weren't allowed to speak in front of the family and there were things that men talked about that had nothing to do with women. Aunt Maria and Aunt Emmie and Aunt Bessie just listened when men talked about Mr Gladstone and things like that.

The next morning, Rachel told Sophie that she had been cold during the night.

Sophie laughed. 'You'd better tell Miss Gordon.'

Rachel followed Miss Gordon as they left the refectory after breakfast.

'Miss Gordon. May I be permitted to have another blanket? I was cold last night.'

The girls around her stopped. Rachel saw that Sophie was looking at her in horror.

'Come to my room, Miss Rachel.'

Miss Gordon did not return Rachel's smile as she stood by her desk.

'Miss Rachel. I am sorry to hear you complaining with such impudence at such an early stage in your residence here.'

'I'm not complaining,' Rachel interrupted. 'You wouldn't know I was cold, would you? It's probably just that I got used to the heat in Egypt.'

'Miss Rachel, kindly do not interrupt when I am speaking. The blankets provided are sufficient for any young person. Pray do not let me hear such allegations of neglect on my part again.'

'It's absurd, Miss Gordon. My father is paying you to look after me. I am entitled—'

'Miss Rachel!' Miss Gordon interrupted angrily. Her face was red; she shuffled some papers agitatedly on her desk as she composed herself before adding, 'Never let me hear you speak so again. I shall report this to your parents if I hear any more of it. I do not know what they would think, when they have been so concerned for your welfare in sending you here.'

Rachel was silent. Doubt entered her mind. Would they believe this woman because she was grown up? Would papa think she had been insolent? For the first time since they had gone, she felt a sense of isolation from her parents which had nothing to do with their departure. She felt separated not by distance but by the impossibility of communication.

There was a note of finality in Miss Gordon's voice as she

continued, 'Now, Miss Rachel, I hope this is but an aberration on your part. Your papa has told me of your rather undisciplined life in foreign parts. That is why he has sent you here. I shall ensure he is not disappointed. I know that when he returns, he will be proud of the nice young English lady you will have become.'

Rachel walked slowly down the corridor. The pain and longing for her parents had returned, but now she had also begun to feel a deep resentment towards her father. Did he know what this stupid woman was like? Had he taken the trouble to find out? No. All he wanted was to be rid of her because he thought she was a trouble.

Well, she didn't care. In future she would be even more troublesome. She would not be dominated by petty rules and regulations. There were tears in her eyes as a bell pealed loudly beside her and she followed the girls as they walked from the chapel into the school room.

Sophie whispered, 'Don't worry about her. Here's a sweet.'

Over the next months, Rachel discovered that unhappiness was never a total state, that her sense of loss and misery was overladen by day to day events and new experiences. The classroom lessons began each day with arithmetic, which consisted of endless calculations of domestic accounts, from the cost of servants, household furnishings, flower and plant displays to the expenses of food, cooking, domestic appliances and the entertainment of guests.

This was followed with the reading of suitable literature, much of which dealt with the happy home lives which the young ladies themselves would one day be responsible for creating. Writing involved copying from handsomely produced books of copper-plate script so that they could develop a neat and impressive hand. Many hours were spent designing and studying appropriate cards for At Homes, invitations, memorials, announcements of engagements, weddings and funerals.

Twice a week, an elderly French lady tutored them in the elements of her language, all of them repeating in unison phrases and sentences as she uttered them.

Household management encompassed a vast field of feminine activity, from the organisation of the servants to the education of children. Rachel learnt that a lady's chief purpose in life was to create a haven of peace and beauty for her husband and sons. This was achieved by ensuring that all domestic activities ran quietly and smoothly. Social values dictated that young ladies did not entertain worldly ambitions; the home was the correct and desirable place in which all feminine virtues and accomplishments should flourish. The only acceptable outside activity was unpaid charitable work – acceptable as long as it did not interfere with the comforts of husband and sons.

Rachel enjoyed the piano and viola lessons, although the music teacher decided early on that she had no voice for singing drawing-room songs and ballads.

Unfortunately, the novelty of these activities soon lost its appeal. After Egypt it all seemed an unreal and temporary world which she could defy and treat with contempt.

Her days were interspersed with criticism and rebuke from Miss Gordon about matters which Rachel considered trivial and irrelevant. On one occasion when Miss Gordon was inspecting their rooms, she reprimanded Rachel for the untidiness of her drawers. Rachel instantly snatched all the clothes out and cast them on the floor.

'Then let the maids do it. It is their job.'

Miss Gordon grabbed her by the arm, hissing, 'Pick them up.' She then turned to Sophie, and added, 'Kindly leave, Miss Sophia.'

Sophie cast an anxious glance at Rachel.

'Go.'

Sophie crept out.

'Now, Miss Rachel, your insubordination has gone too far. I shall report your conduct to your guardians. Perhaps Mr Damarell can inject some respect into you.'

'If you complain, they will take me away. They are concerned for my happiness.'

Rachel noticed with satisfaction that Miss Gordon hesitated. It occurred to her that Miss Gordon had no wish to lose her, even if she was a nuisance, for it would not be good for her reputation. In any case she was more interested in the fees she extracted from papa.

'I will give you one last chance, Miss Rachel. I fear very much for your future happiness. I see nothing but trouble ahead for you. Try to be more ladylike in future.'

Miss Gordon walked briskly from the room.

Rachel stood at the window watching a gardener sweeping up leaves on the path below. The Gorgon's words gave her a momentary feeling of apprehension, as though the woman had cast an evil spell on her. Would her life really be miserable, would she never find the happiness she had known in Egypt? Looking at the fallen leaves, she reflected that it was about this time of year that she had gone with her parents to the opening of the Canal at Port Said. It seemed so long ago, but even now she could still visualise the great display in the pavilions and the Empress who had congratulated her on her French.

The only time that life seemed normal to Rachel was when they went, in pairs, on their afternoon walk along the country lanes. It was intended to be a brisk walk, not only to give them exercise and fresh air, but also to concentrate on improving deportment. But the elderly teacher who accompanied them had little taste for briskness and when they were out of sight of the house, the girls would hurry on to their allotted destination and then sit on the grass, waiting for her to reach them.

Rachel had become accustomed to the Sunday excursions to church from her stay at the Damarells and every Sunday as they walked down the hill in a crocodile, the older young ladies at the front, they passed the ragged children on their way to Sunday school. She remembered, with a curious feeling of guilt, the faces of some of these children. She had visited them with Aunt Maria when she was dispensing charity. A part of her suspected that their world was more real than the one she inhabited for the expressions on their faces seemed to reflect feelings, whether of joy or misery, rather than the correct, undemonstrative behaviour demanded by the Gorgon.

The period between the afternoon and evening church services was devoted to letter-writing.

Rachel would look gloomily around at the other girls in the school-room, most of them diligently writing, dipping their pens in their inkwells every few seconds, as though they feared they would be unable to impart all their news in the allotted time. Yet what did they have to say? Having divulged the contents of her daily time-table in the first few letters, there seemed to be nothing to add to the daily repetition. All she wanted to tell her parents was of her longing to see them, to be with them, to ask papa to come and get her and take her back to Egypt.

But Rachel knew that the Gorgon read all correspondence before it was dispatched; she could never reveal her true feelings. She yearned for letters from her mother, but each time one arrived telling her of all their activities in Cairo, she was plunged into an even greater longing and despair. Only Charlotte's little notes, composed mainly of drawings and squiggles, could raise her spirits a little.

When Rachel returned to the Damarells for Christmas, she was surprised to hear Aunt Maria reveal that she was pleased with the report she had received from Miss Gordon.

'She hates me,' Rachel retorted. 'She's always criticising me.'

'What nonsense,' Aunt Maria said severely. 'You should not speak of your elders in such a manner. It is her job to be concerned with your behaviour.'

Rachel pursed her lips disdainfully. Adults were always concerned for her welfare; it was simply their way of imposing restrictions, making demands.

'She's only interested in the fees she receives from papa.'

'That may be true,' Aunt Maria said in a matter of fact way. 'Obviously, a woman in her situation occupies an inferior position in life. But she has made the best of her lot and that does not invalidate her right to courtesy from her pupils.'

'It's so irksome,' Rachel said, looking hopefully at Aunt Maria. Perhaps she would understand?

But Aunt Maria only said sharply, 'We all have irksome things to accept, Rachel. You should think more of the benefits which life has bestowed upon you.' As she began to walk away, she added, 'Sometimes I fear that your recalcitrant behaviour will only bring unhappiness upon you in the future.'

Rachel went up to her room to unpack her suitcase. The same doubt assailed her that she had felt at the Gorgon's prognostication. How could her behaviour now lead them to foresee an unhappy life for her?

After the restrictions of the Establishment even the limited celebrations in this household seemed exotic. She and Bertha took presents to the poor people in the neighbourhood and the whole family went to the carol service in the church on Christmas Eve. One day James took her to see a roof he had thatched in Loddiswell, and she was permitted to visit the mill with Richard. He told her about the history of the mill, how it had been started by his grandfather and now employed twenty men. He looked with pride at the buildings and the giant wheel turning.

'Of course, I shan't inherit it.'

'What do you mean?'

'Well, when father dies, it goes to the eldest son. James will have it then.'

'James! But he's a thatcher, isn't he?'

Richard's face clouded.

'Yes. I know. But that's what happens.'

'What will you do?'

'I intend to start my own business,' Richard said. 'I shall work hard and have a mill of my own.'

Rachel paused. 'I wonder what I shall do.'

Richard looked surprised.

'Well, you'll marry, of course, and run a household. That's what you are learning about, aren't you?'

Rachel nodded. 'Yes.'

She thought about the Establishment. Some of the older girls looked so grown-up and elegant and they talked so nicely about all those womanly pursuits. On Sunday afternoons after church they were required to give little talks about how to be attentive to your husband and about modesty and decorum. They would obviously have lovely households. Of course, they all thought Miss Gordon was a dragon but none of them complained about their education.

Except Sophie. Sophie had confided that she never wanted to marry. Yet when Rachel asked what she would do instead, Sophie had been unable to say.

'My mama doesn't seem to be like them,' Rachel admitted. 'Our lives seemed so different.'

'Well,' Sophie said. 'She sent you here to learn all this.'

'Yes. I know. I suppose when she comes back she will run her household in the same way.'

She was walking back down the hill from the mill with Richard and said, 'Not all girls want to marry.'

Richard's serious face showed amusement as he replied, 'Well, there are those unfortunate ladies who remain spinsters. But that would not be choice, Rachel. Every lady would prefer to enjoy the protection of a husband.'

She thought of Miss Gordon. Perhaps Richard was right . . .

Winter turned to spring, and Rachel realised with relief that a year had nearly passed. Although every letter from her parents re-awakened her longing to return to Egypt, the routine and rigidity of school was something she had slowly become accustomed to. She knew it was largely because of Sophie, with whom she shared a secret, often unspoken, attitude towards the school. They adhered to the rules and regulations, but they always retained an implicit and detached observation of events, almost as though they were on the edge of rebellion. In her heart, though, Rachel realised that Sophie did not share her deep resentment towards authority. Sophie just seemed unperturbed by events.

The following summer mama was going to come for the holiday and Rachel decided that she would persuade her that she had learnt enough by then. If papa were not with her, she might even manage to persuade mama to take her back to Egypt.

But the beginning of the summer term brought with it a series of events which, looking back, seemed to Rachel to mark the start of a period of disasters.

One evening, she and Sophie were reading in their beds and since it was getting dark Rachel lit a candle. Turning to pick up her book again, she knocked the candle over. It fell on the blanket and, before she could grasp it, the bed was alight.

Rachel screamed, Sophie jumped from her bed and, in her panic, flung open the window to call for help. The breeze sent the flames higher and they both dashed from the room, calling frantically. In an instant, bells were ringing, servants were dashing in with bowls of water and the flames were put out. Miss Gordon appeared on the threshold, a black woollen robe tied tightly around her, her long grey hair loose and dishevelled, asking, 'What has happened?'

Her soft, sweet voice had become shrill.

'It was an accident.' Rachel crept back into the room and walked, through the smoke, across the wet floor. The servants had thrown the damaged blanket out of the open window, and a smell of burning pervaded the room.

Miss Gordon remained in the doorway.

'Is it all controlled?'

'Yes, ma'am.'

'Then clear up the mess.' She glanced around to satisfy herself that all was well. 'Miss Rachel and Miss Sophia, put on some clothes, if they are still suitable, and come with me.' They followed her to her study.

'How did this occur?'

'It was an accident,' Rachel repeated.

'How could something suddenly start burning?'

'I knocked over the candle.'

'Why was the candle lit?'

'I was reading.'

Miss Gordon stood up and walked around the room.

'Reading, lighting candles, defiance of rules,' she said in a low voice as though she could scarcely comprehend the event. 'What are you?' Her voice rose to a shriek. 'Monsters? Evil, ungrateful, dangerous creatures? I shall have to consider the desirability of retaining such persons in my establishment.'

'It wasn't Sophie, it was me.'

'Sophie! And who is Sophie?'

'Miss Sophia.'

Miss Gordon was breathing heavily.

Rachel and Sophie glanced at each other and then watched Miss Gordon as she pulled the bell-rope.

A distraught-looking servant appeared.

'Mary, escort Miss Sophia to one of the empty bedrooms on the first floor. You will return to your room tomorrow after it has been cleaned. Miss Rachel, come with me.'

Rachel followed her up the stairs, along a corridor, up further flights of stairs until they reached an attic on the top floor, where the servants slept.

'You will sleep in this room until I have decided what is to be done.' Miss Gordon walked out, closing the door behind her.

Rachel stood on the bare wooden floor and peered into the darkness. Only a tiny window high in the wall admitted a ray of light which revealed a narrow bed and a small cupboard. There was nothing else. She crept into bed in her petticoats.

It was hard and there was only a sheet and a thin blanket to cover her.

She lay still, looking up through the narrow window to the sky. For the first time, she began to feel an uncontrollable anger towards Miss Gordon and all she represented. Until now, she had attributed her feelings to her separation from her parents. Mama's letters had always reassured her; one day she felt life would return to normal. In the meantime, she was doing as they wished.

Now she began to feel hatred of Miss Gordon welling up inside her. How could she conceal her defiance? Suddenly she remembered another incident long ago, when she had gone off into the desert and papa had been very angry with her. Doubt entered her mind. Would papa agree now with the Gorgon?

Then she told herself that it would be all right when she returned to the room she shared with Sophie. Sophie was the only one who understood. She could always talk to her.

But she did not return. The next day, after prayers in the chapel, Miss Gordon announced that there had been a disaster the previous night. Due to the insubordination of two young ladies, the lives and safety of the whole community had been put at risk. As a result, one young lady, the real culprit, had been consigned to an attic bedroom while Miss Gordon pondered on her future.

In the school room, Sophie whispered, 'Don't worry. She won't expel you. She's too interested in your fees.'

'I don't care. If she does, I can go back to Egypt.'

'No. Your parents would probably send you to another place. It might be worse.'

Rachel frowned. Could there be worse places? She remembered going to the poorhouse with Aunt Maria to visit one of their old servants. But that wasn't an establishment for young ladies.

She waited for Miss Gordon to call for her but no command came and every night, she climbed up to the cold attic. After a week, she resolved that her next letter to her parents would acquaint them with all the terrible things she suffered at Miss Gordon's.

She told Sophie her plan.

'Don't do that, Rachel. You know Miss Gordon reads all our letters before they are posted. Your parents would never get it and what do you think she would do at such insolence?'

'I can't stay in that room. It's so cold and I can hear rats up in the roof.'

'Why don't you just apologise to the old cow. Pretend you're full of remorse.'

'No.'

'Have you got any of your allowance left?'

'Yes, of course. But she's got it.'

'Well, say you'll pay for the damage and order some flowers from the village as a present.'

'Sophie!' Rachel's voice rose. They were in the music room, so their conversation was drowned by the cacophony of sounds issuing from pianos, violins, two girls practising a duet and the beat of a metronome.

'It's not important, Rachel.'

'Oh, Sophie.' Rachel's voice was disconsolate. Her whole being rebelled against such a course of action. 'I can't.'

Sophie wrinkled up her nose. 'It's easy,' she said.

Lying on her boards that night, Rachel knew that Sophie was right. Sophie had learnt about saying the right things, about behaving correctly. And perhaps you didn't have to believe the things you said. She remembered Mr Damarell's words after grace – 'Only God sees into your soul'. As far as she could see, it meant that whatever people like Miss Gordon said or did to her, they could never control her thoughts or see into her mind, could never tell her what to believe.

The next day, Rachel went to Miss Gordon's study and knocked softly. There was no reply. She waited. After a few minutes, Miss Gordon bade the caller to enter.

'Could I speak with you, Miss Gordon?'

Miss Gordon frowned but Rachel went on hastily, 'I'm sorry about the accident, Miss Gordon. Perhaps I could make some recompense by donating the remainder of this term's allowance towards repairing the damage.'

'Ah.'

Rachel remembered how she had used that syllable at that first interview with her father. Perhaps it reflected her anticipation whenever she thought money was involved.

'I hope you have come to your senses at last, Miss Rachel. And let us not call it an accident. It was deliberate insubordination. However, I will accept your donation, although this is not the appropriate place in which to accept your apology.'

Rachel frowned. 'In what way?'

'An apology must, of course, be made to the whole establishment whose lives you endangered. I shall expect that to be done after prayers tomorrow.'

After morning prayers, Miss Gordon always glanced down at the assembled girls and asked in her patronising tone, 'Has any young lady anything she would like to add to our prayers this morning?' She did not expect a reply to her question and always swept from the rostrum virtually before the words were out of her mouth. But the next morning, she paused significantly and glanced triumphantly in Rachel's direction.

Rachel hesitated but Sophie whispered, 'Go on. Get it over.'

Rachel walked slowly down the hall, watched in silence by the whole establishment.

'Ah, Miss Rachel.'

Rachel stood beside her on the rostrum and looked at Miss Gordon and the sea of faces beneath her.

'I wish to apologise, Miss Gordon, for the insubordination perpetrated by myself and for the danger in which I placed you and the rest of the school.'

She glanced up and met Sophie's eyes, and her encouraging smile, then suddenly she burst into tears, overwhelmed by humiliation and the bitter anger seething inside her. She saw now that she could not defeat this woman, could not escape until papa returned to take her back to Egypt.

Miss Gordon looked at the girls.

'I am pleased to observe that Miss Rachel is aware of her monstrous behaviour and now feels suitably contrite. Let her shame be a lesson to you all. You may go now, girls.'

The next day Rachel returned to the bedroom she shared with Sophia. She now knew that the restrictions which had irked her, the difficulty she had found settling into a routine of lessons and timetables and regulated activities was not simply caused by the contrast with her life in Egypt. It was the content of those lessons, the emphasis on trivial matters of etiquette and needlework and feminine accomplishments. Even the French language was taught as though it consisted entirely of pleasant and ladylike phrases to be learnt by heart. Papa and mama had talked to her about all sorts of things, about the history of Egypt and the Pharaohs and the explorers going up the Nile and the slave trade and how the English were trying to end it. She longed to read books and listen to interesting talk. Although she appreciated Sophie's loyalty and her personality and her advice, even Sophie talked only about events at school.

The books Aunt Maria gave her as suitable reading were just like the ones at school, concerned only with advice on how to have a satisfactory marriage and how to bring up children. When she went to the Damarells for the summer vacation, she resolved to read some of the books in Mr Damarell's study, books that seemed to be reserved solely for the male members of the household.

But before she returned to the Damarells, another event shattered her peace of mind.

Rachel awoke one morning with a violent pain, and when she stepped from her bed she found her nightgown was covered with blood.

'Sophie! Look! What's happened? I've got a terrible pain. I'm going to die. I shall never see Charlotte and mama again.' She burst into tears and flung herself on the bed.

Sophie blushed. 'Hush, Rachel. It's all right.'

'How can you say that, Sophie? It won't stop. I shall bleed to death.'

'Rachel, I'll have to get the Gorgon.' Sophie hurried to the door.

'It's all her fault. If I die, she'll be responsible.'

But Sophie had gone already and almost immediately Miss Gordon appeared, closing the door behind her as she came in.

'Miss Gordon, I'm ill. Will the doctor be able to help me?' Rachel glanced fearfully up at Miss Gordon, standing by the side of her bed.

'Miss Rachel, you are not ill. This is an unpleasant matter we must discuss.'

'Unpleasant?'

Rachel feared that Miss Gordon was going to blame her even for this tragedy.

'This is something which occurs to all young ladies at about your age. It is a feminine matter which you must accept.'

'What do you mean? When will it stop?'

'This will continue until your middle age.'

'But I shall bleed to death.'

'It is not continuous, Miss Rachel. It will occur every month and last for a few days.'

'But how can I go out? Go to my lessons?'

'The maids will provide you with the necessary equipment. You will obtain one from them each time you go to . . . the ladies' room.'

'But how—'

'Miss Rachel, that is enough. Matron will demonstrate what to do. Now, during these days you will not participate in exercise of any kind or do anything strenuous. You may walk quietly in the garden when the weather permits. It is to be hoped that the pain you experience now will not persist, but that is a burden you may have to bear.'

'Can the doctor give me nothing?'

'There are various pills and potions in current use, but I do not believe in such notions. It is a womanly complaint which must be accepted from the outset.'

Miss Gordon moved towards the door, saying, 'I will summon Matron.'

She looked back at Rachel.

'I do not need to tell you, Miss Rachel, that this is a topic which is never mentioned. It is a distasteful event which you bear in silence. And I need hardly add that it could never be alluded to in masculine company. Gentlemen understand that ladies are the weaker sex and they do not enquire further if you say you are indisposed. In fact, when you are older, it will be better to shun male company during such periods.'

Rachel sat on her bed awaiting Matron. Total bewilderment overcame her. Why had no one told her? Did it happen to Aunt Maria and Mama? Did Papa know about it? And Miss Gordon? Did it happen to her? And Sophie? Here, sleeping in this same room with her, how had Sophie kept it such a secret?

When she went downstairs later, protected by Matron's equip- ment, she looked around at the other older girls and realized that some of them must be wearing this horrible contraption, must be feeling pain like hers. It was as though each female body suddenly held a hidden shame, to be concealed for ever.

Even Sophie was uncommunicative about it when they went to bed that night.

'When will it stop? How do I know?' Rachel asked.

'It just does.'

'But how will I know when it's going to happen?'

'Remember the date. It's about twenty-eight days.'

'It's horrible,' Rachel frowned.

Sophie pursed her lips dismissively.

'Grandmama says it's nature. It's getting rid of all the impurities women have. It's better if you don't think about it.'

Rachel decided that she would ask grandmama in London about it during the summer holidays, but when she arrived at the Damarells she was greeted with the information that grandmama was ill and she would not be going to London this holiday.

The summer passed taking Bibles to the poor in Kingsbridge with Aunt Maria and visiting the sick with Bertha.

One day they all went in Mr Damarell's carriage to Buckland Down. There had been military manoeuvres on Dartmoor and this was followed by a march-past of the soldiers before His Majesty the Prince of Wales.

Mr Damarell stood in line with the other local notables behind the Prince, and even managed to have a few words with him as the Prince walked along the line.

'My son Jacob is currently with your army in Ashanti,' Mr Damarell said proudly, 'helping to defend the great British Empire.'

The Prince nodded affably. 'Good,' he said.

Mr Damarell spoke frequently of his son Jacob and Rachel sensed that he cared more for him that he did for Richard and Thomas and James. Rachel had never seen Jacob. He had joined the army when he was seventeen and had left Kingsbridge before Rachel arrived. But Mr Damarell frequently took his photo down from the mantelpiece in the drawing-room to show to visitors. Jacob was obviously a brave and adventurous young man and Rachel hoped she would see him when he came home on leave. With his curling hair and laughing eyes he would surely bring some fun to this plain household.

She was almost relieved when the holiday ended and she returned to the Establishment for Young Ladies where Sophie greeted her gloomily.

'But I thought you saw your papa,' Rachel protested.

'I did. I told him I was too ill to return here, but he took me off to a doctor who verified my good health.'

'Oh, Sophie, what would I do here without you?'

'Well, don't worry, I think we're both here for ever.'

'Well, it's almost better here than with my relatives.'

'Aren't they kind?'

'Oh, yes. But Aunt Maria rules our lives and I see more of her than I do of the Gorgon.'

'Don't you like Bertha and the sons you talk about?'

'Oh, James is warm-hearted and takes me for walks, and sometimes I go to the mill with Richard, who is so serious, sort of gloomy. But they are at work all day. And all Bertha does is embroidery and we go visiting.'

'But when you're older you'll go to balls and you'll meet young men and—'

Rachel laughed. 'Not in Kingsbridge I won't. In any case, I shall go back to Egypt with mama and papa.'

Then she remembered another event. She was about to tell Sophie but somehow she couldn't share it, even with her. Arranging flowers one day in Mr Damarell's study, she had looked at the books in the locked glass book-case, reached up on impulse and taken the key from the high mantelpiece. She eyed the titles: books about English history and the army, the Bible and prayer book and, higher up, books by a man called Darwin and another one called *Anatomy*. Idly, she had taken that book from the shelf and begun to look through it. There were drawings of apes and other animals and, further on, pictures of bones and skeletons and then sketches of bodies, of what she recognised as a woman's body, and on a preceding page, another strange drawing. She stared in astonishment. It must be a man. She had peered at it in disbelief and then guiltily thrust the book back into the bookcase and locked the door. She had not gone into the study again, feeling the same kind of shame that she had experienced when that awful monthly event had begun. It was the reason, she knew, that she had returned to school with more equanimity. The world outside had begun to seem threatening.

It seemed so long since she had seen her parents that even they no longer represented protection. Mama was not coming until next summer and the long year stretched before her interminably. Yet it was more than the restrictions of school that worried her. She felt a sense of dread, as though something awful was going to happen. Every month, when the ghastly event occurred, a depression descended upon her, and she would walk up and down the garden paths with other girls who were currently denied exercise, listening in silence to their chattering.

Even Sophie said to her one day, 'Where is your sunshine, Rachel? You mustn't let the Gorgon defeat you.'

Rachel frowned. 'It's not that, Sophie. I feel as though the world isn't what it seems to be.'

'But this isn't the world, Rachel. When we leave here, we'll be grown up. We'll be able to choose what we do.'

'I don't know. It's so . . . dreary . . . at the Damarells.'

The year rumbled slowly past and at last as spring turned into summer, Rachel began to feel her excitement growing. Soon, mama would be here.

She was to go to the Damarells for a week and then she would be escorted to her grandmother's in London by a friend of Aunt Maria. When she arrived at the Damarells, she and Bertha went up to her bedroom.

She began to pull her dresses from the trunk in which they had been stored. 'I shan't need all these, Bertha. You can have any you like. My grandmama will provide me with some new ones.'

Then they both began to laugh helplessly as they tried to struggle into them.

'Oh, Bertha, I was going to give some to you,' Rachel giggled. 'We must both have grown so much this year, I suppose.'

Aunt Maria came in and surveyed them.

'What a waste of money,' she said. 'I hope your grandmother won't make the same mistake this time.'

'What shall we do with them, Aunt Maria? Perhaps we could give them to the servants for their children.'

'I don't know about that, Rachel. This kind of finery might turn their heads. In any case, they are hardly appropriate for Kingsbridge. I think you must wear your school attire to London.'

Rachel

Even that fact could not dull Rachel's sense of excitement as the train steamed out of Plymouth Station on its way to London. At last she would see mama.

Chapter 4

It was a brilliant summer's day as Rachel alighted from the Hansom cab at her grandparents' house and there they were, standing in the drive, as she ran towards them.

'Oh, Grandmama, it's so good to see you. Oh, you look so elegant.'

Her grandmother laughed as she kissed her. 'Ah, dear Rachel. But what is it that you are wearing?'

'Oh, Grandmama, these are my school clothes. I have grown beyond all those lovely dresses you gave me.'

'Well, we shall soon remedy that.'

Her grandfather put an arm around her, saying affectionately, 'Dear girl, I should scarcely have known you.' He looked approvingly at the tall girl before him. 'A real young lady.'

'Well, your hair will surely be your crowning glory, dear,' grandma glanced at the thick, auburn hair, coiled around Rachel's head in tight plaits. 'Perhaps we could dress it less severely while you're in London. Although I'm sure it's quite appropriate to Kingsbridge,' she added kindly.

Rachel followed them into the house, feeling a sense of hope and freedom. It seemed light and open after the dark furnishings and heavy furniture of the Kingsbridge house.

'Are you fully recovered, Grandmama?'

'Ah, yes, long ago. It was but a minor ailment.'

Rachel noticed an anxious look on grandpapa's face and he quickly added, 'But your grandmother should not tire herself too much, Rachel.'

Grandmama laughed. 'Never mind that, dear. We have so many things planned for your enjoyment.'

And indeed the very next day the dressmaker provided her with a dark blue silk gown and a velvet jacket and while grandpapa was at

77

his business in the city, grandmama took Rachel in a carriage to see the exotic shops in Regent Street.

They went to elegant tearooms and rode along Rotten Row and bowed to other fashionable ladies passing in their carriages. Her grandfather took her to the British Museum and to art galleries where he showed her pictures of the Renaissance and of what he called the Dutch School. One day they passed another smaller gallery exhibiting paintings of a different kind of art called the Pre-Raphaelites. Grandpapa said that these were executed by a group of strange persons with undesirable views and notions about society.

She was taken to the theatre to see *Hamlet*, and on those evenings when they were not involved in social engagements she was permitted to select books from the shelves in her grandfather's study. She read books by Charles Dickens and Anthony Trollope and some of the books of Thomas Hardy selected for her by grandpapa.

He talked to her about the government and of how Mr Gladstone had had to call the General Election in February because of earlier by-election defeats. He had made himself unpopular in the country because his views were becoming too liberal, and as a result Mr Disraeli had formed a Conservative government.

'Of course, Mr Disraeli is a bit too flamboyant for my liking. But at least he tries to keep the country together.'

'Mr Damarell says that,' Rachel said. 'But he never discusses it with me. He only talks about it with the boys.'

It seemed strange to her that Mr Damarell held the same views as her grandfather. Grandpapa seemed so different from Mr Damarell, but perhaps men all thought the same about such matters. At least grandpapa talked to her and didn't treat her in Mr Damarell's distant way.

Grandpapa smiled.

'Well, I don't agree with these latest notions about females having the vote and equality with men. Men and women are not the same, thank God. But ladies should be informed to the extent that they can be proper companions to their husbands. Nowadays, ladies take an interest in a womanly way in matters which were closed to them in the past.'

Rachel recognised that although grandpapa talked to her, there was still a great division between men and women. She wondered why it was that men all went out to business and ladies all stayed at home.

When she asked grandmama about it, she smiled cheerfully. 'It's natural, isn't it? We are the weaker sex and we are fortunate enough to have gentlemen who take care of all those difficult elements of life.'

'I don't feel weak, Grandmama.'

Grandmama laughed.

'It isn't just a question of physical strength, dear. Although it is inadvisable for ladies to exert themselves beyond their powers. But it is more than that. Your grandpapa has told me that it has been scientifically proved that too much mental activity can seriously affect a woman's health.'

'I suppose that's why all our lessons at the Establishment are concerned with running a home properly and how to deal with servants and things.'

'And quite right, too. And all those other accomplishments like music and deportment that I saw in the brochure. It is all valuable training for when you become a wife.'

'Supposing I never marry?'

Grandmama smiled.

'That possibility is unlikely to arise. I think one day there will be many young men begging for your hand, dear.'

'My friend Sophie says she will never marry.'

'Ah, young girls say many foolish things. She will soon come to appreciate its attractions. Men and women all have their correct and allotted roles in society.'

One day Rachel looked through the *Saturday Review* which grandfather took every week and realised that some women evidently didn't believe this. The articles she read all referred to someone called the Girl of the Period, who seemed to be a brash, selfish creature who was agitating for what they called women's rights. Her aim was not to be the supporter of her husband, a tender mother or an efficient mistress of her home, she wanted freedom to do as she liked – which appeared to be to do the same things as men.

As the days passed, Rachel's thoughts were occupied with the anticipated arrival of her mother. It was only when mama came that she would be really happy again. She had told her grandmama all about Miss Gordon, her unhappiness at the school and how she wanted to leave and return to Egypt. Grandmama had been sympathetic.

'I was always doubtful about the efficacy of going to such a remote place as Kingsbridge,' grandma said. 'It is so important for young ladies to mix in the right circles.' Grandpapa disagreed, arguing that these matters were for Rachel's father to decide, and adding that he had no doubt that the persons with whom she mixed at school were entirely proper and suitable.

Then, a fortnight before mama was due to arrive, the terrible news came. She was in the drawing-room with grandmama, waiting for the carriage to take them to Hyde Park, when the telegraph boy came up the drive.

Grandmama went to the hall to receive the message and told the boy there was no reply. She came slowly back into the drawing-room.

'Dear girl, we have a disappointment.'

'What is it? Can't we go?'

'No. It is not that. It is your mama.'

'What?'

'She is unable to come, Rachel. It has been made impossible, she says, by unexpected circumstances.'

'Oh, Grandmama!'

Rachel's lips began to tremble and grandmama came and put an arm around her, saying, 'Dear Rachel, it is a great shame. But I am sure there is a reason. We shall hear when we get a letter from mama. Perhaps she is merely delayed and will come later.'

'But what circumstance could it be, Grandmama? How could she ... forget me?'

'Rachel, dear, you are not forgotten. No doubt it is concerned with your father's commitments, or perhaps some financial matter.'

'Financial, Grandmama?'

Grandmama shook her head. 'I don't know.'

Rachel looked fearfully at her grandmother. What did she mean, financial?

'What is that, Grandmama?'

'I am not acquainted with such things, but I am sure it is of no concern. No doubt your mama will come later,' she repeated.

Rachel controlled the anguish she felt as she turned and walked over to the window. She was assailed by the same, cold feeling of loss that she had felt when they had said goodbye two years ago.

Her grandfather looked concerned when he was given the news that his daughter's visit had been postponed.

'I wonder what the problem is,' he said reflectively.

'It's such a pity for Rachel.' Grandmama looked apprehensive.

'Well, you don't need to worry your pretty head about it, Rachel.' Grandpapa smiled at her. 'You must just enjoy the rest of your holiday. Perhaps you can come again at Christmas?'

'No. She will not come.' Rachel moved away. 'Let us not discuss it.'

'Don't be sad, Rachel dear. We'll go out to tea in the Gardens.'

Rachel swung round on them angrily.

'I'm not going back to Kingsbridge if she doesn't come.'

'Come, Rachel.' Her grandmother's coaxing tone had a note of anxiety. 'You will have a nice holiday with us first.'

'No, Grandmama. She promised she'd come. Why should I go back to that horrid place if she doesn't care about me?'

'Rachel.' Her grandfather was looking at her in surprise. 'This is a foolish attitude to adopt. You have to realise that the affairs of the world cannot always be adapted to our own selfish wishes.'

'Selfish, Grandpapa! I have suffered boredom, insult, oh, you don't know how ghastly it is. I hate it.'

Suddenly the whole bitter experience of the past two years welled up inside her. She was trembling with fury, overcome by the sheer impossibility of making anyone listen to her. Then self-pity overcame her and she burst into tears.

'I'm so unhappy, Grandmama.'

Her grandmother took her in her arms and sat with her on the chaise-longue.

'Dear Rachel,' she murmured kindly, 'I know. I know. It is very hard for you. If only you had come to us, things would have been so much easier for you. Perhaps it is still not too late.'

Rachel saw her grandmother glance up, but grandpapa said firmly, 'No, dear. That is not possible. Your own health has to be considered.'

'Rachel, dear,' her grandmother went on, holding Rachel's trembling body. 'You know that we are always thinking of you. We must arrange that you come here more often.'

Her grandfather sighed. Rachel knew that men did not like scenes like this; Aunt Maria always told Bertha that ladies' little emotional disturbances should not be allowed to intrude upon gentlemen's preoccupations.

'When you get older, you will no doubt see the wisdom of your parents' decision, Rachel,' he said kindly. 'Try to see your present situation as a necessary experience in life.'

'It's all right, Henry,' grandmama said, stroking Rachel's hair. 'We shall go upstairs and refresh ourselves and then Rachel and I will go to the park as we planned.'

Rachel's sobs subsided. She leaned against her grandmother; it was so long since she had felt her mother's arms around her.

'Come, dear, everything will be all right.'

Rachel followed her up the stairs. She knew she would have to go back to Kingsbridge but she vowed that if it became too awful, she would simply run away. Then her parents would have to listen.

Rachel returned to Kingsbridge with her trunk full of the new clothes which grandmama had insisted upon buying.

'I shan't be allowed to wear them,' Rachel protested.

'You can leave them at the Damarells' and wear them during the vacations,' grandmama had said.

Misery overcame Rachel as she stood looking along the platform at Plymouth, waiting for Aunt Maria who had arranged to meet her. A tall young man came hurrying towards her, dressed in a military uniform of dark blue trousers and a vivid red jacket with gold trimmings.

Rachel did not move.

'Miss Rachel Cavendish?'

Rachel nodded uncertainly.

The young man extended his hand.

'I'm Jacob. I recognised you from the likeness which your Aunt Maria showed me.'

'Jacob? Oh, Jacob! Oh, I can see. You're like Richard.'

'Ah, but more handsome, I hope.'

'Yes,' Rachel said seriously. 'You are.'

She looked into the dark brown eyes, at the smiling red lips and curling black hair.

Jacob laughed. 'Ah, good. Then we shall be friends.'

He hailed a porter to take the luggage and added, 'I prevailed upon Papa to let me bring the carriage. Shall we take a walk on the Hoe before we return to Kingsbridge?'

'Well, I don't know—'

'It will be all right. You are in my care. My, your likeness does not do you justice, Miss Rachel.'

'It was taken some time ago. I'm not a child any more.'

Jacob smiled.

'Indeed not.'

'And how old are you, Jacob?'

'I'm nearly twenty.'

'That's old. Your papa talks about you all the time, but Aunt Maria didn't say you were coming home.'

'It was unexpected. The Campaign ended and we were given leave.'

'What Campaign?'

'I've been in Ashanti with General Wolseley. I'll tell you all about it.'

Jacob told George to wait with the carriage as they alighted on the Hoe and he took Rachel to the same tearoom that she had been to with Aunt Maria.

She listened to Jacob's story of his exploits in the War, of how, under the command of General Wolseley, he had landed at Cape Coast Castle in Africa, with thirty-three other English officers. General Wolseley had assembled an army of native troops to serve under them and they had had to build over two hundred bridges on their long march through densely-forested, hilly and unhealthy country. At Amoaful there had been a great battle with spears and muskets, and King Koffee had been defeated. He told her how the enemy had fought in long robes, that none of the natives had proper uniform.

'They wear robes like that in Egypt,' Rachel said. 'I'm going back to Egypt with my parents when I leave school.'

Jacob didn't seem to hear her interruption, but went on to recount how their army had gone on to occupy the Ashanti capital of Kumassi. General Wolseley had made the king pay for the war; he was a great hero.

Rachel looked up at Jacob as she held a cup of cocoa to her lips. His eyes shone with enthusiasm and she could imagine the excitement of the battle, the exhilaration of danger. She could almost hear the shouts of men, the crying of horses, see blood flowing from sword wounds, and feel the awful silence of victory and defeat. She knew how brave Jacob must be. With a sense of relief, she realised that while Jacob was there, the house would be a more cheerful place.

Aunt Maria appeared at the door as their carriage came to a halt in the drive and Jacob bounded up the steps and put an arm around her.

'I trust you have not been concerned, dear Mama. We were delayed. The train was late.'

'Oh, I wondered—'

'But all is well. Here is young Rachel, looking a picture, if I may say so.'

Aunt Maria kissed Rachel lightly. 'Come, dear. You must be tired. I notice your grandmother has equipped you once again with the London fashions.'

'They are quite charming,' Jacob nodded to Rachel.

'But perhaps rather advanced for a fourteen-year-old . . .'

As Rachel had expected, Jacob bought a welcome lightness to the house, and even Mr Damarell reduced the time he spent at the mill in order to be with his son.

'You are not here for long,' he said, 'the mill can wait. Richard is there to attend to matters, in any case.'

Jacob went walking with his older brother Thomas and even helped James with his thatching. Rachel noticed that only Richard seemed unresponsive to Jacob's charms. There seemed to be an unspoken reserve between them, but when she asked Bertha if they didn't like each other, Bertha only said, 'They were both upset at my mother's death. My mother was drowned, you see.'

'How awful, Bertha. But weren't you all upset?'

'Of course we were. But I think Jacob was jealous of Richard.'

'Jacob jealous of Richard!' Rachel said in astonishment. 'But why?'

'Well, after Richard was born, I think Jacob felt neglected. Mama seemed to pay more attention to Richard.'

'Well, you would with a baby, wouldn't you?'

'I suppose so. But Jacob was only about three, you see. He'd been the baby till then.'

As the days passed, Rachel saw little of Jacob, who spent more and more time in Kingsbridge and further afield, visiting the homes of young ladies. He seemed to receive constant invitations from their mothers and he would come home and regale them all with details of his visits.

'I hope you won't be breaking any hearts,' Aunt Maria observed one day after Jacob had returned from taking a young lady and her mother to the theatre in Plymouth.

'Hearts are not involved, dear Maria,' Mr Damarell said. 'Jacob is not yet twenty. These are merely social occasions.'

'They are indeed. But young ladies get strange notions.'

'Don't worry, Mama,' Jacob said cheerfully. 'I am always circumspect.'

On one occasion when Rachel went into the library she came upon Richard and Jacob engaged in a violent argument. Jacob was saying angrily, 'It happens to be mine.'

Rachel was so astonished at the expressions on their faces that she hesitated in the doorway. She had never heard raised voices in the Damarell household.

'You know quite well that mother gave it to me.'

Richard was speaking in a low, menacing tone.

'You were just a spoilt little—'

Rachel hastily closed the door behind her and crept down the hall. Were they going to fight? She remembered Bertha's remark, 'Jacob is jealous of Richard'. How could Jacob be jealous of Richard? He was so handsome, he had such an exciting life, there seemed to be so many young ladies anxious for his attentions. Was it something to do with their mother? The spectacle of their emotions made Rachel realise that problems were not confined to childhood; the kind of fear and unhappiness that she suffered could go on, even when you were grown up. Behind a façade of certainty, adults presumably sometimes also felt lost.

That night she watched Richard and Jacob at dinner. They were behaving as though nothing had happened. Neither of them appeared to be bruised or injured, and Jacob was talking in his usual carefree, animated way. Perhaps all adults were like that, appearing cheerful on the outside, while inside they might be as angry or miserable as she was.

The day came for Rachel's return to the Establishment and when Jacob offered to take her in the carriage, Mr Damarell accepted the offer. Rachel had sensed that Mr Damarell found it a trial, returning her to school. He always seemed to be looking for something suitable to say.

Other girls were arriving as their carriage curved around the drive and they alighted at the front door. Rachel felt a sense of power as she saw the looks of curiosity and envy directed at the handsome young man in his military uniform. She saw Jacob glance at them and then he winked at her.

'Goodbye, dear Rachel,' he said, and he bent down and kissed her on the lips.

Rachel blushed.

'Goodbye, Jacob.'

'I shall see you when I return from my next battles.'

Rachel smiled, trying to look cool and sophisticated in front of the watching girls.

'Goodbye, dear,' she said softly and watched as he turned with a flourish, climbed back into the carriage and clattered down the drive, waving as he went.

She turned back towards the gloomy, red brick building, looking triumphant, while secretly dreading the coming term. Then Sophie was running towards her, asking about Jacob. Indeed, Rachel found that Jacob's visit had changed her status in the school. Because of Miss Gordon's frequent rebukes, she and Sophie had been looked upon as dangerous rebels, as two girls who thought themselves superior. Now the older girls seemed to see her as someone with a secret, mysterious life; the young ones looked upon her with awe.

She found that Jacob had also changed her own attitude towards school. Somehow he had given her new hope, for when she had told him about her longing to return to Egypt, Jacob had said reassuringly, 'You only have to get through all these obligations, day by day, and one day it will all be over.'

A long letter from her mother explained that it had been impossible to leave papa, for he had many social duties to perform which required her presence. A few days later, a letter arrived from her father, apologising for the disappointment they had caused her.

'I know that you have found your present situation difficult after your childhood in Egypt. But life here is not typical of an English lady's life. One day, when you are married with a household of your own, I think you will be glad of all the accomplishments you have acquired at Miss Gordon's Establishment.'

Rachel read the letter aloud to Sophie. They were sitting quietly in the garden, relieved of the necessity to go on their walk with the French teacher for a few days.

'If you're going back to Egypt, why do you need all this boring knowledge?' Sophie protested.

'Papa says we shan't be there for ever.'

'But you might marry an Egyptian.'

Rachel laughed. 'Oh, I don't think people do things like that. When we heard that mama couldn't come, grandmama suggested I should remain with them in London. She told grandpapa I was so unhappy and I could go to a school there.'

'Why didn't you?'

'Well, grandpapa wouldn't hear of it. He said it was papa's wish and he knew best.'

'Perhaps you'd find it just as limited in London, if you lived there. You seem to have to do what men say wherever you are.'

'Grandmama says it's just growing up. She says one day I shall be happy to be looked after and be respected. But I'm determined that when I grow up, I'm never going to be told by anyone any more.'

Sophie laughed, arguing, 'How about your husband? He'll expect to tell you.'

Rachel shook her head. 'No. He won't. I shall only marry someone who listens to what I say.'

Sophie pursed her lips.

'The only thing is not to marry,' she said knowingly.

'You always seem so wise, Sophie, but I expect your papa will find some nice young man for you and you'll be swept off your feet, as they say in the novels Bertha reads.'

Autumn turned to winter and winter to spring. Rachel went through the motions of school life, trying to avoid confrontation with Miss Gordon, but her thoughts constantly turned to that last week of her holiday, when Jacob had been at home.

She would sit in the school room, looking through the window across the gardens, visualising their trip up to the Hoe, their brief conversations, his entertaining talk during meals, with Mr Damarell listening attentively and James and Richard asking questions and Thomas making silly remarks. One day he had taken her and Bertha to Dartmoor. They had gone on a horsebus to Princetown where they had tea and hot scones in a tiny café and he had told them stories about Princetown Prison, of how it had been built to house French prisoners during the Napoleonic Wars and American naval prisoners during the War of Independence. Then, about twenty years ago, it had become a prison for criminals and now there were hundreds of dangerous men locked up there.

'They are shut in dark cells with iron bars and during the day they have to break great granite boulders into stones to put on the roads. Sometimes they try to escape,' Jacob had said, 'and then the mist comes down and they are lost. There are terrible bogs on the moor and the prisoners are drawn down to their deaths. Drowned.'

Lying in her bed at night, Rachel would shudder at the awful spectacle and then she would think of Jacob's laughing face as they had walked a little way along the edge of the moor. They had stood on an ancient bridge which, he told them, was haunted by a young and beautiful nun who had committed suicide. She had been enticed from her convent by a wicked knight home from the wars and, overcome with shame and disgrace, she had taken her own life.

'Oh, you're making it all up, Jacob,' Bertha had said, laughing. 'I remember all those stories you used to tell us when we were children.'

Rachel began to invent stories of her own about herself and Jacob, walking along sunlit beaches, riding through the desert with him on a camel, sitting beneath the palm trees. Then they were sitting alone in a drawing-room, and she was his fiancée. He would take her out in the carriage, he would hold her hand and when they got married he would kiss her like he did when he left.

She would have to undress in the dressing-room. She knew married people did undress because she had seen Aunt Maria's night-gowns and Mr Damarell's night-shirts in the laundry room. Then they would go to sleep side by side.

Each holiday when she went to the Damarells', she hoped that Jacob would be there. There were letters from him, extracts from which Mr Damarell read to them at the breakfast table. He was in Africa and he said there was trouble now in the Sudan, but he hoped to be home again soon.

But he did not come and that summer holiday Rachel went to London, not to visit her grandparents, but to attend her grandmother's funeral. Aunt Maria had received the news from grandpapa. Rachel now knew why her grandfather had looked concerned last time they met. Grandmama had already been suffering from consumption when Rachel was there the previous year. During the past months she had become very ill and grandpapa said that it was a happy release.

Her death seemed another landmark to Rachel. She would always remember that grandmama died the summer before her parents returned.

She was taken to the funeral by Aunt Maria and when they entered the house with its black drapes and wreaths along the walls, they were greeted by a grandpapa whom she scarcely recognised. He had been tall and upright and now he looked bent, his hair was white and he spoke in a distant voice. Rachel was taken to the drawing-room, converted to a funeral parlour, where candles burned around the coffin and mutes stood one at each corner.

When she saw her grandmother, lying pink and still, dressed in what looked like an elaborate, embroidered night-gown, Rachel turned away abruptly. Suddenly, she found herself thinking of Jacob, of her fantasies. 'That's what married people would look like in bed,' she thought. 'In an embroidered night-gown.' She blushed at her thoughts. Poor grandpapa was standing beside her.

'I envy people who have some faith in eternity,' her grandfather said. He put an arm around her. 'We all come to this one day. Let us hope it is not the end.'

Years later, Rachel remembered that remark. With those few words he had implicitly introduced her to a world of doubt, to a new philosophy that had no place in the world in which she lived. It was almost as if heaven didn't exist.

But now, she only said sadly, 'Oh, I wish she hadn't gone, Grandpapa.'

When they returned to Kingsbridge, the whole family was clothed in semi-mourning attire.

'I am only a distant relative,' Aunt Maria announced. 'So that is all that is required for the sake of decency. But it is your immediate relative, Rachel, so of course you will wear proper mourning.'

Rachel was clothed in black and new school clothes were hastily run up by the dressmaker.

In keeping with her sense of social progress, during the past year Aunt Maria had had a tennis court laid out on the lawns, having observed that two other wealthy households in Kingsbridge, the doctor and a rising young solicitor, had had them installed.

Mr Damarell had initially demurred at the notion of installing a tennis court, but Aunt Maria had pointed out that it was expected of a family of their standing. She had also added that domestic arrangements were her province, and that such judgments should be left to the lady of the house.

'Women are the moral vanguard of our society,' she had said firmly.

But during that summer, Rachel's state of mourning meant that she could not participate in family games.

She sat on the grass, watching Bertha and her friends hitting the ball to each other and Aunt Maria feared that even her attendance at tea parties might appear frivolous. Her only outings consisted of going to chapel on Sundays with all the other members of the family, her afternoon walks with Bertha distributing gifts, or going with Aunt Maria to leave bread at the workhouse.

Mr Damarell had recently switched his allegiance from St Thomas's to the Baptist faith and had become the chief lay preacher at the chapel. She would listen to his long, precise sermons, dreaming of Jacob and wondering what battle he was involved in. She found that her memories of Egypt and even of papa and mama, were becoming indistinct.

It was only when she returned to school and Sophie greeted her jubilantly with, 'This is our last year, Rachel. Then we'll leave here for ever', that her thoughts began to return to Egypt and her parents.

So that when Miss Gordon commented on the untidiness of her hair, Rachel retorted, 'I shall be leaving here at the end of the year. I can do what I like then.'

Miss Gordon had halted in astonishment.

'Miss Rachel, I had thought that your insubordination had long since ceased. Am I to assume that all my efforts have been in vain?'

'Miss Rachel is only expressing a hope that we shall do some good in the world. We were discussing that very matter,' Sophie interposed hastily.

'Then it was inopportunely expressed,' Miss Gordon said. She looked thoughtfully at Rachel's black blouse and skirt and then at the bow which tied back her hair, and added, 'May I express my regrets at the loss of your grandmother, Miss Rachel. But perhaps a purple bow is rather premature, so soon after the bereavement. A black bow might be more appropriate.'

'Aunt Maria suggested it.'

'Ah, then,' Miss Gordon smiled, 'I suppose you must make do with it.'

Miss Gordon turned away to address other girls coming up the garden path.

'Sophie, how can we bear her for another year?' Rachel asked, rolling her eyes in irritation.

'Come. We have privileges this year, remember. We can even go in pairs down to Kingsbridge once a month.'

Rachel laughed. 'What an opportunity! I suppose I shan't even go to London now that grandpapa is alone. Though grandmama's maid, Lucy, could always be my chaperone,' Rachel reflected.

'Purple suits you,' Sophie smiled. 'So whatever the Gorgon says, your hair looks lovely with that bow. You'll be able to wear a purple blouse in six months' time. And you've got such a nice figure, Rachel. In spite of all my efforts, my waist is still twenty-two inches.'

Rachel went to the Damarells' that Christmas, knowing that it was the last one she would spend there. Even Jacob had receded into the background, a cheerful, happy memory. The new year would bring her parents, her education would be over, she would go back to Egypt.

Her mother's letters became more excited, she no longer spoke of fortitude and duty and the desirability of a ladylike education. She revealed how much she had missed Rachel, what a sad burden it had been, how she was counting the days to their reunion.

She and Sophie spent the spring term discussing their future hopes and plans. Sophie would join her father, wherever he happened to be, and she would come to Egypt to stay with Rachel. When Rachel married, they would spend time at each other's homes and she would never send her children to horrid boarding schools.

Then, during the Easter holidays, Rachel was summoned to London. Her grandfather had been taken ill and wished her to come.

She was accompanied by Aunt Maria, who warned her that her grandfather was suffering from the consumption which had killed his wife.

'You must be prepared for the worst,' Aunt Maria said.

Her grandfather was not in bed when they arrived but sitting in an arm chair in the conservatory.

'I like to sit in here. You get the sun. Forgive me, ladies, but I cannot rise.'

Rachel looked anxiously at the frail body and the bright red spots on his white cheeks, as though the colour had been painted on.

'Grandpapa, are you strong enough to be out of bed?'

'I shan't be strong enough again, Rachel. But there is no point in wasting my few last hours in bed.'

'Grandpapa, do not speak so.'

'My dear Rachel, we must face the inevitable. There is no cause for distress. I merely wished to see you once again. You have brought me much joy on your visits here.'

'Oh.' Rachel could think of no reply.

She sat down beside him and Aunt Maria went to inspect the servants to ensure that everything was being organised properly.

'I regret that I shall not see your parents again. Your dear mother.'

'But how do you know, Grandpapa? Perhaps you may recover. They are coming in the summer.'

Her grandfather did not reply to that remark, but spoke of his long life, of the changes he had seen since Victoria came to the throne, of the great future that faced the British Empire.

Just then Aunt Maria returned, saying that they had talked long enough, that he should rest while they unpacked their trunks. Rachel rose obediently and turned at the door as she went out. Grandpapa was smiling at her.

'Goodbye, dear. May you have a beautiful summer, a beautiful life.'

Rachel did not see him again. An hour later, a servant appeared to say that he had passed on.

She and Aunt Maria remained for the funeral but when she returned to Kingsbridge, even his death and the agonised letters from her mother could not take away her excitement. The last term. The last endless weeks.

Her parents had arranged for her to leave school before the end of term. They should arrive at Plymouth in June. She imagined them boarding the ship at Alexandria, the vivid jellabahs of the fellahin, the pontoons at the quayside, the crowds in the streets, the shouts of the traders selling their oranges.

The day came when Mr Damarell arrived to collect her for the last time from the Establishment. Her trunks were placed in the carriage, and he had a private word with Miss Gordon while Rachel bade a tearful farewell to Sophie.

'Dear, dear Sophie,' Rachel sobbed. 'When papa and mama arrive, you will come to Kingsbridge to stay with us, until we depart for Egypt. And we'll write every week.'

Her excitement returned when Aunt Maria took her to see the house which she had rented for Rachel's parents. It was a large, airy house near the toll gate at the top of Fore Street and Rachel went from room to room, imagining how lovely it would be when they were all there, Charlotte and mama and papa.

'This will be my bedroom,' she said decisively, viewing the wide windows and the pretty pink covers on the bed.

Aunt Maria smiled indulgently, saying, 'I expect your parents will be quite agreeable.'

'And look at the lovely garden. Oh, Aunt Maria, it has been such a long time.'

Two days later, she boarded the horsebus with Aunt Maria for their journey to Plymouth. Thinking of her parents, of her return to Egypt, she could almost smell the incense in the temples, see the black robes of the Arab women, the silver sand and the sparkling waters of the Nile.

Tomorrow, the ship would dock. At last, her education was over. Now, she would begin a new life.

Chapter 5

Ursula awoke early and watched the sky slowly turn from dark blue to grey and then to a pearly white. The light came up in horizontal lines, followed by pale yellow and then amber rays, as though the sun had been lying beneath the desert, slowly forcing the light upwards. Finally, the sun itself appeared, a fiery semi-circle on the horizon.

Charles was still sleeping and, glancing over at him, she realised with a shock that even in repose he looked desperately tired. Over the past months, he had seemed to become more and more worried, though when she had questioned him he had merely said there were difficult decisions to be made. It was strange, for his work had never worried him before. He had always seemed so calm and efficient, as though it were something he did naturally. Apart from discussing the personalities he met, he had never mentioned the details of his work, so it remained a part of his life which was closed to her.

Then one day he had returned to say that he was leaving the bank. Alarmed, Ursula had asked what would happen to them, what he intended to do. And he had quietly replied that he had been offered a post in the High Commissioner's office. When they returned to Egypt, he would be an assistant secretary.

'But that's wonderful,' Ursula had exclaimed with delight. 'It is such progress for you.'

Yet Charles had not seemed greatly excited about the event, as though there were other problems on his mind. What could be more important than that? Perhaps he simply needed a holiday; it had been a long four years since Rachel left.

She turned back to the window, looking down on the crowded street below. It was filled with fellahin pushing carts and dragging donkeys, shouting and gesticulating, the shabbiness of their jellabahs emphasising the vividness of the colours. An orange seller had already perched his stand opposite the hotel, awaiting the tourists who would shortly be arriving at the harbour.

'Charles, we have to make an early start.'

Charles opened his eyes instantly, as though he had been awake all the time. Perhaps that's why he had looked worried, she thought. He wasn't asleep, he was thinking.

'It's very hot in here.'

'Yes.' Ursula opened the window to the sound of horns, voices, the whistles of the cart owners, the sirens of ships. 'I'll go and call Charlotte.'

Charlotte was in the adjoining room, examining the dresses in her trunk.

'What shall I wear, Mama?'

Ursula smiled. 'Don't look so concerned, dear.'

Charlotte was so like her father, she seemed to have a serious approach to everything, as though every detail had to be settled before she could enjoy anything. She was very different from Rachel. Rachel was so spontaneous, so light.

'You can wear a thin dress for at least a few days. We shan't be getting into colder climates until we reach the Bay of Biscay. You look delightful in the yellow one. It goes with your fair hair.'

As she spoke, Ursula was still thinking of Rachel. The pain she had felt at their parting had never gone, it was still with her now, along with a deep sense of guilt at having parted with her. Had Rachel been happy? Would she have changed after four years? She had said so little in her letters, they had almost been formal, as though her real thoughts and personality had been hidden away. Had she lost that wild streak of hers? Well, at least, it wouldn't happen to Charlotte, for an increase in the number of English residents had led to a new English school being established in Cairo during Rachel's absence. Charlotte would go there. She had warned Charles that she could not go through the agony of leaving Charlotte in England and, suddenly and inexplicably, a few months ago, he had agreed to her plans. Ursula had not enquired into the reason for his change of mind, fearful that any questions might lead him to alter his decision.

As though guessing her thoughts, Charlotte smiled and exclaimed,

'Oh, Mama, it will be so lovely to have Rachel back with us.'

'You will have to work very hard at school, Charlotte, so that papa does not regret his decision.'

Charlotte nodded. 'Don't worry, Mama. I shall like going to school.'

'Yes, I know you will.'

Charlotte had caused Charles no anxiety. She fitted in with the English community, never rebelling against the restrictions of ladylike behaviour. She seemed almost naturally pliable, as though she sensed the right things to say and do. Perhaps it was this fact which had made Charles decide to keep her in Cairo.

Ursula was dressing as she talked.

'Aren't you wearing a thin dress, Mama?'

Ursula smiled. 'No. I've put those away until I return. They're not suitable for England. This silk gown will be more appropriate.'

Whenever she spoke of England Ursula thought only of Rachel. Now, on the point of returning there, a depression came over her. She remembered the winters, the rain, the long periods of darkness. Even Alexandria, where it rained constantly during the winter, had never had that damp, gloomy atmosphere. She thought of dark days in London, of fog and the lights of cabs shining through the mist.

Yet, Ursula reflected, she had been happy there once. She remembered sunny summer days spent in gardens, and, of course, she had loved the theatre and the musical concerts. You didn't get those in Egypt. But what could ever compete now with the splendour of Karnak and Luxor?

After breakfast, they walked down to the harbour. The Citadel of Qait Bey cast a great shadow across the bay.

'There's our ship.' Charles pointed to a large, three-masted schooner-rigged steamer.

'They seem to be loading more cargo than passengers.'

'Cotton, probably. I believe there are only about twenty passengers.'

They watched the fellahin carrying great trunks, pulling boxes and containers along the quay, loading them into the hold. Ursula thought of the stories Fatima had told her about their harsh lives, their sufferings, how they were swindled and bullied and treated with terrible cruelty. This was the other side of Egypt, the reality.

But she still wanted to return. To the European Egypt meant sunshine and light and colour, an opulence not possible in England, and a freedom, too, from obligations. The restrictions of correct English behaviour could not be applied in Egypt; it was as though whatever the English did was bound to be acceptable, simply because of their natural superiority.

They looked back from the ship at Pompey's Pillar and the new houses being built along the seafront.

'Alexandria has grown even since our last visit.'

Charles nodded.

'Isma'il has changed Egypt, hasn't he?' Ursula went on. 'Since we've been here, look at all the railways he's built, the hundreds of bridges, and all his palaces and gardens.'

Charles sighed. There was a strange smile on his face but Ursula had no opportunity to question him, for he was leading them along the dock to the waiting ship.

It was to call only at Trapani in Sicily and then go through the Mediterranean and the Bay of Biscay to Plymouth. The other passengers were bank personnel and their families or government officials, going on leave. It began as a calm, sunlit voyage and even Ursula was undisturbed by her usual sea-sickness. Charles spent much of his time with the male passengers in the smoking-room, playing bridge. Charlotte and the other children were entertained by an English governess who was returning with one of the families. Ursula sat on the deck with the wives, listening to their plans for their vacation: visiting relatives, buying clothes, going to the theatre. It was a world she had left behind; she could enjoy a pleasant nostalgia without wishing ever to return to it. All that mattered was that Rachel would soon be with her. There were plenty of young men in Egypt, she reflected; young army officers, government personnel. Rachel would not be deprived of a social life.

As the days passed, Ursula began to feel a rising excitement. At last, she could think about Rachel without sadness. In a week's time, they would be together again. The misery would be over.

After dinner one night, she and Charles went on deck. It was a mellow moonlit night and Charles slumped down into a deck chair. Ursula stood on the deck, leaning against the rail.

'Are you all right?' she asked.

'Too much brandy, I think.'

Ursula smiled. 'That's unusual. Perhaps it's something you've eaten.'

'No.'

'We'll be home in a week. The house Aunt Maria's taken for us looks lovely, doesn't it?'

Charles frowned. 'It's larger than we need.'

'But . . . I thought you agreed. And it's only for two months, isn't it?'

'It's a greater expense than is necessary.'

Ursula looked at him in astonishment. Charles never discussed financial matters. He made all the decisions, he would surely have known the rent involved.

'What do you mean?' Ursula spoke hesitantly.

Charles was silent for a moment, then he said, 'Sit down, Ursula.'

Ursula sat uncertainly on the seat beside him. She had a sudden feeling that her smooth life was about to be destroyed, but she said firmly, 'What is it, Charles? There must be something you should tell me.'

Charles sighed, looking tired. 'There have been complications,' he said at length.

'What complications?'

He was silent for a moment. Ursula watched the lights of another ship, far away on the horizon. They sat in silence as two passengers walked slowly past them along the deck.

'I don't expect you to understand.'

'Charles, what are you speaking of? I am quite capable of understanding. What has happened?'

'I am in grave financial difficulties, Ursula.'

'Financial difficulties? What do you mean?'

A picture flashed across Ursula's mind of ledger books and balance sheets and Charles's bank; the great mystery of percentages and loans and rates of interest.

'I can understand perfectly well,' she added.

Charles smiled bleakly. 'Yes, I suppose it's quite simple really.' He paused. 'Last year, the bank gave Isma'il a loan of £8 million.'

'Surely all the banks give him loans?'

'Yes, but unfortunately his finances have now reached a desperate state.'

'What do you mean?'

'Egypt is bankrupt. That's why Isma'il sold his shares to Disraeli last November. The banks wouldn't lend him any more, so Britain got control of the Canal for £4 million.'

'But isn't that a good thing for Britain?'

'It may be good for Britain, but his debt to my bank almost ruined them.'

'Oh.'

'They were only saved by the Anglo-French agreement to take over financial control of the country. The two governments have re-organised all the debts.'

'What does that mean?'

'Basically, they've given the Egyptian government a longer period in which to repay. Sixty-five years, in fact.'

'Well, that's all right then.'

'Not exactly.'

Ursula frowned. What did this have to do with Charles's financial problems? Then she remembered that it was Charles who seemed to arrange all these loans for his bank. Was that why he was leaving? Did they blame him?

'And you, Charles? Is that why you're leaving the bank?'

'Not exactly,' he repeated.

'What then?'

They sat in silence, gazing across the dark sea streaked by the light of the moon. Charles looked haggard in the shadows. His lips moved silently as though he had difficulty in voicing his words. He swallowed.

'The bank doesn't blame me for that, Ursula. All the banks were lending. That's what banks do.'

'So?'

'Some people also lent Isma'il their own money. Many of the French and Prussian bank officials were doing it. It was a good investment with high rates of interest. But these turned out not to be loans to the Egyptian government but to Isma'il's personal account. It was never clear which was which.'

'Ah.' Ursula breathed deeply. 'So that's what you did.'

'Yes.'

'Very much?'

'More than can ever be repaid. Very large amounts of money.'

'Haven't you anything left?'

'It's not quite like that. I also owe it to the bank.'

'Oh, God!' Words like fraud, cheat, swindler, criminal flashed across her mind. Was that how it was?

'That's why I resigned, Ursula. The bank won't do anything about it. It would be bad for their reputation.'

'But how are you going to the High Commission?'

'I was offered the post when the British government came in to run the country. They don't know,' he added.

They sat in silence again. A breeze began to blow in across the sea. Ursula shivered.

'Why didn't you tell me?'

'I didn't want to worry you about such matters. I thought it would be all right.'

She tried to imagine Charles taking such a gamble. Perhaps at the time it hadn't seemed a risk. She could not visualise him taking chances, yet she knew that long ago he had thought he was taking a chance in marrying her. By what means did Charles arrive at decisions? Then she thought of Rachel and Charlotte.

'Is that why you're not sending Charlotte to England? Because of the expense?'

Charles did not reply.

'Well, you don't need to worry about that. I am sure it will be better for her in Egypt.'

'What it means, Ursula, is that we can't go back to England. I mean, I wouldn't be employed in a bank there. But there is a chance that a job here, in the High Commission, might provide some opening in London in the future.'

'But how can you ever repay your debt, Charles?'

Charles shook his head. 'We shall just have to organise our lives more frugally,' he answered.

Ursula sighed. She had heard of financial disasters, of men being ruined, but she had always supposed that it was people who had squandered their money, betting and gambling. It didn't happen to respectable people.

'You don't gamble any more?' she queried, remembering his visits long ago to the gambling dens in Cairo and Port Said. Was there another personality beneath the cautious man she knew? Was there some part of him that longed for excitement, even risking the well-being of his family?

'No.' Charles smiled bleakly. 'That was just child's play.'

'You will get a salary from the Commission, Charles?'

'A very good one. But the debts will swallow that up for some time to come.'

Ursula frowned. How could she suddenly consider abstruse financial matters like this? All it meant to her was disaster. She stood up. 'It's getting cold. Let's go down to the cabin.'

Charles hesitantly put an arm around her. 'I'm sorry, Ursula. I wouldn't have told you except—?'

'What?'

'It's the future, Ursula. If anything should happen to me—'

His voice trailed off into silence.

Then, with a sudden feeling of relief, she remembered her father, the property and its contents, the considerable fortune he must have left her. Charles had been dealing with all that, through the lawyers in England. He had naturally taken over the supervision of such matters.

'But Charles,' she exclaimed, 'there is the inheritance from my father. It must have been considerable. Indeed, you mentioned the figures some time ago. That will surely . . .' She became silent as she saw the expression on his face.

Charles blushed, his lips trembled as he said, 'It was, Ursula. But that has all been committed. There was nothing else I could do.'

'Do you mean—' She could scarcely formulate the thoughts breaking into her mind. 'Charles, do you mean that I and the girls would not be provided for?'

Charles shook his head, a look of despair on his face.

Ursula took a deep breath, trying to work out what would happen to her and the children. 'Charles, do you mean we would be penniless?'

Charles sounded as though he were trying to inject a note of hope into his reply as he said, 'That is only the immediate future, Ursula.

God willing, I am not likely to die yet and obviously, as time passes, the situation will improve.'

Ursula walked slowly along the deck by his side. She could not comprehend the magnitude of what Charles was saying. At the moment she wanted to hear no more. For the first time in her life she saw that the male world was full of perils and anxieties, problems with which she was suddenly being faced without knowing any of the solutions. Her bewilderment was mingled with a sense of betrayal.

The next day, they entered the Atlantic and sailed up the coast of Spain. For the first time, the sea was rough and great waves rocked the ship as a violent gale blew from the west. Ursula was confined to her cabin, too ill to think about anything. A few days later they entered the Bay of Biscay and unexpectedly the storm abated. Only a light breeze ruffled the sea and Ursula sat on deck in the sunshine with Charlotte. For the moment, she forced herself to dismiss Charles and his problems from her mind. She would not let anything spoil the joy and anticipation of seeing Rachel again.

Then early one warm June afternoon they were on the last stage of their journey, passing along the north-west coast of France, sailing towards the Channel and England.

'It's almost like Egypt,' Charlotte said cheerfully. 'Perhaps it will be hot in England.'

It was a clear, sunny evening as they turned into the Channel and Charles pointed north to the far horizon.

'Up there is the Lizard,' he said. 'We shall be rounding the coasts of Cornwall and Devon.' He began to tell Charlotte about the places he had visited as a child, when he was living in Kingsbridge with his aunt and uncle.

A mist began to form as they sailed slowly past the distant coast and Charles tried to estimate where they were, but the mist turned to a fog which became more dense as darkness fell. A cold dampness surrounded them and the ship almost seemed to grind to a halt as the fog thickened. The fog horns began to wail and Ursula and Charlotte went down to the cabin. Charles remained on deck, peering into the impenetrable fog, trying to see the flash of a lighthouse.

There was no moon, only a weird silence. As a precaution, the captain called for all available men to go up on deck and position themselves around the vessel, to look out for any passing ships or for the lighthouse and to listen out for the sound of the fog bell. As Charles looked into the darkness, there was a strange, uneasy roll of the ship. At the same moment, he felt a sudden violent break of waves and the unexpected whistle of wind in the rigging after the previous deathly silence.

He glanced round him at the other men. No one spoke but as the wind blew harder he heard the captain giving the order to take in top-gallant sails and to reef the topsails. Yet even as the violence of the gale increased, the fog still engulfed them and the waves began to batter the ship. The sea suddenly appeared to rise around them, the waves rising up to a great height, seeming to confront each other and then crash down in foam around them.

The captain was shouting instructions to the crew to lighten the ship. Anything that could be lifted was cast overboard but the violent motion of the ship made it a dangerous activity. There was a terrible scream as one of the sailors was washed overboard and the captain yelled at them to cease the operation.

Then suddenly three huge waves struck the vessel beam-on and the ship trembled as though it would break apart. There were shouts and screams from the passengers below and the captain and crew appealed for calm; it was only a freak wave, he said.

At the same moment, there was a thunderous crash as the ship struck broadside on to the rocks. Her mainmast dipped forward into the sea and the captain called for rockets and signal-guns to be fired.

Charles dashed down to the cabin. His face was white as he grabbed Ursula's arm, urgently shouting, 'Ursula, we must prepare to leave the ship. When it's possible, the lifeboats will be launched. Put on some warm clothing.'

'What's happening, Charles?' Ursula demanded, terror in her eyes.

'Hurry,' he shouted at them. 'Do what I say. Don't just stand there.'

They snatched up their coats, Charlotte clutching Charles's jacket as he pushed them out of the cabin, and climbed the stairs to the deck, to be confronted by screaming and shouting passengers and children clinging to their mothers' skirts. They began dashing up and down the deck, as though desperately seeking some way of escape. The captain appeared, shouted at them without effect, grabbed the revolver in his belt and fired it into the air. The passengers were silent. He yelled at them through his speaking-trumpet but against the boom of the waves his words were heard only by those immediately beside him.

'Our rockets and signal-guns will be seen on the shore,' he was bellowing. 'We are off-course and nearer to land than we estimated. Two of the boats have been damaged but be ready to go when we launch the others.'

Everyone watched in silence as the first boat was launched, only to be smashed to pieces against the hull as it was being lowered. A second boat followed, but it capsized as soon as it reached the water.

There was a violent crash as the fore-topmast and yard rigging crashed down into the sea. The vessel immediately began to roll uncontrollably, but the captain screamed, 'We must wait. The risk is greater than remaining here.' He looked at the terrified passengers. There was another crash as the ship was once again thrown on to the rocks. It was now listing more heavily, and the captain ordered all the women and children to gather on the deck-house roof, over the midships saloon, pointing desperately to where they should go.

Ursula peered at Charles in the darkness, and said, 'We'll stay with you.'

'No,' Charles yelled violently. 'Do as he says, Ursula. It's your only hope.'

He pushed her towards the stairs. She led Charlotte, weeping now with fear, up the gangway with the other women. Ursula peered through the windows. The sea was raging below them, she could see the giant waves sweeping across the deck beneath and the crew with their red tasselled caps trying to stem the rush of water with buckets. She saw Charles clinging to the side-rail and then a huge wave swept over the deck-house and hurled its occupants into the sea.

There were brief screams from the water, but after another enormous wave hit the ship, no one could be seen. Charles, calling helplessly, saw Charlotte's fair hair floating for a second on the foaming surf before she disappeared. He did not see Ursula. He shouted urgently to a seaman, another boat was lowered and Charles flung himself down into it, followed by half a dozen passengers.

'Row,' Charles screamed, peering anxiously into the dark waves. He snatched an oar and tried to plunge it into the sea. It was swept away and the next minute the boat crashed against the rocks, capsized and flung its passengers into the water. Charles tried to swim, but his right arm wouldn't function and another giant wave seemed to throw him upwards and then drag him down. He thought he heard Ursula's voice, he called frantically but he heard only the slap of the waves. As the water closed over him, he saw a brief kaleidoscope of the main events of his life: his aunt and uncle, Kingsbridge, London, the bank in Cairo, Ursula smiling at him, Charlotte running. Then he saw Rachel, a solitary figure in a flimsy dress standing on the water, waiting. The waves broke against the rocks.

Chapter 6

It was a calm, sunny morning as the horse-bus trotted along Union Street, through Devonport and down Fore Street to the docks. As they reached the harbour, Rachel looked with anticipation at the smooth sea and the soft rolling of the waves.

Aunt Maria pointed out the schooners and brigantines and barques which rose gently up and down, their sails flapping lightly in the westerly breeze. A pilot was leading a liner in, to wait off-shore until there was space at the landing stage.

'Perhaps that's it,' Rachel said, pointing eagerly.

'Don't point, dear. No. I think that must be one of those large vessels from America.'

Rachel stood at the edge of the wharf, looking hopefully at each ship.

'The ship we came in last time was like that one over there.' She pointed to a large three-masted schooner anchored at the quay. 'Do you think that's it?'

'Perhaps we should walk in that direction. The passengers are not yet disembarking.'

They began to walk along the quay, watching fishermen shaking their nets, laying them out to dry in the sun. A man was shouting as he walked towards them, carrying what appeared to be a large poster.

'Disaster at sea. Terrible scenes in storm,' he shouted. He stopped near them and pasted the poster on a board. Instantly, men appeared from the fishing sheds, from the warehouses and workshops, and crowded round the poster. Rachel saw a look of gloomy expectation on their faces.

'Aunt Maria, what is it?'

'It's all right, child. They always put up news about vessels in

107

distress. There are many ships passing around these shores.'

Nevertheless, she took Rachel's hand and led her over to the board. 'Let us look,' she said imperiously.

The men turned and made way for them as Aunt Maria read the announcement: SCHOONER CRASHES ON STAGS IN FOG AT 3 a.m. LAST NIGHT. SOUTH OF LIZARD POINT. MANY LOST.

'What's the Stags?' Aunt Maria turned to the man who had pasted up the poster.

'A reef, Ma'am, south of Lizard Head. Treacherous in fog. Specially if the captain lost his bearings.'

'What ship was it?'

'Can't say yet, Ma'am. There was a sudden mighty storm and the seas were too high to launch the lifeboat last night; they'll be doing the rescue this morning.'

'Not much chance,' one of the fishermen observed. 'Even if they got clear of the ship, no one would survive on those rocks.'

'All I heard,' the poster man said importantly, 'was she's broken her back and her mast has disappeared. Fragments of boats have been seen further up the shore.'

'But where was she coming from?' Aunt Maria said impatiently.

'Oh, somewhere south. The Med most like.'

'Was it a cargo vessel or a passenger ship?'

'A bit of both, most likely.'

The men began to turn away, planning amongst themselves to take out boats to go to the wreck. The sinking of a ship was a profitable event around these perilous coasts, and they would go out to collect valuables washed ashore and then raid the wreck for what remained.

Aunt Maria hesitated, looking at Rachel anxiously.

A fisherman said, 'If you go to the Custom House, lady, they'll most likely know a bit more.' He pointed to a building further up the quay.

Aunt Maria nodded and began to walk away. Rachel stood stiffly, looking at the poster.

'Come, Rachel.'

'Aunt Maria, it can't be—'

'No, dear. It can't. But we must enquire.'

Rachel slowly followed her. Was it possible? Was it really their ship?

The Customs official looked at Aunt Maria solemnly. 'We have little information yet. But it was a schooner, called the *Good Hope*. Left Trapani about three weeks ago.'

'Oh.' Aunt Maria sounded relieved. 'That was its port of departure?'

'Well, no, Ma'am, that was a port of call. It was coming from Alexandria.'

'Oh, no! It must be them. What's happened to them?'

The official turned to Rachel in concern. She was trembling violently.

'Miss, the lifeboats and other vessels were out early this morning, looking for survivors.'

'Survivors?'

'Yes, Miss. There's always hope.'

'Aunt Maria, can we go? We must go and see!'

'There must have been boats,' Aunt Maria said. 'There would have been survivors, wouldn't there?'

The man hesitated. 'Well, I can't say yet. But they'd be taking them in to Falmouth, I reckon. Did you know of people on board?'

'It's my mama and papa and my sister,' Rachel shouted. 'Are they all right?'

The man shook his head. 'Well, I reckon your best bet, Ma'am, would be to get on down there. Then, if they are brought in—'

Rachel saw the man look at Aunt Maria. It was that meaningful adult look she had seen so often, a glance that warned her they weren't telling her the truth.

'Aunt Maria, let's go. We must go.'

'It will take so—'

'There's a bus going from here in five minutes. Then you would get the information,' the official added to Aunt Maria.

Hours later, it seemed, the horse-bus trundled into Falmouth Harbour. As they alighted at the Custom House, they were confronted by groups of people who all seemed to be talking about the shipwreck and who all seemed to have information.

Rachel hesitated, trying to hear their conversation, but Aunt Maria hurried past them, saying, 'We don't want to listen to a lot of ignorant rumours, Rachel. I'll talk to the officials.'

Rachel stood quietly by her aunt's side, with the sun shining through the windows on her blue tussor dress, made specially for this long-awaited home-coming, as the Custom official finally gave them the details.

There had been an impenetrable fog and a sudden huge sea had forced the vessel on to the rocks. It had broken in half and evidently the boats which had been launched from the ship had been dashed to pieces.

There were only four known survivors among the crew who had been found clinging to rocks. One of these had since died of exposure. All the others, passengers and crew, were feared lost, including the captain and his officers. From information received from Egypt, its place of departure, it appeared there had been twenty-six passengers and a crew of thirty aboard.

'But have no . . . people, bodies been recovered?'

'The boats are still out there searching, Ma'am. But I fear they will have been taken out into the deep. That will be their final resting place.'

Rachel looked uncomprehendingly at Aunt Maria. She frowned. 'But is there no message, Aunt Maria?'

'Message, child?' Aunt Maria's eyes opened wider. 'Message? No, dear. I fear there will be no message.'

Rachel stood gazing through the window as Aunt Maria explained to the official about Rachel's parents.

'It is a terrible coast, Ma'am. For people in these parts it is more of a graveyard than the cemetery.'

He looked uncertainly at Rachel, and added, 'There are no words of condolence I can offer, Miss, that could be sufficient for your grief.'

'What can I do, Aunt Maria?' Rachel sat down on the bench, absently smoothing the folds of her new blue dress. She felt as though she were choking, as though giant hands were clutching her, squeezing her life away. 'It can't be, Aunt Maria. It can't be.'

Aunt Maria and the man glanced at each other.

'We can only ask for God's strength to help us through these catastrophes,' the man said.

Rachel stood up again. She must go, make sure. There must be something.

'Aunt Maria, can we go to this Lizard?'

'The Lizard? But there is nothing there, dear. There will be only the wreck. It would only cause you more distress.'

'No, Aunt Maria. I wish to see it. Please let us go there.'

Aunt Maria looked at the official. Such a decision seemed to be beyond her feminine capabilities.

'Perhaps it would help,' the official said. 'It might help to see this . . . last resting place. She will have no grave to visit.'

Aunt Maria sighed. 'No doubt my husband will by now have heard the news in Kingsbridge. Could I get some message through to him of our delay?'

'I can telegraph the Custom House at Plymouth. They would see that a message is delivered to him.'

Aunt Maria nodded. 'Then I will take the child, as she wishes.'

That afternoon, they stood on the rocks above the Lizard and Rachel looked down on the broken vessel far below.

'Perhaps they're in the water somewhere. They might still be in the ship. Why don't people go and look in the ship?'

Aunt Maria did not answer; there was an expression of dread on her face as she stared down at the rocks.

'Aunt Maria, there's a path down.'

'No, child, I can't go down there.'

'Aunt Maria, let me go.'

'Rachel, it's dangerous. You could slip. Please be sensible, Rachel.'

Rachel looked at her. 'Aunt Maria, I must go down.'

Aunt Maria frowned. She knew she could dismiss Rachel's demand as insubordination, but something in Rachel's expression told her that this was not such an occasion.

She turned. 'I'll get one of the fishermen to accompany you.' She spoke to a group, standing near them, contemplating the wreck far below. 'Would one of you gentlemen accompany my niece down the cliff. She wishes to see the wreck nearer at hand.'

The fishermen looked at her in astonishment.

'Is it a dangerous venture?' Aunt Maria asked, seeing their indecision.

'No, Ma'am, it's not dangerous,' one man said. 'It's an easy enough path down. But it's a forlorn picture when you get there.'

'Yes. It's a forlorn event for my niece.'

'Ah.' One of the older men came forward as though he had suddenly understood. He looked at Rachel thoughtfully. 'I'll take yer, Miss. Follow me. The path isn't too steep and there are rocks either side you can hold on to if you want.'

Rachel followed him as he went slowly down the long, winding path. They turned the last corner and reached the beach. Great rocks rose up from the sand and there, in the receding tide, the ship lay, the front half buried beneath the waves. The man turned to Rachel. She sat down on a rock and he stood beside her.

'That's what the sea does, Miss.'

Rachel stood up again and peered across the water and then along the water's edge. The man followed her gaze.

'Just flotsam and jetsam, Miss.'

'It's so calm and quiet.'

'Most of the time it is. The fishermen say it's like a quiet woman. All peaceful and benign until she suddenly erupts and the whole world shakes.'

But Rachel did not hear his words. The longing for some evidence, some tangible proof of what had happened to them overcame her. She looked agonisingly at the wreck, forlorn, solitary, its aft-sails tattered, its decks broken. Then she looked out at the smooth sea. Were they there, out there beneath that huge ocean?

He looked uncertainly at her pale face, at the misery in her eyes.

'There must be something,' she said.

The man cleared his throat. 'Who was it, Miss?'

'Mama and papa and Charlotte.'

'Oh.' The man sighed, his eyes widening at the extent of her misfortune, then he sat down on the rock beside her and contemplated the sea.

'I reckon I was younger than you when it happened to me,' he said thoughtfully. 'About twelve.'

Rachel continued to look at the wreck.

'A bit further up the coast, around Kynance. My father and brother out fishing one day. The sea just as calm as now. But they never came back. Wasn't even a storm.'

'What happened then?' Rachel asked absently.

'Freak wave. Must have capsized them. Only an old boat.' He lapsed into silence.

Then Rachel said suddenly, 'What happened to you?'

The man looked at her. He thought for a long time, as though he were weighing the importance of his words.

'Well, living round here, you know that sea's always out there, waiting to get its prey. It was hard for my mother with seven kids to rear. Course, me and my brother started work then. We had to take the place of me dad and me brother. After it happened, I used to come down to the beach and look out, always expecting to see them. For a long time, you can't believe it. It seemed such a mystery. But when you're young, life goes on. You've got to live in this world, Miss.'

There was a sudden shout from the cliffs above.

'They're wondering what's happened to us, Miss.'

He stood up and shouted back, then turned to Rachel and gently said, 'We'd better be going, Miss.'

Rachel stood up. The desolation she felt now was worse than before. Somehow, they had become more remote, as though that vast, smooth, impersonal sea with the sun dancing on it deceptively, and the cruel rocks jutting out from the water, had hidden them from her forever.

Then she recognised what she had come for, to see evidence of their last moments, to know what they had done, what they had said. She tried to imagine them, but it was so long, so long, that even their memory evaded her. She tried to imagine their faces, but every time her mind clouded over and she could see only the blue water and the broken ship.

She began to cry, her body shaking with anguish, overcome with her own loneliness. She was aware of her complete helplessness, of the helplessness of all human beings. The man stood by her side, a hand on her shoulder but he did not speak. 'I wish I were dead,' Rachel said, but even in that she was helpless, because here she was, alive.

'No, Miss,' the man said. 'That's what life is. We have to go on with the living.'

There was another shout from above and he gently steered her around and led her back up the cliff path. Aunt Maria was sitting on a bench at the top of the cliff, surrounded by the fishermen.

'There's little enough to be seen,' the man said. 'But it was better for her to go and see. It's the only thing you have.'

Aunt Maria nodded, as though she understood, as though the fishermen had been telling her the same thing.

She had evidently discussed other matters, too, because she said to Rachel, 'We shall stay in Falmouth tonight, dear. It is too late to return to Kingsbridge this evening. There is a suitable inn, these gentlemen tell me, opposite the harbour in Falmouth. It is possible that more information may be forthcoming by tomorrow.'

They returned to Falmouth in the pony and trap which Aunt Maria had hired to bring them to the Lizard. Rachel was silent. She tried to see her mother's face, tried to remember Charlotte's voice, but all she could summon up was the rocks and the wrecked vessel.

When they entered the dining-room, Aunt Maria said, 'You must be hungry, Rachel. You have eaten nothing today.'

Rachel looked around her. She frowned, feeling as though she had suddenly emerged from a nightmare. The terrible loss she felt, standing on the rocks near the wreck, had changed to a cold void inside her. The violence of her feelings had gone; it was as though that desolation had forced her to accept the truth. There was to be no answer, no hope. They were gone for ever. She was alone.

She began to eat the bowl of soup which was placed before her and then pushed it away. 'What will happen to me, Aunt Maria?'

'Don't worry about that now, Rachel, dear. We shall take care of you.'

For a second, Rachel visualised the house at Kingsbridge, Bertha and Mr Damarell, Church Street, long steep Fore Street, leading up to the mill and the big elegant house where they were to have spent their holiday. But superimposed on that was another picture of sand and temples and the hectic streets of Cairo.

'I shan't go to Egypt any more.'

'No. Probably not, Rachel. Now, would you like a pudding instead? You must eat something, you know.'

The next morning, Aunt Maria made further enquiries but there was no fresh news. The local paper carried a long and graphic account of the events of that night as related by the three survivors. The fog, the sudden gale and giant waves, of how the women and children had all been herded up to the deck-house for safety, to be clear of the waves crashing across the deck. And of how a giant sea had torn off the roof, flinging them into the ocean. The three survivors had jumped into a boat but they had seen another one capsize and its occupants sucked down into the waves. They had been thrown clear on to the rocks and managed to cling there until the storm subsided. It was a miracle, the paper said.

Aunt Maria sat in silence while Rachel read the article. Then she said, 'Rachel, dear. We will return to Kingsbridge. It is not for us to understand the ways of God. We must bear misfortune with fortitude. In the end, we shall all go to our eternal home.'

Rachel suddenly remembered the words her grandfather had uttered when her grandmother died: 'Let us hope that we may meet again one day'.

'Perhaps there is no eternal home,' she said.

'Dear child, do not speak so. The Lord will protect you in your misfortune.'

'How can he? I am here and they have gone. They will never come back.'

Aunt Maria stood up. 'Such matters are beyond our grasp, Rachel. We have to learn to bear our suffering. I remember when my dear mother passed on, I thought I should never survive. But you must go on living. It is what your dear parents would have wished. Come, we must take the bus.'

When they reached Kingsbridge, the curtains had already been drawn across the windows and Mr Damarell was awaiting them as the carriage turned up the drive.

He came down the steps towards them. 'Rachel, may I offer my sincere condolences in your terrible loss.'

Rachel frowned. It was as though mama and papa and Charlotte were being wrapped up in words, put out of her reach.

He took her arm awkwardly. 'Come in, dear girl. The Lord will sustain you in your hour of need.'

'Rachel has been very brave,' Aunt Maria said. 'But I am glad to be at home again.'

She smiled as though the strain of the past hours had been almost too much for her. Now she had returned to the protection of her husband. It was here that she could operate with confidence, organise the domestic side of grief.

Bertha came from the drawing-room, already dressed in half-mourning, a black gown with a purple lace neckpiece, suitable for distant relatives, although it was actually only Aunt Maria who had been related to poor dear Ursula. Bertha's black hair was wound round her head in a plait. Her dress clung too tightly to her figure and Aunt Maria observed that it would be necessary for her to have a new one.

Aunt Alice was contacted with a request that she should come and measure Rachel and Bertha for dresses, and coats. Shoes were ordered from Mr Tanner in Fore Street and accessories from Mr Burgoyne. Rachel would wear full mourning for a year and then change to half mourning, then semi-mourning, until she could return to normal attire.

When James and Thomas returned from work, they changed from their working clothes into black suits before greeting Rachel in the drawing-room.

They expressed the same regrets at her sorrow, the same certainty that the Lord would sustain her in her hour of need. They also added that only time would heal. Rachel listened to their words with animosity. It was almost as if they were encouraging her to forget, to lay them to rest in the past.

Only Richard, returning later from the mill, seemed to understand what had happened to her.

Rachel was standing in the conservatory when he came in.

'I'm sorry, Rachel,' he said seriously.

Rachel looked at him belligerently. 'Don't say the Lord will look after me, or that time will heal.'

Richard looked surprised at her vehemence. 'Perhaps it's true, Rachel.'

'How can it be? How can time heal? They're gone but I don't want to forget them. I'll go on wishing for ever that they were here.'

'Yes. I know. But I think they're only trying to help you. Perhaps the Lord does help, if you believe enough, Rachel.'

'Do you, Richard?'

Richard turned away uncertainly. 'Everyone's soul is his own,' he said enigmatically.

'I just can't see their faces, Richard,' Rachel said anxiously. 'It's as though I've gone blind.'

116

'No. It happened to me, when my mother died. I just couldn't imagine her. I used to go up to her room and sit there. But it was no good.'

'And do you remember her now?'

'After a time, it came back. But I think it was only when I could cope with it. It was as though my mind was protecting me from the truth. Perhaps that's what they mean by time healing.'

Rachel's eyes suddenly widened. 'Richard, I'd forgotten. Your mother drowned, didn't she?'

Richard nodded. A remote expression came into his eyes. He put an arm around her awkwardly, saying, 'You have to believe me, Rachel. I know it's terrible but you will get over it. It's not that you forget. You just learn to carry the sadness with you.'

Rachel looked at him bleakly. For a moment she leaned against him, longing for her mother's arms. Never again would anyone just cuddle her and kiss her like her mother and Charlotte had done. She realised suddenly how much she had missed their loving embraces. Aunt Maria's kisses were always formal and remote. Tears sprang to her eyes, she felt renewed panic inside her.

'I can't bear it, Richard.'

Richard stroked her hair lightly.

Aunt Maria appeared and looked at them quietly and then said kindly, 'Come along, Rachel. Let's go to the music room.'

Rachel followed them both. Large candles were burning on tall brass stands and the piano was decorated with wreaths. Heavy curtains were drawn across the windows.

'What is it for?' Rachel looked bewildered. 'We can't have a . . . funeral.'

'It's in respect, Rachel dear. When you wish you may come in here and sit quietly.'

At dinner that night, Mr Damarell incorporated a long remembrance talk into his saying of Grace. Rachel had heard the words before, when he had been speaking of other relatives who had passed on. She imagined them all congregating in some heavenly place of sunshine and green fields with many mansions and angels with gold wings, singing, floating in a blue sky. But what about those gods in Egypt, did they have another heaven? Would Mama and Papa be seeing those giant gods from Karnak and Luxor?

The next day, Rachel was placed in the study to read the letters of condolence which had already arrived, the cards and messages. She remembered all those afternoons at school, when they had sat in the school room, practising their copper-plate handwriting on invitation cards and congratulations and similar letters of condolence.

'They must be replied to,' Aunt Maria said. 'It is appropriate that you should write them yourself. Would you like my help?'

'No, Aunt Maria. We learnt it all at school.'

'Ah. Then that is something for which you must be grateful to your dear parents.'

Then the relatives arrived, Aunt Bessie and Uncle Robert, the fishmonger; Uncle Wesley, the grocer and Aunt Emmie and Uncle James who was a carpenter in Salcombe. Uncle Jonathon, the gentlemens' tailor and draper and his wife Aunt Alice, who had brought the new patterns with her for their mourning attire. During the day, Aunt Maria's relatives arrived; Aunt Martha, the straw-bonnet maker who now owned two establishments in Dartmouth and her husband, Uncle Albert, who owned a fleet of fishing vessels and who supplied the royal household. Uncle Roger who also lived in Dartmouth and was the Port Reeve and Uncle John from Brixham, dressed in his uniform of a ship's captain. Uncle Henry sent a message to say that his practice in Kingswear did not permit of his visiting the bereaved family; he had that very day to attend upon Lord Kinlare of Mount Castle House who was sick with distemper.

Rachel noticed that Mr Damarell seemed to address Aunt Maria's relatives with greater formality than normal, as though he wished to impress upon them the importance of his own situation. Each of them discussed the shipwreck, the mystery that no lifeboats had managed to launch on that fateful night, that perhaps there had been negligence somewhere.

As they talked, Rachel felt a new, terrible doubt, wondering if perhaps they could have been saved. However Uncle John, who reminded them that he had been a seaman all his life, said that in those seas, no such rescue was possible.

Aunt Bessie said what a shame it was that there could be no funeral. It helped so much to have that final gesture of respect and tribute. After that, you could get down to putting your life together again.

'Rachel is young,' Mr Damarell said. 'She has not seen her parents for four years. It was a disappointment for her then, but in the event it may help her to recover more easily from their loss.'

'Yes. I think we may hope so,' Aunt Bessie agreed.

'Myself, I didn't have much enthusiasm for her going to that school. I don't believe in this education of young women,' Mr Damarell went on. 'Quite unnecessary. What do they need with all this highfalutin' learning? Gives them ideas not suitable to feminine requirements. They can learn all they need to know at home, with a proper mistress of a household and a decent governess.'

'Well, dear Arthur,' Aunt Edith said quietly, 'I think they have taught her useful accomplishments. She is conversant with all those qualities desirable in a lady.'

Rachel noticed that Mr Damarell did not dismiss or ignore her comment, as he often did with the women in his own household. It was almost as if he felt inferior. Were these relatives of Aunt Maria's different from the people in Kingsbridge? Was this what Aunt Maria meant by a better class of person?

'Well, perhaps in this case it may come in useful,' Mr Damarell was saying.

Rachel listened to their words in silence. They spoke as though she weren't there, as though like her parents she had vanished into the sea.

But their words worried her. There had been no mention of what would become of her, where she would go. Aunt Maria had said they would look after her, but would Mr Damarell want her in this household? And where would she go if he didn't?

A week later, when the candles had been removed, the letters had all been written and the visits of sympathy had been completed, Rachel was passing the drawing-room door when she heard her aunt and Mr Damarell speaking inside. She could hear Mr Damarell's voice raised in indignation.

'It's a disgrace,' he was saying. 'Whatever happened to the man?'

'I cannot understand such matters, Arthur. What does it mean?'

'It means that he was financially insolvent. It means that Rachel is completely unprovided for.'

'But how did that happen?'

Rachel heard Mr Damarell exclaim, as though in anger, 'I don't know. Must have been a rogue and scoundrel, or an improvident fool. The bank simply say there are no funds.'

Rachel crept along the hall and into the music room. What were they saying? Were they speaking of papa? And what did he mean, a rogue?

She turned, hurried back to the drawing-room and burst in. 'Aunt Maria, what are you talking about?'

They both turned round, and Mr Damarell said sharply, 'My dear young lady, you must kindly knock when your aunt and I are engaged in conversation.'

'I heard you,' Rachel said. 'Are you speaking of papa?'

Aunt Maria was about to reply, but Mr Damarell waved a hand to silence her, saying, 'She will need to be told. It might as well be now. Close the door, Rachel. Sit down.'

Rachel sat on a high-backed chair in front of him while Aunt Maria went over to the settee. Mr Damarell stood erect before the fireplace, a thumb stuck each side in his waistcoat, his eyes raised to the ceiling as though he were about to deliver a sermon. He pondered for a moment, then he looked at Rachel.

'I have today received a communication from your father's – your late father's – place of employment.'

'The bank?'

'Do not interrupt, please. This is a serious matter. From his bank. They have presented me with information to the effect that his finances were in a desperate state when he passed on.'

Rachel frowned. 'Do you mean money?'

Mr Damarell ignored her interruption.

'They have informed me that in view of the unfortunate circumstances and also the protection of the bank's reputation, they have dealt with his commitments in Egypt, though they do not go into detail about what they were.' Mr Damarell breathed heavily. 'They state, however, that they cannot be responsible for any further creditors there may be in this country.'

Rachel shook her head in incomprehension.

'What it means,' Aunt Maria began, but Mr Damarell silenced her with a look.

'I have been in contact with Miss Gordon at the Establishment for Young Ladies. It seems that your late father had contracted to settle

120

his obligations to that good lady when he returned to England. That obligation has, of course, not been met.'

'But how—'

Mr Damarell raised himself up and put a hand on each side of his waist. 'As your guardian, it falls to me to honour this debt and any other that may emerge.'

'I'm sorry.'

'It means, of course, that any funds that a young lady in your position might have expected to inherit are non-existent. You are substantially without any source of income and, of course, bereft of any capital.'

Rachel frowned. 'Mr Damarell, I recollect that Mama communicated to me in a letter that Grandpapa had left her a considerable sum. Would not I now be entitled to that benefit?'

Mr Damarell looked at Rachel with an expression of disapproval. 'I have been in touch with your father's lawyer in London. Unfortunately, your grandfather's estate was settled very speedily, at the request of your father. That inheritance to which you would have been entitled was swallowed up in repaying his monstrous and mysterious debts.'

Aunt Maria sighed. 'When one thinks of the money wasted on those elaborate dresses you were unable to wear, on school fees—'

'Pray, Maria, if I may be permitted.' Mr Damarell's tone changed to one of regret. 'It is a misfortune, but not one for you, Rachel, of unparalleled gloom.' He rose up to his full height and smiled benignly towards the ceiling. 'I have, fortunately, the wherewithal to accommodate you under my roof. Having laboured assiduously from youth, I am, perhaps, one of the most successful gentlemen in the neighbourhood. It is something of which, I have to confess, I am justly proud. And as the Lord has seen fit to reward me, so it is my duty to assist those in distress. You will be treated as a member of the family and, in spite of your disadvantages, it is to be hoped that in good time you will make a satisfactory marriage.'

Rachel stood up and demanded, 'What did you mean by the word rogue?'

'Rachel, I trust you do not listen at keyholes like a common servant.' Mr Damarell's voice was indignant.

'I could not help over-hearing, Sir.'

Mr Damarell raised his eyes to the ceiling again. 'We do not speak ill of the dead, Rachel. They have passed to that higher authority who sits in judgment on us all. It is not for us mortals to see into the hearts and minds of others. It is for us to pray for his immortal soul.'

'But what—?'

'The circumstances of his apparent financial ruin can only be conjectured. It is better if we do not go into pointless speculation, Rachel. It is enough for you to know that at least you have a roof over your head.'

Mr Damarell looked at Rachel benevolently. As he left the room, he added, 'It is to be hoped that the investment your father made in you in sending you to that Establishment will now be of benefit. I am confident you will assist your dear aunt in adding to the comfort and well-being of this household.'

Rachel looked at Aunt Maria questioningly but she only said, 'Let us not discuss it any further now, Rachel. Mr Damarell will deal with everything.'

It was not until she was at chapel the next Sunday listening to Mr Damarell who, as the lay preacher, was delivering the sermon, that she saw the full implications of her position. What Mr Damarell had meant was that papa had deliberately spent all his money, he had not paid for her school, he had not been concerned about what happened to her at all. She felt a wild anger inside her. He had never cared, he had sent her to England when she wanted to remain with them, he had left her destitute and then he had died and taken mama and Charlotte with him.

She clutched her hymn book as she sang the words of the final hymn, selected by Mr Damarell, 'Oh, hear us when we cry to thee, for those in peril on the sea'.

Her fury seemed to choke the words in her throat. James, standing by her side, whispered, 'Are you all right, Rachel?'

She nodded but as they left the chapel and began to walk down the hill, James came back and joined Rachel and Bertha. 'I prefer to walk with you ladies,' he said, smiling. 'Papa proceeds at such a great rate.'

Rachel looked at him. James was very thin and he was always pale. Aunt Maria often said that he had a poor constitution and that his thatching job was too demanding for him. But Mr Damarell said the fresh air would do him good, it would build up his strength.

'It is a difficult time for you, Rachel,' James smiled at her sympathetically.

'It is papa's fault,' Rachel said angrily. 'He was a rogue.'

'Rachel! Do not speak so. How can you utter such words?' Bertha said in a shocked voice.

'Your father said it was so.'

'Rachel, he could not have meant that,' James protested. 'You have misunderstood his words. It appears your papa had some misfortune. That is not a disgrace, Rachel.'

'He has left me penniless. Abandoned.'

'Rachel, you are not abandoned. My father will provide for you as long as necessary. We are all pleased to have you in our household.'

Bertha took her arm. 'I am so glad to have you, Rachel. I have found my domestic duties very burdensome. Of course, I am sad for you but—'

'But what?'

Rachel looked at Bertha's plump, pink face, her curly black hair fixed neatly back with combs beneath her wide straw bonnet.

'It is such a change to have you visit with me and attend to errands instead of being chaperoned by Lizzie or Gert.'

Rachel thought about the visits she and Bertha had made in the past. Was it possible that life could be composed of those endless calls and At Homes and polite conversation and tea parties and tidying drawers and arranging flowers? Panic seized her again but Bertha was saying, 'It's not only that, Rachel. Perhaps I can help you to get over your tragedy.'

Rachel looked at Bertha's encouraging smile, the tender way she was looking at her, and suffered a pang of guilt.

'Yes, Bertha,' she said slowly.

Chapter 7

As Rachel entered the Damarell house her feeling of guilt grew. She recognised that to her they were just people who had inhabited the periphery of her life while she waited for the time to pass. She realised that she had never really thought about this household or the lives of the people who inhabited it. She had thought only of surviving until her parents returned and she could escape. Yet they were people with their own thoughts and feelings and she had abruptly appeared in their household, deposited amongst them almost without warning. Perhaps they had had no greater desire to receive her than she had had to come? They had seen her, still did see her, as a strange and undisciplined girl. Yet they had taken her in, made her welcome; even Mr Damarell had accepted that she was now a member of his family.

In fact, she had never thought about any of them, except Jacob when he had come on leave that time. She remembered how she had been infatuated with his laughing face and all the wild stories he had told her about his life in foreign parts. Jacob had only been home briefly once or twice since then, while she had been in London visiting her grandfather. Now he was in Africa somewhere, and although Mr Damarell still read his letters proudly to visiting relatives, Jacob seemed remote and unknown, someone from another era.

Rachel thought about her years at the Establishment. All of that life, too, had passed in a kind of dream. Her whole life, at school and at the Damarell's, was a void, because she had been living for the moment when she would return to Egypt.

As she followed Bertha into the drawing-room and Gertie took their coats, her thoughts made her feel more of an interloper, her guilt grew even greater. She was living on their kindness and Mr Damarell's generosity.

125

The anger she felt towards her father returned as she thought about all the hopes which had been demolished and his now broken promise, that if she would only endure necessary hardship she would be rewarded and return to a real, normal life. As they ate their cold Sunday lunch, Rachel listened to the men's conversation. They were talking about how Queen Victoria had been proclaimed Empress of India. Mr Damarell said that was all very well but Disraeli would be better employed keeping an eye on the Russians and the Afghan border. Thomas said he should be paying more attention to problems at home. Trade was getting bad, the fishing industry in the south-west was losing out to ports on the east coast.

'He ought to pay more attention to the needs of working people,' Richard said.

'Working people!' Mr Damarell frowned. 'It's my opinion people don't work like they used to.'

'Many of the underpaid workers need protection. They want proper unions to look after their interests.'

'Underpaid! What do you think they are going to be paid with? If the owners don't make enough profit, that's the fault of the workers.' Mr Damarell looked severely at Richard. 'We're running a mill, not a charity. If you want to do your job properly, don't start listening to those employees. They should think themselves lucky that they are in secure positions. Let them look around at those who don't have the benefit of a weekly wage.'

Richard was silent. Aunt Maria took the opportunity to observe that the workmen who were engaged on the extension to the drawing-room were frivolous in their conversations with the housemaids.

'It is for you to deal with domestic matters of that nature,' Mr Damarell said shortly. 'If the girl is unsuitable, dismiss her.'

'Yes, of course, dear.' Aunt Maria accepted the mild reproof with a smile. Her husband was not required to concern himself with such details. She nodded to Lizzie to clear the table. 'It will be a relief to have the extra space when it is completed. So much more suitable for social occasions.'

Mr Damarell nodded briefly and said, 'I hope you will be satisfied.'

Rachel recalled that it was Aunt Maria who had mooted the necessity for more space. First she had intimated that it might be advantageous to move to Salcombe. There were more substantial houses in that vicinity; usually inhabited by a better class of person.

Mr Damarell had been indignant at the mere suggestion. He had lived in Kingsbridge all his life; the mill was there. This was the community in which he had some responsibility and influence. He did not intend to consider such a proposition.

Aunt Maria agreed that he was a person of much prestige and as such he was expected to have an establishment befitting his station. It was not merely his activities in the community which were of significance; his domestic arrangements were also of note in the neighbourhood. He would surely desire to have a house appropriate to his importance.

'Do you have any complaint?' Mr Damarell had asked.

'Ah, no, dear Arthur. It is no complaint. I am merely desirous of seeing that your success is recognised. A number of homes in the neighbourhood have introduced modern facilities. Gas lighting in all the rooms, including the bedrooms, more commodious bathroom arrangements, larger rooms for the entertainment of guests. It would seem fitting that we should be seen to be leaders in those fields.'

As a result, improvements to the house had been set in hand. During the weeks and months that followed, Rachel tried to tell herself that this was her home, this was where she belonged. Of course, Mr Damarell had never actually said that, he had only said he would provide for her. It was as though she was a permanent visitor who might one day pack her valise and leave. Sometimes she thought that Mr Damarell was looking at her critically, as though he was wondering if she had outstayed her invitation. Aunt Maria and Bertha and the young gentlemen were always kind and polite, and yet she still felt insecure, an onlooker, rather than a family member.

It was very different from the Establishment, because that had been all females. Watching Aunt Maria in action, Rachel reflected that women had ways of getting round the fact that men made all the decisions. Or was it just that women were allowed to have some influence in domestic matters, but not beyond? It seemed strange to her that men and women were so separate.

Even the house was different without the men. While they were there, it was as though everything was being run for their benefit. Aunt Maria was constantly preoccupied with their comfort. Cushions were adjusted on chairs and settees in the drawing-room, windows were opened and closed according to their wishes, they were served first at meals, Lizzie or Gert were constantly hovering in the shadows, awaiting the expression of any wish.

When they departed early each morning to their various places of business, everything changed. Richard and Mr Damarell would leave first, riding down the drive in the gig. The carriage was only used for social visiting or when Mr Damarell had an important business or official appointment. Then James would go. He walked because he was usually working on houses in the neighbourhood. James had two young apprentices, but Mr Damarell frequently berated him about his treatment of them.

'You are not severe enough,' he would say. 'In my opinion, they are laggards. I have seen them, when they're supposed to be up there, on the roof, sitting on the ground in the sun, as though it were a holiday.'

James would always say, 'They're good lads, Papa. They're only young.'

'Young! It's when they're young that they need to have some sense of discipline knocked into them.'

A further point of conflict between the two men seemed to be that his father considered James insufficiently ambitious. James made no secret of the fact that his main interest was in music, and spent most of his free time in the music room, practising the piano. He was also the organist at the chapel. When the opportunity arose, he intended to abandon thatching and take up a paid position as an organist or as a music master in some educational establishment.

His father had expressed the opinion that it was a poorly-paid occupation and, in his view, more suitable as an unpaid recreation for a lady with some time on her hands.

Arranging the flowers in the music room one day, Rachel had broached the topic with Aunt Maria.

'I think it would be nice for James to be a pianist. His playing is so delightful.'

Aunt Maria smiled, agreeing. 'It is indeed. I believe, too, it would be a more felicitous occupation. He might be requested to play at desirable social functions. He would meet different people.'

'But Mr Damarell seems not to approve.'

'Ah,' Aunt Maria said hastily. 'Of course my dear husband knows best. He is concerned for James's welfare.'

The last one to depart in the mornings was Thomas. Although he said that he enjoyed the walk down to Date's yard, he usually seemed to manage to get a lift in someone's trap. As he left the house, he always turned and waved to Aunt Maria and the girls, his round, plump face smiling cheerfully. Thomas was always cheerful. He seemed unperturbed by Mr Damarell's stern view of life and he chatted to the servants in a way that no one else did. Aunt Maria revealed to Rachel that when Thomas had completed his apprentice-ship and had become a fully-fledged foundryman, his father had promised to set him up in a foundry of his own.

'In a way,' Aunt Maria said, 'I believe it is because Thomas reminds him of his favourite son, Jacob.'

'Why should Jacob be his favourite son?'

'I don't know, dear. But fathers always seem to have a favourite son. He is so proud of him.'

'Is Thomas like Jacob? I scarcely remember him, except that he used to tell Bertha and me all sorts of stories.'

'In some ways they're alike,' Aunt Maria said reflectively. 'They both have a happy disposition. Of course, Jacob is very handsome, perhaps too handsome for his own good, I sometimes think. And he has a certain worldliness, a sophistication that Thomas lacks.'

'Is that a good thing, Aunt Maria?'

'It is neither good nor bad, Rachel. Such attributes depend upon how they are employed.'

With their departure, the house seemed to enter into a routine of its own. When only the women remained in the house, Rachel often felt that she was back at the Establishment. It was there that she had learnt about the correct running of a household, the form all its activities should take. She occasionally thought that Aunt Maria had absorbed all that information more assiduously than Miss Gordon. Perhaps Mr Damarell was right. She had never needed to go there; Aunt Maria could have taught her just as well.

The morning began with Aunt Maria summoning Mrs Greeve, the housekeeper. Aunt Maria observed to Rachel that when she came here, the house had been sadly understaffed. She did not know how poor Elizabeth had managed with only two general maids and a coachman to attend to Mr Damarell and the carriage. Even the gardener had only been a visiting lad from the village. But now, as was proper in such a household, there was a housekeeper, cook, the housemaid, Lizzie, and the two under housemaids, Maggie and Gertie, as well as her own maid, Betsy, and the footman and gardener. Aunt Maria had suggested a valet for Mr Damarell, but he had been adamant that such a person was unnecessary. He wasn't having a man entering his bedroom.

Having discussed the duties of the day with Mrs Greeve and then proceeded with her to an inspection of the kitchens and the other servant quarters, Rose, the cook, and the upper housemaid, Lizzie, were given their various requirements from the store-closet. Aunt Maria accompanied Lizzie to the bedrooms and to what she called the public rooms to give any special instructions about their cleaning or arrangement. Rachel and Bertha then followed Aunt Maria to the drawing-room, where she consulted her diary to ascertain their duties for the day, the visits they expected from friends and acquaintances, the At Homes, the calls they would make and any evening events they would attend. Next, she and Bertha went to their bedrooms to examine their wardrobes, to ensure that anything needing repair or attention was handed to Lizzie.

After this, they were free to indulge in useful recreation and answering and sending invitations on behalf of Aunt Maria. Rachel had told Aunt Maria that she had no interest in embroidery or tapestry.

'I remember you executed a very fine crochet table-cloth at the Establishment,' Aunt Maria protested.

'It took me about a year,' Rachel said gloomily. 'Sophie did most of it for me.'

'Ah. How is your friend Sophie?'

'She is in London,' Rachel sighed. 'She goes to India soon to be with her father, but hopes to return next summer. She has invited me to visit her.'

'That would be very pleasant,' Aunt Maria smiled. 'By then, you will be out of mourning. Though, of course, we must be as moderate as possible in expenditure on a new wardrobe.' Then she added thoughtfully, 'I am sure your friend Sophie mixes in advantageous circles.'

'I suppose so.'

'It is so important for young ladies to meet desirable persons.'

'Mama means young men,' Bertha said, laughing.

'Ah. You may think it amusing, Bertha, but you will wish to maintain the standard to which you are accustomed, or even beyond, when you marry.'

'I'm not yet eighteen, Aunt Maria. For me marriage is a distant prospect.'

'That may be, Rachel, but you should wish to cultivate suitable and interesting contacts. But now, girls, let us get on with our various activities. I must have a look around the garden to see that James has enough jobs to occupy him during these winter months.'

'I think I shall go to the music room and practise the violin,' Rachel said.

'In that case, I shall take my paints into the summer house where I can't hear you,' Bertha laughed. 'I have my water colour to complete.'

Rachel did not play the violin but stood at the window watching Aunt Maria speaking to the gardener. There always seemed so much to do, every moment was filled with activity, just as it had been at school. Yet there was something missing in her life, as though she was constantly waiting for something that would never happen. She wondered if it was different for men; perhaps that world of work they went to was what was missing. Perhaps it was different when you were married? Yet when she thought of Aunt Maria, her life seemed to be the same. Of course, it must be different, having a man in the same room as yourself at night, but that seemed a disadvantage. It no doubt caused terrible difficulties at certain times of the month. Whatever did Aunt Maria do? She sighed, closing her mind to that distasteful topic.

After lunch that day, they went to their rooms to change into their afternoon clothes. Rachel looked gloomily at her black dress, with its neat, tight, high-buttoned bodice and her black kid boots and black straw bonnet, tied with black ribbon. Soon the mourning period would be over and she could wear bright colours again. It seemed so long since she had worn any pretty dresses. At the Establishment, it had been those ghastly black skirts and white blouses that made you look like a housemaid.

She gazed at her face reflectively in the looking-glass and

remembered that Aunt Bessie had said that black suited her with her auburn hair and grey eyes. But black didn't really suit anyone but old women like Aunt Maria. Well, in a couple of months she could wear purple; even that would be better than this gloom. She went down to the drawing-room. Aunt Maria was consulting her diary again, checking the morning calls, to ensure that she had made no mistake about the date.

'First of all,' she said, 'we must visit upon the Hyamson establishment to acknowledge their kindness in entertaining us to the dinner party on Thursday last. In view of the distance, and the fact that much of the route is uphill, we shall go in the carriage. It also looks more suitable when calling on such persons. We must then leave dinner invitations at various households as we pass. Finally, we must leave a condolence card at the Trewin household. Now, where did I put that mourning card.'

Aunt Maria looked round.

'It's on the mantelpiece,' Bertha reached up. 'You put it there to remember.'

'Ah, yes. Now, girls, let me look at you. Maggie kindly wipe over Miss Rachel's boots. They are scarcely shining.'

Gertie took a duster from her overall pocket and polished the offending articles.

'And while we are absent, Lizzie, kindly wash down the shelves in the conservatory. And also the windows. Now, remember, girls, we do not overstay our visit to the Hyamsons.'

They set off along the road to Salcombe. The house lay at the top of a hill, overlooking the estuary, and Aunt Maria commented approvingly on the wide, lawned gardens and the new conservatory which had been erected.

'They have a tennis court,' Bertha remarked. 'Perhaps we could arrange a game with Jane and Felicity.'

'They have two sons as well,' Rachel said. 'I was talking to them at dinner.'

'Yes, I noticed,' Bertha frowned.

Rachel blushed. 'It is normal courtesy. I found them entertaining.'

'Yes. They found you entertaining, too. Young men always do. It's not fair, just because you're pretty.'

'That is nonsense,' Aunt Maria said sharply. She was wearing a high, black hat which made her look even more regal than usual. 'You must learn to cultivate polite conversation, Bertha. Always have a list of topics in your mind that may appear amusing or interesting. In any case,' she added, 'young men are more interested in your listening to their own words rather than hearing yours.'

A servant led them into the drawing-room at one end of which stood a grand piano. Rachel saw Aunt Maria observing the object thoughtfully. Shortly, she thought, the old piano would be removed and a grand piano would be installed at Mill House. Mrs Hyamson, a small, plump woman in a silk dress with an old-fashioned bustle, received them graciously and bade them be seated.

She smiled kindly at Rachel, saying, 'Your discussion at the dinner table about the beauties of the Egyptian landscape was the source of much interest to the assembled guests, Miss Rachel.'

Rachel blushed as she suddenly pictured Miss Gordon. Had she been too forward?

'Dear Rachel was at one time in that country,' Aunt Maria said approvingly, 'and has many interesting observations to make.'

The conversation turned to general matters, a winter vacation which Mrs Hyamson and her family had taken recently in Bath, the sad demise of Mr Trewin, and the joys of the approaching festive season.

When further visitors were announced, Aunt Maria looked meaningfully at Rachel and Bertha. After the new arrivals were seated and had exchanged a few pleasantries, Aunt Maria rose quietly, said farewell to her hostess, and bowed to the other guests. They were escorted to the front door by a servant and climbed back into their carriage.

'Well, I think that was most satisfactory.' Aunt Maria looked pleased.

'I didn't like her dress,' Bertha observed. 'That awful cerise colour with those white gloves.'

'I confess I found it rather lacking in taste, but that is not an important matter. She runs an impressive establishment and she and her family will be most suitable guests at my next musical evening. Now, we must leave these invitation cards and then visit Mrs Trewin.'

When they returned to Mill House, Aunt Maria collected the cards which had been left by callers during their absence.

'There is one from a Mr Montgomery.' Aunt Maria looked mystified. 'I do not recollect his name.'

'He was at Mrs Hyamson's the other night,' Bertha said. 'He comes from Loddiswell. He's probably hoping for an invitation so that he can see Rachel.'

Aunt Maria smiled. 'Then you must ensure, Bertha, that young gentlemen are just as desirous of your company. Remember, you are twenty-four in a few months' time. It is to young ladies of your age that young gentlemen are directing their attention.'

Bertha frowned. 'I'm almost on the shelf,' she said gloomily.

At Aunt Maria's next dinner-party, Rachel found herself observing the male guests, elderly husbands like Mr Roache, whose dinner jacket seemed to be strapped across his large stomach; the dentist, Mr Markham, who wore a monocle and talked with Mr Damarell knowledgeably about the situation in Afghanistan. Mr Damarell instantly turned the conversation to his son Jacob, as though Jacob's presence in the army made him an authority on its activities throughout the world. Then there was Mr Waldorf, an accountant, who talked about the financial affairs of the country and expressed the view that Mr Disraeli's foresight in buying the Suez Canal shares would prove to be in Britain's long-term interests.

Her eyes rested finally on young Mr Cresswell, who was only a visitor, currently staying with his aunt and uncle. He had smooth brown hair and what Rachel mentally called a plain face, and he talked about farming in Dorset and how the grain market was being ruined by the growth of imports.

Would marriage to any of them make life seem better, would they fill her emptiness? She tried to imagine living with Mr Cresswell, running his household, sharing the same room with him at night.

Then she felt Richard's eyes on her. She smiled across the table and said, 'Bertha and I are to play tennis tomorrow afternoon at Mrs Hyamson's. Could you not come, Richard?'

'I shall be working, Rachel.'

'No, it is Saturday. Surely you could be available.'

'That is a good idea, Richard,' Aunt Maria remarked. 'You must not spend too much time studying, you know. Richard is such a studious young man,' she observed to the assembled guests generally, nodding approvingly at him.

Most of Richard's evenings and free time were occupied in the library, studying, and although his father approved of his endeavours, Aunt Maria frequently pointed out that progress in this world also meant mixing with the right people.

'Will you come, Richard?' Rachel persisted.

'Yes, perhaps I will.'

Rachel always enjoyed being with Richard. He was quiet and thoughtful and in a way she liked him just because he was so serious. Also, he seemed to talk to her in a different way from Mr Damarell and James and Thomas, almost as though she were a boy. Of course, he never made all those polite remarks that other young men made to her, about how charming she looked and how delighted they were to make her acquaintance. But he told her about his work and all about the countryside and the books he was reading. He even encouraged her to read what he called interesting literature, although Richard's recommendations were always examined first by Aunt Maria to ensure their suitability.

Yesterday, in the library, she had suddenly remembered the terrible book she had discovered there when she was a child, with its pictures of the male and female anatomies. She remembered how disturbed she had been at the time, yet she had forgotten about it almost instantly. At the recollection, she had blushed and glanced up at the glass bookcase to see if it were still there.

'Those are the books James collected,' Richard said, following her gaze. 'When he was thinking of becoming a doctor.'

'Oh, I see.'

'I think they would not interest you.'

'No. Why didn't James become a doctor then?'

'When he left Crispin's, he was offered an apprenticeship to train as a thatcher. Father thought it an excellent opportunity, so he gave up his medical studies.'

Richard had passed her a book by Mr Hardy called *Under the Greenwood Tree*.

Rachel smiled at him now and mentioned that she had almost completed it. 'The people in the novel have a strange form of speech.' Rachel frowned. 'I find some of it tiresome to translate.'

Mr Cresswell observed that Mr Hardy came from his own Dorset and had apparently trained to be an architect. He nodded knowingly.

'That is how the working men speak in my part of the world. Mr Hardy has interpreted them very well.'

'But the female persons do not speak like any I know,' Rachel protested. 'Our servants do not speak so.'

Mr Cresswell smiled, remarking, 'No doubt the lower classes in Kingsbridge also speak with a different intonation from a lady like yourself. In fact, I have heard them on my uncle's farm up at Loddiswell. It is simply a different dialect from Dorset.'

'Yes, I suppose so.'

It wasn't just the dialect that Rachel found unsatisfactory. These books never answered her questions. They talked about men and women and about people being married but never actually said what that meant. Of course, she knew it involved living in the same house and being provided for and even sleeping in the same room as your husband. But there were children, too, and women had them. So how did they get there?

Aunt Maria would say that a lady was in a 'certain state' and had to rest, and a few months later the woman would remain at home for weeks on end, so when you visited she was either lying on the couch, with her stomach getting larger and larger, or else she was indisposed and you didn't see her at all. You just left your card and a message of what Aunt Maria called encouragement. Then she would say one day that the lady had been confined – which Rachel assumed from Aunt Maria's serious demeanour meant that she had suffered some strange illness – it often seemed from her tone that it was a kind of disgrace for which the lady was only half responsible, a bit like the monthly shame. Naturally, that was never mentioned in books either, and all that Aunt Maria had told her was that it went on happening for a number of years and then it stopped.

Then the pregnant lady had the infant and after a further period of resting, her life appeared to return to normal.

Richard interposed, 'Perhaps you have no interest in the rude behaviour of Dorset labourers, Rachel. I will suggest something more suitable when we are next in the library.'

Rachel raised her eyebrows in astonishment. Richard was looking with distaste at poor Mr Cresswell, as though he had been discussing some forbidden topic.

But Mr Cresswell seemed unperturbed.

'I hope Mr Hardy may find his new career as financially rewarding as his previous profession. I believe that the fortunes of a writer may be insecure.' Then he smiled in a strange way. 'Perhaps you should not read *Far from the Madding Crowd*,' he said. 'In that volume his young ladies seem to behave with the greatest impropriety.'

'Oh, indeed?'

Mr Cresswell nodded. His eyes rested on Rachel. He looked at her auburn hair and her black gown, fringed now with purple and adorned with a silver necklet.

'No doubt the artistic life has much appeal for young ladies such as yourself. I think you must have many such accomplishments.'

Rachel glanced at Richard. There was a look of irritation on his face and when the ladies were rejoined in the drawing-room, she asked him, 'Don't you like Mr Cresswell?'

'Like? I have never considered the matter. I scarcely know the man.'

'But you seemed to be disapproving when he was speaking to me.'

Richard frowned. 'I did not care for his attitude.'

'He seemed quite proper. What do you object to?'

'I think he was making advances.'

'Advances, Richard?'

'You are too young for such attentions.'

'Well!'

Rachel sat down as the guests subsided into silence. James had been requested to play the piano by Aunt Maria.

'Rachel, dear. Will you turn the pages for him?'

Rachel went over and stood behind him, as he performed some pieces by Bach and then a request by Mrs Markham, the dentist's wife, for 'The Lost Chord'. James seemed so frail, even his fingers looked delicate as they moved over the keys.

Rachel was distracted as she followed the music, thinking about Richard's words. She knew she liked young men to say she looked charming, but she had supposed that this was simply part of correct behaviour. It had seemed to confirm that she fitted in to this household, that she belonged. But did they actually mean it, did it imply they were interested in her, personally?

She looked at Richard who was standing by the mantelpiece. When she smiled, he turned away. Had she offended him? She did not want to offend Richard. It was always Richard to whom she turned during the black days of depression when she was overcome with longing for her parents. They would walk along the Estuary to Salcombe on warm summer evenings, or over the hills to Loddiswell, and he would tell her about his childhood. She discovered that he had been as isolated at St Crispin's as she had felt at the Establishment, but for different reasons, she reflected.

'I was always so studious,' Richard had said ruefully. 'Most of the boys weren't interested in study.'

Rachel's eyes fell on Mr Cresswell, who was watching her approvingly. She smiled slightly. Suddenly she understood what Aunt Maria meant – that this cultivation of suitable young men was not simply a question of invitations to dinner parties. It was a kind of play where people acted out parts, a situation that could be varied according to mood or inclination. But how encouraging should one be? There seemed to be some question of judgment and she imagined the eyes of the married ladies upon her, observing whether she was behaving suitably. She became aware that there was a line of correctness beyond which it would be only too easy to pass.

The problem crystallised when Aunt Maria gave a large Christmas celebration. Rachel had now abandoned her black attire and wore a dark grey gown trimmed with lilac-coloured lace. There was no high collar to conceal her neck and the full skirt was gathered neatly behind, so that when she sat down it was pulled up slightly to reveal pretty kid boots and silk-clad ankles. Bertha had given her a gold choker necklace for Christmas and on her hair she wore a gold Spanish comb. The rest of the family were long past their mourning period and Bertha wore a dark red gown with wide frills and a velvet jacket decorated with sequins.

Rachel peered over the bannisters, watching the guests arrive. Aunt Maria and Bertha were already in the drawing-room and she descended slowly, feeling with satisfaction the eyes of the visitors on her.

Mr Cresswell was coming towards her, a hand outstretched to assist her as she came down the stairs. His black jacket hung loosely on his person as though, Rachel thought, he had had it made a size too large to allow for growth. She almost giggled at her own absurd thoughts and then nodded coolly in greeting.

'Ah, dear Miss Rachel. What a delight to see you again.'

Rachel hesitated, noting his eager face, his glance of approval. But it was more than that. Looking at him, it was as though she had a sudden revelation. So this was it. His expression, his whole attitude, everything about him in that moment in time was giving her the answer to the mystery. As she had suspected, she knew now that there was something more between men and women, something she couldn't understand but which was reflected in his whole demeanour. It was a totally different expression from the one people normally had when they were addressing her.

It had some special meaning; that was all she knew at the moment. But as she lightly held his hand, quickly released it, and said, 'Good evening, Mr Cresswell,' she felt an unexpected sense of power. It occurred to her that perhaps this was a kind of balance between men and women; men were the strong, decision-making individuals, but the weaker woman had this unspoken possibility, whatever it was, to make a gentleman focus his attention on one particular female, virtually to become her servant.

During the musical soirée which followed dinner, she noticed other young men observing her. She found herself half-smiling in a calculated way and recognised that a certain expression in her eyes aroused a corresponding response in theirs. It seemed like a new game she had discovered.

Young Philip Waldorf was heading towards her as she sat down by Bertha, whereupon Richard quickly occupied the only vacant chair beside her.

'Mrs Roache is going to sing,' Bertha whispered, rolling her eyes.

James's fingers rippled across the piano keys and the violinist tuned his strings.

'Have I heard a request for "Come into the Garden Maud?",' Mrs Roache looked round at the expectant guests. The ladies were arranged in a semi-circle of chairs, their voluminous gowns making it necessary for them to sit some way apart so that they had to lean across to talk to each other. The gentlemen were in the next row, their long black jackets buttoned up, their hands clasped behind their backs.

'Ah, that would be charming,' Aunt Maria smiled.

Mrs Roache stood by the piano, her pink silk gown, with four frills on the skirt and an elaborate lace shawl cast around her shoulders, accentuating her plump figure. After each song, Mrs Roache protested that she could not sing another but was easily persuaded to do so by her appreciative audience. After an hour, Mrs Waldorf rose, making signs of impending departure to her husband.

'Perhaps you would like one final tune?' Mrs Roache suggested. She turned to James. 'I remember you have the music sheet there for "The Lost Chord"?'

James looked through his music. 'Yes, I know it is here somewhere.'

'Do you have it in A? That, of course, is the key most suitable to my particular talents.'

It was discovered that the music James had was rendered in E flat, but Mrs Roache decided that the guests should not be deprived.

'I will do my best with that,' she said graciously. She then decided that the guests could not leave without the benefit of hearing her rendering of 'I Dreamt that I Dwelt in Marble Halls', for which there was much applause. The evening ended with everyone singing 'Home Sweet Home' and then the carriages arrived to take the guests away.

When Rachel came down the next morning, the rest of the family had almost finished breakfast and Thomas had already departed for work.

'I'm afraid I didn't hear the gong,' Rachel apologised.

'Perhaps we are undertaking too many social engagements, Maria,' Mr Damarell observed to his wife. 'Perhaps we are abandoning all sense of sobriety.'

'Dear Arthur, I do not think that is the case. It is such an important aspect. Perhaps Rachel is a little indisposed?'

'Oh, no,' Rachel said hastily. 'I am perfectly fit.' She felt anxious at the thought of her social activities being curtailed, having finally found something to entertain and excite her.

'We have to plan Bertha's twenty-fifth event now,' Aunt Maria continued. She spoke as though she thought this were a good opportunity to broach the subject. 'It is only a few months away.'

'Event?' Mr Damarell smiled at Bertha.

'I thought we might have a ball,' Aunt Maria said. 'It is becoming quite usual, you know.'

'A ball? I don't think I am one for the dance.'

'Ah, dear. It is for the young people, accompanied of course by their parents.'

Rachel listened quietly. She knew that Aunt Maria would get her way. Over the past two years, she had realised that the sobering influence of the Methodist church was gradually being eroded. The whole family still went to the chapel three times on Sundays, and Mr Damarell gave much thought to his sermons, but the time spent on Grace and the reading of Bible texts in the evenings had both decreased – particularly as many evenings were now occupied with dinners and musical events.

Aunt Maria even permitted her and Bertha to go down into Kingsbridge unchaperoned, and on one occasion they had walked to a neighbouring house when they had a tennis engagement. That particular event had not been repeated, as Bertha had foolishly revealed that all the other young ladies had arrived by gig.

For Rachel, the great significance of the ball was that now that mourning was over, she could wear anything she liked. She spent the next few months praying that no one else would die. A week before the ball she was plunged into anxiety when Aunt Martha was involved in a pony-trap accident. The pony had been startled by a lad careering down Fore Street on a bicycle, had run into a post and Aunt Martha had been thrown from the trap. It was feared that she would not survive and Rachel and Bertha had waited anxiously for news.

'Oh, how awful it will be if I have to wear black to my ball,' Bertha moaned.

But Aunt Martha survived, although it was feared she might be confined to her couch for ever.

Rachel knew that it was as a result of the ball that Mr Damarell began to view her in a different light. Aunt Maria had engaged a small group of musicians and it was observed that Rachel had three successive dances with a young man to whom she had only just been introduced. She then spent a large part of the evening sitting with him, laughing and talking, and on one occasion even refused Mr Cresswell a dance. 'My card is full,' she had said instantly and then continued to sit. When the young man had suggested they go out on the balcony to observe the moonlight, Rachel had agreed. She had stood by his side, leaning over the balustrade, looking across the fields and houses to the estuary beyond. As they turned to go back to the ballroom, he had been observed with an arm around her waist.

It was not until the next morning that Aunt Maria broached the topic.

'Rachel, Mr Damarell was not pleased with your behaviour last night.'

'But, Aunt Maria—'

'Rachel, you must have known that your actions were quite reprehensible.'

Rachel laughed but she said instantly, 'Yes, Aunt Maria. I know. But it was just fun. I had no interest in the person concerned.'

'Then that is even worse. If you were to behave like that again, your reputation would be ruined for ever.'

'But I did nothing, Aunt Maria. I just find it amusing that men behave so. It is a sort of weakness.'

'Rachel, how can you speak so,' Aunt Maria said impatiently. 'You must understand, it is no weakness. Gentlemen will get quite the wrong impression from your attitude. I fear they would abandon any serious intentions towards you.'

'Serious? Aunt Maria, it wasn't serious.'

Aunt Maria sighed. 'Rachel, you know as much about etiquette as I do. I am speaking of more than that. Young ladies do not encourage gentlemen in the way you did unless they are engaged to be married. And even then, it would be inadvisable to behave as you did.'

Suddenly, Rachel was serious. 'Aunt Maria, why would anyone marry me?'

'My dear girl, you have many natural attractions. You can be quite charming when you see fit. These are attributes you must cultivate.'

'But I have no – what did Mr Damarell call them – assets. I am not like Bertha.'

'That is true, Rachel. Naturally, Mr Damarell will provide Bertha with a suitable portion on her marriage and it is a circumstance of which gentlemen are not unaware. Although I have no doubt that you will receive some gift from him, it is even more reason why you should behave with circumspection. You must make it clear that although you have no worldly assets, you have other desirable graces which will enhance their lives.'

'Yes, Aunt Maria.'

Rachel left the drawing-room and went upstairs to examine her clothes. Lizzie was looking at the gold silk ball dress Rachel had worn the night before.

'It's lovely,' Lizzie said, 'and you looked beautiful in it, Miss.'

Rachel sighed. 'Put it in the closet, Lizzie. Oh, I did enjoy it Lizzie, but I suppose—' Her voice trailed away.

'I noticed the young gentlemen were much impressed, Miss.'

'Were they Lizzie?'

'Oh, yes, Miss.'

Rachel smiled and went downstairs to the drawing-room. She had invitations to write for Aunt Maria. Perhaps Aunt Maria was only annoyed because she had looked more attractive than Bertha.

That evening, however, she found that Richard was equally disapproving. She went to the library to find a new novel, but Richard said acidly, 'Perhaps it would be more appropriate if you re-read some of the books on etiquette.'

Rachel smiled at him. She knew that the looks and glances that other young men found so disturbing had no effect on Richard. He didn't seem to notice.

'It was only a game, Richard.'

'It is not a game with my sex,' Richard said firmly. 'Your actions may be misinterpreted.'

'Come, Richard, it is a lovely evening. Could we not walk down to the quay?'

Richard hesitated. 'I have some studying to do, Rachel.'

'Oh, come. You do so much studying.'

'I mean to make some progress in life, Rachel.'

'Yes, I know. I am sure you will. But I can't go alone and Bertha does not feel like walking today.'

'Well, just a brief walk then.'

They went down the drive, along Wallingford Lane, over the junction with Duncombe Street and into Batts Lane. The villagers were sitting outside their cottages in Church Street, enjoying the evening sunshine. Chickens were scratching in the dust of the road and as she passed a cottage door, Rachel could smell baking bread. They waited at the narrow part of the road while a horse and cart ambled past and walked on down to Dodbrooke Quay. Fishermen were repairing their boats there as they passed them and walked on towards Crabshell.

'I don't come here often,' Richard said suddenly. 'It doesn't have pleasant memories.'

'Why not?' Rachel asked in surprise.

'It was here that my mother drowned.'

'Oh, Richard, how awful.'

Rachel looked along the quay and down into the water lapping against the stone wall. 'I didn't think. Shall we go back?'

'No. It's all right. It was along here.'

Richard went on down the path and then took Rachel's arm. 'Keep away from the edge. They took her from the water and laid her on this seat.'

'What happened?'

Richard sighed. 'It just happened,' he said abruptly. 'Come along, we must return.'

Rachel frowned. Was there some secret about his mother's death? 'Richard, is the animosity between you and Jacob something to do with your mother's death?'

He stopped and turned. 'Animosity? There is no animosity, Rachel.'

'I think Jacob feels some resentment towards you.'

Richard shrugged. 'It is merely that I was the youngest son. He feels I replaced him in Mama's affections.'

Rachel looked at him with sudden understanding. 'Richard. You never said. You saw it happen, didn't you?'

Richard nodded. 'Yes, Rachel.'

'Richard, you don't blame yourself, do you? You were only a child.'

Richard thought for a moment. 'No. Not any more. But at the time, I was convinced I was to blame. You see, I persuaded her to come for a walk. But of course, I realise now she would have refused if she had not wanted to.'

With a sudden insight, Rachel said, 'Ah, but Jacob blames you, doesn't he?'

Richard did not reply.

'Come Richard, we won't come here again.' She took his arm.

'When my parents were drowned, I went down to see the wreck. But somehow, it made it worse. At least, your mother was here. But I had nothing.'

'No,' Richard said. He looked at her kindly. 'Perhaps I was hard on you earlier, Rachel. In spite of my family, you must have felt much alone. But I say these things only for your own good.'

Rachel smiled. 'Yes. I know. But these young men, Richard. They are so odd. If I look at them like this—' she looked ardently into his face, her eyes gazing into his, 'they seem to become quite entranced.'

Richard breathed deeply. 'Rachel, men do not feel like women. It is improper of you to look so. It is provocative.'

'But what does it provoke?'

'Let us not discuss it further, Rachel.' Richard looked impatient. 'You should listen to the advice given to you by your Aunt Maria.'

When she discussed it with Bertha later, Bertha simply said, 'I suppose it might make them want to kiss you or something and that would be improper, wouldn't it?'

'Imagine kissing Mr Cresswell,' Rachel laughed.

'Mama says we shouldn't think of such matters. I suppose that happens when you get married.'

Rachel found it increasingly difficult to attend to her domestic duties, waiting eagerly for every dinner and tennis party and even the occasional ball to which they were invited. Those events held an attraction which her day to day routine manifestly did not. It occurred to her that perhaps there was some occupation to which she might devote her energies. She knew that there were governesses. Would it not be possible for her to attain such a position?

One evening, she broached the topic with Mr Damarell. They were assembled in the drawing-room. Aunt Maria was engaged on a large tapestry, depicting Raleigh's boyhood; Bertha was cutting up cardboard, out of which she made painted decorations for flower-pots. They could hear James playing the piano in the music room; Richard was studying in the library. Only Thomas was not at home; he had gone sailing with a group of young men from the foundry. Mr Damarell was reading *The Times*. Rachel noticed an advertisement offering just such a vacancy for a superior school-mistress, with a knowledge of French and music.

'Mr Damarell, could I engage your attention for a moment?'

Mr Damarell looked across at her, asking, 'What is it, Rachel?'

'It has been on my mind that I might become a governess or a school-mistress, Mr Damarell.'

'A what?' Aunt Maria said sharply. Bertha laughed.

Mr Damarell looked at her, pondering. Rachel always felt that his slowness in replying resulted from his need to think up impressive words and phrases.

'Did I hear you correctly, Rachel?'

'It is not that I have any complaint about my life here,' Rachel said hastily. 'It is merely that I thought it might assist in some way.'

'In what way would such a course of action assist?'

'Well, I should earn some small income.'

'Income? And why would you want money? Are you not well enough provided for?'

'Oh, yes. Mr Damarell.'

'Do I sense an unfortunate ingratitude for my generosity?'

'No. Certainly not. It is just—'

'Your aunt tells me that you perform your domestic tasks satisfactorily. Is not everything provided that you would require?'

'Oh, that is true.'

'The females in my household do not take paid employment, Rachel. Are you trying to bring disgrace upon us?'

'No, Mr Damarell. I meant no harm.'

'Then let us hear no more of it. Remember your position, think of your duties.'

'I thought merely that it might place me in a more advantageous position in relation to marriage.'

'More advantageous! A governess! A school-mistress!' Mr Damarell's eyes opened wider. 'I fear in spite of your education, you have remained without judgment.'

'I thought I should use some of those talents which I acquired through my education.'

Mr Damarell put down his paper and stood up by the marble fireplace.

'Those talents are of use only in one sphere, Rachel. They should enhance your life and that of those around you. Your education is of small account in comparison with other matters. I trust that your Aunt Maria has not failed to acquaint you with those desirable requirements which are of paramount importance. It is the apprehension of those maidenly virtues, proper ladylike conduct, the ability to command a household and fulfil all those matters concerned with the home which will bring any gentleman to consider your possible wifely virtues.'

He looked at Rachel's lost expression, adding less severely, 'Perhaps your aunt needs to find more tasks for you to perform. It is idleness which leads to morbid thoughts in young women.'

'Yes, Mr Damarell.'

Mr Damarell sat down and returned to his paper.

Rachel took up her book again. Miss Austen was quite amusing. Her young men and ladies often behaved in a fashion which Mr Damarell would have thought frivolous, but she still answered none of the questions that were always in the back of Rachel's mind. Yet she had to admit to herself that he was right. This was the life that all women had and she should be grateful that she had balls and entertainments to look forward to. She could only hope that domestic life really would be more exciting when she married. Perhaps the apparent barrier between men and women, this talk that said nothing, would end. Perhaps Aunt Maria and Mr Damarell had all sorts of conversations when they were alone.

She resolved to concentrate on impressing young men with her accomplishments, make the most of her opportunities, and so as the weeks and months passed, she set about making herself attractive and charming. Hostesses found her an agreeable guest and she and Bertha were invited to every event in the neighbourhood. They attended balls and musical soirées, tennis and boating parties and were taken to the Regatta at Dartmouth accompanied by Richard and Thomas.

On those evenings when there were no social engagements, she frequently went to the library to talk to Richard and sometimes they walked across the fields or down to the quay.

'It's funny,' she said one evening as they stood on a hill-top, looking down on the estuary. 'I am permitted to walk out with you, but must be chaperoned with anyone else.'

'I see nothing funny,' Richard said. 'We are relatives.'

'No. We're not really, are we? I am related to Aunt Maria, and she's not actually your mother, is she?'

Richard shook his head dismissively. 'It is as if we were,' he said shortly.

Rachel smiled at him. 'You're so serious, Richard, but somehow I prefer to be with you rather than anyone else.'

Richard blushed but he looked pleased. 'Well, we are in the same household.'

'Yes. With these other young men, I can never suggest any activity. It would be thought to be forward.'

'And it would be, Rachel. You are too young to think of young men at all.'

'You said that before, but I'm nineteen, Richard.'

'Yes. I know.' Richard nodded and looked at her thoughtfully.

She smiled at him, looking into his eyes, but he turned away. 'And you're twenty-one, Richard. You're an eligible young man. Do you have no interest in the young ladies you meet?'

'I am concerned with my prospects, Rachel. I have told papa that I intend to move into ship-building as soon as an opportunity presents itself.'

'Oh, I am sure you will succeed. But why do you speak so sharply, Richard?'

'I didn't. Come, let us return.' Richard turned away abruptly and started walking down the hill.

Even Richard was the same as the other young men, she thought, following him. As though there were a wall between them, some barrier that she was unable to see.

It was not until some months later that Rachel had a different view of Richard.

She had met a young gentleman farmer, Rodney Parrish, at one of Mrs Hyamson's New Year celebrations. He then called upon Aunt Maria and requested that Rachel be permitted to come to see his riding stables, in which she had expressed an interest. He would send his carriage and Rachel would be escorted by his sister. Rachel could see that Aunt Maria was delighted by the invitation, but had replied that of course Mr Damarell must first be consulted. Mr Parrish had called again two days later to learn that permission had been granted.

'It's not fair,' Bertha said gloomily. 'You can't be betrothed before I am, Rachel. I'm over four years older than you.'

'Bertha, please be sensible. The young man has merely expressed an interest. It is for Rachel to conduct herself in a decent fashion.'

Rachel stood in front of the looking-glass. She was wearing a blue silk afternoon dress in the new style, with the skirt straight and tight in front and gathered up at the back.

'I'll lend you my dark blue cape,' Bertha said. 'I hope you have a lovely time, really.'

Rachel smiled.

'Oh, you've got such a slim waist, Rachel.'

'If you would desist from eating all those pastries that Rose produces, yours would be the same, Bertha,' Aunt Maria laughed.

Rachel sat down while Lizzie combed her long hair and drew it up with combs.

'Do I need a hat, Aunt Maria?'

'Of course, dear. It would be quite unsuitable without.'

They all looked through the drawing-room window as the carriage came up the drive. Mr Parrish's sister, Valerie, was tall and elegant in a green gown and velvet jacket and she seemed not much older than Rachel.

As they drove up the hill to Loddiswell, she confided to Rachel that Rodney had spoken of her frequently during the past days and much looked forward to her visit. Rachel smiled but she had difficulty in recollecting the conversation which had taken place between them. She remembered that he had spoken about his horses and how he would be delighted to take her up to Dartmoor to ride. At the time, owing to the fact that it had happened to be an unfortunate time of the month, she had felt uncomfortable and was more concerned that nothing dreadful should happen to her dress.

Rodney greeted them as they arrived and asked the coachman to take them all to the stables to show Rachel the horses. Rodney was very tall and thin and he wore wide riding trousers which Rachel considered inelegant. Then Valerie showed her around the gardens, although it was a cold January day, while Rodney walked by her side, wearing the expression that Rachel was accustomed to precipitating if she looked at gentlemen and smiled. Then they went to a tall glass building which had been built on to the side of the house.

'This is what Valerie calls the orangery,' Rodney said, smiling.

'It is very charming,' Rachel said, as tea was brought. 'I find the climbing plants particularly agreeable.'

'We are going on a riding expedition next week to Dartmoor,' Valerie informed her. 'Perhaps you would like to accompany us.'

'I fear I am not much of a rider,' Rachel frowned. 'I have attempted it only a few times.'

'You will be perfectly safe with me,' Rodney assured her. 'Perhaps I could give you some lessons.'

'That would be delightful.' Rachel was enthusiastic. It would be a new activity, a new interest.

As they drove back in the carriage, Valerie observed, 'I am so delighted that we have met you. Rodney seems to have little interest in most female company.'

Rachel waved as she watched the carriage go back down the drive and walked slowly up the steps to the house. She could see the future. She would make more visits to Rodney's house, he would call upon her more frequently, they would dance together more often and one day Rodney would call upon Mr Damarell to ask for her hand. She would wear a lovely bridal gown and they would go to the church, there would be a great reception at Loddiswell Farm and she would move in with her new husband.

Aunt Maria was delighted with her visit but instantly frowned when Rachel mentioned the Dartmoor expedition.

'The date you mention is a Sunday,' she said. 'I fear Mr Damarell would not permit such a thing.'

Indeed, Mr Damarell expressed doubt about the desirability of Rachel continuing to maintain such contact.

'I know that the congregation of the Established church are less fastidious than those of us who are of the Methodist persuasion,' Aunt Maria observed. 'I think for them it means no harm.'

'Then that is for their consciences. The members of this household do not act in such a frivolous fashion.'

A message was dispatched to the Parrish household that such an engagement, on such a day, could not be countenanced. When Rachel expressed disappointment, Aunt Maria said, 'It is of no concern, Rachel. It will merely make the young man more eager to see you.'

It was only later, when she was walking on the hills with Richard, that she first realised the meaning of his silences and irritated manner.

'Mr Damarell won't let me go on Sunday,' Rachel said.

'Go where?'

'Ah, of course, you were not here. I went to visit Rodney Parrish this afternoon. It was pleasant enough and he wishes me to ride with him on Sunday.'

'Ride with you! Where?'

'We were to go to Dartmoor. With his sister and a party, of course.'

Richard stopped, shouting, 'To Dartmoor! You scarcely know the man. He might be a scoundrel.'

'Richard! Why are you so angry? He is harmless enough.'

'Harmless.' Richard's eyes flashed at her contemptuously. 'What would you know about that?'

'I only know he pays me attention.'

'But what is that to you?'

'Perhaps he will wish to marry me.'

'Rachel.' Richard spoke in such a despairing voice that she looked at him in consternation.

'What is wrong with that Richard? Would it not be an excellent opportunity for me? Aunt Maria appears to think so.'

Richard sighed, calmer now, and added, 'It is more fitting that you discuss such matters with her, but what is your view of him, Rachel?'

Rachel thought for a moment, then she shrugged her shoulders. 'I find him unexceptionable. As an individual, he is neither more nor less worthy of comment than any other. But what he offers must be acceptable. Is that not what marriage is about?'

'No!' Richard looked at her angrily.

'Then what? Pray tell me.'

Richard shook his head. 'It is about respect and—' He turned away abruptly but not before she had seen the misery in his face.

'Richard, is it that you fear we shall cease to be friends? That you will have no further call on my company?'

Even as she was speaking the words, she realised the truth.

'No,' Richard said slowly. 'It is not for me to say.'

She looked at him, her eyes widening in surprise as she began to remember things he had said, his disapproval when she seemed to enjoy the company of other young men. Involved in her own ambitions, she had failed to notice Richard's attentions, his pleasure in taking her for walks, talking to her. In any case, it was difficult to appreciate his feelings behind that serious façade. Yet he could not be thinking of marriage to her. He was devoted to progress, only a lady who could further his career and worldly ambitions would be suitable. And Rachel was firmly convinced that Mr Damarell would not have approved of her as a daughter-in-law. Did Richard love her then? Was he like these young men in novels, harbouring a secret, wild passion? Could that happen to Richard?

'Richard.' She spoke in a different tone.

He looked at her in silence.

'Richard, is it—'

'Come, Rachel. It is time to return. I think you are letting your imagination run away with you. I was merely advising you for your own good.'

He spoke curtly now and began to walk briskly across the fields. He talked lightly of a swallow, high up in the sky, and showed her a badger sett hidden beneath a bank of the stream. He made no further comments about her future visits to Rodney Parrish and treated him with cordiality when Rodney attended social functions at the Damarell home.

Yet somehow, Rachel found that the dream of marriage as a solution to her present boredom had lost its attractions. She felt that she had seen a brief hint of something in Richard which she had never observed in other young men – a strange kind of intimacy which seemed infinitely compelling. Yet even if Mr Damarell would have permitted it, marriage to Richard did not offer a solution. There was something more, she was convinced of it.

Then, on a warm summer evening, she was returning with Bertha from a tennis game with the Hyamson girls.

'Isn't Jane fortunate? She is to be married at Christmas,' Bertha sighed. 'Though I find her fiancé singularly unattractive.'

Rachel made a face. 'Sometimes I find all of these young men unattractive. If only—'

'If only what?' Bertha looked puzzled.

'I find many of them pleasing enough. I don't know. It's just . . . there must be something more.'

'More than what, though? It is surely a great compliment to have young men paying you attention.'

'Oh, yes. I find it agreeable. But would you care to be married to any of them?'

Bertha smiled. 'Perhaps we should not be speaking in this frivolous fashion, and of course this is a secret, but I have noticed that since you have made your lack of interest in Mr Cresswell so apparent, he pays me a great deal of attention. Perhaps I would consider a proposal from him.'

Rachel began to smile, too, thinking of his beady eyes and his obsequious manner, but she hastily stopped smiling and said kindly, 'Then I hope he will, Bertha. I am sure he would provide well for you and he appears to be settling here, although I thought he had interests in Dorset.'

'Yes, I believe he has. Of course, I should wish him to buy some property in these parts.'

They walked round the house to leave their rackets in the summer house by the side of the tennis courts. As they began to cross the lawn, they saw a man standing by the fish-pond, looking down into the water; a young man dressed in an army officer's uniform.

Bertha hesitated, then called, 'Jacob! Oh, Jacob, how delightful to see you.' She ran eagerly towards him.

Jacob looked up smiling, walked towards her and flung his arms around her. 'Ah, dear Bertha. How lovely to see you.' He kissed her on the cheeks, holding her away from him, so that he could contemplate her. 'Bertha, my little sister. You are such a young lady now.' He kissed her again, laughing with pleasure.

Then he turned to Rachel, holding out his hands. She remembered the smile, the dark laughing eyes, the curly black hair, his tall, upright body, that warm voice that made all his words sound interesting.

'Hallo, Rachel.' He put his arms around her lightly and she felt his warm lips on her cheeks. He looked at her as he had done Bertha. 'Well, Rachel, what can I say?' He shook his head in disbelief.

Rachel felt a glow of triumph. For once, even Jacob seemed lost for words. He just stood, looking at her, a strange expression in his eyes, a compelling, embracing expression of intimacy.

Suddenly, everything had changed. Somehow, that look was one she recognised, had always anticipated. It was as though Jacob held the key to the mystery that she had never been able to define. That look represented experiences which she had never known, a world beyond the confines of Kingsbridge; he would know the answers.

She smiled coolly.

'It is a pleasure to see you again, Jacob.'

Chapter 8

Aunt Maria decided to hold the celebration for Jacob's return in the Assembly Rooms. The walls were hung with Union Jacks and the hall was festooned with ribbons and gold and silver paper decorations and coloured lights, shining through the stained-glass windows to the street outside. The carnival atmosphere was to honour not only Jacob's arrival but also the victory in Zululand, of which he had been a part.

For months, the inhabitants of Kingsbridge had been reading newspaper reports of the ineffectiveness of the British Army against the barbarian Zulu. There had been much criticism of the officers, who seemed incapable of achieving a decisive victory over an inferior foe, and a growing sense of shame that such a great nation as this should be unable to subdue a horde of black savages.

Mr Damarell had been vociferous in his condemnation of the command and supported demands for more troops to be sent to the battle zones. He knew that the defeats could not be attributed to officers in the field such as Jacob, and that it was upon them that final victory depended. As the weeks passed, fear of a humiliating defeat had seemed to come over the nation. Long lists of casualties and honours and awards given to those killed in battle appeared in the *London Gazette*. Battle after battle seemed to be a catalogue of slaughter and rout. The public at home could not understand the events of Rorke's Drift. How was it possible that although five hundred Zulus had been killed or mortally wounded, compared with only forty British troops, the final result was a humiliating defeat for the British Army? Then, in the summer, events took a turn for the better. Under the command of Chelmsford, the capital Ulandi was at last taken and the Zulus appeared to be overcome. But the king, Cetshwayo, had escaped into the forest and it was not until

Wolseley took over, that he was finally caught and brought back to Ulandi.

The British drew up their armistice conditions and Mr Damarell let it be known in Kingsbridge that his son Jacob had been the chief executive of final victory.

Rachel stood before the looking-glass, dressing for the evening's celebration. Since Jacob's arrival a week ago, the house seemed to have taken on a new life. She felt as if she was living in a permanent state of expectancy. He behaved so differently from the other males of the household, going to the kitchens to talk to the maids, making calls without card or previous engagement, commenting on the appearance of ladies who had visited in words which Aunt Maria found too daring.

'But it is true,' he would protest, 'she *is* frumpish and fat.'

Some mornings, he rose before dawn to ride across the hills, returning when breakfast was officially over and then going to eat in the kitchens. He came home late at night or failed to return at all, saying that he and his companions had consumed too much wine and he had not felt like making the journey.

At first Rachel had been surprised that Mr Damarell seemed to accept his behaviour with equanimity. Then she heard him saying to Aunt Maria that Jacob had been subjected to much hardship and that was why he behaved in this fashion. With maturity, he would settle down.

As she looked at her pale blue gown, with its rather low-cut neckline, she thought about Jacob. He had said that blue suited her, with her auburn hair and her lovely eyes. Jacob's intimate glances were nothing like the furtive looks of admiration she received from other young men. He made her feel that she was someone special. Since that first meeting on the lawn, it was as though she had become a new person.

Bertha called her from the downstairs hall: 'Are you ready yet, Rachel? We are about to depart.'

Aunt Maria, in a silver voile gown with pink roses around the neckline, and Mr Damarell in his long black dinner jacket, were awaiting them in the carriage. Bertha's hair was dressed in ringlets with a large purple bow, to match her bright purple gown.

'Is Jacob to go with us?' Rachel asked.

'No, dear,' Aunt Maria replied. 'I believe he is escorting a young lady.'

'Ah,' Mr Damarell smiled. 'Jacob naturally attracts much admiration.'

Rachel repressed a sigh of disappointment. Jacob had observed to her on two occasions, making a face, that he must fulfil his social obligations. He was expected to show his appreciation to the worthy inhabitants of Kingsbridge for their natural interest in and concern for the dangerous life he lived. Jacob had given her the impression that he did not greatly welcome the necessity. He had looked at her and smiled as though social demands were of little interest to him. His smile had seemed to suggest to Rachel that he would prefer to be with her.

When they arrived at the Assembly Rooms, Jacob was standing on the steps in full dress uniform of dark red jacket and blue trousers, greeting the guests as they arrived.

Before the dancing began, Rachel watched him going round the room, putting his name on the young ladies' cards. She saw Rodney Parrish coming towards her and hastily rose to cross the room and engage in conversation with Aunt Maria. Supposing Jacob should ask her for a dance for which she was already engaged; perhaps he would want the first dance? Indeed, how many dances should she leave vacant in anticipation? Then Jacob appeared and before Rodney reached her he was saying, 'Could I engage you for the polka, Rachel?'

She smiled, waiting to see what other dances he might request, but he nodded to her and said, 'I must ensure that I remember all the ladies who may be anxious to dance with me,' and walked across the room towards Valerie Parrish.

She noticed that Jacob danced first with Aunt Maria, then with Bertha, followed by Aunt Edith and the other aunts who were present. Rachel realised that, in spite of his unconventional behaviour, Jacob was observing protocol; it was proper that he should dance with his Mama and sister first, then with all the other young ladies.

It was only when her card was full that Jacob appeared again and asked Rachel for a further dance.

'Oh, Jacob,' she said in disappointment. 'I am already committed.'

'Ah, that is no matter, Rachel. It is natural that you should be much in demand.' He smiled cheerfully.

'Oh, Jacob, I would so much prefer to dance with you.'

Jacob grinned at her anxious expression. 'It's not important. No doubt we shall have many more opportunities.' At the end of the evening Jacob returned with them in the carriage, thanking his father for the celebration in his honour.

'Ah, son, I am gratified that God has seen fit to return you to us.'

Jacob laughed. 'There have been occasions in the past months when I have felt that to be unlikely.'

'What was it like?' Bertha asked.

Although Jacob had talked extensively about his companions and their day to day living, he had said little about his experiences of the fighting.

'I expect your brother would wish to forget those events,' Mr Damarell said.

'No, Papa. It is not something which one forgets lightly.'

'Indeed not, son. These heathens need to be subdued once and for all.'

Jacob sighed as though the topic were too large for conversation.

'They are brave men, Papa. They were fighting for their country.'

'Indeed! But it is the British who are taking civilisation to them.'

'They are an incredible race of men, Papa. They are not to be despised.'

'Ah, I do not despise them. They are also God's creation. But one must suppose they are a lower form of mankind at this time.'

Jacob frowned. 'No, Papa, I would not say that.'

Mr Damarell bowed his head. 'No doubt, you have a different perspective from that which we have in England, son. And it is natural that a soldier such as yourself would not refer to his own courage and the dangers to which you have been exposed. But the whole nation will be eternally grateful to you. It must have been a great consolation to you when Wolseley arrived.'

'The war was over by then, Papa, and I have seen nothing of Wolseley. I left with Chelmsford.' Jacob yawned and said lightly, 'Well, Papa, I find the demands of this social life equally exhausting. I think tomorrow, I shall not be rising early.'

In the event, Jacob departed in the early hours of the morning and did not appear at breakfast. After going to her room to examine her clothes, Rachel went to the library to deal with some cards for Aunt Maria. She glanced constantly through the windows and down the drive, longing for Jacob to return. Her mind was flooded with pictures of his laughing eyes, his provocative smile and the memory of everything he had said. Finally, there he was in the flesh, cantering up the drive with Rodney Parrish. She felt a surge of delight that they would be taking lunch.

Rachel listened in silence to their conversation. They had been across the hills to Aveton Gifford and Loddiswell and then come back through Ledstone. For a second, she feared he may have been calling upon a young lady, but then she calculated that they would not have had time for such an undertaking.

She looked at them across the table, remembering what Aunt Maria had once said about Jacob – 'Sometimes I think he may be too attractive for his own good.' Then Rachel looked at Rodney. How could she ever have contemplated marriage with him? He was, of course, a kind and considerate person, but he was also cold and formal. With him, she could never have broken through the barrier that separated men and women. In fact it was only with Jacob that she had seen such a possibility. Lately, when Rodney had requested the pleasure of her company, she had made the excuse that she was much employed at the moment. Fortunately, he had understood and had said that it was natural that the family should wish to spend as much time as possible with Jacob. When he was not involved with social engagements, Jacob did indeed take her and Bertha and Aunt Maria to Dartmouth and Torquay and Paignton. Sometimes he took them out on a boat at Salcombe.

He also visited his father at the mill, went down to the foundry to see Thomas and was encouraging James to give up his thatching and take up a musical career.

Today, Jacob disclosed that he and Rodney were to take tea with some young ladies in Alvington. He smiled at the girls, adding, 'I wish I could take you with me, Rachel and Bertha. But I think it might not be correct.'

159

'Certainly not,' Aunt Maria agreed. 'If it is a specific invitation then, of course, it would be inappropriate.'

Rachel walked with them to the front door. Rodney bowed politely but Jacob turned and said, 'Perhaps tomorrow, Rachel, I might be permitted to take you to Brixham. I have some brief business there and then we could walk around the harbour and see the fishing boats.'

'Oh, that would be lovely, Jacob.'

Rodney smiled. 'Ah, Jacob, as I surmised you are occupying much of her time. Before you arrived, I was sometimes given the pleasure of her company.'

'Oh, Rodney,' Jacob protested, 'I have but a short time at home.'

'Of course. It is right that Rachel should consider her family first.'

The summer was passing and there was a feel of autumn in the warm air when they set out for Brixham. The leaves were beginning to turn to gold, and as they rode in the gig through the rolling countryside, Rachel felt as though she had never been as happy in her life. When they were alone, Jacob seemed quieter and more intimate, and he talked to her about his life in a way which made her feel she was a special confidante. He told her about his plans, how he hoped to rise to a position of some importance in the army, and of how he loved the adventurous life which it offered.

'Do you intend always to live so?' Rachel asked.

'Perhaps not always, but for as long as I am able.'

'And do you not intend to marry?'

'Ah, that must be desirable one day. But I have not yet found a lady to engage my attentions.' He smiled. 'Though I think she would have to be someone like yourself, Rachel.'

Rachel looked at him uncertainly. 'Are you making polite conversation, Jacob?'

He looked astonished. 'Polite, Rachel? I always mean what I say at the time that I say it.'

Rachel smiled. No. He wasn't just being flattering. She could see by his expression that he really meant what he said. 'Tell me about the war, Jacob. You only talk about your companions.'

Jacob frowned. 'You don't need to concern yourself with such matters, Rachel,' he said dismissively.

To her surprise, Rachel found herself thinking suddenly of

Richard. Richard never said things like that. If she asked him anything he always replied seriously. He never talked as though the female mind were somehow inferior to men's. She felt irritated with herself at such a comparison. Jacob wasn't treating her as an ignorant, uneducated female, it was just his way of protecting her.

'I would like to hear what it's really like.'

Jacob looked at her thoughtfully, as though he realised that she was serious in her enquiry. She was not asking for a report of heroic exploits.

'Well, Rachel. It's horrific,' he said slowly, then hesitated.

'I can't imagine it, Jacob,' she prompted him.

He suddenly became serious. 'These Zulu have no fear of death. They come down upon you in hordes, thousands of black bodies brandishing assegais. They wear nothing but feather skirts around their lower parts and thin leather boots also decorated with feathers. They have a piercing war-cry that chills your blood. I have seen hundreds of our soldiers hacked to death, dismembered. And the Zulus never give up. When they should capitulate, they still come back for more, in the early light of dawn, in the darkness of night, suddenly they are there again and launched into another battle.'

'Aren't you afraid?'

Jacob hesitated again; perhaps she shouldn't ask questions like that. Mr Damarell said Jacob was a hero.

'Yes, Rachel. Terrified. Most of the time. All those heroic deeds you read about – it's simply a question of survival.'

Rachel frowned. 'There's no other way out, I suppose.'

'No. You're a thoughtful little girl, aren't you Rachel?'

'I'm not a little girl.'

'No. I know. I have never spoken about this to anyone else. It is too painful. What men do in war is beyond heroism. But now, let us speak of more cheerful topics.' Suddenly, he laughed. 'Talking to you so.' He shook his head. 'You must have won my heart, Rachel'

'I think you spend much time winning the hearts of young ladies, Jacob.'

Jacob put an arm lightly round her shoulders. 'They are of no account,' he said briefly. 'Let us enjoy this lovely English day. My leave will end soon enough.'

Rachel felt a sense of panic, thinking of his imminent departure. Her face clouded. Was life always to be full of partings from people she loved? She blushed; for the first time, the word had come into her mind. She looked at Jacob. Yes, of course, she was in love with him. That was what had been missing before. Love. Although he would go away again, she knew she would love him for ever.

He took her hand as she stepped down from the gig.

'You have some business to attend to, Jacob?' she enquired.

Jacob grinned. 'I have decided not to concern myself with it. Come. We will walk around by the harbour and then we shall have tea and cream cakes.'

They wandered along the quay, talking idly, laughing at some urchins who were jumping in and out of the water, panting breathlessly as they climbed a hill to look down at the boats rocking in the harbour, the sun casting a yellow light across their sails.

Jacob pulled her arm through his as they walked back down into the town. Rachel felt as though the sun was shining for them alone, but she was keenly aware of the glances of other young ladies at the handsome young man walking by her side.

After tea, they looked in the little shops in the town. Although they sold nothing different from those in Kingsbridge, every window appeared interesting, everything was filled with meaning. Brixham seemed a magical place to her.

As they rode back through the countryside, the great circle of the sun was casting its rays across the sea. The sky was striped with orange as the sun slipped slowly beneath the horizon and when they reached the house, Jacob kissed her gently on the cheek, saying, 'Would you like to go out with me again, Rachel?'

Her eyes shone with excitement. She looked at him eagerly. 'Oh, yes, I would, Jacob.'

In bed that night, she went over every moment of the past day, so that she would remember it for ever. She thought of his smiling lips and that expression in his eyes. With a shock, she realised that she never looked at him with that meaningful look she used on other young men. Somehow, it would have been false. This was much more important. She simply looked at him as she felt; he could surely see the love in her eyes, in her smile, just as she thought she could see the same feelings in his face. Then she realised that Richard never looked at her like Jacob did, with that meaningful expression in his eyes. With another shock, she also realised that she had scarcely thought of

Richard since Jacob's arrival. She had a vague twinge of guilt that she had neglected him when he had always been so kind to her. Well, he had his studying to do; she would make up for it when Jacob was gone.

In fact, she had scarcely noticed anyone. She went to the dinners and musical evenings with the rest of the family; she assisted Aunt Maria and Bertha in the running of the house, making visits, receiving calls, walking down into Kingsbridge on errands. She graciously received compliments from young men, danced with them dutifully, talked politely about their interests and activities. But in her mind, she and Jacob were inhabiting another world because her heart told her that Jacob shared her feelings.

The next morning at breakfast, Jacob revealed that he was going to spend the day with a fellow officer who lived in Plymouth.

'Pray, invite him here, Jacob. We have spare bedrooms. Would he not care to visit you?'

'Perhaps, Mama. But first, we have a long-standing engagement in Torquay. We are meeting two young ladies whom we first met long ago.'

Mr Damarell looked at him thoughtfully. 'I know you mean no harm, Jacob, but you must consider these young ladies' reputations. I presume you are to visit them at home.'

'That is correct, Papa. And I will invite my friend Maurice to visit in a day or two.'

That day, Rodney Parrish called and Aunt Maria told Lizzie that she was at home. He was shown into the drawing-room and Aunt Maria rang the bell for tea to be brought.

Rodney commented politely on Aunt Maria's tapestry and asked Rachel what book she was reading.

'It is a history of Africa,' Rachel smiled.

'Ah, I see you are influenced by Jacob. I fear Rachel has little time to spend on external activities while he is here,' he observed to Aunt Maria. 'Though I appreciate her duty to her family is of paramount importance.'

'Oh,' Aunt Maria said hastily. 'Rachel does not need to concern herself to such an extent. I appreciate your sense of devotion,' she added kindly to Rachel. 'But neither I nor Jacob would wish you to neglect your own obligations.'

She smiled in turn at Rodney. 'In fact, though of course Jacob is a dutiful son, we see but little of him. He is involved much of his time with social calls and seems to have achieved a wide circle of acquaintance.'

'Ah, then perhaps I might be permitted to invite Rachel to an entertainment in Plymouth next week. She will, of course, be accompanied by my sister.'

'Rachel will be delighted to accept, Mr Parrish. Will you send your carriage?'

Rachel sighed and politely accepted his invitation. She was relieved when Mrs Waldorf was shown in and Rodney rose to depart. She could now visualise the situation she would be in when Jacob left. Everyone would be expecting her to make a suitable marriage. But what about Jacob? If he loved her as she loved him, what would happen? Her mind could envisage no course of action. She would simply wait for him, that was all. Somehow, she would have to evade the question of marriage. Well, she would think about that later, after Jacob had gone.

Jacob did not return for dinner that evening. She went to bed, looking up at the bright full moon and listening for the sound of the gig. Then she heard the wheels on the gravel and listened for voices. Had he brought anyone with him? There was silence and then she heard the pad of his footsteps on the stairs and she sighed with relief that he was safely home. As she turned in her bed, still listening, the door opened quietly and Jacob came in.

'Jacob!' She feared that some calamity must have befallen him, that there must be some terrible news for him to enter her bedroom.

But he whispered, 'It's all right, Rachel. It's only me.'

'What is it?' Her voice was anxious.

'Shush. Don't be alarmed.'

'Has something happened? Shall I light the candle?'

'No. It is not necessary.' He sat down on her bed. 'I simply came to say goodnight.'

'Jacob, supposing Aunt Maria—'

He put his fingers over her lips. 'It's all right, Rachel. You look beautiful with your hair loose. Why don't you wear it so?'

'It's so long. When I came here from Egypt, it was cut short. It was so hot in Egypt.'

'Like the rest of Africa. Perhaps one day we will go there together, Rachel.'

'Oh, I wish we could! But Jacob, you must leave now.'

'Yes.' He smiled down at her. 'Goodnight, Rachel.'

He went out quietly and she lay still, her heart beating so that it seemed almost to choke her. Jacob must know that his behaviour was wrong, but she felt an even stronger sense of joy; he had wanted to see her, simply to say goodnight. She fell asleep, now sure that he must love her as she did him.

At breakfast the very next day, indeed, when Aunt Maria observed that Bertha was attending a party in the church rooms to be given for poor children, Jacob requested that he might take Rachel to Buckfast Abbey. He had not been there for a long time and understood that the country house which had been built on the site of the old monastery had certain attractions.

'Perhaps you will wish to acquire it one day,' Mr Damarell observed.

Jacob smiled. 'It would depend upon my fortunes, Papa. But I have heard there is some acreage around it. Perhaps I shall become a farmer.'

Thomas laughed. 'The operation of the plough is different from wielding a sword, Jacob.'

'But probably less hazardous,' Jacob said cheerfully. There was continual banter between all the brothers about the value of their various kinds of work. It seemed to Rachel to be a good-humoured kind of competition which none of them took seriously.

Jacob seemed to be in a reflective mood as they made their journey to Buckfast. They were travelling today by local horse-bus to Harberton, where they hired a gig for the remainder of the journey. They stood on the green hill looking down over the few remaining ruins and the house perched in the centre.

'I have read something about this place,' Rachel observed.

'Yes. We heard much about its history at St Crispin's.'

'Richard has some journals of the antiquarian societies who have been employed for many years in discovering information about its past. From the ruins, they appear to have evolved complete picture of what the abbey looked like. I believe that old building over there must be the fourteenth-century building they mention and which is all that remains of the original.'

Jacob put an arm through hers, and said, pensively, 'You are a strange creature, Rachel. You have many of those feminine attributes which are so attractive yet—'

Rachel looked enquiring. 'Yet what?'

'It seems often that your thoughts do not lie in feminine interests.'

Rachel shook her head. 'Jacob, sometimes I find female activities tedious.' She looked at him doubtfully; would he understand what she felt? 'It is as though there is something more in life than I have yet encountered. I cannot describe it.'

'Well, indeed, Rachel, there are many things in life. But you are young. They will all be revealed to you in time.'

'Will they, Jacob? I see so little sign of it in Kingsbridge.'

Jacob laughed. 'Come, let us walk down the hill and see the monastery and then we can walk along the lane.'

They encountered few people as they walked round the remains of the abbey and strolled along the curving narrow lane between high hedges, already turning brown and yellow.

'There are many unaccustomed experiences in foreign parts,' Jacob went on as though in reply to her question. 'For one thing, the young ladies behave differently.'

'Do they? I scarcely remember.'

She tried to recall her years in Egypt; she could remember only that they wore long black gowns and that usually their faces were masked by yashmaks.

'You were but a child.'

'Yes. How do they behave, Jacob?'

'I can only illustrate, Rachel.' Jacob stopped and looked down at her, smiling, put his arms around her and kissed her on the lips. Rachel stood still, unmoving, but she did not resist. He tightened his embrace around her and kissed her again and this time she raised her arms around his neck.

'Jacob.'

He gently smoothed her hair back behind her ears, held her face between his hands and kissed her eyes, her ears, her cheeks. And then his arms were around her again and she waited for his warm lips to be pressed against hers.

166

He dropped his arms then, took her hand and said softly, 'That is only for you, dear Rachel.'

Rachel stood still, feeling that she would fall if she moved but Jacob put an arm around her, steering her slowly back along the lane towards the abbey. She felt elated; the world, after all, could be a beautiful, exciting place. Perhaps none of the people in Kingsbridge had experienced what she and Jacob had; it was only a love like theirs that could change her world.

As they jogged through the countryside in the gig, Rachel asked, 'Jacob, is that what you do with foreign girls?'

Jacob smiled. 'No, Rachel. That is what I have been informed by other officers. They have told me of its delights.' He laughed. 'I have not felt so inclined previously.'

Rachel smiled. 'Then you must tell them that their information was correct.'

As they neared Kingsbridge, Jacob observed suddenly, 'I think such behaviour would be thought improper in this country, Rachel. It would not be thought correct by your Aunt Maria, or by the young men with whom you mix.'

Rachel laughed. 'But how could I wish to behave so with anyone but you, Jacob? It is not a problem that will arise.'

'No. But your aunt would not think it was appropriate for us, either.'

'Dear Jacob, I understand that.'

She lay in bed that night, waiting to see if Jacob would appear, but he did not come. Her days passed in a kind of dream. It was as though there were a mist before her eyes through which she dimly perceived the world around her, pitying Bertha and Aunt Maria and Aunt Bessie that they knew nothing of that other, secret experience. She smiled when Bertha revealed that she thought she was in love with Mr Cresswell; Bertha was like those silly heroines in novels.

She would smile at Jacob when they were all dining at home, or entertaining guests and he would raise his eyebrows and return her smile. Even when he was talking with other ladies at dinner-parties or musical evenings, he would look at her suddenly and wink. None of them knew the Jacob that she knew.

She did not see Jacob alone for another week. His popularity with the mothers of Kingsbridge involved him in constant social engagements and although Rachel and Bertha were frequently invited, she and Jacob were never alone.

Then one evening, when they returned late from an entertainment at Mrs Markham's and they had all retired to their rooms, Rachel heard the soft padding of his shoes on the stairs. She held her breath to listen for the turn of the handle in the door.

Jacob stood by the bed, looking down at her as she peeped at him from above the white sheets. He was wearing a loose black jacket and trousers and a frilly white shirt. He looked just as beautiful in ordinary clothes as he did in his uniform.

'Rachel, I have ascertained from Aunt Maria's appointments book, that she and Bertha have engagements tomorrow. Would you like a day out at Hope Cove?'

'Oh, yes.'

'We can go by gig and there is an excellent inn there where we can partake of lunch.'

'Have you asked Aunt Maria's permission?'

'Oh, that will be no difficulty, Rachel.' Jacob paused and looked at her reflectively. 'You looked so charming this evening, Rachel, in that lovely white gown, that I longed to kiss you again.'

There was a strange expression in his eyes that made her feel almost afraid. She had unfamiliar feelings in her own body, too, as if she were being overtaken by some power she could not control.

'Jacob,' she began, but he interrupted.

'I have been told there are other, um, expressions of love that foreign girls display.'

'Oh, Jacob, perhaps we should not emulate them. I am not foreign.'

'It is not dangerous, Rachel,' Jacob smiled as he sat down on the bed, put his arms around her and kissed her gently on the lips.

She sighed.

'There. That is not undesirable, is it?'

'Oh, Jacob.'

He put his hands on her shoulders, and they moved slowly down her arms and then rested lightly on her breasts.

'Jacob, this cannot be. It must be wrong.'

'Rachel, dear, nothing is wrong in love.'

168

She felt his fingers caressing her lightly. No, it could not be wrong.

'Jacob, suppose someone should find you here.'

'Dear Rachel, I will go now.'

He took her in his arms again and kissed her, a long, slow kiss. Then he was gone.

She lay in the darkness, her hands on her breasts, imagining the fingers which had caressed her. Her heart was beating violently. This must be what marriage was, she thought, this must be what happened. If she were married to Jacob, they could do this every night. She would lie by his side and she would go to sleep with his arms around her. But the feeling of guilt would not go away, because they were not married and she was not a foreign girl. Yet when she thought of Jacob, she knew that she could not resist him. She tried to sleep, but she could not rest. It was no longer her mind that he occupied; it was as though he had taken over her body.

It was a misty day as they drove down the steep hill towards Hope Cove. The little houses nestled together in the village, as though trying to protect themselves from the great gales and storms that blew in from the sea.

As they stepped from the gig, a violent wind almost took their breath away.

'Look at those huge rocks rising up like terrible demons from the ocean bed and those fantastic waves, pounding over the stones. Is it not exciting, Rachel?'

Rachel laughed. Suddenly she felt a great freedom, as though she and Jacob were a part of those violent elements.

'Can you walk up the hill, Rachel? It is quite sheltered behind the walls and from there you will find an impressive view.'

'I wonder why it is called Hope Cove,' Rachel queried as they climbed. 'It must be a forlorn harbour for any ship to approach.'

'I remember when I was but a young lad, I came here with some friends and we went out in a boat. The wind changed and we were almost lost on the rocks, but for the skill of the lifeboats.'

'You must always have liked adventure, Jacob.'

Jacob nodded. 'Yes. I suppose I always found Kingsbridge confining. Life should be an adventure, Rachel.'

His eyes were bright with excitement, the wind was ruffling his long black hair. Rachel took his hand. 'Kiss me now,' she said softly.

Jacob took her hand and led her through a gap in the wall on to the grassy hill. The tall bushes and shrubs protected them from the wind, she could hear the waves crashing on the rocks far away beneath them.

He took her in his arms and kissed her. 'We can sit here, Rachel. We are protected. It is warm in the sun.' He pulled her down beside him and she closed her eyes as he took her in his arms.

'Rachel, if you love me, there are other things we could do to express that love.'

'Jacob, what do you mean?'

'Rachel.' He ran a hand down her leg and pulled up the hem of her skirt.

'Jacob, what are you doing?'

Jacob did not reply. Suddenly he grabbed at her skirt and pulled it up to her waist. His eyes were shining in a different way, it was as though he had suddenly been possessed by a wild spirit. Then he flung himself across her.

'Rachel,' he said passionately, 'I am bewitched by you. I must know you. Oh, you are so lovely.' His hands grabbed at her bodice and he tore it open, kissing her violently.

'Jacob, stop. Stop! What are you doing?'

She struggled against him, but he forced her legs open. She shouted that he was hurting her, but he continued, his body enveloping her, tearing into her, until he suddenly ceased and lay silently by her side, one arm still holding her to him.

Rachel pulled her skirts down over her naked legs. It was beyond fear, beyond shame, what had happened was beyond any thoughts she could recognise. Did these things happen only in foreign countries? Was it just . . . she could not find the words. Perhaps the mystery she'd tried to fathom had not been the love which she had found, but this bitter experience. Was this to be the price of love? Was this a part of marriage?

'No one ever told me,' she said quietly.

Jacob squeezed her gently. 'No. Of course not. There are no words to describe these things. I was overcome by desire for you, Rachel. Do you hate me now?'

'Hate you? If this is a part of love, then it must be.'

Jacob sighed. 'Dear Rachel. Life is not so simple.'

'Why did you do that, Jacob?'

She saw an expression of impatience flit across his face.

'It's quite normal, Rachel. Though perhaps your provocative attitude made me behave in too abrupt a fashion.'

'Normal, Jacob? Provocative!' Rachel's voice wavered; tears misted her eyes. What did he mean?

'You have made your feelings quite clear, haven't you, Rachel? I assumed you would welcome it.'

'Welcome! But I knew nothing—'

Jacob looked at her thoughtfully. 'No,' he said slowly. 'You didn't, did you? Dear Rachel, I did not mean to disturb you.' He stood up and pulled her up beside him. 'Are you all right, Rachel?'

Rachel smiled bleakly. 'I must accommodate myself to these things, Jacob, if this is a part of love.'

Jacob nodded slowly and stroked her hair. 'Rachel, such things should only be experienced in marriage.'

'Yes. I know that now. But it is different for us, isn't it? Soon, you will go away. We have so little time.'

Jacob sighed again. He put an arm around her. 'Come. We will take lunch in the inn. Then we must return. The mist will come down as soon as the sun goes.'

Jacob seemed subdued as they walked slowly down the hill but after he had imbibed some wine with his lunch, his spirits seemed to return and he began to look forward to that evening's ball at the Hyamsons'.

Rachel found that the experience of that day had changed her attitude to Jacob. She felt an anxiety, an uncertainty that had not been there before. Would he think less of her for what had happened? Would he find these ladies who did not indulge in foreign behaviour more desirable? She could not rid herself of the sense of shame that she felt. Did he really love her? Perhaps he would not want her now? She remembered a phrase used in the novels that Bertha read, 'a fallen woman'. Was this what it meant?

Her days passed in the usual flurry of calls and domestic duties and visits to the dressmaker with Aunt Maria. She felt at first that the whole family must know what had happened; surely she must appear different? But no one seemed to notice anything strange; she and

Jacob had, after all, rarely been alone together. No one could have suspected the love that had arisen between them.

Then, a few nights later, Jacob came to her room again. He was wearing only a nightshirt and a silk robe. The fear of what was to happen silenced her, she closed her eyes and prayed that she might not scream out. But, this time, it was less violent and afterwards Jacob lay by her side and whispered that one day they would be together for ever.

She spoke the words for the first time, words that had been in her mind almost since she met him: 'I love you, Jacob.'

Jacob looked down at her pensively. 'Yes, I know, Rachel. And of course I love you. But soon I shall be recalled to my regiment. We must enjoy these days that are given to us.' They lay for a long time in silence and the black sky was already turning to blue when he left.

Later that morning she remembered that this was the day of her visit to Rodney Parrish and she pleaded with Aunt Maria that she had a head-ache.

'Surely this is not the time of the month,' Aunt Maria said doubtfully.

'No. It is not that, Aunt Maria. I think perhaps we returned late from the ball.'

'No later than usual, dear. Do you wish me to send a message?'

Remembering that she must behave as normal, that no suspicion must be aroused in her aunt's mind, Rachel said, 'No. I am sure I shall be all right. I will go.'

'Perhaps he makes his attentions too transparent, dear. But I am sure he is a sincere young man.'

'Yes, Aunt.'

She walked dutifully round the stables with Rodney and even went for a short ride with him across the fields. Rodney asked her when Jacob would be returning to his regiment but Rachel only said vaguely that she did not know.

It was at breakfast one morning, early in the new year, that Jacob received an advance warning that he was to proceed to Plymouth in two months' time. There he would embark upon the ship which would take him and his regiment to Egypt. They would be held there in preparation for any activity that might present itself in the Sudan.

'Ah, the Sudan,' Mr Damarell said. 'I knew there was trouble brewing there. Let us hope it will not be like the trials and tribulations of the Zulu war.'

'You know all about Egypt, don't you, Rachel?' Jacob smiled at her.

'Yes.' Rachel tried to go on, but no words came. Both the thought of Egypt and of Jacob leaving her seemed to combine into one terrible catastrophe. If only she could go there again, if only she could go with him. Egypt reminded her once again of her parents. She realised that the misery of their loss had receded since Jacob came; he had helped her to recover. It wasn't time which had healed, but Jacob's love.

Then he had another communication to say that departure had been delayed until April and Aunt Maria began to make plans for all the persons to whom he must bid farewell, of appointments she must make for him to visit the tailor, of new luggage he would require.

'You are always gone for so long,' Bertha said gloomily. 'Perhaps when you come again, I shall be married. And you will have missed the wedding.'

'Ah, dear Bertha, that is one of the trials of a soldier's life. This time I may not be absent for so long.'

The days were filled with all Aunt Maria's arrangements, so that Jacob seemed to have ceased to have a life of his own and on the last evening, all the aunts and uncles were invited to dinner at the house. It was very late when they departed and Rachel climbed the stairs to her room, knowing that it must be too late now for Jacob to come to her. Tomorrow, there would be an early start.

She lay in silence, waiting for the dawn. Then, when she had fallen asleep he came in and lay down beside her. She felt no more shame or fear, this was what she wanted, to be with Jacob for ever. He spoke words of love now and she responded, holding his naked body against hers, caressing him as he had taught her.

His brothers bade him farewell as they departed for work the next morning and Rachel and Bertha went with Aunt Maria and Mr Damarell in the carriage to see him on to his ship at Plymouth. She stood once again on the quayside where she had stood years before, waiting for her parents to arrive. Was her life to be an endless series of departures and loss?

Jacob introduced them to some of his fellow officers who had already assembled on the quay and they all talked cheerfully about the impending journey. Rachel could sense the latent excitement which Jacob was already feeling, the anticipation of new worlds and new experiences.

Finally, Jacob came and kissed Bertha and Aunt Maria and shook his father's hand. Then he came over to Rachel and kissed her on either cheek. 'Goodbye, dear Rachel.' He bent over her, smiling, and whispered, 'You will wait for me, won't you?'

Rachel smiled at him. 'Yes,' she said.

They watched him climb the gangway to the ship, turning to wave as he reached the deck. Aunt Maria and Bertha were waving back and Rachel noticed Mr Damarell, standing alone, a look of pain on his face. For the first time since she had known him, she felt sympathy for him. He was always so remote, his expression always so forbidding, but for a moment, she saw only a lonely father contemplating his son leaving, a son he might never see again. Every time Jacob left, he must suffer this agony.

Rachel went over to him and put her arm in his. 'It is very hard, Sir,' she said softly. 'But Jacob will return.'

Mr Damarell turned to her and then he smiled. 'Thank you, dear.'

Rachel had a momentary feeling of fear and guilt. What would Mr Damarell think, what would he do, if he knew of the things which had happened between her and Jacob? He would never blame Jacob though; he would always believe that she was responsible. She had a cold feeling of dread; he must never discover.

Mr Damarell held her arm in his and they both turned and watched in silence as Jacob disappeared into the bows of the ship.

Chapter 9

Aunt Maria looked irritated at Maggie's excuse.
'Forgot, girl? How could you have forgotten? You pass the shop on your way to the Shambles.'

'I'm sorry, Ma'am. The basket was heavy coming up the hill and I forgot my other assignment.'

'Basket heavy! Well, if you are unable to perform your duties properly, perhaps you had better seek alternative employment.'

'Oh, no, Ma'am.' Maggie's lips began to tremble.

'Let me go, Aunt Maria. I would enjoy a little fresh air.' Rachel spoke eagerly. 'I have nothing particular to attend to this afternoon.'

She longed to be out of the house. It was so silent and dead since Jacob had gone and there was no longer the anticipation of his return from one of his expeditions. Even the calls on elderly relatives and the visits she and Bertha made delivering provisions to the poor seemed a liberation.

'You're not a servant, Rachel. One would scarcely expect you to carry out errands that Maggie neglected.'

'But Aunt Maria, I want to go to that very shop myself. I have to get some new ribbons.'

Aunt Maria hesitated. 'Well, I do want the feathers for that new bonnet. Aunt Alice will be here tomorrow to attach them for me. And none of the servants are free.'

'I don't need anyone to accompany me, Aunt Maria. I would like some fresh air.'

Aunt Maria looked at Rachel thoughtfully. 'Very well, dear. You have been looking a little peaky lately. You need to get out in the sun a little more. You and Bertha haven't had any of your tennis parties lately.'

'Perhaps you would tell me exactly what you require,' Rachel said

175

hastily. She had no wish to go to tennis parties or anything else. All she wanted was to get out of the house and be alone, so that she could think about Jacob, re-live their brief days together. When he first left, she had been grateful when Rodney Parrish called and requested her company at social events. She had thought it would help her to get through the desolate days ahead, but his conversation was tedious and his attentions intrusive. Yet she knew it was necessary to fulfil her usual duties because she had to conceal from everyone the agony she was suffering.

She was almost grateful now that her parents had sent her to England as a child, for she had learnt then to bear her misery in silence. Without that experience, she felt she could not have listened with such apparent equanimity to Aunt Maria's speculations about where Jacob's ship might be at the moment, or when they would be likely to receive a letter from him.

'You'd better wear your large straw hat,' Aunt Maria said as she followed Rachel to the front door.

Rachel walked slowly along the drive and down into Fore Street. It was a warm day, the trees cast deep shadows across the pavement and she stopped and leaned over the garden wall at Mount Pleasant, looking at the forget-me-nots and alyssum and the fading primulas. It was just like a garden she and Jacob had looked at in Dartmouth one day; the street was quiet in the afternoon heat and sunny just as it had been then. Jacob had laughingly leaned over the wall and picked a forget-me-not. 'Will you forget-me-not?' he had said.

She walked on past St Crispins where some young boys were running out of the gate, their satchels slung carelessly over their shoulders. That was where Jacob had gone to school. When she told him about the Establishment, he had said that he had never liked school, either. Jacob had understood her feelings.

The sun was pouring down on her back and when she reached the corner of Duncombe Street, she sat on the wooden seat, feeling a curious ennui. Then she thought of Jacob's laughing eyes, his enthusiasm. He wouldn't want her to behave in this listless fashion. She sprang up. No. It was her spontaneity he had liked; she mustn't lose that. When he came back, he would not want to find a dull, colourless girl.

176

She walked on down to Mr Curtis's shop and stood looking absent-mindedly in the windows at the bonnets and ribbons and silk flowers. Yes. They would have a tennis party and she would go to the ball that Rodney had invited her to next week.

As the days passed, she found she could even begin to think about Jacob and their brief months together; she did not try to eliminate him from her mind as she had had to do with her parents. And his last, whispered words sustained her. Yes. She would wait for him for ever. She could never marry because one day he would return. Then they could tell Aunt Maria and Mr Damarell of their love and they would be wed.

About a month after Jacob departed, another thought had also begun to occupy her. The horrible monthly event had not happened. At first, she could not remember exactly when it should have come, but as time passed, she knew that it was late. She wondered if all the anxiety about Jacob had upset her stomach; it had happened like this once before when she had had influenza. However, when two months had passed, she began to fear that she must have some disease and spoke about it to Bertha, who looked equally mystified.

'Perhaps you have some stomach disorder,' Bertha said doubtfully.

'Do you think it is ending? That I shall no longer be cursed with this unpleasantness?'

'I don't know.'

'Aunt Maria said it goes on for some years and then it stops. Could that be what is happening?'

'I think you must speak to Mama,' Bertha said. 'She will know what is wrong.'

The next day, she went into Aunt Maria's bedroom.

'Aunt Maria, I believe I may have some illness.'

'Illness, dear. Do you feel unwell?' Aunt Maria looked concerned.

'Well, no. But the monthly visitation has not happened.'

Aunt Maria frowned. 'For how long, dear?'

'It must be two, perhaps nearly three months.'

'Nothing at all?'

'No. I think perhaps it is ceasing, as you said it would one day.'

'Ah, no. It could not be that, Rachel.' Aunt Maria shook her head decisively. She looked thoughtfully at Rachel.

'Although I know I advised it, perhaps you have been indulging in too much exercise with your tennis. Or have you been eating anything which upsets you?'

'I have done nothing out of the ordinary. In fact,' she smiled, 'since Jacob departed, we seem to have had a somewhat quieter life.'

'Yes. That is true.' Aunt Maria seemed to be considering her words. 'Rachel, you have not done anything untoward?'

Rachel frowned. 'In what way, Aunt Maria? What could I have done?'

'With young men, Rachel.'

Rachel looked puzzled. 'Well, I have danced as usual. I went riding with Rodney and then there was the pantomime last week.'

'No, Rachel. I don't mean that.' Aunt Maria shook her head dismissively. 'No. Of course not. Rachel, I think perhaps we should visit Dr Scott. It may simply be some minor complication.'

'But what will he do?'

Aunt Maria breathed deeply. 'Well, he will have to examine you, Rachel. I am afraid that may be rather a distasteful event, but it will have to be done.'

'Could I not take some tonic, Aunt Maria?'

Aunt Maria hesitated. 'No, dear. I think it would be better to get some medical advice.'

Next day, Aunt Maria and Bertha accompanied her on her visit to Dr Scott. He lived in a large white house on the other side of Dodbrooke and he opened the door himself when they arrived, a tall, elderly gentleman with a kind smile and white hair that flowed down to his collar.

'Ah,' he said to Aunt Maria when he heard the problem. 'Perhaps Miss Bertha would like to wait in the drawing-room while I expect you would wish to attend on Miss Rachel.'

Rachel felt a growing sense of dread. Did he think she was really ill? 'I don't feel ill,' she volunteered.

'Don't worry, dear. I am sure we'll soon come to the root of the problem. It's probably some small stomach complication that will soon be put to rights.'

They followed him into a large room, at one end of which was a large screen.

'Now, dear. Will you go in there and remove your outer garments and any tight-fitting under-garments you may be wearing. Then cover yourself in this robe and we will see what we can find.'

Rachel undressed with trembling fingers. She had never been examined by a doctor in this manner before. She pulled on the white robe, which covered her from head to foot and then hesitantly emerged from behind the screen.

'Now, Miss Rachel, I shall be as unobtrusive as I can.' He glanced at Aunt Maria who removed herself to a chair with her back to them. 'I must just try to make a cursory examination—'

With the robe still around her, he slipped a hand inside and felt across her stomach. Rachel blushed and looked at the ceiling.

'Have you noticed any discomfort in the past few weeks?'

'No. Well, actually,' Rachel added thoughtfully, 'I have felt somewhat sick on one or two occasions. When I rose in the morning. But it has passed.'

She saw Aunt Maria turn her head suddenly, looking in alarm at Dr Scott. Dr Scott coughed and cleared his throat.

'Miss Rachel, I have to ask you if you can think of any other reason why—' He lapsed into silence.

Rachel shook her head in dismay. 'No, I have no knowledge of medical matters.'

Dr Scott asked her to sit down. He glanced at Aunt Maria as though seeking her consent for whatever was to follow. Aunt Maria merely pressed her lips together and turned away.

'Miss Rachel, I have to tell you that pregnant ladies find themselves in the same condition as you find yourself. Their monthly periods cease.' He spoke the last sentence in a subdued tone, as though the words were being forced from him.

Rachel experienced a new feeling of dread. She was aware of all those secretive conversations she had heard between Aunt Maria and Aunt Bessie and Alice about ladies being in a certain state. Miss Gordon's warning that you never mentioned these matters in front of gentlemen somehow suggested that in a mysterious way they were connected with it. 'Yes. But these ladies are pregnant because they are married. I'm not married, though.'

Rachel looked at him anxiously. Her mind, trembling on the edge of understanding, was suddenly clear. Even before he continued, she knew the truth; she felt as though, buried inside her, the knowledge had been there all the time. She had always known. That was how you got pregnant. What she and Jacob had done. That was why she had felt such anxiety.

'No. But it is possible for any lady to become pregnant, given the circumstances. You see, there are foolish girls who behave as though they were married. They permit gentlemen to behave in a fashion in which only husbands should behave.'

'Oh, no,' she said in an agonised whisper.

'Rachel, it can't be true.' There was an expression of horror on Aunt Maria's face.

Rachel began to tremble.

'It is so then, Miss Rachel?' Dr Scott looked at her in disbelief.

Rachel did not reply.

'Perhaps you should inform your aunt of the individual who is responsible for your condition.' Dr Scott's manner had changed. He looked at Rachel distastefully.

'Rachel, are you sure you understand what Dr Scott has said?' Aunt Maria whispered.

Rachel looked at her blankly. 'Yes, Aunt Maria. I understand.'

'Miss Rachel,' Dr Scott began, but Aunt Maria interrupted.

'Dr Scott, I think this matter must be left to be settled by Mr Damarell. Rachel, we will depart now.' She stood up, looking severely at Rachel.

'Dr Scott, I presume upon your fullest confidentiality in this dreadful matter.'

'Madam, how can you doubt my professional honour?' Dr Scott looked insulted.

'Forgive me, Dr Scott, I am distraught. Pray go, dress yourself, Rachel.'

Rachel climbed into the gig behind Aunt Maria and Bertha. What would happen to her? What would Mr Damarell do? Her first thoughts had been of Jacob. Had he realised the possible consequences of his actions? Had he knowingly put her into this situation? But the shock of Dr Scott's revelation seemed to have stopped any coherent thought.

In answer to Bertha's sympathetic questions about the cause of Rachel's indisposition, Aunt Maria replied curtly that they would not discuss the matter at the moment – Mr Damarell must first be consulted.

'But what has Papa got to do with it?' Bertha queried in astonishment.

'Bertha, please desist, as I requested. You will know soon enough.'

'But Rachel, are you very ill?'

Rachel shook her head. 'No, dear. Don't talk about it now. I'll be all right.'

Mr Damarell was at the mill when they returned, so that it was not until that evening that Rachel was summoned from her room where Aunt Maria had requested her to remain.

Aunt Maria and her husband were standing side by side in the drawing-room, as though they were presenting an impenetrable, united front. Mr Damarell asked her and Aunt Maria to be seated and stood in front of the fireplace, his arms folded.

'Now, young lady,' he said in a harsh tone she had never heard him use before. 'What is this I hear?'

Rachel looked at him in silence.

'Speak, girl,' he shouted. 'Explain yourself.'

'I can't explain. I didn't know.'

'Didn't know!' Mr Damarell's face went red. 'How dare you say such a thing in this respectable household! And after your father's concern in sending you to a decent school.'

His anger seemed to release her own.

'That's the reason. It's because no one ever explains such things in respectable households and decent schools. No one told me. How would I know that this would be the result?'

Mr Damarell raised his arm as though he would strike her, his face red and tense.

Aunt Maria moved agitatedly in her chair.

'Arthur—'

'And why should you know,' he shouted. 'Why would any respectable female need to know? And how could such a possibility have arisen in the first place?'

Rachel had a momentary vision of Hope Cove, of the wind whistling high above them, the waves crashing on the rocks below. 'It just happened.' She felt herself building up a barrier of speechlessness. If she did not reply, they could not find out.

181

'Rachel,' Aunt Maria began but Mr Damarell silenced her with a wave of his hand.

'I will deal with this, Maria. Now, girl, let us have the facts. With whom did this happen?'

Rachel saw now the implication of his words, the horror of revealing to them, to all the family, what she and Jacob had done. It could never be. She would never tell them, never let them treat their love as something to be despised.

'I don't know,' she repeated firmly.

Mr Damarell stood looking at her, controlling his violent emotions. He waited disdainfully for her to succumb to his demand.

'Arthur, dear. Do not disturb yourself.' Aunt Maria interposed hastily. 'Perhaps it is a shock to Rachel. She must collect her thoughts.'

'A shock! Are you condoning her actions? Collect her thoughts? She will collect her bags and go but not before I have ensured that her seducer is brought to book. Now girl, when and with whom did this occur?'

'I don't know,' Rachel repeated.

Mr Damarell frowned as though he were contemplating an even worse possibility, bitterly adding, 'I trust that you have not fallen so far from grace that there could be – more than one?'

'No.'

'Then, who is it?'

'I shall never reveal that to you, Sir.'

Rachel stood up. Her aggressive expression concealed the fear she was feeling, the anxiety about what he intended. 'Collect her bags and go.' But where?

'Sit, girl!' Rachel sat down.

'Maria, have you no idea who this wretched creature might be?'

'Dear Arthur, it is scarcely possible. She is always with Bertha or chaperoned by one of the servants. When she visits Mr Parrish his sister commonly comes to collect her.'

'Parrish. Ah. Is he the scoundrel, then?'

Rachel was silent.

'Is he?'

'No, Sir.'

'I know of no one, Arthur.' Aunt Maria was speaking soothingly.

'All the dances are properly regulated, the musical evenings, the entertainments—' Aunt Maria was clearly reflecting as she spoke, trying to visualise some possibility. 'No, apart from her walks with Richard, there is no chance.'

Aunt Maria spoke Richard's name dismissively, as though he would never be entertained as a candidate, but Mr Damarell said, 'Richard. It cannot be that you have brought my own son to such disgrace.'

Rachel shook her head violently, afraid to speak. His thoughts would surely lead him to those few excursions she had made with Jacob. He would surely see the truth in her eyes if he mentioned that name.

But it was Aunt Maria who said dismissively, 'And those trips to Buckfast Abbey and Hope Cove and elsewhere with Jacob.'

Rachel glanced furtively at Mr Damarell, her heart pounding. She saw a strange expression come over his face and he said shortly, 'Jacob would never be such a fool. He would not bring disgrace on his family. Let us not malign him in his absence.'

'Sir,' Rachel said suddenly, 'it is someone unknown to either of you.'

'Ah.' He seemed to sigh with relief. 'Then if you have been violated by some unknown creature, give me his name.'

Rachel looked down in silence.

'Does Bertha know of this, Rachel?' Aunt Maria asked.

'Oh, no. She is quite unaware.'

'I should hope my own daughter would not be connected with such—'

Mr Damarell turned his back on them, resting his arms on the mantelpiece. Rachel and Aunt Maria watched him uncertainly. The grandfather clock chimed its sombre notes, the minutes ticked past. When Mr Damarell spoke, it was in his usual sanctimonious tone.

'I have made my decision, Rachel. You will go to your room and consider your position. Reveal the name of this scoundrel and I will get you married off in due haste. You will then move to another part of the country where your disgrace may go undetected. And may the Lord forgive you both.'

'No. I can't do that.'

183

'Very well. Go and pack your clothes. I shall contact the workhouse and you will depart there in the morning. In the meantime, confine yourself to your room.'

'No!' There was terror in Rachel's voice but Mr Damarell had already left the room.

'Aunt Maria, I can't go to the workhouse.' Rachel had visited it on occasion with Aunt Maria; she thought of the destitute girls there and their puny babies and of the old toothless women and ragged old men.

'You have brought it on yourself, Rachel. You could not remain in this household.' Aunt Maria looked unhappy but she led Rachel firmly upstairs.

When the door closed behind her, Rachel walked over to the window and looked out across the lawns and beyond to the hills. Her fear became submerged in anger. She would not go to the workhouse. All her life she had been told where to go, what to do. She was grown up now. She would deal with this problem herself. She would run away. But where could she go, what lay beyond those hills? She began to pack her valise. As darkness fell, there was a knock on the door and Bertha entered with a tray of food. The servants were not to be permitted to see her; it was not desirable to risk the knowledge of her disgrace leaking out to the village. Bertha looked at her in embarrassment.

'Oh, Rachel,' Bertha said tearfully. 'Whatever will become of you?'

Rachel almost burst into tears but she said quietly, 'I don't know.'

'Rachel, would it not be better to reveal the identity of . . . It must then be possible for you to marry the . . . father.'

Rachel frowned. Supposing she did tell Mr Damarell. Would Jacob return and marry her if he knew? But, no. He could not return. His regiment would not allow that. In any case, even if Mr Damarell believed her, he would not want his son to marry her. He would blame her for what had happened.

'No,' she said. 'I can't do that.'

'Rachel, Mama says you are to go to the workhouse.'

'I can't Bertha. It's terrible there.'

'Yes, but when you've had . . . it, perhaps Papa will allow you to return.'

'I don't want to,' Rachel said obstinately. 'I'll go away. Get a position somewhere.'

Bertha looked at her uncomprehendingly, then walked over to Rachel, tears in her eyes, saying, 'Goodbye, Rachel. Perhaps Mama will allow me to visit. Oh, Rachel!' She kissed her and hurried from the room.

Rachel ate her meal and finished her packing. She was troubled by the doubts that had assailed her. Would Jacob have married her? The truth slowly forced itself into her mind. The reason she was unwilling to tell Mr Damarell was because of her doubts about Jacob. Had he loved her? Would he acknowledge his responsibility? A feeling of desolation came over her, prompted by the growing conviction that she had been betrayed and she was utterly alone. The pain of that knowledge seemed to give her a new determination. She would escape from this house, she would leave tonight.

Her mind began to work more clearly. If she was to escape, she could take only a light case with her. She might have to walk a long way. But what about money? Where could she get it? What did destitute people do?

As darkness fell, she listened as the other members of the household went to bed. She waited, then crept up to Richard's room and cautiously turned the handle. There was no one there. He must still be in the library. She paused on each stair, listening, and went quickly along the hall.

Richard was sitting with his back to her, looking through the windows into the darkness. She gently closed the door behind her.

'Richard.'

He turned, startled. 'Rachel. What are you doing?' He looked angry; she thought she saw an expression almost of hatred.

'I came to say goodbye.'

'Then say it and go.'

'Richard, surely you will not desert me.'

'Desert you! How dare you speak so after what you have done. You have betrayed us all.'

'How dare you accuse me. I am the one who will suffer.'

'You knew what you were doing.' His voice was trembling with emotion. 'You . . . disgust me.'

185

Rachel controlled the anger that enveloped her. 'Richard, please help me.'

'Help you! You are beyond that.'

'Richard, I need money. I will not go to the workhouse. I could go away.'

'Where? There is nowhere to go. You can't escape from what you've done.'

'I could go to London. Sophie lives there. She would help me.'

'No respectable person would countenance your presence, Rachel.'

'Richard, if I go to the workhouse, I shall die and you will be responsible.'

Richard stood up. 'Leave this room, Rachel. Go!'

'Richard, I thought that you once loved me.' She looked at him appealingly. 'Richard?'

He walked abruptly to the door. 'If I did, that would be my misfortune. I hope never to see you again.'

Rachel ran over to him. 'Richard, won't you help me?'

He opened the door without looking at her and went out; there was a muffled sound in his throat but he did not speak.

Rachel crept back to bed. It was dark now, a cloudless sky. She would wait until it was getting light. Then she would go. She lay on her bed in her clothes and the hours passed. With the first pale light of dawn she got up and put on her coat. As she was about to leave, the door opened and Richard came in. She feared for a second, looking at his angry expression, that he had come to prevent her escape. Then he put a linen bag into her hand.

'Here. Take it. Go now.' He pointed to the door and she crept down the stairs behind him.

He stood with her on the steps, forcing himself to speak. 'There is an early horse-bus down at the quay. It goes to Plymouth at five o'clock, for the farm workers. Get a train there to London.'

Rachel looked at him uncertainly. 'Goodbye, Richard. Thank you.'

He stood on the steps, watching her, a stony expression on his face.

In the icy morning mist, Rachel hurried along the road, down Fore Street to the quay. The little houses with their white door-steps, the familiar shop windows filled with goods, looked remote and eerie as though they were already ghosts of her past. As she climbed into the horse-bus, she felt a mixture of elation that she had escaped and a terrible foreboding of what was yet to come.

Chapter 10

For the third time, Rachel peered into the bag of money which Richard had given her.

The first time had been at Plymouth when she bought a ticket for the train. Apart from her school allowance, spent on small items of food and sweetmeats, she realised she had never handled money in her life. At Kingsbridge, when she and Bertha went on any small errand for Aunt Maria, all transactions were placed on an account.

The second time had been on the train, when she had gone to the dining-car for breakfast. When the waiter came to her table, he had asked if the lady was unaccompanied.

Rachel had remembered Aunt Maria's treatment of the lower classes. She said disdainfully, 'Yes and I wish to order breakfast.'

After that, the waiter had treated her with respect and when the moment had come to pay, she had once more had to peer into her bag to find the right coins. She remembered that in tea-rooms Aunt Maria had occasionally added what she called a tip, so Rachel added another two pence to the amount she laid on the silver tray. The waiter thanked her and bowed. Perhaps she had left too much.

Now she stood by the cab which had brought her to Kensington, the driver by her side.

'That's the house, Miss.'

She handed him the money and picked up her valise, looking up at the tall building on the corner of the square and through the railings to the basement. A white cat peered up at her. That must be the Marmaduke that Sophie had always talked about. It was nearly four years since they had met, although they had corresponded regularly. Sophie seemed to divide her time between residence with her father in India and the house in London where her grandmother lived. Yet

189

what would she think of Rachel's situation now? Sophie had been so different from everyone else at school, but they had never discussed matters of this nature. Well, at that time, they had never even known of such things, she reasoned. Surely she would not condemn her as everyone else did. But would she be able to help her? Could she expect Sophie and her grandmother to take her in? Walking up the steps, she felt a flash of panic. Finally, she was going to be destitute. When Richard's money was gone, what would she do?

If Sophie was unable to help her, she might end up in the workhouse. The very word brought terror to her mind. She remembered a visit to the workhouse in Kingsbridge one Christmas with Aunt Maria, when they had taken food and clothes for the inmates. She remembered the stone floors, the smell, the dejection of the old men and women, the young girls with babies in their arms. They had been sitting around on wooden benches, not doing their usual work of oakum-picking because it was Christmas Day. Some of them seemed to be lunatics, one young girl was sitting in a corner crying. No. She would never go to a place like that.

The door was opened by a footman who bowed automatically, as though that were his normal response to every visitor.

'Is Miss Sophie Curzon at home?'

'Miss Sophia, Miss? I fear not.' He smiled. 'She is not likely to be, Miss. She is currently in Egypt.'

'Egypt! I understood her father was in India.'

'Ah, yes, Miss. But he was in the past months transferred to Egypt.' Then he abruptly stopped speaking, as though he had committed some fearful impropriety. 'But I have failed to ask your business.'

'I am a friend from school, we correspond regularly, but I fear I have been away and lost touch with her movements.'

'Ah. Would you wish to leave your card? I fear there is no one here of the family.'

'No. Thank you.'

'No doubt Miss Curzon has your address.'

'No. Yes.'

Rachel knew she had no address to leave. She sighed.

The footman looked at her doubtfully. 'Are you quite well, Miss?

Would you care to come in and rest? It is a warm day.'

'No. Thank you.'

Rachel turned and descended the steps carefully. The footman watched her anxiously for a moment and then went in and closed the door. She clutched the railings. It had happened once or twice before, a sudden giddiness as her heart seemed to beat faster, and then she was all right again. She stood for a moment in the sun, looking at Sophie's house. It seemed impossible that both Jacob and Sophie had gone to that beautiful land of Egypt that she had been forced to leave. She had visions of Jacob meeting Sophie, of his falling in love with her, behaving with Sophie as he had done with her. She turned away. Now she was really alone. Where could she go? Then she thought of her grandparents. She had some kind of recollection of grandmama saying that some of the houses in their square were let out as apartments. People rented them in the same way that she and grandpapa had once rented a house before purchasing one. She hailed another cab and asked the driver to take her to Suffolk Square.

Riding along, she reflected that London seemed much more confusing and busier than it had done in the company of her grandmother. There seemed to be so many people, so much noise.

'This is Suffolk Square, Miss. That is number 40.'

'Yes.' She nodded dismissively. 'I remember.'

The cab driver touched his cap as she handed him some coins and she began to walk over to her grandmother's house. When he had gone, she stood looking at the short drive up which she had once run with such joy, and the tall white house where grandmother had waved to her from the top of the steps. Then she turned to look reflectively at the other houses in the Square. She walked along slowly, then saw a brass plaque with various names printed on it. Perhaps it was this sort of place? She mounted the steps and pulled the large brass handle.

A uniformed person came to the door.

'I have come to enquire if you have an apartment to rent,' Rachel said in the tone in which she imagined Aunt Maria would have spoken.

The man looked at her in bewilderment. 'Apartment, Miss?' He looked at her valise and at her deep blue woollen coat and her short leather boots. 'Perhaps you should come inside, Miss. I will call the proprietor.'

Rachel entered a wide, high-ceilinged hall.

'Pray be seated, Miss.' He went off down the hall and a few seconds later a short, plump gentleman appeared.

'Yes, Miss. Can I be of assistance?'

'I wish to rent an apartment. Quite a small one will be adequate.'

'Ah.' The man smiled obsequiously. 'May I assume that your father – or some gentleman, perhaps – will deal with the contract for such an agreement.'

Rachel frowned. 'No.'

'Oh.' He shook his head. 'Of course, these apartments are let only on long contracts. At least a year. Is that what you would wish?'

'Oh, no. Just for some months. I am not sure how long. I thought we might come to some monthly arrangement.'

The man smiled. 'I think perhaps you are looking for something slightly different, Miss. May I suggest you proceed further along towards Oxford Street. Behind that street you will find large houses where rooms are let out by the week or month.'

'Are they respectable?' Rachel was not sure what the word meant in this context but she knew that Aunt Maria would have asked such a question.

'Oh, yes, Miss. They are of the highest reputation. I know, indeed, of a suitable address off Margaret Street which I shall be pleased to furnish you with.'

'Thank you. And could you also call me a cab?'

'Certainly, Miss.' He looked at her reflectively. 'Pray do not think me impertinent, Miss, but this is a dangerous city for young unaccompanied ladies. Young ladies of your standing are not often seen alone. Perhaps you would be advised to pursue your enquiries with some relative.'

Rachel smiled briefly. 'Thank you for your concern,' she said, picking up her valise and going down to the cab.

It went briskly along Oxford Street and stopped in front of a tall house similar in appearance to the one she had just left, except that here all the houses were joined together and there were no gardens around them. Rachel glanced down the street, crowded with horses, carts, cabs and what seemed to be a multitude of people after the comparative quiet of Suffolk Square, then went up the steps.

The door was opened by a maid in a starched white apron and cap, and she was shown into what the maid called a reception parlour. A tall, amply-bosomed lady soon appeared in a stiff black dress with a wide, lace collar and a large jet brooch at her throat. The lady smiled at her and introduced herself as Mrs Wentworth.

'I wish to rent a room for a few weeks or months,' Rachel said quietly. 'It is not convenient for me to stay with my relatives, who are nearby.'

Mrs Wentworth seemed to find this sufficient explanation. 'Nowadays, it is not always possible, I believe. But will you be dealing with the financial arrangements yourself?'

'Yes.'

'Then I will show you a room and you can consider its suitability, Miss—'

'Miss Cavendish.' The maid appeared and took her valise.

'Right, Miss Cavendish.' Rachel followed Mrs Wentworth up the stairs.

The room was on the second floor and looked out on to the busy street, but at the back there was a small garden in which Mrs Wentworth said she could sit.

'Thank you. Now,' Rachel tried to speak confidently, 'perhaps I may be permitted to unpack the few belongings I have with me at the moment, and then I will come down and complete the financial arrangements. And what will the rent be?'

'Eight pounds monthly, in advance.'

'That will be most convenient.'

When she was alone, Rachel sat on the bed and hastily poured out the money from the linen bag. It came to £46. There must have been £50 there to start with. She must already have spent £4. Would there be enough to last? And how about food? If she ate very little, perhaps it would last for five months. She knew now that a pregnancy lasted for nine months. Already, at least three months had passed. But what would she do then? She remembered that she had her jewellery. She could sell that and if it became necessary, she could sell some of her clothes. But what about the baby, where would it be born? Could she go to a hospital? She stood up. Now that she was settled, she could start finding out.

For a second, looking round the small room, she felt a surge of panic. Her anxiety began to make her feel giddy again and she poured herself a glass of water from the jug. Then she remembered the plans she had made on the train. After the baby arrived, she would find a position as a governess. She would say she was a widow; she had even invented a sad tale of a husband killed in a hunting accident.

That afternoon, she found a small, elegant restaurant in the vicinity of Margaret Street. She would dine there in the evenings and restrict herself during the day to fruit she could buy in the nearby market. In the afternoons, she would walk in the Park or wander along Regent Street as she had done with grandmama, so that she would confine herself to using a cab only in the evenings.

But as the days passed, Rachel began to feel the burden of her loneliness. She avoided conversation with any young men she observed in the Park, knowing that this would be unseemly. The chaperoned young ladies only glanced at her unaccompanied state with curiosity; without introductions, how was it possible for her to meet anyone or engage in any social life?

There was also the further complication that she feared her situation would soon become obvious. She let out her dresses and was thankful for the full skirts, and she extended the bustle so that it was difficult to assess her real size.

After a few months, she counted her money and knew that it could not last. She tried to remember Miss Gordon's financial instructions. During their household managements lessons, the actual expenditure of money had never been mentioned. They had worked out series of accounts, but they always related to the running of a household. The maxim had been that the good housekeeper, of whatever standing, always managed within her budget. But what was a budget?

As her money diminished, she began to sell items of her jewellery in a pawnshop she had noticed while wandering down into Piccadilly; a gold necklace given to her by her father, an Egyptian bracelet mama had sent to her with the carved heads of pharaohs and the words Kismet imprinted on the clasp, some jet necklaces and bangles Aunt Maria had given her. It was as though with the loss of those objects she had severed her last connection with her old life. Nothing remained.

Self-pity overcame her, remembering the familiarity and ease of that old world which she had once treated with contempt. The boredom she had felt at Aunt Maria's, the endless round of calls, the tedious musical evenings, her violin practice and wax-flower making and Aunt Maria's Berlin woolwork, now seemed like an idyll. She even thought of the hymn singing on Sunday evenings and the visits to chapel with a kind of longing.

By the end of the autumn, all her jewellery was gone. In spite of the approach of winter she decided to go down to the pawnshop and sell her coat. She would have to make do with a cashmere shawl. At the same time, she would have to leave this house. Mrs Wentworth had been away, as a result of which Rachel already owed a month's rent, but it would be impossible to pay that and have sufficient left over to see her through the winter. She knew with a terrible feeling of shame that she would have to deceive Mrs Wentworth – she would have to leave surreptitiously, without paying. Momentarily she had a picture of Mr Damarell's stern demeanour, of the expression of horror that would come across Aunt Maria's face.

It was a warm, sunny day as she packed her valise. She surveyed herself in the looking-glass: the skin beneath her eyes appeared smudged with shoe-black and her face seemed to be thinner, in contrast with the increasing size of her body. She combed her long hair and tied it back neatly, put on the small blue hat which matched her pale blue gown and pulled on her gloves. She needed to look respectable to see the proprietor of her next accommodation. Then she took up the leather valise her father had given her long ago and crept from the house. The money from the sale of her coat and the little she still had in her linen bag, would pay the rent of some inferior place and keep her until the baby arrived. As for that, she had no clear picture of how the baby would come, she felt a terrible fear contemplating the future and the impending birth. She had been unable to mention the problem to Mrs Wentworth; perhaps, when she moved to her next room, she would find some female person whom she could ask.

As she walked down the street, she saw a tall army officer coming towards her. He did not look like Jacob, but she was overwhelmed by the memory of him.

For weeks, sitting alone in her room, she had tried to put him from her mind, because every time she thought of him she was overcome with despair. Although she had doubted it at first, and believed that Jacob had been as ignorant as she was about how babies were conceived, she was convinced now that he had known all the time the possible outcome of his actions. She had really loved him but he had just been using her. She realised that he had never actually said that he loved her, had never made any promise of marriage. In her situation, his request that she should wait for him seemed almost cynical. Of course, what she had done had been wrong. Yet even now some part of her refused to feel any shame. After the initial horror, the shock of that totally unimagined assault, it had seemed a natural thing.

When she reached Leicester Square, Rachel went into the pawn shop and deposited her coat. The old man behind the counter was accustomed to her visits and asked her if she also wished to pawn her valise. He would give her some shillings for that, he said. Rachel shook her head; that would be the final item she had to sell.

'Could you recommend a room I might rent in this vicinity?'

The old man looked at her thoughtfully. 'Depends on the kind of room,' he said, grinning.

Rachel frowned. 'Something as reasonable as possible.'

The man nodded slowly, asking, 'Just for your own occupancy?'

'Yes. Of course.'

'Well, depends on the rent you want to pay. Two shillings?'

'I could manage more than that. Four shillings, perhaps.'

'Well, Miss. If you turn down that street opposite, you'll find some tall houses. The better-class ones are further along the street. Outside, you'll likely see a prosperous-looking gent with a big gold chain across his person. He's the owner of the whole block. You'll see his brougham drawn up outside. You talk to 'im.'

Rachel nodded, took the money for her coat and crossed the road. The streets were narrow and she looked anxiously up at the high buildings. She had supposed they were derelict warehouses. Was it possible that these crumbling exteriors concealed furnished rooms?

She saw the man the pawnbroker had mentioned and walked up to him. 'Would it be possible for me to see you in your office?' she asked.

The man looked at her blankly through narrow eyes, the upper and lower lids seemed to be squeezed together by the puffiness of his face. 'What d'yer mean?' he replied in an aggressive tone.

'I wish to enquire if I could rent a room.'

He eyed her up and down, then shrugged his shoulders indifferently. 'D'you want one to yourself?'

'Yes.'

'Well, the better class ones are six shillings.'

Rachel hesitated. 'Yes. I can manage that.'

'Up 'ere, then.'

He led her along the road to the next block of houses, which looked no different from the first and pushed open a side door. They were in an alley which was crowded with very young bare-foot children playing amongst great piles of rubbish and refuse. They were all in rags and some of them were naked. An open sewer ran down by the side of the buildings.

Rachel was about to retreat back through the side door, but the man said peremptorily, 'Come and see the room.'

She followed him into a dark stone-floored corridor, with doors on either side. There was a smell of decay, as though bad food, human bodies and excrement had all been deposited there from time immemorial. Although little sun filtered through the high, narrow walls, the weeks of summer heat had turned the place into a bowl of smouldering and suffocating airlessness. When they reached the end of the corridor, they mounted a wooden staircase which creaked and shook as they ascended. As he walked along the narrow passage, the proprietor pushed the doors to the rooms open and thrust his head inside.

In one room, Rachel saw a dirty child of about four, sitting on a sack, her clothes ragged and filthy, her face pockmarked and grey. But it was her expression that Rachel noticed, the face of a care-worn old woman. On the bare boards by her side lay a baby, a piece of dirty shawl flung across it. When the girl saw the proprietor, a look of fear crossed her face, but the man only closed the door again.

'Looking after the kid,' he said in the same indifferent voice. 'Her mother's out all day.' He leered. 'Making money. By the time she gets back, she'll have spent most of it on drink.'

Rachel stopped as the man opened another door. She had been following him more and more slowly, but somehow she felt powerless to turn and escape. She knew there was no escape. Where else could she go?

'I don't know if this is quite suitable,' she said timidly. She had a

197

feeling that if she appeared to insult this man, he might strike her.

'Look, Miss. I can tell you that this is the best you'll get in these parts for six shillings. There's those who are queueing up to get one of these rooms.'

'Yes, of course,' she said hastily. Perhaps he was right; her room with Mrs Wentworth had been eight pounds a month and that was sparsely enough furnished.

She followed him into the room. There was a wooden chair with only three legs and a small wooden table was balanced against the wall as though it might collapse at any moment. The walls were black with damp and mildew; the wallpaper was hanging in shreds. The single window was broken across the centre in a jagged line, so that only the lower half retained any glass. The bedstead consisted of an old iron frame on which rested a few layers of straw which served as a mattress. The bedding consisted of two sacks, covered with dark stains which appeared to be congealed blood.

Rachel sighed. Wouldn't the workhouse be better? But even as she considered the idea, she knew she could never go there. Her experience of Kingsbridge had convinced her that she might never escape. She had seen old men and women who looked as though they had been there for years. There had been young girls with babies, who would never be able to leave because they had nowhere to go, no money, no family, it had seemed. She realised now that those girls had probably been rejected by their families, just as she had been. She thought with shame that she was looked upon now as one of those same disgraced females. Well, at least here, once the baby had been born, she could get away. She would get some kind of job.

'Course,' the proprietor remarked, 'if you want something cheaper, you can have an unfurnished apartment for four shillings.'

'No. I'll have this.' She put down her valise and felt in her linen bag. 'Do you want the rent in advance?'

'Ho! You're the kind of young lady I like. My deputy comes round every day. You pay daily.'

'I'll pay you now for the week,' Rachel looked at him distantly. She felt that if she remained in his presence any longer she would suffocate. 'Here.' She passed him six shillings.

He nodded and walked over to the door. She sat down on the straw and despair overcame her. How could she, how could anyone live in these conditions? Then she felt a bitter anger against her aunt and Mr Damarell at their cruelty in turning her out. She thought about Mr Damarell's sermons and his constant references to purity and sin and hell fire. What did he know of places like this?

Suddenly there was a great commotion from the next room. She heard a man shouting and children crying and screaming with fear, a woman shrieked, there was a crash as though someone had fallen and then there was silence.

Rachel went to the door and peeped out. Two children were standing in the corridor, the face of the boy was bleeding and the small girl was crying. Rachel beckoned to them and they came towards her uncertainly.

'Is your Mama in there?'

'My dad's drunk. He always hits us then,' the boy replied. Both the children smelt so putrid that she could not go near them. They stood hesitantly in the doorway. She felt too overwhelmed to speak. Then they turned away and went back to their door.

Rachel closed her door behind her and walked down the corridor. She would have to go out, keep away from here as much as possible and only return when she was too weary to walk any longer.

The door to the next room adjacent to hers was open and as she passed a voice croaked, 'Is that you, Ellie?'

Rachel stopped and looked into the room. 'No,' she said. 'I'm in the next room.'

A young woman was lying on a straw mattress on the floor, surrounded by half a dozen small children, the eldest of whom could only have been about seven years of age. She had large, dark eyes and must once have been beautiful but now her face was yellow and lined, and every breath seemed to cause her pain.

'You're expecting,' the woman said in her rough voice. 'Poor soul.'

Rachel frowned, then understood the woman's words. 'Yes.'

'How are you going to have it here?'

'I don't know.'

The woman turned to the eldest child. 'Bert, take her down to Mrs Boot. She can help you.'

Rachel followed the boy down the rickety staircase and into a room on the floor below. A scrawny, middle-aged woman was sitting on a wooden box. She looked up as they came in. She was wearing a black dress covered by the remains of an old overall. Her hair was so thin that she seemed almost to be bald.

Rachel shuddered. A dead cat lay on the floor beside her but the woman seemed not to notice it.

'Mum sent her,' the child said and turned and went out.

Rachel stood in the doorway.

'What is it?'

'I'm expecting,' Rachel said. 'I don't know where I can have it, but I'm not going to the workhouse.'

'Turned out by your family, was you?'

'Yes,' Rachel agreed.

'Why didn't you get rid of it?'

'Rid of it?' Rachel looked astonished.

'Yeh. Slippery elm. A bottle of hot gin. Jump down the stairs.'

'Would that have—' Rachel looked at her uncomprehendingly. Was it possible? Perhaps none of this need have happened.

'Sometimes.' The woman made a face. 'It's too late now, anyway. Too far gone.'

'Oh, is it?'

'You'd kill yourself.'

'If only I'd known. Are you sure?' Rachel looked at her anxiously.

The woman pursed her lips dismissively and looked at Rachel with an expression she did not understand, before saying, 'Well, you don't have to keep it, do you?'

Rachel frowned. 'Don't I, Mrs Boot?'

The woman shook her head impatiently. 'It might not live, might it?'

'Oh. No. I suppose not.'

'Well?'

'I am sure it would be best for the child if it didn't,' Rachel said in a bewildered tone.

Mrs Boot nodded. 'Anyhow, when's it supposed to be?'

'I don't know.'

''Ere. Come 'ere.'

The woman stood up, felt across Rachel's stomach as Dr Scott had done and said firmly, 'Any minute, I should say. D'you know what to do?'

'No. I don't.'

200

'Well, I reckon you better not go out. When the pains start, give me a shout. Or knock on the floor. You'ms above me.'

'Pains?' Rachel looked terrified. What would happen?

'It's all right. You won't mistake 'em when they come.'

'Supposing the proprietor should find out.'

The woman laughed humourlessly. ''E don't care if you have a giraffe as long as he gets his money. Now go back upstairs and don't leave any belongings about, if you got any.'

But the advice came too late. When she returned to her room, her valise containing her one remaining dress and petticoats was gone.

She sat down on the straw again. Now she had nothing more to sell. If only the baby would come. She felt no interest in the creature she carried inside her. It was as though that protrusion in her stomach was something totally separate from herself. But now she was filled with anxiety. What sort of pain was it? How did the baby ever get out? Would they have to cut open her stomach and who would do that, in any case? Surely no doctor would come to a place like this.

The days passed and apart from going for bread, which was all she could now afford, and walking up the alley to the tap for water, or to the privy which all the tenants shared, she did not move from her room.

She felt in a trance, as though she must be as still as possible so that she did not come into contact with the world around her. Looking through the filthy window down into the alley below, she could dimly make out other people. There was an endless noise of shouting, crying children swarmed up and down the stairs, and the alley was congested with tenants coming and going, and also with cats, dogs, pigs and chickens. She could see into a room opposite which was occupied by two men, three women and four children. During the day, the men went out and did not return till the candles were lit. Every now and then one of the small boys came back with a piece of bread or bits of wood. One of the women spent the day sewing buttons on to a card. On the second day, two of the women began to fight, pulling each other's hair and screaming. The sewing woman came between them and then the younger woman, her face bruised, went out of the door, dragging one of the children with her.

A minute later the door was re-opened and the woman who had left slung something back into the room. Rachel saw that it was a rat. One of the children caught it and flung it back through the doorway.

Rachel watched it all as though she was seeing a scene in some awful drama. Although it had an air of total unreality, she knew that it was real, that these were people, breathing, speaking, inhabiting the same world as she did. Yet there was nothing she could recognise.

But the baby did not come and when she went out one day, she heard Christmas hymns being sung in St Martins in the Fields. She stood, shivering in her thin summer dress, and then hurried back to her room.

That night, she felt a violent pain in her back. She sat bolt upright, but the pain went as quickly as it had come. Half an hour later, it happened again and she knocked loudly on the floor. What would happen if the woman didn't come?

Rachel heard her climbing the stairs and as she came in, Rachel felt as though she had been seized by a convulsion. 'Mrs Boot. It's a fearful—' she screamed.

''Ere. 'Ave a drink of this.'

Rachel took the dirty cup from the woman's hand. The violent smell of brandy made her feel sick.

'Go on. Drink it. And you better take that dress off.'

'No. No. I can't do that.'

The woman looked at her with her hand on her hips. 'What d'yer mean, you daft thing? 'Ow d'yer think you'll get the little bastard out?'

Somewhere beyond the pain, Rachel seemed to hear echoes of Kingsbridge; remarks she had heard Thomas and Richard making about how the lower classes deserved to be poor because they spent their money on drink. This woman was drunk. Rachel looked at her in horror.

'It's all right,' the woman was saying. 'The pain will get worse before it's better. Now, take off your clothes.'

Rachel slowly unbuttoned her bodice and slipped the dress down. 'Mrs Boot, how does it get out?' she asked, her lips trembling.

The woman sighed impatiently. 'Blimey. 'Ow d'yer think?' Then, seeing the terror in Rachel's face, she added, 'It comes out between your legs. Now, get down on the bed. 'Ere.' The woman laid the blood-stained sacks over the straw. 'That'll be more comfortable.'

The pains were becoming more persistent and Rachel lay down.

She sank into semi-consciousness as the pain flooded her body and the woman shoved her legs apart and thrust her hand upwards into Rachel's body.

'Push,' she said sharply. 'Don't just lie there.'

Rachel tried to do as she was told, but she felt as though she were being torn apart and then the woman said, ''Ere it comes.' But the struggle went on for what seemed like hours after that until Rachel felt as though her body would burst, and then suddenly the pain went and she lay in a pool of blood.

The woman picked up the infant and carried it across to a corner of the room. 'Keep still,' she said to Rachel. 'I'll deal with you in a minute.'

Rachel could not see what she was doing. Then she put the infant on the floor.

'Black hair,' she said. 'Would have been a lad.' She came over to Rachel.

In a daze, Rachel said, 'Would have been?'

The woman looked at her, mystified. 'Course. You didn't want it to survive, did you?'

Rachel looked at her in bewilderment. 'What do you mean?'

'That's what you said, didn't you? You said it would be best. What the 'ell were you going to do with the little bastard, in any case? How d'you think you were going to feed it? What sort of life would you have?'

Rachel sank back on the sacks. That was what Mrs Boot had meant; it might not survive. She had never even thought of such a solution; of course this woman would have understood that was what she meant. She felt a violent sense of loss; a strange feeling of longing came over her; it was the words 'black hair' that had aroused the feeling in her.

'Now, dearie. We got to get rid of the mess inside you.'

'What do you mean?'

'It don't matter. Just lie still.' Mrs Boot began to press on Rachel's stomach and then she thrust her hand inside again.

'Oh, you're hurting me. And why am I bleeding all the time?'

'There. That's done. 'Ere, clean yourself up.' She brought a bucket of water from the corner where she had been with the child. 'Then put on your dress.'

Rachel did as she was told.

'You better keep still for an hour or two. You'll be all right. I'll bring you up a bit of bread.' She looked at Rachel's body. 'Well, you ain't got much milk there, so that won't be troubling you.' Then she looked at the body on the floor.

'Now, I'll deal with that for you. 'Ere, have a drink.' She poured some more brandy into the cup and this time Rachel drank it eagerly.

She looked at the woman. 'Couldn't he,' she nodded towards the baby, 'have a proper burial?'

The woman looked at her as though she were crazy. 'Are you a lunatic? Who's going to pay for that?'

'No. I don't know. But will you leave it. I'll do it myself.'

The woman shook her head. 'Please yourself. I'll be off now. You'd better leave it till tomorrow.'

Rachel had some more brandy and sank into unconsciousness. When she awoke it was dark and she peered across the room. How long had she been there? She could faintly remember Mrs Boot coming up with bread and a cup of tea, and another occasion when the deputy had opened the door and asked for the rent. She remembered Mrs Boot telling him to clear off because Rachel had paid rent in advance. There had been an argument but finally he had gone away. She also remembered the small boy from the next room looking in and saying – what was it – his mother had died and they were all going to a cheaper place, one of the nightly boarding houses. But everything had faded away, as if she had fallen into a recurring coma. She peered across the room. She could just make out the outlines of the tiny body, still lying there.

She pulled off one of her petticoats, crept weakly over to the child, picked it up and wrapped the petticoat around him. Its face was blue and wrinkled and she looked in agony at the dark eyes, staring at her as though at any moment it would come to life. Looking at him, she was overcome with longing, with the wish that he had lived, that she could have kept him with her. She pressed him against her, her whole being concentrated on the tiny creature in her arms, as though he might suddenly be alive. His death was worse than the agony she had suffered in giving him life. If only he had lived. After a few minutes, she sighed. It was too late.

She fumbled around her waist to ensure that her linen bag was still there, tied beneath her dress. It contained her last few shillings. Then she crept down the stairs, along the alley and out through the side door. Although it was apparently the middle of the night, there were still people in every dark alley and on every street corner, women who seemed to be going up to every man who came along, men reeling against doorways, children running in and out of houses.

Rachel peeped into the bundle in her arms. If she took him to a church, someone would find him and then he would get a proper burial. She went along St Martin's Lane and reached the steps of St Martins in the Fields. There were beggars sitting on the steps but she went up to the top and looked around. No one was paying any attention to her.

She took one last look at the small face. The woman was right. How could she have supported him? She went behind one of the pillars and laid it gently on the ground and then turned and began to walk absently towards Piccadilly.

She began to feel faint. Perhaps having a child made you ill, she thought gloomily. But she couldn't be ill. With her last few shillings, she must find some way of getting a decent position. She could never return to that place.

She bought a cup of hot cocoa from a stall and as the sun rose she began to feel better. How could she get a position as a governess? It was her reflection in a shop window which reminded her that she must look respectable. She went to a wash-house, arranged her hair and brushed down her gown. She would call on one of the houses in this neighbourhood. Someone might be able to give her advice.

She turned off Piccadilly into a street of large houses in their own grounds. It occurred to her that these were more opulent than anything the Damarells or even her grandparents had ever aspired to. How did one get an entrance into that magical world? How could she become one of these people, with their carriages and gardens and retinue of servants?

Perhaps she would meet a romantic young major, like the handsome young men she had seen in Cairo as a child, someone who would make her forget Jacob and who would marry her and take her back to Egypt. But, no. Perhaps not Egypt. That was where Jacob had gone. She would not want to see him again. Even as she thought this, she felt a longing for him and for those few idyllic months she had

had with him. Would there ever be anyone like Jacob?

Feeling faint again, she entered a small park and sat down. She watched a middle-aged lady coming towards her. Her pale pink dress was made of silk and a fur cape was draped across her shoulders. Her neat grey shoes matched the velvet handbag she carried. Rachel noticed the lady was looking at her flimsy dress and cape and then she smiled at her and nodded.

Rachel said, 'Good morning, Madam,' and the lady sat down beside her on the seat.

'It is a most pleasant day,' the lady observed in a genteel voice. 'Are you taking an early morning walk?'

Rachel smiled. 'Only a stroll.'

'And do you live in this area, Miss?'

'In the vicinity.'

'It is not usual to see a young lady walking alone.'

'No.' Rachel sighed, suddenly feeling tired. Every event, every encounter, seemed fraught with difficulty. If only life could go back to the simplicity she had known in Kingsbridge. Perhaps, after all, ladies needed protection. Perhaps it was better to let men conduct all worldly affairs. 'I am, at the moment, alone in this city.'

'Alone?' The lady spoke in a tone of incredulity. 'But how can that be?'

'I have had an unfortunate difference with my parents and have escaped from the parental home.'

'Escaped, dear girl. But where are you now staying?' The lady looked even more alarmed.

'I have not yet found suitable accommodation.'

'My dear. But this is ... incomprehensible. You are a beautiful young lady. What will happen to you in this great city? Surely you are not yet of age?'

Rachel shook her head. What had already happened to her was beyond any speech or explanation.

The lady suddenly patted Rachel's hand. 'Now, tell me your name, dear. I am Mrs Rowbotham.'

'And I am Rachel. Rachel Cavendish.'

'And where do you come from, Rachel?'

'Before I tell you that, you must undertake not to reveal my whereabouts to my parents.'

'My dear girl, you must have full confidence in me. I will undertake never to reveal this information without your specific consent. I merely wish to help you.'

Rachel smiled. 'Well I have come recently from Kingsbridge.'

Mrs Rowbotham frowned. 'Kingsbridge? In Devon?'

'Yes.'

'Well, that is some good distance, Rachel. I am most distressed to see a young lady such as yourself placed in such a vulnerable and dangerous position.'

'I intend to find a situation as a governess. I suppose, madam, you do not know of any appropriate household who could use my talents.'

'And what are your talents?'

'Oh, I have had a good education. I am accomplished in the violin, painting, embroidery, as well as having a good knowledge of the English classics. And, of course, I am versed in household management.'

Mrs Rowbotham smiled approvingly. 'I think I may have the very place for you, Rachel. In the meantime, I am prepared to take you home with me. You may remain there until you have sorted out your intentions.'

'I have very little money,' Rachel said uncertainly.

Mrs Rowbotham pursed her lips, as though money were not a pleasant topic to introduce. 'Of course not, dear. Now, come. I am sure you are in need of some light breakfast.'

Rachel looked at her doubtfully. 'It is most considerate of you, Mrs Rowbotham. Are you sure you can accommodate me?'

'Come. You shall see. It is but a few yards from here.'

Mrs Rowbotham's house was similar to those Rachel had been studying, large and white in a beautiful tree-lined garden. She followed Mrs Rowbotham up the steps and the door was opened by a uniformed footman. As they walked through the wide hall, a gentleman appeared from one of the rooms.

'My dear,' Mrs Rowbotham said eagerly to him. 'I have met this unfortunate young lady in the park. At the moment, she is without bed or board. Her intention is to seek a position as a governess. I have offered to take her in, so that we may offer her some protection while she pursues her enquiries.'

The man looked at Rachel. He was very tall and thin and his teeth were brown when he smiled. He extended a hand, and Rachel smiled, controlling the unaccountable sense of revulsion she felt.

'Miss Rachel Cavendish,' Mrs Rowbotham said, 'she has had a most excellent education and would, I believe, fit excellently into any situation.'

'How do you do, Mr Rowbotham.'

'Mr Grainger,' he corrected her. 'Welcome, Miss Cavendish.'

Rachel felt he was looking at her as though he were uncertain whether to believe the truth of what Mrs Rowbotham had told him and hastily added, 'I trust I shall not cause inconvenience, Mr Grainger.'

Then he seemed to relax. 'It is, of course, for Mrs Rowbotham to decide. This is her establishment. I am merely a business associate. But I am sure she will provide you with the protection that is so necessary in this city.'

'Now, dear, pray accompany me upstairs. I will show you to your room.'

Rachel followed Mrs Rowbotham up the wide staircase. It seemed almost incomprehensible that she had come upon such good fortune. At last, she could begin to escape from her past and look forw..rd to her future.

Chapter 11

Mrs Rowbotham led Rachel along the wide upper hall. The doors of the surrounding bedrooms were all closed but finally she flung open a door and went in. Rachel followed her and looked in astonishment at the extravagant furnishings: the large bed was covered with a red silk frilled counterpane on which lay a lavish pink eiderdown; the pillow-slips matched the counterpane and the cushion covers on the arm chairs and the chaise longue seemed to be all frills and flounces; the thick carpet was patterned with large flowers on a vivid pink background and the elaborately-frilled curtains were pale blue; the wall-paper was a matching colour with vivid red roses; two large brass gas lamps with ornate glass shades stood on either side of the fireplace. Rachel stood by the door, hesitating to step on the sumptuous carpet. What perplexed her even more was the heavy smell of perfume which seemed so overpowering that she looked around seeking to find its source.

Mrs Rowbotham was watching her and said rather sharply, 'I hope you will find this acceptable.'

'Oh, madam, I did not mean to be impertinent. It is simply ... somewhat overwhelming. I have never seen such a bedroom before.'

Mrs Rowbotham smiled. 'Probably not. I have spent much care and attention on designing my establishment. I hope it will strike anyone as being of the highest class.'

'Oh, Madam, I am sure it is.'

Rachel looked round uncertainly. It seemed an affront to sit on those chairs or lean against that bed.

'Now, Rachel. I presume you have no luggage anywhere.'

'No. I am afraid not. I have but a small amount of money in my bag.'

'Very well. First of all, we must supply you with some gowns and other necessary items.'

'Madam,' Rachel said anxiously. 'Your generosity is excessive. If you could allow me to remain here briefly until I have acquired a situation, then I need trouble you no longer.'

Mrs Rowbotham looked offended. 'Rachel. Do not reject my concern for you. May I suggest that you have a wash and then come down to breakfast.' Mrs Rowbotham walked from the room, closing the door behind her.

Rachel sat carefully on the chaise longue. She began to feel now that there was something strange about this place. How could Mrs Rowbotham suddenly accommodate her? How could she be so greatly concerned for such a chance acquaintance? Was she so rich that she could easily dispense such hospitality? And that man, Mr Grainger. Rachel knew nothing of business organisations, but she could not imagine what kind of business partner he could be? Why would a lady like Mrs Rowbotham associate with such an individual? Then she told herself that her experiences of the past months had probably made her suspicious even of good intentions. Indeed, what right had she to be suspicious? What would Mrs Rowbotham think if she knew her real story?

As she stood up, she began to feel faint again. She felt a pain in her stomach as though she were having the baby all over again. She realised that blood was trickling down her legs and she pulled the bell cord frantically.

One of the maids answered the bell, looked at her and then dashed from the room, calling for madam.

'Oh, Mrs Rowbotham,' Rachel said agonisingly, 'I shall spoil the carpet.'

'Here, girl.' Mrs Rowbotham placed a large sheet on the floor for Rachel to stand on. 'Is this your normal monthly experience?'

'Oh, no. Oh, Mrs Rowbotham, I feel so ill.'

Rachel collapsed on the floor. When she awoke, the room was in darkness and the curtains were drawn. She could see Mrs Rowbotham standing on the other side of the room, talking softly to a man. Who was he? How long had he been here?

'It is quite certain,' the man was saying. 'There can be no mistake.'

'And she will be all right now, doctor?'

'Yes. Keep her in bed. I will call again in the morning.' Rachel watched them creep from the room. The pain had gone but she felt desperately weak. She realised she had felt ill ever since the birth of the baby but had simply attributed her condition to lack of food and the horrors of her experiences. But what had the doctor been saying? Did Mrs Rowbotham now know the truth of her situation? Would she turn her out as Aunt Maria had done?

She lay still, dreading Mrs Rowbotham's return. When she came back, Mrs Rowbotham pulled back the curtains and a maid placed a tray by the side of her bed and left. Mrs Rowbotham came and looked at her.

'I'm sorry to have caused such trouble,' Rachel said weakly.

Mrs Rowbotham sighed with a pained expression on her face. 'I fear you did not tell me the truth, Rachel.'

'Mrs Rowbotham, I could not bring myself. You could scarcely have befriended me if you had known of such circumstances. I will leave as soon as I am able.'

'Rachel, I found it a most distressing revelation. When I invited you to my house, I could never have anticipated such a thing.'

'No. It is why I was turned from my home. And it was not my parents, Mrs Rowbotham. It was an aunt who had taken me in. I am an orphan.'

'An orphan, Rachel?' Mrs Rowbotham seemed to greet the information with interest. 'Then you have no legal guardian?'

'Well, I suppose my aunt would be that.'

'But she has evicted you.'

'Yes.'

'Well. Well.' Mrs Rowbotham paused. 'I am willing for you to remain here, Rachel, in spite of your ... unfortunate situation. But, of course, it must have some influence upon my sense of responsibility. I have told the doctor that you are my daughter or he might insist that you be removed to a hospital.'

'Oh, no!'

'No. That will not be necessary. You must remain in bed until he permits otherwise. And then I must insist that you do not venture forth alone. I feel it is only prudent that I protect you from your own weakness.'

Rachel blushed. 'Mrs Rowbotham, it will never happen again.'

'Indeed, I hope not. Now, take some breakfast. Of course, the maids are not aware of your situation and I would not wish you to discuss anything with them.'

'Oh, no. I would never do such a thing.'

The doctor called the next day and confirmed that Rachel was making a satisfactory recovery. He remarked that it was fortunate that she had received prompt medical attention.

Rachel remained in bed for a further week, attended only by Mrs Rowbotham. In spite of her kindness and caring attention, Rachel still felt an unease. The fact that Mrs Rowbotham had accepted what must to her have been a disgraceful revelation seemed even more strange than taking Rachel into her home in the first place.

When she was well enough to go downstairs, Mrs Rowbotham summoned a dressmaker who measured her for her new wardrobe. Rachel protested at such generosity but Mrs Rowbotham only smiled. A few days later, she announced that Rachel was well enough to accompany her when she received callers.

'I am sure I shall fulfil any expectations you may have in that respect,' Rachel smiled. She thought of all the At homes and visits and calls she had undertaken with Aunt Maria. It was a relief that Mrs Rowbotham had not enquired further into her family, nor shown any disposition to find out how she had become pregnant.

To Rachel's surprise, Mrs Rowbotham's callers all proved to be gentlemen. Most of Rachel's contacts with the opposite sex to date had been prospective husbands at dinner parties and musical evenings and balls. But all Mrs Rowbotham's callers appeared to be very prosperous-looking older gentlemen. Perhaps Mrs Rowbotham was a widow; she had heard Aunt Maria frequently remark that wealthy widows were often more sought after than young ladies. Yet they all seemed to observe her with more interest than they did Mrs Rowbotham. Perhaps they were surprised to discover that Mrs Rowbotham had a daughter. And why were they never accompanied by their wives? Were they all widowers?

She mentioned the topic to Mrs Rowbotham who looked irritated by the question. 'I am introducing you to gentlemen,' she said sharply, 'to ensure that you know how to behave suitably. Perhaps one day they may be prospective suitors.'

Rachel laughed. 'Oh, they are far too old.'

'Rachel, that is not the way to speak of my visitors. Older men are frequently more desirable as marriage partners. And I must request you to behave in a more inviting fashion when they address you.'

'Inviting, Mrs Rowbotham?'

'You are most attractive, Rachel, but you fail to exhibit your charms sufficiently. You must learn to be more . . . welcoming.'

'Oh, Mrs Rowbotham, I did not mean . . .'

'No, I am sure not. But you need to be more lavish with your feminine charms. You will notice that the indoor gowns I have ordered for you are slightly more mature than the gown you arrived in.'

'Yes. I suppose I am only acquainted with the kind of behaviour expected in Kingsbridge,' Rachel said doubtfully. And indeed, Rachel blushed when she tried on the scarlet silk gown with its dipping neckline, and a vivid blue voile gown which one could almost see through.

'This is the kind of thing worn in better circles in the capitals of Europe,' Mrs Rowbotham told her. 'It is fortunate that I am here to advise you.'

As the days passed and Rachel's strength returned, she began to long for the open air. She requested that they might go for a walk and Mrs Rowbotham took her to the park where they had met. 'This is not a suitable place, by the way, for unaccompanied young ladies.'

Rachel laughed. 'No. I think you were somewhat upset when we first met.'

'Ladies meet gentlemen in the house, not outside. It creates an erroneous impression. Any day, you will see young women in the Haymarket and Regent Street and in the Argyle Rooms whose reputation is scarcely to be considered.'

'Mrs Rowbotham, I think I shall not be venturing to such places. Now that I am recovered, I can endeavour to find a situation as a governess.'

Mrs Rowbotham looked at her with barely-concealed impatience. 'Before we discuss such matters, I have arranged for us to go on a vacation. I think it would be well for your health.'

'Oh, I did not realise. That would be delightful. But I cannot impose further upon your hospitality.'

'Nonsense. Mr Grainger has purchased tickets for us on the channel steamer. We are going to Belgium for a brief period.'

'Oh, that will be charming.' Then Rachel added doubtfully, 'Will Mr Grainger be there?'

'No. We have a mutually owned establishment in Brussels. We shall stay there but in the meantime Mr Grainger will be here in London and will attend to the running of this house in my absence.'

Rachel frowned. It seemed most unusual for a gentleman to run a house but then she reflected that when her grandmother died, her grandfather must have had to attend to such matters.

On the morning of their departure, Rachel waited in the hall. Her cases had all been packed by the maid; all her new clothes were included; Mrs Rowbotham had explained that she would need many changes of clothing because there were many social functions in Brussels which they would attend.

The footman carried the luggage out to the waiting carriage. Rachel looked in astonishment when Mrs Rowbotham came down the stairs accompanied by a girl of about twelve. She had long fair curls and blue eyes and she was dressed in an elegant little yellow dress with a laced bodice and a frilled skirt which reached just beyond her knees. The child smiled at Rachel.

'Rachel,' Mrs Rowbotham said, 'we are taking little Grace with us. Her parents are not comfortably off and are happy that she should be going with us for a holiday.'

'Oh, Mrs Rowbotham,' Rachel said in surprise. 'You are a most generous lady. Has Grace been staying here? Why have we not met?'

'No. Grace arrived only last night,' Mrs Rowbotham spoke rather curtly. 'And is very pleased to be here, aren't you, Grace?'

'Oh, yes.' Grace smiled cheerfully. 'I am going for a holiday and then Mrs Rowbotham has undertaken to find me a nice situation in a respectable household.'

Rachel took Grace's hand. 'You look like a little sister I once had,' Rachel said. She had not thought about Charlotte for a long time; the sudden memory took away for a moment the hope she was beginning to feel about her new life.

'I have six brothers and sisters,' Grace said. 'But when Mrs Rowbotham offered to take me, Mam was pleased. She couldn't afford to feed us all.'

They went in a carriage to the port and then boarded the steamer which would take them to Ostend.

Grace chattered about the other passengers and was frequently interrupted by Mrs Rowbotham.

'You must learn to be more subdued,' she said. 'It is not good taste to comment upon other people's behaviour. And you must lower your voice and speak in more modulated tones.'

'Oh, I remember what a naughty child I was,' Rachel laughed. 'I am sure Grace will learn very quickly when she gets older.'

'With proper training, it is perfectly possible for Grace to learn now,' Mrs Rowbotham said firmly.

They reached Brussels as darkness was falling. Grace had fallen asleep on the journey from Ostend but as they came into the station, she sprang from the carriage and began to dance along the platform.

'Come here,' Mrs Rowbotham said severely. Rachel looked with surprise at her violent expression. For a moment, she seemed to see a different person standing there.

Grace turned and came back.

'I'm sorry, Mrs Rowbotham.'

'Kindly put aside your rough ways,' she said firmly.

Rachel held Grace's hand as they walked in silence from the station. Doubt entered her mind again. There seemed to be a growing hostility in Mrs Rowbotham since they had left England. It began to seem strange that she had brought them to Brussels for a holiday. If she thought that Rachel needed to recuperate, why had they not gone to the country?

Mrs Rowbotham hailed a carriage. As they drove along the wide boulevards Rachel and Grace gazed with awe at the old buildings, the magnificent squares and avenues. When they reached the Grand Place in the old part of the town, Mrs Rowbotham pointed out the great churches and the Hotel de Ville, drawing their attention to the fine decorations on the great walls. 'An appreciation of art is most desirable in these parts,' she said as the carriage turned into a street off the square.

As they ascended the steps of a large house, Rachel was surprised to find two or three gentlemen leaving. She asked Mrs Rowbotham if other people lived in the house.

Mrs Rowbotham frowned. 'No. This is my house, but I have a number of ladies and other persons living here. These gentlemen are no doubt calling upon them.'

She led them into a large drawing room. Sitting by the window were two young girls of about fifteen and in another seat by the fireplace a girl of Grace's age. They looked up anxiously as Mrs Rowbotham entered. 'Good evening, girls.'

They all stood up and mumbled a reply. Rachel gazed in astonishment. Their young faces were made up with rouge and powder and their hair was dressed in styles fitting only to adults. But it was their clothes which gave her a feeling of disapproval. Their dresses were over-decorated with frills and flounces, the bodices were so tight that she could almost see their half-formed breasts beneath. Why were they dressed in this ridiculous fashion? How could Mrs Rowbotham countenance such behaviour? A picture of her bedroom in Mrs Rowbotham's house in London flashed across Rachel's mind. Was this woman in fact not a lady after all?

Grace was looking with admiration at the gaudy dresses of the girls. 'Oh, how lovely. Oh, Mrs Rowbotham can I have a dress like that?' She went over and gently touched the frills and then stepped back slightly as she noticed the low necklines, a look of incomprehension on her face. Then she laughed. 'You'd be cold in winter though, wouldn't you?'

None of the girls replied, looking doubtfully at Mrs Rowbotham.

Rachel turned apprehensively to Mrs Rowbotham. Had she made a terrible mistake in associating with this woman?

Mrs Rowbotham noticed her expression. She said pleasantly, 'These young girls are under my protection, as you and Grace are. They were in very poor circumstances when I befriended them.'

'You are most charitable, Mrs Rowbotham,' Rachel said slowly. She began to feel she was taking part in a charade, like the ones they had had at Mrs Hyamson's entertainments.

There was a perfunctory knock on the door and an elderly gentleman came in. He had long white hair and a grey beard which reached almost to his waist.

'Mrs Rowbotham,' he said quietly. 'It is good to see you again.'

Mrs Rowbotham smiled and shook hands but she did not introduce him to Rachel. 'Good evening. And have you come to call upon Veronica?'

The old man smiled and held out his hand to one of the fifteen-year-olds. 'I think she must be expecting me. A good girl, Mrs Rowbotham.'

Veronica came stiffly towards him, her eyes averted.

'Say good evening, Veronica,' Mrs Rowbotham said evenly.

'It is of no concern, Mrs Rowbotham. I prefer young ladies to be rather shy.'

He took Veronica's hand and led her from the room. Watching them, Rachel had a sudden overwhelming fear. Something awful was going to happen. She was trapped. She was about to speak to the girls when Mrs Rowbotham said firmly, 'Now, Rachel and Grace, I wish you to come upstairs with me. I want to have a talk with you.' They followed her. Mrs Rowbotham showed Rachel into a bedroom. 'This will be your room, Rachel. I shall take Grace along the hall and then return and talk to you.' She went to the door and before Rachel could speak, the key had turned in the lock.

Rachel dashed to the window. Her bedroom looked out over the street. Should she fling the window open and scream? But she saw that it too was locked. She walked around the room and idly opened a drawer in the dressing-table. A pile of photographs lay inside. She drew them out; perhaps they were pictures of Mrs Rowbotham's relatives, her late husband, or perhaps she had had children. Her fingers clutched the pictures as she looked in disbelief. There were naked men and women; young girls in strange positions.

She looked again at the room, the ornate furnishings which now told their own story. How could she have been so blind, so stupid? But how could she have known? Young ladies were never told of such things, they were not even told about marriage or having babies. From birth, she seemed to have been cocooned in a blanket of deception, a protection that had ironically exposed her through her ignorance. But always on the perimeter of her life there had been an awareness of sin and vice and all the other words Mr Damarell had used. Was this what he had meant? In the back of Rachel's mind were vague memories of things she had heard, suggestions she had seen in newspapers about women who lived immoral lives, the fallen women of the streets. She remembered the degraded women around Leicester Square. Was that what they had been doing? But these were young girls; Grace was only a child. What could it have to do with her?

The door opened and Mrs Rowbotham came in. 'Now, Rachel, I wish to speak with you.'

'What sort of place is this, Mrs Rowbotham?'

Mrs Rowbotham breathed deeply. 'This is a high-class establishment, Rachel. I pride myself on the way in which I look after my girls. You are fortunate to have the opportunity to live under such a roof.'

'What are all these men doing, Mrs Rowbotham? And what was that man doing with Veronica?'

'Rachel, kindly stop this absurd pretence. You are not a child.'

'Mrs Rowbotham, it is no pretence. It is only now that I have realised. I have seen those revolting pictures in the drawer. I scarcely comprehend their meaning but I have no intention of remaining in such a place.'

Mrs Rowbotham looked at her coldly. 'Don't tell me that such activities are unknown to you. And before you make any precipitate decisions, I think you should consider your position.'

'My position is that I shall return to England.'

Mrs Rowbotham laughed. 'And how does a young lady with no resources whatever achieve such an objective? It seems to me that the only way would be to follow the very course you are rejecting.'

'Then I can get a situation in an English household over here.' Sudden memories of her life in Egypt flashed across her mind. 'I can go to the British Embassy.'

'Rachel, let us stick to the facts. First of all, can you tell me what became of the child you bore?'

'Mrs Rowbotham, what has that to do with it?'

'A great deal, Rachel. It is my opinion that you killed that child.'

'Killed!' Rachel sat down on the bed. 'What do you mean? That is an infamous suggestion.'

'Perhaps. But did it receive a proper burial?'

'No. I had no money.'

'Then, what became of it?'

'I left it on the steps of a church.'

'Left perhaps to die?'

'No. It was already dead.'

Mrs Rowbotham laughed scornfully. 'Then I fear that you will be accused either of infanticide or of causing the death of your child by abandonment.'

Rachel gripped the brass bedstead, staring at Mrs Rowbotham, feeling an overwhelming desire to strike her. She felt that she would choke with the anger that seethed inside her. Anger heightened with the fear that perhaps what Mrs Rowbotham said was true; she could be treated as a criminal.

'I want to go immediately.' Her voice was shaking with hatred.

'However,' Mrs Rowbotham continued as though Rachel had not spoken. 'As long as you are in my care, you will be safe. In return, you will earn your keep.' Then she added patronisingly, 'And don't tell me that you were unaware of what was happening. I believe you will be willing enough.'

'Willing! How dare you suggest such a thing. I believed you were an honourable person. I had no idea.'

'Indeed.' Mrs Rowbotham blushed with anger. 'Do not presume to insult me. It was quite apparent to me, when I observed you in the park, the kind of girl you would become. Be thankful that I rescued you from such degradation.'

'Rescued.'

Rachel began to feel weak with emotion. She sat down on the bed. 'And what about Grace?' she said faintly.

'Some gentlemen prefer these young creatures. I cannot see the attraction myself, but it is not for me to judge.'

'It cannot be legal,' Rachel said angrily.

Mrs Rowbotham smiled complacently. 'I have nothing to fear. I offer these positions only to young girls from poor backgrounds whose lives would have been destitute. They would have ended up on the streets in any case. With me, they are rewarded with a standard of living unimaginable to them previously.'

'Mrs Rowbotham, you cannot keep me here under duress. Your ... patrons must know that.'

'May I assure you that the gentlemen who visit here are not concerned with either morality or duress. I advise you not to bother them with your small concerns.' Then she added, smiling, 'It is also my experience that many young ladies come to enjoy the life. No doubt, you may also come to appreciate its advantages. I expect to have these problems when they first arrive. The young girls in particular provide me with disagreeable situations. But I ensure that they are initially protected from too many demands.'

Rachel glared at her angrily. 'There would be no point in trying to imprison me here. I shall not behave as you wish.'

Mrs Rowbotham said abruptly, 'Let us not waste time on your abuse. First of all, perhaps you would examine the garments laid out on the chaise longue.' She went over and picked up a black lace undergarment which looked to Rachel like a bathing suit with no skirt and what appeared to be scarlet petticoats.

'What are they?'

'These are garments some of the gentlemen like. I hope you will find they are comfortable. You will discover that some persons have peculiar tastes but it is for you to accommodate them.'

'I shall accommodate nothing.'

Mrs Rowbotham smiled benignly. 'I may also say that all gentlemen enjoy a tussle. I believe the sort of firebrand you appear to be, with your lovely auburn hair, will cause much enjoyment.' Then she added, 'It would not be wise on your part to invite too much . . . force.'

She walked briskly to the door.

'You will not be working for the next week. During that time, you will meet with the other young ladies who will give you some advice about conduct. If you can behave with dignity, you will be permitted to dine with them tonight. Of course, any recalcitrant attitudes would involve your being locked in your room. I will come and fetch you at ten o'clock.'

'Ten o'clock?'

'Perhaps that seems late to you. But the young ladies appreciate a break; there is a long night ahead.'

Rachel sat on the bed again. As soon as she got out of this room, she would inspect the house, find some door or window to escape. She would write to Aunt Maria; she would not be able to ignore her terrible plight.

Rachel went briskly down the stairs when she was summoned and was shown into a room with half a dozen young ladies. Mrs Rowbotham ate in a separate room with the children and young girls.

Rachel looked at the girls around her in their scanty dresses and rouged cheeks. 'Why are you here? Why haven't you escaped?' she asked indignantly.

'You'll find out,' a fair-haired girl called Rosa said. 'If you try to escape, you will either be drugged or even killed. No one would know, would they?'

'Killed!'

'A girl disappeared only last week. She proved to be too awkward.'

'But why haven't you told anyone?'

Rosa laughed. 'We're never allowed out, are we? The doors are permanently locked. What do you think we can do?'

They told her incredible tales about their clients, so that even the horrors of Leicester Court began to seem less awful. At least there she had been free, there she could leave.

Rachel asked them what would happen to Grace.

'She won't know what's going to happen to her. She'll be given plenty of brandy beforehand to make her amenable. Even then, the children always make a fuss.'

Rachel spent the next week discussing her escape plans with the other girls. She would break one of the bars in a downstairs window. Even if she could not squeeze through she could scream to passers-by. Or she could do some injury to herself which would necessitate the attendance of a doctor.

The girls only laughed at her suggestions.

'Mrs Rowbotham has many accomplices. She would simply say that you were mentally deranged.'

'I don't think you want to get away,' Rachel said indignantly.

'Have you forgotten what England is like?' Rosa asked. 'What hope do we have there? At least here we have food and a roof over our heads.'

A week later, when Rachel was descending the stairs to go for her evening meal, she met Grace coming up with a tall, middle-aged man. He was breathing heavily and walking as though he had been drinking and Rachel stopped and said anxiously, 'Are you all right, Grace?'

The man pushed past her. 'Course she's all right. Come on. Get a move on.' He shoved Grace before him. Rachel looked at her terrified face, aghast, as they went into the bedroom.

A feeling of despair came over Rachel when she returned to her

221

room. First she tried to force the window again. Looking around her in frustration, she picked up a hair brush and smashed it against the glass. It had no effect; the glass was so thick that it was difficult even to see through. Next, she went over to the door and began to hit it harder and harder with the brush, with a shoe, and finally picked up a chair and crashed it against the door. Nothing happened, no one came.

Rachel lay down in exhaustion. The screams from Grace's room went on far into the night. Rachel realised that to get out of the house, she would have to use more than arguments with Mrs Rowbotham. She would have to use her brains, and get hold of those keys Mrs Rowbotham carried around with her.

Grace's voice sank to a low whining sound. Then there was silence.

The next day, Mrs Rowbotham made no mention of Rachel's behaviour the night before. She informed her that in future Rachel would go down to the drawing-room at five o'clock and wait with the other young ladies. If she was selected by a gentleman, she would take him to her room. Should she be engaged at ten o'clock, she would be permitted to take her meal later. All young ladies must have a proper meal to ensure their good health.

At five o'clock, Rachel sat waiting downstairs with her three companions. They were dressed in similar flamboyant clothes to her own, but she was surprised to find that they did not appear as dejected as they seemed during the meals. In answer to her question, Rosa said, 'It's no good eating your heart out about something you can't change.'

'I shall never submit,' Rachel said firmly. 'I shall threaten to report them, to tell their wives.'

The door opened and a man who looked like Mr Damarell came in. His eyes ran up and down her body, her low-necked gown and tight bodice. Rachel felt her heart beating violently; now was the moment when she must act. As he ran his hands through her hair, Rachel stepped back and pushed him away.

'Ho, ho. So you don't fancy me, eh?'

'Don't touch me,' she said defiantly.

'Well, well, we shall see about that. Let's repair to your apartment.'

Rachel stood where she was, but he grabbed her arm and dragged her from the room. She hit him violently across the face and he turned on her in fury, his arm raised. At the same moment, she heard a commotion at the front door, a woman's raised voice demanding entry and a man threatening to call the police if they were not admitted. Rachel's client immediately dropped her arm.

'I understand there are girls here who are under age and other persons held against their will,' the woman was saying.

The man pushed Rachel aside and hastily ran along the hall in the opposite direction, towards the back of the house. Rachel clung to the bannister, scarcely believing what she had heard.

The couple came into the hall followed by a protesting footman. The woman was tall and dressed in an elegant black coat with a small cloche hat on her fair hair. Rachel was astonished to see that the man wore a vicar's collar.

'Where is the mistress of this household?' the woman demanded. She saw Rachel at the bottom of the stairs and called out, 'Wait a moment. Do you reside in this place?'

'I am a prisoner in this place,' Rachel said quickly.

Before the woman could reply, Mrs Rowbotham appeared and said sharply, 'Go to your room, Rachel. I will deal with these intruders.'

Rachel hesitated. If these people had really come to help, what would they do if they discovered her past? Would they inform the police, as Mrs Rowbotham had threatened to do? Would she be condemned for abandoning her baby? Would they think she had killed it? The fears tumbled through her mind – but nothing mattered, except to escape from this place.

The woman saw her hesitation and added, 'We are here to help you, Rachel.'

'Please get me out of here,' Rachel shouted. 'I was coerced here. I have nowhere to go.' She spoke quickly, afraid that at any moment Mrs Rowbotham might somehow stop her.

'How dare you come into this establishment,' Mrs Rowbotham said angrily.

'We are here to ascertain what English girls live here and to return them to England,' the woman replied calmly.

'I shall call the police. You are intruders.'

Rachel pushed past Mrs Rowbotham and clutched the woman's arm. 'Don't leave without me. If you go, I shall never escape. There are other girls in the drawing-room. We are all imprisoned here.'

'Lead us to them.' The vicar lightly took her arm.

Mrs Rowbotham was instructing the footman to call the police as the man and woman followed Rachel. There were four girls in the drawing-room.

'I have come from England,' the woman said to them kindly. 'If any of you are here under duress, I will see to it that you are freed and return to England with me.'

The girls looked at each other uncertainly and then at Mrs Rowbotham standing in the doorway.

The clerical gentleman added quietly, 'You may return to England under our protection, ladies. Do not fear.'

Rachel looked at him, suddenly doubtful. Who were these people? Would they abduct her just as Mrs Rowbotham had done, perhaps take her somewhere even worse?

'Protection!' Mrs Rowbotham jeered as though in response to her fears. 'Who do you think these people are? These creatures will simply snatch you away and put you in some low-class den of iniquity. Or else they will take you to England and hand you over to the police. Beware of them, girls.'

Rachel waited. She looked at the woman's face. Surely she was genuine. But how could she know, what should she do? The four girls also stood in silence.

'Are you here under duress?' the woman asked. They did not reply.

'They are afraid of Mrs Rowbotham,' Rachel said anxiously. 'They will not speak in front of her.'

At that moment, the footman appeared. Behind him were two policemen. To Rachel's surprise, Mrs Rowbotham looked relieved to see them.

'Gentlemen, I should be grateful if you would remove these intruders from my house. They are making disgusting accusations,' she declared.

'What is your complaint?' The policeman spoke in French but Rachel could understand his words as they addressed the newcomers.

'Sir,' the fair woman said. 'I would like you to inspect this house. It is my belief that this is a house of ill-repute and that there are young people here who have been kidnapped and brought here against their will.'

The policeman looked at Mrs Rowbotham questioningly. 'Is this so, madam?'

'Certainly not.'

He then looked at the four girls but they did not speak.

'But they are afraid,' Rachel repeated impatiently. 'You know what you have told me,' she said to them. 'Why do you not take this opportunity to escape?'

'I have nowhere to go,' one of them said briefly.

'Then let us inspect the premises,' the woman said quietly.

Rachel quickly led the way upstairs and flung open the bedroom doors. There were no men to be seen; some of the girls were in bed, others were attending to their toilet.

'I see you are accustomed to police raids,' the vicar commented cynically.

Rachel said urgently, 'There are young girls here. And where is Grace?'

Mrs Rowbotham smiled at Rachel. 'I think you are imagining things, dear.'

'She is only a child,' Rachel said to the woman. 'She was enticed away and came over to Brussels with me and Mrs Rowbotham.'

The policemen turned to descend the stairs. 'We can see nothing untoward here, madam,' one of them said in English. 'I fear your allegations are without foundation. If you wish to take this matter further, you must lodge a formal complaint with the chief of police. We do not need persons coming from England to tell us how to conduct our department of justice. Perhaps you would both be good enough to depart.'

The vicar gentleman glanced at Rachel. 'Then we shall take this young lady with us. At least we can rescue her.'

Rachel felt a terrible fear that, even at this last moment, Mrs Rowbotham would prevent her from leaving.

Mrs Rowbotham said threateningly, 'Take her. And see what happens to her when I place information about her misdeeds before the English police. She may wish she had not returned.'

Rachel took her rescuer's arm and cried out, 'Oh, madam, it's not true. Don't leave me alone. I'm coming with you.'

They began to walk towards the front door and then Rachel stopped. In her anxiety to flee from the house, she had almost forgotten.

'How about Grace? I cannot leave without her. I promised I would rescue her.'

The woman looked at the policemen and demanded drily, 'It is a criminal offence in England to abduct children. Have you no such law in this country?'

'It would have to be proved, madam, and we have found no children here.'

Rachel said suddenly, 'Wait. They've hidden her.' Before Mrs Rowbotham could stop her, she dashed up the stairs to the second floor and burst into Grace's room, calling 'Grace, are you here?' There was no answer. She looked under the bed and then remembering what the girls had said about people being killed flung open the door of the ante-room. Grace was lying on the floor, her mouth bound and gagged with a man's tie, her arms and legs tied together.

'Come quickly,' Rachel called to the woman and the vicar. 'She is here.'

The man and woman dashed up the stairs, followed by Mrs Rowbotham and the police.

Once she was released, Grace clung to Rachel in terror. 'I know I shall die, Rachel. I told you I would.'

'No. No, you won't. We're going away, Grace. It's going to be all right.'

Mrs Rowbotham looked at the police. 'Let them take her,' she said contemptuously. 'She is a ward in my care, but she has been nothing but trouble. There is no gratitude for all I have done.' She turned to the woman. 'Now, get out of my establishment.'

The woman took Grace's hand and Rachel and the vicar followed them down the stairs and into the waiting carriage.

As the carriage began to move away, Rachel felt a sudden panic. Perhaps these people were really in league with Mrs Rowbotham and they were being taken away to some worse destination. Perhaps she and Grace would be killed. She looked back and saw the policemen appearing to remonstrate with Mrs Rowbotham.

'No doubt telling her to be more circumspect in future,' the woman commented contemptuously.

'Where are we going?' Grace began to look worried again. Rachel noticed the change in the child since she had last seen her. There was a permanent expression of fear on her face and she sat in a crouched position, as though she was shrinking into herself.

'We shall take the night boat to England,' the woman said. 'Then we will go to my house in London and we will find your parents and take you back to them.'

Grace looked even more fearful. 'But supposing my Mam lets some other person take me off to find me a situation.'

'No,' the woman said. 'I shall see it does not happen again.'

Then she turned to Rachel, and asked, 'And where is your home, Rachel?'

Rachel hesitated. 'I haven't got a home.'

The woman looked at her thoughtfully. She had vivid blue eyes that seemed to look into Rachel's soul, and when she smiled, her face appeared to light up with kindness. In spite of her doubts, Rachel had a sense of safety.

'Well, when we reach home, you must tell me all about it. I am sure we can help you.'

Rachel felt a gnawing anxiety at her words. She would never tell anyone about the child, it was that which had brought all this misery. It must be kept hidden for ever.

Overcome by their experiences, she and Grace both slept on the boat which took them to England and the train which rocked them all the way to London. Finally they transferred to a carriage which took them to a house in Hampstead. As they alighted, Rachel looked out in the early morning light across a large heath.

'It's the country,' she said, suspiciously. 'I thought we were going to London.'

'Yes. It is London, but quite far from the centre. But I have not told you my name, have I? I am Mrs Robertson. Josephine Robertson. And this gentleman is the Reverend Jonathon Bryant. Now, let us go in and have a warm drink and then I think you might both like a hot bath and a good long rest.'

Grace was still subdued, as though she feared some tragedy might yet befall her, but when Mrs Robertson suggested that, for a day or two, she might feel happier sharing a room with Rachel she managed to smile and said, 'Yes'. She followed Rachel into a neat, plainly furnished bedroom with two beds.

Rachel glanced at Mrs Robertson's calm face; if they were being tricked once again, she felt too tired to think about it. She would deal with that later.

They slept for most of the day and were woken by Mrs Robertson, who escorted them downstairs for a meal. The vicar had left and they ate alone with Mrs Robertson, who said that her husband was a barrister and would be returning later that evening.

They briefly met Mr Robertson, who said how glad he was that his wife and Reverend Bryant had been able to rescue them, but it was not until the next morning at breakfast that Mrs Robertson began to speak of their experiences.

'We are very anxious that these terrible practices should cease,' Mr Robertson said at the breakfast table. 'My wife intends to see that young people like yourselves do not suffer such abuse.'

When he had left for the Courts, Mrs Robertson said, 'Now that you are both rested, I am going to ask a lady doctor to come and see you, to ensure that you are well.'

Grace looked terrified and exclaimed, 'Oh, no! That happened to me in Belgium.'

'No,' Mrs Robertson said gently. 'It will not be like that. This lady will only wish to ensure that you have not contracted any disease.'

'Disease?'

'I am sure it would be nothing that cannot be cured.' She smiled. 'She will soon bring you back to health. But I think it unlikely that it will be necessary.'

'I have no knowledge of lady doctors,' Rachel looked puzzled.

'No. There are only a few, although we hope that there will be more and more. It has been a great struggle to establish that ladies have as much right to be doctors as men.'

Rachel frowned. She thought back to Kingsbridge, the men going to their places of work in the morning, the household of women following their domestic pursuits. Was it possible that ladies could partake in the professions that men followed? Since leaving Kingsbridge, she had almost longed for that protected world which had once seemed so restrictive.

Rachel looked at the doctor with interest when she arrived. She had almost expected her to be wearing masculine garments, but she had a pretty face and wore a dark green silk gown with a frill round the hem and a green velvet jacket.

'This is Dr Caroline Roach,' Mrs Robertson said.

'I think you have both had an unhappy time,' Dr Roach said in a soft voice. 'Now, Grace. I expect you would like Rachel to come up with us and we'll make sure you're both fit and well.'

In a quiet and unobtrusive way, as she chatted pleasantly to Grace, she confirmed that the young girl appeared to be unaffected. 'I'll just examine you again in a week's time, to make sure,' she said casually. 'I can tell you that such activities frequently cause terrible diseases.'

She turned to Rachel.

'I have no need of such an examination,' Rachel said firmly. 'I did not suffer the same privations as Grace.'

Dr Roach hesitated. 'Are you sure it would not be wise to—?'

'No. There is no need.'

Dr Roach nodded pleasantly. 'Of course, it must be for you to say,' she said lightly.

Rachel felt as though a burden had been removed from her mind. They were not to be imprisoned; she could make her own decisions, she was free.

Dr Roach turned to Grace. 'I fear your experiences will have had other effects, dear. We must make sure that your heart and mind recover as well as your body.'

The examination concluded, they returned to the drawing-room.

'Now,' Mrs Robertson said. 'I must tell you a little about what we are doing. We have heard that there are frequent instances of the enticement and kidnapping of young persons on both sides of the Channel. It is called the white slave trade, and a number of persons in this country are determined to stop these practices. We have formed a committee and are making efforts to bring these people to book and also to persuade Parliament that new laws should be passed.' She paused. 'I fear it will be distasteful to you, but we must know the whole story. We must know exactly what happened to you both. You see, Members of Parliament are reluctant to commit themselves to anything which involves the greater freedom of women. So we must have real evidence. Do you understand?'

Rachel nodded. 'Yes, but I fear Grace's experiences are worse than mine.'

'Perhaps. But I must also have your story as well, Rachel.'

Rachel sighed. She thought of Mrs Rowbotham's threats. 'I have done nothing criminal,' she said slowly.

Mrs Robertson looked surprised. 'Rachel, dear, we are not here to accuse you. You must have faith in us.'

The front door-bell rang and a maid brought in another lady.

'Ah,' Mrs Robertson said with pleasure, 'It is a delight to see you again, Alice.' She turned to Rachel and Grace. 'This is Miss Alice Grenville. She is an important and devoted member of our committee.'

Rachel took Alice's hand. Although she appeared to be no older than Rachel, Alice gave an impression of dignity and confidence. She was tall and elegant and dressed in a neat black gown and jacket with a white silk blouse beneath. She had an olive complexion and her long, golden hair was tied back with black ribbon.

'Hallo, Rachel,' she said in a deep, soft voice. 'I am sure we shall be friends.'

'Yes.'

Rachel took Alice's outstretched hand with a curious feeling of expectation and almost of fear. She knew instinctively that she had never met anyone like Alice before and that Alice's words were not just a polite formality. It was as though everything she said would always be the truth. Rachel had a premonition that this beautiful woman was going to change her life in a way she could not yet anticipate.

Chapter 12

Rachel followed Grace into the parlour with a feeling of apprehension, seeing the long table surrounded by high-backed chairs. Would other people be interviewing them? What sort of questions would they ask? Looking at her expression, Miss Grenville smiled and said, 'It is not meant to appear inhospitable, Rachel. We use this room for meetings.'

'It merely appears rather formal, Miss Grenville.'

'Please call me Alice. I think there is little disparity in our ages.'

Mrs Robertson was already sitting at the head of the table on which lay large sheets of writing paper.

'As I explained this morning, we are conducting a campaign to get this corruption of young girls stopped. In order to do that, we have to be formal in our methods and present coherent evidence to the various committees. It is essential that we appear business-like.'

Caroline Roach and Alice sat by her side, facing Rachel and Grace. No one else appeared.

'Now, Grace,' Mrs Robertson said when they were all seated. 'I want you to tell us all you can remember about what happened.'

Grace frowned and Caroline Roach smiled at her encouragingly.

'Where did you meet Mrs Rowbotham?'

'I was going on an errand for my mother.'

'And where was that?'

'Near Waterloo, where we live. It's called the Rookeries.'

'What was the errand?' Alice asked.

Grace blushed. 'We didn't have anything to eat. I was going to nick some bread.'

Mrs Robertson said slowly, 'Have you ever been in trouble through performing these errands?'

231

'Oh, no. I only went when I had to.'

'Where was your father?'

'He was out looking for work. But he didn't always find it.'

'And Mrs Rowbotham?'

'She saw me walking along and she smiled at me and asked where I was going. I said I was going shopping for me Mam.'

Grace explained how Mrs Rowbotham had asked about her family and then said she might be able to help them. So she went back with Grace to the two rooms where she lived with her parents and her six brothers and sisters. Mrs Rowbotham had told her Mam that she could find Grace a situation as a maid in a nice house and how she would be looked after. Her Mam had looked doubtful at first, but Mrs Rowbotham had promised that Grace would write and tell her how she was getting on. Next, Mrs Rowbotham gave her a document to sign. Her Mam couldn't read or write very well, but she signed it as best she could.

'She took me to this house where I met Rachel and the next day we went on the ship,' Grace concluded.

'And how did you get these clothes you are wearing?'

'Mrs Rowbotham had lots of girls' clothes in her house.'

'Didn't you wonder why?'

'She said she helped lots of young girls.'

'And then?'

Grace looked tense. 'I don't want to tell you any more.'

Mrs Robertson was silent for a moment. 'Grace, we are trying to save you further embarrassment. In order to put your case before Parliament, we must have the evidence. You would not want to give such information if there were gentlemen present, would you?'

'No!'

'Then if you tell us, we will write down your words and you can sign the document. Can you read, Grace?'

'Yes. I went to the board school till I was eleven.'

'Good. Then we will never have to refer to these unpleasant matters again. When that is done, I shall take you to see your mother, tell her what has happened and request her permission to place you in a safe home where you can learn a trade of some kind. She will be able to visit you there.'

'Will Rachel be there?'

Mrs Robertson was about to say yes when Alice interrupted. 'Although Rachel will visit there, it is unlikely that she will remain. We do not wish to misinform you. But we promise that she will come to see you often.'

'Now, Grace.'

Grace told them in a low voice of the humiliations to which she had been subjected. The man was violent and when she shouted he hit her and forced her to the floor. He made her remove her clothes. She thought he was drunk and all night he repeatedly attacked her and forced her to do terrible things. She kept calling but no one came to help her.

'You need not tell us any more, Grace,' Mrs Robertson said. 'Now, I have made a note of what you have said. I will read it to you and then you must sign it.'

Dr Roach said she would take Grace for a walk while Rachel related her story.

When they were gone, Mrs Robertson turned to Rachel, asking, 'How did you meet Mrs Rowbotham?'

'I was sitting in a park, early one morning.'

'Alone?'

'Yes.' Rachel blushed. 'I had run away from my home because I had had a disagreement with my aunt and uncle.'

She told them about Kingsbridge and the death of her parents, and of how the Damarells had adopted her. As she described her departure from Kingsbridge and her arrival in London, she dismissed the thought of telling them the whole truth. The agony of those months, the days in Leicester Court and the final loss of the baby were experiences she could never share with anyone. It would also have meant speaking of Jacob – the humiliation of her trust in him, the even greater humiliation of his desertion, were things she could not yet confront. She felt a bitter anger that, even now, she still could not forget his final words, 'Wait for me'. It was as though a part of her would be waiting for ever, as though no matter what happened, there was a bond between them that she would never experience with anyone else.

'But why were you in the park at that hour?'

'I had nowhere to go. I had been forced to leave my previous accommodation. My money had almost run out.'

'And what did you intend to do?'

'I intended to find some inexpensive accommodation. And then Mrs Rowbotham offered to take me in until I found a situation as a governess.'

Rachel looked from Mrs Robertson to Alice. She knew there were questions they could ask which would reveal her lies. If they asked for the name and address of Mrs Wentworth they would find out about her dishonesty. Supposing they asked for the address of the Damarells? Surely they would want her to contact Aunt Maria, to settle the disagreement and return home? Then she would be exposed. And what if they insisted on a medical examination – would Dr Roach know what had occurred? Luckily, they seemed to be more interested in Mrs Rowbotham.

'What happened to you in Brussels?'

'I was not subjected to the same humiliation as Grace.'

'But why not? Surely you were taken there for that purpose.'

'Yes. But Mrs Rowbotham was concerned that I should behave correctly . . . with the visitors. I spent about a week with the other girls and they told me what was expected. The very night you arrived was to have been spent with my first . . . client.'

'So you remained . . . unviolated?'

'Yes.'

'I see now why you did not desire a medical examination,' Alice nodded.

'It is not necessary.'

'No,' agreed Mrs Robertson. 'How old are you, Rachel?'

'Twenty.'

Mrs Robertson sighed. 'Well, although you are under age it will be difficult to prove that any evil intentions were harboured by Mrs Rowbotham as nothing had yet occurred.'

'I was locked in my room and never permitted to leave the house.'

'Yes. We can prove that much. But the trouble is that you went willingly to Brussels.'

'It was under a false impression. I did not know her intentions.'

'No, dear. We understand that. But the problem lies in persuading a Select Committee of the House of Commons. You see, they persist in believing that any female found in that situation is a willing accomplice.'

234

'That is monstrous. How could Grace be responsible?'

'Grace is a different case. Young persons are protected by law up to the age of thirteen, but beyond that you are presumed to know what you were doing.' She glanced at Rachel's clothes, the low-necked red silk gown and lace and velvet cape which she was wearing when they escaped from Brussels. 'Perhaps you would like to borrow a gown of mine. We must be about the same size.'

Rachel blushed. 'She forced these clothes upon me. And we had to rouge our cheeks and colour our lips. And there were black lace under-garments in the bedroom which I was supposed to change into when the gentlemen came.'

Mrs Robertson nodded. 'That must also be in your statement, Rachel. It provides evidence of Mrs Rowbotham's intentions.'

Alice shook her head. 'It would not prove to a Select Committee that Rachel was not disposed to wear them. Well, we must do what we can. We must depart now, Josephine. We have the meeting to attend.'

'Yes.' Mrs Robertson stood up. 'Perhaps you would like to accompany us, Rachel. It is important for you to know what is happening.'

They went by carriage to a large hall in the centre of London, while Alice briefly explained that their committee were trying to get support for the abolition of the Contagious Diseases Act. Rachel was silent, almost ashamed of her ignorance. She had never heard such topics being discussed before. She had never even been to a public meeting. In Kingsbridge, Mr Damarell had attended parish meetings and those connected with the affairs of the church. She had also heard Richard and Thomas discussing what they called union meetings – although these had never been mentioned in front of Mr Damarell – but ladies had never been involved in such matters. She remembered how she had wished to get beyond the restricted interests suitable for females, how she had always felt there must be more meaning to life. Perhaps this would be what she had been seeking.

When they entered the hall, it was filled with both men and women eagerly talking to each other. She listened with curiosity to ladies ardently discussing the political situation and the absurdity of an Act of Parliament of which they disapproved.

To her surprise, Alice said, 'I am addressing the meeting tonight, Rachel. Would you like to come on the platform with me?'

Rachel's eyes opened wide in astonishment. 'Me? Oh, no, Alice. I have never taken part in such an event.'

Alice laughed. 'Then this will be an introduction.' She looked at Rachel with her forthright expression. 'Come, Rachel. You must begin to think about the world beyond domestic walls.'

What did Alice mean by that, what world was she thinking about? Rachel realised that in spite of her impatience with feminine activities, her hopes and fears all centred around the question of what would happen to her – would someone propose to her one day, would she have a home and children, would she enjoy that social life which, even if it had been circumscribed, she had enjoyed in Kingsbridge? It had not seemed within the orbit of a woman's world to initiate events beyond that. In her own mind, she had always been a rebel, yet she saw now that her childhood rebellions were not the sort of thing that Alice was talking about.

'Rachel, we have so much to discuss,' Alice said, as though she knew Rachel's thoughts. 'But that will be later. Come.' She led Rachel up to the platform, where the Reverend Bryant was sitting. He stood up and shook her hand.

'Good evening, my dear. And have you come to help us? Perhaps you would like to tell us about your experiences in Belgium.'

Rachel blushed, shaking her head. 'Oh, no. I couldn't do that. Not in public.'

The Reverend Bryant smiled. 'We must all do what we can, you know, to get these pernicious practices stopped. I expect you will soon want to join us in our campaign.'

Rachel nodded doubtfully and sat down. He introduced Alice as a member of the committee formed to combat the Contagious Diseases Act.

Alice rose and began to speak. Rachel reflected yet again how elegant she looked. Alice was the kind of lady of whom Aunt Maria had approved, but what would she think of this situation? Rachel listened with pleasure as Alice spoke unemphatically in her soft, deep voice. The audience seemed to be entranced.

Alice told them how the Act had been passed to protect soldiers and sailors from diseases they might contract from prostitutes.

Rachel blushed. For a lady to use such a word seemed almost an immoral act in itself. She glanced sideways at the Reverend Bryant. Although he looked pained, he did not seem to find it unacceptable. The audience appeared to have no reaction.

'The terms of the Act reflect the thinking of those who initiated it,' Alice said. 'In the first place, it accepts the idea of prostitution as a natural state. It implies that it is acceptable for these practices to continue, as long as men are protected from its dangers. Nowhere is there any suggestion that men should be discouraged from such practices, or that they are in any way responsible. Ladies and gentleman, it is the committee's belief that these men are responsible and that if the Act exists at all, then they should be similarly subject to its provisions. In other words, men should have regular medical inspections to see if they are fit to consort with women. As to the prostitutes themselves, they can be arrested by the police on mere suspicion. There is evidence to prove that the police themselves molested young women who were not prostitutes, merely because they were seen in music-halls or talking to soldiers.'

A voice from the audience protested that as far as the prostitutes were concerned, the medical examinations were voluntary.

Rachel watched Alice's eyes flash in anger, but she continued quietly, 'I am afraid that is not the case, sir. There are plain-clothes policemen circulating in our garrison towns who can bring before the magistrates any woman whom they suspect of prostitution. They need only suspect. They need present no evidence. The Morals Police can then request her to submit voluntarily to medical examinations for up to a year. If she refuses, she is taken before a magistrate who can then order her to be medically examined. If she persists in her refusal, she can be sent to gaol. That does not appear to me to be voluntary and merely places a woman, if she does submit voluntarily, in the position of incriminating herself.'

Alice paused and said quietly to the man, 'Would you find that acceptable, sir, if it happened to your wife or daughter?'

'It would never happen to my wife or daughter,' the man replied indignantly. 'They don't go out unaccompanied as the likes of you do.'

Another voice from the back of the hall shouted, 'These women deserve all they get. A disgrace to our wives and daughters.'

'It's men who make them so,' Alice retorted quietly.

Rachel eyed the speaker indignantly. What did he know about such things? She stood up suddenly.

'Perhaps you are unaware that there are prosperous houses in this vicinity where young women and even children are imprisoned. They are held there to serve the purposes of men.' Her voice was shaking. She realised she was speaking too softly for anyone to hear.

'Speak up, Miss,' the man shouted in a mocking voice.

Rachel cleared her throat. She tried to raise her voice, but she could not control the trembling as she continued. 'Young women do not choose this way of life. They are forced into it by circumstances.'

'I bet you didn't take much forcing.' He laughed.

A man near him interrupted. 'There is no need to insult this lady,' he said sharply. 'You only show your ignorance.'

'Oh, ignorance, eh?' The first speaker turned on the man and began to advance towards him. 'And what sort of thing are you?'

Rachel watched in horror as two or three others followed him. Someone began to shout, a whistle blew and two policemen appeared from the back of the hall. There was a brief scuffle and the group were ejected unceremoniously.

'I'm sorry,' Rachel whispered to Alice guiltily. 'I shouldn't have spoken.'

'It was brave of you, Rachel. Don't worry. You will become accustomed to these interruptions.' Alice calmly turned to the audience. 'Now, ladies and gentlemen, perhaps you may have questions you would like to ask.'

To Rachel's surprise, almost everyone seemed to agree with Alice, and they all produced facts and figures to support the view that the Act was immoral. She then asked for contributions to the expenses of the campaign and explained that next week she was to meet members of the Select Committee to put her case.

As the audience began to depart, Alice turned to Rachel and smiled. 'A bit bewildering for you.'

Rachel nodded. 'It's just that I know so little about such matters, Alice. I just couldn't think of what to say.'

'It's all right, Rachel. It took us all some time to learn. It's hard to talk to an unsympathetic listener.'

'Then I must learn, Alice. Even when I was with Mrs Rowbotham, even when I realised what was happening, I never thought about prostitution.'

As Rachel spoke the word, she felt she had taken a step into the unknown. For her to utter such a word was unimaginable. On entering the hall, she had had a sense of danger, but now she seemed to have a sense of security, a kind of hope. Even if you were a woman, you could say what you thought, you were capable of having opinions. The world didn't need to be a menacing place. Women had to fight for the right not to need protection.

Alice raised her eyebrows in agreement. 'There are many other things to think about too.' Then she smiled. 'I'm so glad we met, Rachel.'

'Oh, yes, Alice. So am I.'

When they returned to her home in Hampstead, Mrs Robertson announced that she would be going to the north in a few days' time with her husband. 'He is engaged on a case and I shall take the opportunity to see interested persons there who may further our cause. While I am away, Alice has offered to take you to her home near Hyde Park.'

Rachel felt a surge of excitement. She hesitated. 'It is very kind of you both. But I have no income, Mrs Robertson, and had intended to seek a position as a governess to support myself. I cannot impose upon your hospitality.'

'You will not be imposing,' Alice said decisively. 'We will work out your future together.'

'And in the mean time, I will take Grace to see her mother and then get her settled in the house at Winchester, if they have room,' Mrs Robertson added.

Alice's apartment was in a large block looking out over Hyde Park.

'My grandparents lived near here,' Rachel said thoughtfully.

'Did they leave you no inheritance?'

Rachel shook her head. 'No. I understand my Papa lost everything in Egypt.'

'But how?'

'My aunt never told me exactly. I don't know whether it was through dishonesty or ineptitude. I think he borrowed money from the bank which employed him and ran up horrendous debts. I only know it included everything my grandfather left Mama in the Will.'

Rachel frowned. 'I have never spoken about my parents since they died. It's as though I've shut out their memory because it is too painful.'

'Yes. It probably was,' Alice said. 'But I hope now you're here, you'll have the peace of mind to think about your life. There's so much to do, Rachel,' she said enthusiastically.

They were in the large, airy bedroom which Alice had allocated to Rachel. Alice sat on the white counterpaned bed. She looked at Rachel reflectively.

'When we first met, I saw great potential in you. It's as though you have enormous resources that you haven't yet developed.'

'Oh, and I thought how different you are, Alice, from anyone I've ever known. You make me feel as though life can be so much more exciting.'

Alice smiled. 'Oh, I think it is. I was always determined that I wouldn't be a dreary housekeeper for a dominating man.'

'But how did you achieve it?'

'Well, I can't pretend that I didn't have great opportunities. My parents had liberal views and believed in the equality of men and women.'

'But surely men and women aren't equal in many ways. Women are physically weaker and they need protection from any arduous exertions because their bodies are meant only to cope with child rearing.'

Alice rolled her eyes. 'Yes, I know. And that when menstruating they should rest and that they are prone to hysteria as a result of their enfeebled condition.' She shook her head dismissively.

'Menstruation,' Rachel said slowly. She had never spoken the word before. Alice used these unspeakable words as though they were a natural part of everyday conversation. Would she ever be able to do so without feeling guilty?

'Yes, menstruation is just a normal, if tiresome event. As far as I can see, half the male population don't even know it happens. When one friend of mine married, her husband observed that he understood that ladies had a headache once a month. Can you imagine that?'

Rachel shook her head. 'Well, it's not something that one discusses with gentlemen, is it?'

'Why not?'

'It's not very nice, is it?'

Alice stood up and tossed her long hair back over her shoulders. 'I think it's neither nice nor nasty. It just is. And I think anything is discussable. Anyhow, I don't intend to marry. It doesn't interest me.'

'But why?' Rachel queried. She remembered Sophie saying the same thing, but she had been only a young girl at the time. Yet Alice made her feel now that it was not only possible; life might even be better.

'It seems to me it's a choice between having a career or being a wife.'

'Mrs Robertson is married.'

'Yes. There are some women who manage it, I admit. But whenever it's a choice between her activities and her husband's, she always seems to sacrifice her own wishes. It's as though he permits her to devote herself to the committee, rather than seeing it as a right.'

'Alice, what am I to do about an income? I must find some employment.'

'I think the only path to follow at the moment is to be involved in political activities, try to influence Parliament, get new laws. People like myself who have the income and opportunity to devote themselves to the cause of women have a moral duty to do so.'

'Well, I'm not in that position.'

Alice came over to where Rachel was standing by the window and put her hands on Rachel's shoulders, looking earnestly into her eyes. 'Yes, you can be, Rachel. If you want to.'

Rachel was silent for a moment. Then she said slowly, 'Yes, Alice. I do. You make it seem as though life has some purpose.'

'Good. I have had an idea. The committee are in need of someone who can organise meetings, arrange visits and interviews with influential persons about the Contagious Diseases Act. You could help Mrs Robertson and the Reverend Bryant with their white slave activities.'

'Do you think I could?'

'Of course! It will give you an income and we will furnish one of the drawing-rooms as an office. And you are so attractive, Rachel. I am sure men would listen to you.'

Rachel laughed. 'As they do to you. But I'm afraid I don't know very much, Alice.'

'It's not what you know, Rachel, as much as what you believe, and you'll discover that as you start to think about it.'

During the next few months Rachel felt that she was learning more about life than she had done in the whole of her previous twenty years. She went to meetings with Alice and other members of the committee, and to the House of Commons to listen to debates and meet the few Members of Parliament who supported their cause. In the evenings, she and Mrs Robertson accompanied the Reverend Bryant and members of the Salvation Army to Argyle Street and the Haymarket, where they talked to prostitutes who were offered positions in domestic service if they would abandon their way of life.

At first Rachel was shocked at the prostitutes' wretched appearance and at their ribald remarks and obscene conversations. Yet she knew that their assertions were true. She remembered what the girls had told her in Belgium. They had a better life than they would ever have in service, even if they could get a job. They had clothes and a bed to lie on, even if they never had much sleep in it. How could the dismal life which the Reverend Bryant offered them have any appeal? She confided her thoughts to Alice.

'He deplores the fact that many of them return to their old ways but he forgets how they are treated by the mistresses of many households.'

Alice smiled. 'He is concerned for their souls, Rachel.'

'Is that what you are concerned with, Alice?'

'No, of course not. I am just trying to get equality of treatment between men and women who indulge in the same activities. But at least he is on our side.'

'It seems natural to me that women should be defending other women, but somehow it seems strange that men should be involved in such things.'

Alice laughed. 'Rachel, it is a good thing that you should question motives, even if they turn out to be honest. It's the only way we can discover what we believe ourselves.'

It was on a visit one day with Mrs Robertson to the House of Commons that she met Ramsay. They had gone to give a report to a Committee on the activities of Mrs Rowbotham and the white slave traffic. The gentlemen present then studied Grace's statement but only one of them offered to support their cause. He introduced himself as Ramsay Harris and said he was a barrister. When he heard that Rachel was the secretary of the committee, he suggested that she should return with him to his chambers and acquaint him with the committee's activities.

As Rachel stepped into his carriage, she felt a sense of freedom. For the first time in her life, she was being treated as an equal by a man. He was asking her advice, was interested in her opinions. She was not just a woman; she was an individual.

They went to Ramsay's rooms in the Temple and afterwards he suggested they should go to the Savoy for dinner. Rachel hesitated. She was wearing what she now called her working clothes, a black gown and jacket and no jewels. She was scarcely dressed for an evening occasion. Then she smiled and agreed. It was not really a matter of concern.

Ramsay was tall and she supposed he was handsome and Rachel realised that she had not really noticed any man since Jacob's departure. Suddenly she remembered the joy she had felt on that first occasion when Jacob walked across the lawn towards her in the sunshine. She sighed impatiently. She had no wish to remember, he belonged to a past from which she had escaped. This was her life now, she was free, she could make her own decisions, follow her own course through life.

She had not been to the Savoy before and she looked with pleasure at the sumptuous furnishings and the great chandeliers. Ramsay appeared to be known by all the waiters and clientele who, he told her, were mainly writers and playwrights, artists and City gentlemen.

'What do you do?' Rachel asked.

'I act in the criminal courts, mostly for the defence.'

'Can you choose who you defend?'

Ramsay laughed. 'It depends what briefs you are offered. Presumably most people think I'm better at defence than prosecution.'

'Surely if a person is innocent, that is not difficult,' Rachel said naïvely.

Ramsay laughed again. He had a cheerful face and kind brown eyes. 'It's when they're not innocent that it becomes difficult. Perhaps you would like to come to the courts one day and observe the conduct of a trial.'

Words flashed through her mind; courts, justice, criminals. They represented the apotheosis of the male world and she was now free to enter such a place. She felt a thrill of satisfaction and said, 'Yes, I would.'

'Good. I'll send my carriage for you. Tomorrow?'

'Oh, I don't know. I have work to attend to, you know.'

Ramsay smiled. 'Yes, of course. But I can assure you that this may be all a part of your work. It is to be hoped that the persons responsible for events in Belgium will eventually find themselves in court.'

Rachel frowned. 'Do you suppose that I would have to be a witness in that event?'

'It would be most desirable, Rachel.'

'But I cannot imagine—'

'Then come. Acquaint yourself with the procedure. It can be an intimidating experience if you don't know what to expect.'

Rachel breathed deeply. 'Yes. I will.'

The extended route they took on their return journey to Alice's apartment happened to pass the house in which Sophie had lived. Looking at the house, Rachel had a sudden longing to see her. It seemed to link up with the thoughts she had had recently about her life. At last, she was beginning to look back on the past without fear, as a continuous process that had brought her to where she was.

'I have a friend living in that house,' she observed. 'I must call upon her.'

'Now?' Ramsay asked doubtfully. 'It is almost midnight.'

Rachel laughed. 'No. Not now. She was in Egypt when I last tried to contact her. But I must leave a card tomorrow.'

Rachel followed Ramsay as he went up the steps to Alice's apartment in Hyde Park and rang the bell. Then he took her hand and said, 'It has been a great pleasure to be with you, Rachel. I hope I shall see you tomorrow in court.'

'Yes, you will,' Rachel smiled. Looking into his eyes, she saw the intimate expression she had known long ago, something she had almost forgotten and had no wish to remember.

'Goodnight,' she said abruptly. 'And thank you.'

Alice was reading in the drawing-room when Rachel entered. 'I've been concerned about you, Rachel. Where have you been?'

'But surely Josephine told you. She said she would send a message. I went to Ramsay Harris's chambers to discuss our case.'

'Yes, she did. I cannot suppose that the meeting took so long.'

'No. He invited me to dinner.'

'Ah.' Alice pursed her lips.

Rachel looked at her flushed cheeks. There was a strange expression on Alice's face. 'I'm sorry if I worried you. Are you feeling all right, Alice?' she asked anxiously.

'Of course I am.'

'It was thoughtless of me. Of course, I have never stayed out so before.'

Alice stood up. 'I shall go to bed now.' She turned at the door. 'I just missed you, Rachel.'

Rachel walked slowly up the stairs, feeling bewildered. There had been something she could not understand in Alice's expression. Her thoughtlessness may have been irritating, but why should Alice look so distraught? It was only a trivial matter.

The next day, Ramsay's carriage appeared and took her to the Criminal Courts. She sat in the public gallery and watched the trial of a man who was charged with murdering his wife and child. She felt a moment of panic when it was stated that they had lived in a room in an alley off Leicester Court. Memories of the terrible slums, the rats, the birth of her child, made her feel as though it was she who was being questioned. Those awful words Mrs Rowbotham had used, 'infanticide', 'killing a child by abandonment' echoed in her mind. It could be her, standing there.

Then she saw Ramsay. She had scarcely recognised him in his wig but at one point he looked up and nodded and she managed to smile.

The man was examined by the prosecution, who accused him of deliberately giving his wife and child a poisonous substance which had killed them. His replies were scarcely audible and the judge shouted at him to speak up. He said that it had been a mistake, that he had thought it was a bottle containing gin which he had found on a rubbish heap.

No. He had no employment. And how did he live? Presumably by stealing and thieving, the prosecution suggested.

Rachel stood up. She wanted to shout at the judge, to tell him the horror of these people's lives, that he could not understand what they suffered. She opened her mouth, but the words would not come. Suddenly, she burst into tears and rushed from the court. She called a cab and went back to Hyde Park. She knew that Alice was right about the injustice done to women; they had no rights, no freedom, no careers. Yet how many of the reformers had ever known, as she had, what it was like to live in such degradation? And she had known it for only a few months. In a way, Mrs Rowbotham had been right. These girls in Brussels had a better life than these poor wretches.

'Rachel, are you upset about something?' Alice asked that evening. She looked at Rachel anxiously.

'I suppose I am.' Rachel forced herself to speak. 'You know the trial I've just been telling you about. When I had no money I stayed briefly in that place, Leicester Court.'

'Where? In those slums?' Alice stared at her with disbelief.

'Yes. In a room. That's why I was relieved to go with Mrs Rowbotham. After that experience, I couldn't see what she was really like.'

'But why didn't you tell us?'

'It had nothing to do with the case, had it?'

Alice shook her head, looking offended. 'I wish you had said. It's as though you don't trust me.'

'I'm sorry. It's difficult to talk about it. I just wanted to put it out of my mind.'

Alice sighed. 'Well, I've been thinking. Perhaps you've been working too hard. We never entertain ourselves. It's always meetings and conferences and things like that, isn't it? You seemed to enjoy the Savoy last night with Ramsay. Perhaps we could go somewhere tonight. Just the two of us?'

Rachel smiled. 'Yes, perhaps we could. I thought you had no interest in such things.'

'Well, if it pleases you, I would enjoy it, too.'

'I suppose we should be accompanied by gentlemen.'

Alice frowned indignantly. 'Nonsense, Rachel. That is just an example of this male-dominated society. We'll go to the Carlton Rooms. Why don't you go and change into one of the gowns you have had made?'

Rachel smiled. 'I haven't worn an evening gown for so long. It might be entertaining.'

Rachel contemplated herself in the looking-glass. She wondered briefly whether it was appropriate to her new interests that she was still subject to female vanity. When she went downstairs, Alice was awaiting her, wearing a dark blue gown which enhanced her long golden hair and her blue eyes.

'On, Alice, you look lovely.'

Alice shrugged. 'I wish I could enjoy it, but I can never forget that it is encouraging men to look upon us as objects of their own desires.'

'Oh, Alice. You are so serious.'

The door-bell rang and the maid brought a card for Rachel.

'Oh, it's Ramsay,' she said cheerfully. 'Please request him to come in.'

Alice frowned. 'Were you expecting him?'

'Oh, no. But he saw me at the court today and is probably puzzled that I left so peremptorily.'

Ramsay came in, looking anxious and expressed his concern. 'I saw that you looked disturbed. I should not have suggested that you come.'

'Oh, please. I shall come again. It seems to me monstrous that these poor people are treated so.'

Ramsay nodded. 'I agree with you. That is why I always try to act for the defence. But you get a false impression from only one visit. On the whole the juries are disposed to sympathise with these unfortunates. There are many who go free who really should not.'

'Then that seems to me only justice.'

'There are charitable organisations who are working on their behalf,' Alice said.

'Indeed,' Ramsay agreed. 'I am myself involved with such a charity. We visit those places and try to find employment and accommodation for worthy causes. Perhaps you would like to join us?'

Alice said abruptly, 'At the moment, I think Rachel is fully occupied with her work relating to the Contagious Diseases Act and also in relation to the white slave trafficking.'

'Yes, of course.'

'But I should be pleased to help you, Ramsay,' Rachel interposed. 'You can tell me about it.'

Alice stood up and said peremptorily, 'Now, I fear we cannot delay longer. We are going for dinner.'

Rachel turned to Alice. 'In view of Ramsay's kindness to me last night, might he not be invited to join us?'

Ramsay smiled. 'Indeed, I would welcome that. My carriage is outside.'

Alice looked icily at Rachel but she said nothing as they left the house. She was also silent as they drove along while Ramsay spoke about that morning's trial and how the man was obviously guilty.

During the meal, Rachel became aware of the animosity that Alice felt towards Ramsay, which was highlighted when she began to speak about marriage and its inherent shortcomings.

Ramsay pointed to happy marriages such as that of Mr and Mrs Robertson, who combined their individual activities in what appeared to be complete equality.

'Perhaps,' Alice said. 'But theirs is conducted, as many are, on a religious basis. They believe in the sanctity of marriage. I know that Josephine, if asked, would say that marriage is more important to women than anything else.'

'And you do not believe that, Alice?' Ramsay looked doubtful.

'I think marriage is usually the degradation of women. There are few women who are not at the mercy of their husband's demands.'

'And what do you think, Rachel?'

Rachel looked around her, at the men in their dinner jackets and frilled white shirts and the ladies in their expensive silk and satin gowns, festooned with ribbons and lace; at their necks, arms and fingers covered with jewellery. Yet behind that façade was the reality of the domestic life that held women within its grip. She thought of the long days at Mill House, the calls and visits, the polite conversation and attendance at sick beds, the occupying of one's time in suitable, ladylike pursuits. And then the return of the men in the evening, with Aunt Maria and Bertha and the servants hovering around, attending to their anticipated wishes even when they had expressed none, listening attentively to their conversations at dinner. But most of all Rachel was struck by that vast area of male and female relationships which had seemed to be composed of hints and evasions. It was only at the balls and dances that there had been some sense of contact, a latent excitement, but even there every exchange was evasive, as if each word concealed the real meaning of what was being said.

Rachel said, 'Until I came here, I seemed to live in a sort of dream. It was as if I spent my childhood and adolescence waiting for something to happen.'

Ramsay raised his eyebrows. 'That doesn't answer my question, Rachel.'

'If I thought that marriage would take away the freedom I have enjoyed with Alice, then I would not want it. It is only Alice and Josephine and their friends who have made me feel that I am of any value. I think it is because the women as well as men are engaged in activities outside their own lives.'

Alice smiled at her. 'Marriage is not compatible with equality, Rachel.'

'Oh, come,' Ramsay protested. 'Most of the husbands I know have a great regard for their wives. It seems to me that many of them are pampered and spoilt, with little responsibility being demanded of them. Their days are free, the servants perform all those tasks which are demanding.'

'That's the trouble,' Alice said. 'Men tend to think that that is what women want.'

'Most of them seem content enough with the situation.'

'But that's because they have never been presented with alternatives. It's only recently that married women have acquired a legal right over their own property.'

'And I supported that Act.'

'Yes, I know you did, Ramsay. But you also know that most men prefer to see women in a subordinate role.'

Ramsay turned to Rachel. 'And what do you think?'

'Perhaps it is just the way in which society is constituted. I think men mean no harm. We are all brought up with various expectations. No doubt we would think men churlish if they did not treat us as they do. Perhaps women like to be put on a pedestal.'

'It's not a pedestal,' Alice protested. 'A wife and home are simply an extension of a man's ego.'

Ramsay laughed. 'You are a formidable lady, Alice. I do not think you would ever be subordinated.'

Later that night, when they were drinking cocoa in the drawing-room before retiring, Rachel said thoughtfully, 'Perhaps someone like Ramsay would be acceptable as a husband. He would not expect a wife to be a mere housekeeper.'

'Rachel, you are not contemplating marrying him!'

Rachel laughed.

'I am not thinking of marrying anyone.'

'I have no doubt that the thought is already in Ramsay's mind.'

'Alice! How ridiculous. I scarcely know him.'

Rachel looked doubtfully at the expression of animosity on Alice's face. There was something more than disapproval of marriage in Alice's attitude. In fact, Alice's normally impersonal assessments and judgments were tinged with violent emotion whenever they referred to the topic.

Alice put down her cup and saucer and came over to the armchair where Rachel was curled up and knelt down beside her. 'Rachel, I am being selfish, I suppose. I couldn't bear to be without you.'

'Alice, what are you saying? I'm not leaving.'

'I've been so happy since you came. I simply hoped that you would not leave.'

Rachel put her hand on Alice's head. 'Of course not. I owe so much to you, Alice. But I had not supposed I would be here always.'

'No.' Alice sighed. 'I could not hope that, I suppose. But you are welcome here for ever, Rachel.'

Rachel had an uncomfortable feeling as she lay in bed that night. Alice's attachment to her was greater than she had realised; it was almost what she had expected a husband might feel for his wife. She felt that she did not deserve such devotion and she was painfully aware that, even now, she had not told Alice the whole truth about her past.

Rachel's days were filled with the vast correspondence which was conducted in relation to the Contagious Diseases Act. She went to the Continent with delegations intent on stopping the white slave trade and attended debates in the House of Commons. There were constant attempts to get the Act repealed but after lengthy debates the motions always fell. Many people believed that the law demanding the medical examination of prostitutes had helped to diminish disease and few people were concerned with the committee's belief that it was an insult to women. She went down to Winchester with Josephine Robertson to visit Grace in the house which she had set up for young girls in need and redeemed prostitutes. Grace seemed happy and was soon going to a situation as a lady's maid where, Mrs Robertson said, she would be treated and looked after properly.

As the months passed, Ramsay appeared more and more frequently at the meetings which she and Alice attended in the evenings, after which he would invariably invite them back to his house for a meal.

The evening came when Alice was absent, visiting a house in the East End of London which she suspected was being used for harbouring young girls. Rachel returned alone with Ramsay to his house, thinking of how she would once have been aware of the impropriety of such an action, of how she would have been required to take a chaperone. She knew that, in a way, she was more interested in the freedom that Ramsay represented than in Ramsay himself.

He told her about the case he was currently engaged in, involving a breach of promise suit. A young lady of high social standing had been engaged to an officer in the Queen's Royal West Surrey Regiment. Whilst stationed in another part of the country, he had become involved with the wife of a fellow officer. As a result, he was likely to be dismissed from his regiment. The officer's defence was that he was not yet married, and that he was still willing to marry his fiancée. He had not jilted her.

'Surely he has no case,' Rachel protested.

'It is a moot point,' Ramsay said doubtfully. 'You see, a wife cannot divorce her husband on the basis of one act of adultery. So if the officer could prove that this was a solitary act, it could be disputed whether the lady has a case at all.'

'That is just another piece of inequality for women, isn't it? A wife can be divorced for just one act.'

Ramsay laughed. 'I hear Alice's influence in that remark.'

'But she is right, isn't she?'

'Yes. But if women want equality, then they must also expect to be sued if they break off an engagement.'

'But there would be little point. Few women have money in their own right.'

'So is the lady suing because of her injured pride or for the money it will give her?'

'I sometimes wonder why you champion the cause of women, Ramsay.'

'I champion the cause of justice, Rachel. I truly believe in equality.'

'Yes. You are quite unique, Ramsay. I am so glad I met you.'

Ramsay was suddenly serious. He paused. 'I have wished for some time, Rachel, to approach this topic.'

'What topic?' she said laughing. 'Whether you are unique?'

'I wish very much that you thought so.'

'What are you saying, Ramsay?'

'Rachel, over the past year, in fact ever since I met you, I have thought of you with increasing affection. That must surely have been obvious.'

Alice's words – 'I've no doubt he's thought of it' – flashed through her mind. She felt disappointed that this easy, pleasant life with Ramsay was about to end.

'Ramsay. No. I have not thought of it.'

'Then I must have been most neglectful in my attentions.'

'No. It's not that.' She realised it was she who had wanted it to go on for ever like this, to be undisturbed by the feelings that had ravaged her life in the past. His friendship had given her a security that any more intimate relationship could only destroy.

'Do you care nothing for me?' Ramsay asked.

'No. It's not that.' She thought of Jacob, of the baby, she could never tell him about all that. 'Since coming to London, my life has been involved in all the work I do with Alice. The committee, the children, visiting homes run by the Salvation Army to house destitute people.'

'Yes, of course. But I am speaking of your feelings, Rachel.'

'I've never thought about it, Ramsay.'

'Well, could you bring yourself to think of it now?'

'I don't know.' Rachel blushed in confusion.

'Would you marry me, Rachel?'

Rachel looked at him in bewilderment. 'No I couldn't marry you. I could not give all that up. I can't lose myself again.'

'"Lose yourself!" You wouldn't do that, Rachel. I have no wish to make demands of that nature. I have a sufficient income for you to have a comfortable, even an extravagant life if you so desired. There are servants to attend to all domestic matters. You would always be at liberty to follow all those pursuits to which you are devoted. Indeed, as you know, they are activities in which we are both involved.'

Rachel smiled. She looked at his serious face, his kind eyes, she supposed he was very handsome. There must be many young ladies who would like to marry him. 'Yes. I know. I do not mean to sound churlish.'

'Rachel, dear, it is not churlish. It is an important matter in your life. Marriage is not something one considers lightly.'

'No.' She knew in her heart that there was no possibility, but instant rejection somehow seemed hurtful.

Ramsay smiled. 'Will you think about it, Rachel? You can have all the time you need. It is not a matter on which I shall change my mind. Now, let me take you home.'

Rachel was relieved to find that Alice was in bed when she returned. Although she was in sympathy with Alice's views, she felt a degree of loyalty towards Ramsay. In fact part of herself was attracted by that opulent life, by the opportunities it would provide. With Ramsay's income, they could both do so much more for women, for the poor, the disadvantaged. Nevertheless she knew she would have to tell him the truth and then he would never wish to marry her.

When she went down to breakfast the next morning, the maid brought in a letter for her. She opened the envelope which contained a card and a letter. The card read:

This letter arrived at this establishment today, with a note to Miss Sophia Curzon requesting that it be forwarded to you, if your address were known. In view of Miss Sophia's absence in Egypt, I am taking the liberty of sending it to the address you left here a few weeks ago, when you deposited your card. Yours obediently.

She opened the envelope. Inside was a brief letter. She looked at the signature. Mrs Cynthia Forster. She frowned. What was that half-remembered name? She read:

Dear Rachel,
Perhaps you will have some recollection of me. I am the wife of the Reverend David Forster, preacher of the Methodist Chapel in Kingsbridge. Your Aunt Maria had the address of your old friend Miss Sophia Curzon and hoped that perhaps she might know of your whereabouts. It is my sad duty to tell you that your aunt is suffering from a disease which the doctors diagnose as incurable. I fear, indeed, that she declines daily and will not for much longer suffer the trials and tribulations of this earthly state. In view of the unhappy nature of your departure, which I can assure you is known only to your immediate family and to my dear husband and myself, she is most desirous of making peace with you before she departs for ever from this world. If you are in any situation which makes this possible, it would be a most Christian act if you would come as soon as you are able, to set your aunt's soul at rest. In case your circumstances do not permit, my husband has requested me to enclose the fare which will enable you to travel down on the Great Western Railway. May I hope that God has cared for you since you left this place.
Yours dutifully, Cynthia Forster.

'What's the matter?' Alice asked anxiously.
Rachel passed the letter, shaking her head. A terrible wound had been opened up inside her; all the memories of life at the Damarells, the despair she'd felt when her parents died, the hopes she and Sophie had shared at the Establishment, their dreams of a happy future, Hope Cove and Buckfast Abbey with Jacob, seemed suddenly to spark a fire inside her, a deep longing, an unbearable sense of loss.
'Oh, Alice.'
'Don't be upset. That woman turned you out just because of some disagreement. How long is it since they contacted you?'

'It must be over three years since I left Kingsbridge.'

'There. You have no duty to go.'

'No, Alice. I must go.' She frowned. 'It's that poor pastor's wife sending the money that's so upsetting. It just reminded me of the endless concern everyone had in Kingsbridge. At the time it seemed so suffocating. It was such a tiny world.'

'Rachel dear. I know you must be upset by those memories, but that woman turned you out when you were only nineteen. She didn't care. She showed no concern then.'

'I know. But—'

Alice sighed. She came and put an arm around her. 'If you must go, Rachel, would you like me to come with you?'

'No, Alice. I'll go alone. I probably won't be there more than a day or two. I can't imagine that Mr Damarell will be pleased to see me.'

'Then pack your suitcase and I'll get a carriage and go with you to the station.'

As the train drew out of the station that afternoon, Rachel looked at the solitary, receding figure of Alice in her deep-blue summer gown, her golden hair shining in the sunlight, as she waved goodbye. Dear Alice. It was she who represented Rachel's world now, with her generosity and honesty and striving.

She looked along the platform, thinking of those other stations and ports, of what seemed to be the constant farewells of her childhood and youth.

Chapter 13

Rachel felt a sense of apprehension as the horse-bus plodded into Kingsbridge. Her doubts had increased as the train carried her through the familiar countryside. Would Mr Damarell create some awful scene? He might refuse to speak to her, even to admit her to the house. Then she reminded herself that she had been requested to come by Aunt Maria, that he must have consented to the invitation. And why should she be concerned about his behaviour, he no longer had any control over her. Then she saw James and Thomas standing awkwardly by the side of their gig. They walked towards her slowly, as though they were uncertain that she was indeed Rachel. James was wearing a brown serge suit and looked even more frail than when she had left three years earlier. Thomas seemed to have grown even taller and had put on more weight, but he still had the warm round plump face which had so frequently been transformed by laughter.

Rachel held out her hand. 'It is kind of you to meet me. I suppose that Alice telegraphed.'

Thomas was looking at her almost as if she were a stranger and James said as he kissed her on the cheek, 'Rachel, I should scarcely have known you.'

'Have I changed so much?'

'No. Not your face. You couldn't lose those shining grey eyes or that lovely auburn hair. But you look so . . . confident.'

Rachel smiled. 'It has been a long while. I suppose I had to grow up some time.'

'It's more than that,' Thomas said bluntly as he shook her hand. 'You look so different. Makes me feel a real country lad.'

She climbed into the gig. She had almost forgotten the directness of their remarks. It was as though they were still living in the past, still seeing her as a child. Then she reflected that it was simply the way people talked to each other in a family.

'London is a different world,' she admitted. 'But how is your mother?'

James's face clouded. 'I am glad you have come, Rachel. She so much wished to see you again.'

'And your Papa?'

'You'll notice a change in him, I warrant,' Thomas looked at her doubtfully. 'Well, he hasn't exactly changed, but I can tell you, he hasn't softened with old age, you know.'

'Ah.' Rachel felt that he was warning her of some impending trouble. 'Well, I shall not cause him embarrassment. I can arrange to lodge for the days I am here at the King's Arms Inn.'

'I am sure that will not be necessary,' James assured her. He smiled. 'I think he would find that even less acceptable.'

'And Bertha?'

'She is now the wife of Mr George Cresswell, whom you may remember.'

'Yes, of course.' Rachel had a picture of the opinionated gentleman who had once paid her attention. 'Yes. I remember.'

'At Bertha's behest, he disposed of his estate in Dorset before his marriage and now farms just beyond Loddiswell. Bertha is well provided for and enjoys a comfortable existence.'

'I know she was reluctant to leave this area. I am glad she is happy. And are there any offspring?'

'She is expecting in a few months' time.'

'Her first pregnancy?'

Thomas looked embarrassed at the word. Rachel reflected that she would have to watch her vocabulary in the Damarell household. Even as the thought flashed across her mind, she thought of Alice and Ramsay and Josephine. No. She would not watch her vocabulary. She would not return to the old ways. What she believed in was how she would behave.

'Yes,' James replied. 'But since our mother's illness, she has come almost daily to visit.'

They alighted from the gig and Rachel slowly climbed the steps of Mill House. She frowned, visualising the first time she had climbed those steps with her parents, Charlotte clutching her hand. She remembered all the times she had seen Mr Damarell standing at the top, looking down when she arrived, his hands in his waistcoat, a stern, assessing expression on his face. But he was not there today.

The door was opened by Gertie, who stepped back in astonishment when she saw Rachel. 'Oh, Miss Cavendish, it is a pleasure to see you.'

'Hallo, Gertie,' Rachel bent down and kissed her on the cheek. 'It is a pleasure to see you, too.'

'Oh, Miss. You're such a lady now.' Then Gertie blushed. 'Oh, Mr James, Mr Thomas, let me take your hats.' She hurried down the hall ahead of them.

'Where is Mr Damarell?'

'He's in the drawing-room, Mr James. Shall I announce Miss Rachel?'

Rachel laughed. 'That won't be necessary, Gertie. I'll go in.'

'Shall I—?' James began.

'No. I'll see him first.'

Rachel felt determined not to be intimidated. It was he who should be grateful for her visit. She opened the door. Mr Damarell was standing in his usual upright posture by the fireplace, his thumbs in his waistcoat, staring beyond her at the ceiling.

She looked at him for a moment, her heart beating violently, then walked across the room, saying, 'Good afternoon, Sir. As you will know, I have come at my Aunt Maria's request.'

In spite of her turbulent feelings, Rachel's voice was calm. She realised she had feared coming here, that somewhere in the back of her mind had lurked the suspicion that he could take away all the confidence that her new life had given her. Now, as he slowly brought his gaze down to her level, she knew that he could no longer dominate her.

Mr Damarell did not move as she advanced with outstretched hand.

'I am sorry at the sadness of your current situation,' Rachel said as he reluctantly extended his hand.

'Good afternoon, young lady.'

'It is some three years since we met and I hope that time will have healed any adverse feelings you may have had towards me.'

'Only God can make judgments upon individual souls,' Mr Damarell replied. 'Your past shame lies between you and your maker.'

Rachel had a sudden impulse to laugh at his words. It was as though he were compelled to speak in this fashion, regardless of the circumstances.

'That is so, Mr Damarell, and of course I recognise now that it did not lie within your province to have condemned me. I regret the error of your judgment, but that is all long forgotten.'

Mr Damarell blushed. 'The error of my judgment! How dare you make such a charge. It is only on my wife's behalf that I permit you to enter this house at all.'

'Mr Damarell, do not disturb yourself. We must accept that your opinions are not the same as mine. Be assured I would not be entering this house were it not for my better feelings towards Aunt Maria.'

'Opinions! They are not opinions. They are the words of your maker.'

'About which we all hold differing views. I shall not be detained here longer than is desired by Aunt Maria. And I shall put up at the King's Arms Inn.'

'Young lady. Are you trying to disgrace me? No one knows of the reason for your departure. What would be thought if you did not remain in this house during your stay?'

'Mr Damarell, I am not concerned with what would be thought. Now, perhaps if it is a suitable moment, I might be permitted to see my aunt.'

'Not concerned! Rachel—'

Rachel interrupted. 'Please remember that I am no longer a member of this household. I could only remain if I am requested to be a guest in an appropriate and civil manner. And that would only be for the peace of mind of my aunt.'

At that moment, James entered the room, saying, 'Your aunt is aware of your arrival, Rachel. Perhaps you would like to come up.' He looked questioningly at his father. Mr Damarell looked sternly at Rachel then nodded briefly and Rachel followed James from the room.

Her aunt's bedroom was in semi-darkness when she went in and there was the heavy scent of smelling salts and carbolic soap. Aunt

Maria was propped up on pillows, her head back as though she were asleep, but when Rachel went over to her, she opened her eyes.

Rachel was shocked at the change. Her hair had turned white and her eyes seemed to be two pinpoints of light in her sunken face. The greyness of her complexion was emphasised by her flushed cheeks. Aunt Maria's long, thin fingers grasped Rachel's hand. Rachel bent down and kissed her, struck by the strangeness of her situation, that she should be here comforting this woman who had evicted her.

'Hallo, Aunt Maria.'

Aunt Maria tried to smile but her lips scarcely moved. 'Hallo, Rachel.'

Rachel sat lightly on the bed beside her. Now that she was here, she felt overwhelmed with the weight of having nothing to say. It was too late now for discussion or explanations, any attempt to connect the past and the present; everything had to be compacted into a few reassuring remarks, a subliminal attempt to prove that, in spite of everything, all was well, that accounts had been rendered and settled.

'I'm so glad you managed to contact me,' Rachel said quietly.

'It was Mrs Foster.' Aunt Maria's words were scarcely audible.

'Yes. Her letter was sent on from Sophie's house.'

'How is Sophie?'

'She's in Egypt.'

Aunt Maria nodded vaguely.

Rachel smoothed the bed covers. 'Are you comfortable, Aunt Maria?' she asked, at a loss for words. She had hoped to come and reassure her aunt that she would recover, that soon she would be better.

'Is everything all right with you, Rachel?'

What was she referring to? Did she wish to know what had happened to her when she left Kingsbridge, had she wondered about the baby? Or was she referring to her life now?

Rachel smiled. 'Yes. Everything. I have found much happiness, Aunt Maria.'

Aunt Maria nodded. 'I wanted to tell you ... I have never had a moment's peace since you left ... I tried to find you—'

Rachel had an absurd picture of Aunt Maria walking round the streets of London, knocking on doors, peering into the rooms at Leicester Court. She shook her head.

'Aunt Maria, you needn't explain. It is all in the past. You need have no feelings of remorse.'

Aunt Maria sighed and closed her eyes.

Rachel sat in silence, then Aunt Maria said, 'Will you be able to stay?'

'As long as you wish, Aunt Maria.'

'It won't be long. I am very tired.'

'Would you like to sleep now? I'll come back later.'

Aunt Maria opened her eyes. Rachel saw an urgent expression on her face. What was it? There was something more that Aunt Maria wanted to say.

'Rachel, over there.' Aunt Maria pointed to the dressing-table.

'Yes?' Rachel stood up. 'Do you want something?'

'In that top little drawer. Under my handkerchiefs.'

Rachel went over and pulled the little brass handle. 'A handkerchief, Aunt Maria?' Rachel touched the embroidered squares.

'No. Beneath. There are some letters.'

Rachel put her fingers further into the drawer. An acute feeling of anxiety came over her. It was going to be something she didn't want to know; something from a past that she had forgotten. She felt the envelopes and carefully withdrew them from the drawer.

'Put them in your bodice, Rachel. They're for you.'

Rachel took a deep breath. 'Aunt Maria, I don't—' She looked at the anxious expression on her aunt's face.

'You'd gone. I couldn't send them on. Please take them.'

Was Aunt Maria concerned for her, or did she fear that some secret would be revealed if the letters were found?

She nodded reluctantly.

'It is kind of you to come, Rachel.'

Rachel bent down and kissed her. 'No. It's not kind. I am pleased to be here. My life is very good, Aunt Maria.'

As she prepared to leave the room, Mr Damarell opened the door. He looked quietly at his wife. When she opened her eyes, he said, 'I have requested Rachel to stay here with us, Maria. I hope she will agree.'

Rachel had a momentary feeling of triumph. It was a small point, but he had been compelled to accept defeat. She smiled at him briefly and nodded. 'Yes, I will stay.'

She went to her room and took the three envelopes from her bodice. Without looking she knew that they had been posted in foreign parts, that they bore an army post mark. The pain of the past enveloped her. It was more than she could bear to open the letters in these circumstances, to be suddenly precipitated back into those violent emotions. She had only just achieved calm indifference and the letters would re-open those wounds. She would have to wait before she could read them. Perhaps until she left here. She put them in her valise and went downstairs.

At the evening meal, Rachel enquired about Richard. She had assumed that he would be returning at the end of the working day.

'Richard is now in Dartmouth,' Mr Damarell answered, in the polite and distant manner he had adopted towards Rachel. 'After you . . . three or four years ago, he decided to leave the mill and become a fisherman. He went to Dartmouth and built up a fishing fleet.'

'Oh, he often spoke of starting his own business,' Rachel said.

'He is now in the process of starting a shipyard,' Thomas added. 'I think all his book reading must have done him some good.'

'And is he married?'

'None of my sons are yet married,' Mr Damarell glanced at James and Thomas as though they were guilty of some act of treachery.

'I am engaged, Rachel,' Thomas said. 'I am to marry Miss Felicity Brown in a few months' time. Thirty-one seems a sensible age to marry. I now have my own foundry, Rachel. You must come and see it.'

'And how about your music, James? Did you finally take it up?'

'Yes. A year ago I was forced to give up thatching. The doctor advised that the chest complaints from which I suffered could be attributed to my occupation. I am now the organist for St Thomas's and teach music in various schools.'

Rachel smiled. 'Then you have all achieved your ambitions,' she said, thinking how compact life was in this country town, with its clearly achievable ambitions.

No one asked what had become of her when she left Kingsbridge and she wondered how they could resist questioning her. She realised that James and Thomas were avoiding the topic out of consideration for her rather than lack of interest, also, perhaps, because they might have found it too embarrassing.

It was only Bertha, when they were alone the next morning, who asked her about her life. Bertha was still round and plump but now she wore her curly black hair in a neat bun, and the wide gathered skirt of her gown emphasised rather than hid her impending confinement.

'What happened to you, Rachel? Where did you go?'

'I went to London.'

'And the baby? How about the baby? What did you do?'

'I have no child,' Rachel said briefly. 'Let us not speak of that.'

'But what happened, Rachel?'

Rachel hesitated. Bertha was looking at her with concern. She was the only one who had been kind, uncritical. 'It died,' she said briefly.

'Oh, Rachel, how awful for you.'

'I met people in London who helped me. I am now the secretary of a committee which is committed to reform.'

'What sort of reform?'

'The law relating to prostitutes,' Rachel said calmly. 'The corruption of young girls.'

Bertha's eyes opened wide.

Rachel smiled at her. 'It is absorbing work, Bertha. I spend long hours at my job.'

'Do you mean you have a paid occupation, Rachel?'

'Yes. I needed an income.'

'I have heard that there are ladies in London who act so, but it is only possible in these parts for the lower orders. As you know, people like Papa would never permit such a thing. I think I would not care for it, though it sounds very important and exciting. And you look so impressive, Rachel.'

'You look very well too, Bertha. Are you happy in your marriage?'

Bertha puckered her nose. 'Well there are aspects of it which I would rather forego. Of course I realise now it is the lot of all women. And George is very good and indulgent. He is most correct, Rachel, as you may remember, and it is a pleasant thing to have a house and to run it correctly.'

'Yes, I am sure it is.' Rachel smiled. She remembered how, when she was a young girl, it had been George Cresswell who had made her see the emptiness of the married state.

'And don't you intend to marry, Rachel? Surely the life of a spinster is of a very inferior quality.'

'It does not appear like that to me, Bertha. I enjoy having an income and I believe there is no reason why females should not have careers like men.'

Bertha shook her head in bewilderment. 'Have you no suitors, Rachel? Would you not like a husband and a household of your own?'

Rachel thought of Ramsay. Somehow, since arriving in Kingsbridge, his proposal appeared less attractive rather than more so. Marriage, even in the setting of her London life, seemed restrictive.

'I have thought so on occasion. I have a barrister friend who wishes me to consider the proposition.' She frowned as she spoke. Why was it that some part of her wanted to convince Bertha that she was not unsought after?

'There,' Bertha said triumphantly. 'I knew you must surely desire such a thing. Perhaps now that you have returned, we might be able to visit each other.' Then her face clouded. 'But does he know of—'

'No,' Rachel said abruptly.

Bertha told Rachel that Jacob was now in Afghanistan but Rachel asked no questions and she hastily changed the subject. Why had Bertha mentioned Jacob at that moment? Did she suspect, or even know the truth?

'Oh, Rachel, after you'd gone, Papa was so restrictive with me. I was scarcely able to leave the house and he could think of nothing but my getting married as soon as possible.'

'I'm sorry I caused you such inconvenience.'

Bertha laughed. 'Oh, it was all right because it made poor George speed up his plans.'

The following morning, James and Thomas departed for work. Only Mr Damarell remained in the house, afraid to leave in case his wife's condition deteriorated suddenly, but after his sons had left he went to his prayer room.

Rachel went down to the drawing-room. Maggie and Lizzie were cleaning the brass and silver ornaments. After she had made brief enquiries about their lives in the intervening years, Gertie brought Rachel a letter. It was from Alice. She felt a sense of relief as she opened the envelope, a reassurance that her real world was still there, awaiting her.

The letter was written on pink parchment.

Dearest Rachel,

I hope you had a pleasant journey and that you have not found the condition of your aunt too distressing.

The house is very tedious without you and I sat in the drawing-room last night and thought how only the previous evening you had been sitting on the sofa in your pale blue velvet gown, your lovely hair arranged on top of your head in its soft curves.

Today I addressed a meeting of the Women's Guild concerning the conditions of women workers in the textile trades. I went to tea with Lady Harburton, who has decided to found the Rational Dress Society, which would enable women to abandon the absurd restrictions to which we are currently subject. We spent some time discussing and executing designs which might be more compatible. But I will tell you of all this when you return. Although I miss you sadly, please remain with your family as long as you find necessary. Ramsay has offered to deal with any matters which would be delayed because of your absence. I did not offer him your address, as I feared you would have little time to enter into correspondence. Goodnight, dear Rachel.

Rachel smiled. Alice was a dear girl. She felt enormous gratitude towards her. The idea of marriage seemed unnecessary while she and Alice had such a friendship. She stood by the window, looking across the garden to the hills beyond. In the back of her mind was the nagging knowledge of those letters, lying upstairs in her valise. What did they contain?

She turned abruptly and went up to see Aunt Maria. Rachel spent much of the time at her bedside. Aunt Maria scarcely spoke but seemed to find comfort in having Rachel with her.

Two days later, another letter arrived from Alice.

Darling Rachel,

It was a delight to receive your brief note but please do not concern yourself with writing. The situation for you must be stressful but I am glad that Mr Damarell is behaving with decorum.

Last night, I had a most fearful nightmare. I dreamt that you were to marry, it was not revealed to whom this would be, but I awoke in an absolute panic of apprehension and fear. All day, I was obsessed with anxiety in spite of the fact that I knew this to be but a dream. I thought about the men with whom we consort and of the attitude they have towards you of such respect. I know you have a reputation for judgment and intelligence and impartiality, but I recognise also that they are fascinated by the air of mystery about you and by your beauty and dignity. We mix with many distinguished and important persons, but they treat you as equal to them in every way.

My mind is now concerned with the prospect that I cannot keep you for ever, I fear I shall lose you one of these days to some persuasive suitor who will carry you off to his castle. Dear Rachel, if you have time to write, persuade me that I am wrong.

Your devoted Alice.

Rachel stared at the words, then she folded the letter and tore it into pieces. It was even more disturbing than the thought of the three letters in her valise. There was something strange about Alice's anxiety, something excessive in the feelings she demonstrated. Why was Alice so opposed to marriage? Had she perhaps also had an unhappy love affair?

That night, Aunt Maria passed away and Rachel found herself faced with another kind of emotion. She was drawn back to memories of those other deaths which had so affected her life, that of her parents and Charlotte, and her grandparents. Perhaps her extravagant feelings for Jacob had been prompted by that violent loss when she was too young to cope with it, the need for someone to replace their love. Then her thoughts turned to the baby. That had been an experience of a different kind, as though she had lost something of herself. It was in thinking of Aunt Maria, that she realised she could now look back at the past with a new calm. There was nothing in the future that could cause her such desperation as she had experienced in the past.

There was an atmosphere of sorrow and regret at Aunt Maria's death as the relatives, Uncle Jonathon and Aunt Alice, Aunt Bessie and Emmie, Uncle Robert and Fat Uncle Wesley, descended upon the house. They treated Rachel with a mixture of familial intimacy and disapproval, discussing poor Aunt Maria with her yet almost implying that, by her absence, she had been partly responsible for Aunt Maria's decline.

Bertha had alerted her already to the fact that none of them knew the real reason for her departure three years ago and Rachel was astonished that even close members of the family had been left in ignorance. They had all been given the same story, that she had gone to Egypt with a relative of her father's, who had undertaken to be her guardian. Rachel longed to escape, to be released from all those conflicting emotions and found herself shrinking into silence. This house had had the same effect on her when she was a child, she told herself angrily. This place, these people, had no power to distress her now. Alice's letter made her feel even more isolated, as though her emotions were being pulled in different directions. She consoled herself that it was probably the last time she would visit Kingsbridge anyway. Finally, she admitted to herself that it was the letters, waiting to be read in her suitcase, that were the real cause of her unease. Without those, she would have attended the funeral, said goodbye and left.

She told herself that she could simply destroy them unread, that by reading them she would be forced to re-live what had happened. Yet she knew that it was more than curiosity that would compel her to read them. They represented a final acceptance of the past. Now she could prove to herself that she had grown beyond it.

Bertha confided in her that Richard would not be attending the funeral.

'Did he not visit Aunt Maria during her illness?' Rachel asked in surprise.

'Oh, yes. He came the day before you arrived. But he always arranged to come when Papa was absent.'

'Why?'

'They have not communicated since Richard went to Dartmouth.' Bertha glanced at her doubtfully. 'I think it was connected with your departure.'

'Surely Mr Damarell did not blame Richard!'

Bertha shook her head. 'I don't know. The matter was never discussed.'

'I'm sorry about Richard. Of course, he had nothing to do with it.'

Bertha shook her head in silence.

Rachel went in a carriage with Bertha and George Cresswell to the chapel and then on to the graveyard; a silent Mr Damarell accompanied by his sons went in the first carriage.

After the funeral meal was over and Bertha, George and the relatives had departed, Rachel said that she would be leaving for London in the morning. As they would be going to work early, she said farewell to James and Thomas and then went over to Mr Damarell.

'It must have been a difficult thing for you to accommodate me,' she said quietly.

Mr Damarell frowned. 'The past is the past.' He paused as though he were forcing himself to speak. 'It was good of you to come to visit your aunt.'

Looking at him, Rachel felt no pleasure at his capitulation. She saw him now as a sad human being, uncertain beneath his dogmatic pronouncements. She knew that it was simply this place, this house, the rigid standards, the correct behaviour, the narrow view of society which Kingsbridge represented, that made her feel as though she must assert the values of the world she now inhabited.

The next morning, she took the route down Church Street and along the raised pavement to the embankment, past the small terraced houses where the housewives were washing their steps and cleaning their windows. They all nodded politely then stared, their hands on their hips. She imagined the gossip and speculation which would follow her. Surely they had guessed the real reason for her departure? The lower classes weren't stupid; she knew from her work in London that unwanted children, unexpected pregnancies, were no mystery to them.

When she boarded the train at Plymouth, she found an empty compartment, opened her valise and extracted the three letters. Now that she had left Kingsbridge, she would have the strength to deal with whatever the contents revealed. It seemed a test to her. After accepting long ago that Jacob had never written, that he had forgotten her, would she have to revise her thoughts? Supposing, after all . . .

Abruptly, she tore open the first envelope and looked at the date on the letter. It had been written only a week or two after he left England. She took a deep breath.

Dear little Rachel,
What fun we had, didn't we? You make me regret that my leave has ended and although the sun here makes life pleasant, I miss our little walks and talks in the countryside. We are still passing through the Mediterranean and we see here and there pretty girls, with flowers in their hair, walking along the sandy coast. I believe the Sudan may not have such a felicitous climate but no doubt it will be full of interest and adventure. This is just a brief little note but perhaps you will write to me, as life sometimes becomes tedious so it is good to be entertained with news from home.
With affection,
Jacob.

Rachel frowned, her heart beating violently. She could see his laughing face, his spoilt expression when he did not get his own way. The feeling of delight he had always roused flooded through her. Oh, why had Aunt Maria given her these letters, why could she not have destroyed them, let the past be forgotten? Why had there never been anything, even in her present life, to equal the excitement of those days with him?

Slowly, she opened the next letter. It was dated about six months after the first. She would have been in London by then, she reflected, wandering the streets, living at Mrs Wentworth's, fearful that her money was running out. She sighed.

Dear Rachel,
Everyone in the family has written except you. I do not understand your silence in view of your assertions of such affection for me. I do not understand your behaviour, either then or now. Many other young ladies of Kingsbridge have written to me, whom I assume were more genuine than you. Perhaps after all you were not such a virtuous person. Anyhow, my life here is agreeable and we find

many friends of the opposite sex to entertain us. If you care to remedy your neglect I shall be pleased to correspond with you.
Sincerely,
Jacob.

Rachel clutched the letter and then re-read it. His anger seemed to leap up from the page and strike her. They were not the words of someone who had deserted her. Yet if he loved her, why had six months elapsed between the first letter and the second? She re-read it, blushing now at the words 'virtuous person'. What did he mean? What was he implying? But the last sentence told her he had not forgotten, that beneath his anger was the wish to hear from her. She slowly folded the letter and replaced it in the envelope. The unanswered questions, the doubts ... there was no point now in reliving the past.

With trembling fingers, she picked up the last envelope. Should she simply destroy it, unopened? That final letter might be even more revealing; it might precipitate her into uncontrollable regrets. She took a deep breath. It was ridiculous. She would have to read it. It could not affect her now.

Rachel tore it open. A photograph dropped out from inside the letter. She closed her eyes as she picked it up. Then she was looking at a laughing Jacob, standing beneath a palm tree, in a short-sleeved shirt and light-coloured trousers, his curly black hair evidently blown by the wind. Yet for the first time she saw that his smile seemed to be more of bravado than happiness. He was standing with an arm around the shoulders of a young, dark-skinned girl in a long, flowing robe. Rachel could instantly imagine the vivid colours of her dress, the feel of that soft cotton. The picture blended with her memories of Egypt, of the desert, the Nile, the sunshine. She looked back at Jacob. She unfolded the letter.

Dear Rachel,
I have frequently enquired about you in my letters to Mama and the others without response. Today I have had a letter from Bertha to inform me privately – though why that is so she does not say – that you left Kingsbridge some months ago. It seems that you do not intend to return. I can only assume that my father's generosity

in taking you in has met with little gratitude from you. As I have had no communication from you, I realise that you had the same indifferent feelings towards me. I am therefore writing this merely to inform you that I have no desire to see you again or to hear from you.

Please do not reply. It might also interest you to know that I have found the foreign girls and their behaviour to be just as interesting as my fellow officers had suggested. You will know to what I refer. As you can imagine, this makes your own small charms insignificant.

Yours sincerely,

Jacob Damarell.

Rachel returned the letter to its envelope. There was no need to re-read it. It was as though someone had sat down and explained everything to her. Reading each letter, she knew that her mind was trembling on the edge of understanding, not only of Jacob but of herself.

She saw in his last words the injured pride that someone as handsome and attractive as he knew himself to be should apparently be cast aside. Yet nowhere was there any expression of concern about her, no mention of love, no reference to a future together. There had been long gaps between his letters, at a time when he must have assumed she was still waiting for him. She remembered Bertha saying that Jacob had felt lost and rejected when his mother died. Perhaps he had never recovered, was always seeking love that could be given without responsibility. Like the love of a mother. But she also saw that it had been the same for her. It was the vacuum of her own lost childhood that Jacob had filled. It was not the excitement of love he had given her, merely an illusory sense of belonging.

She looked through the window, realising that her life had been overshadowed by that unresolved memory. At last she was released from guilt or remorse. She and Jacob had each been fulfilling roles dictated by their childhoods. She had come to terms with her loss. Nothing could ever make up for the death of her parents, but she saw now that the sense of rejection was natural. It was over. Her future decisions, her future life, would no longer be affected by one devastating experience.

* * *

As they had arranged, Alice was awaiting her as the train drew in at Paddington and she ran along the platform and eagerly threw her arms around Rachel and kissed her.

'Oh, it's been such a long time.'

'But it's only been a fortnight,' Rachel protested, laughing.

'Didn't you miss me, Rachel?'

'Of course I did. I was looking forward to getting back to my life here.'

'Was it awful?'

Rachel frowned as they climbed into a cab. 'No. Not exactly. It was full of conflicting memories. You know, you want to remember nice things about your childhood, but all sorts of undesirable thoughts kept appearing. I felt as though I'd always been terribly lonely.'

'Well, you're not lonely now, are you?'

'No.' Rachel smiled. 'It was a good thing I went, Alice. Everything is much clearer in my mind, because I saw that life isn't just a catalogue of nice or unpleasant events. Everything added up, somehow. In fact,' Rachel laughed, 'looking back, it all seems quite interesting.'

'Well, I hope you won't be dashing off to Kingsbridge too frequently.'

'I have promised Bertha to go down when her child is born. But what have you been doing?'

Listening to Alice, Rachel felt a momentary twinge of guilt that she could never tell Alice the whole truth. But it was a decision she had made long ago. Her life, finally, was her own.

'Well, I told you about this Rational Dress Society. You'll find that interesting. And Josephine has at last got the backing of Lord Kildare and some other prominent people to speak on the Contagious Act in the House. And we have found the house you wanted to accommodate some of the reformed prostitutes.'

'Where is it?'

'It's just off the Haymarket.'

'That's not an ideal place, is it? They will still be very much in the vicinity of their former activities.'

'Yes. I know. Of course, ideally, it would be better to find houses in the country, like the one at Winchester but that creates problems in finding suitable persons to run them.'

Half an hour later, Rachel entered her study with a sense of expectation. She felt as if she was at a new beginning, as if Jacob's letters had not only released her from the past but also opened the future. Yet there was something beyond that. There were problems she had ignored, and decisions she had evaded which must be addressed. She felt now that she could see them objectively. Why had she rejected Ramsay? Was it because of the past or for genuine reasons in the present? And Alice? Rachel understood in her heart the feelings that Alice was hinting at. Could she accept that situation without making her own feelings clear? And what were her own feelings? Having escaped the sense of loneliness that had pervaded her since childhood, she now wanted to be alone, to truly make her own decisions, to be free to discover herself. However, it was only due to Alice's kindness and generosity that she was here – it was a situation which demanded permanent gratitude, almost inferiority. She stood up decisively. She would talk to Alice.

Only two days later, before she had had an opportunity to speak to her, Rachel received a telegraph from George Cresswell, saying that Bertha had been delivered of a boy. Could she come immediately? Rachel experienced an unaccountable sense of expectation as she packed her valise. She smiled at her own attitude, remembering the distaste with which she had previously travelled to Devon. But when Alice returned that evening, Rachel was faced with an unexpected situation. She watched her running up the steps to the apartment, her face red and agitated.

'Alice, what's the matter?'

Alice looked at her in fury. Her words came out in gasps, as though she would choke. 'Don't speak to me! You are a liar, a cheat!'

Rachel blushed. 'Alice, what are you saying?'

'Why didn't you tell me? You're absolutely—' Words failed her; she threw her coat to one of the servants and walked past Rachel into the drawing-room. 'Come in here!'

Rachel followed her. Alice closed the door firmly.

'I've just come from a meeting of the committee. We were interviewing people about the corruption of young girls.'

'Yes,' Rachel said calmly. 'You said you were going.'

'Mrs Rowbotham has finally been apprehended whilst in this country and today she was called,' Alice said violently.

Rachel breathed deeply, looking at Alice with an instant understanding. The attempt to find Mrs Rowbotham had gone on for so long that Rachel had dismissed the fear that she ever would be caught. It was another problem that she had put to the back of her mind. Now Alice knew.

'She made accusations about you.' Alice looked at her with pleading eyes, as though even now she hoped they could be denied.

'Yes,' Rachel said.

'What do you mean, yes? Are they true?'

'I don't know. What did she say?'

Alice's voice rose again in anger. 'That you had a child. That you were a corrupt little . . . whore. That she rescued you.'

'Yes, I had a child,' Rachel said calmly.

'And how about—?'

'No. I wasn't a whore.'

'Rachel, how could you deceive me? Why?'

'Perhaps it was wrong, Alice. But my life is my own. I had to work it out for myself.'

'You had no right. You are here under false pretences.'

'No, I am not. I have a right to privacy. I have worked for the committee as agreed. In any case, Alice, I have already decided to leave here. I do not wish to be dependent on you any longer.'

'Dependent! Is that all you can say? She made other allegations, too,' Alice added suddenly. 'That you disposed of the child, murdered it.'

Rachel turned on her indignantly. 'And did you believe that? Who are you to criticise me for disloyalty?'

'I don't know,' Alice said in a desperate tone. 'What am I to think?'

'You can think as you wish. It does not concern me any more.'

'It concerns the committee, though. It means we cannot put Mrs Rowbotham up to be questioned by the Select Committee. If she made these allegations about you, and you admitted you had a child, our whole case would fall.'

Rachel frowned. 'Yes. I regret that. But it is not true.' Then Rachel added apprehensively, 'Alice, what will happen to me if Mrs

Rowbotham makes her allegations about the child in public?'

Alice looked at her coldly. 'You need not concern yourself with that. She knows that if she puts herself for one moment in the public eye, she will end up in gaol.'

Alice looked at her, suddenly bewildered. 'Rachel, apart from your deception, don't you know what my feelings are?'

'Yes, Alice. I do know now. Perhaps I've always known really. But I could never share them.'

'But you were willing enough to make use of them. Didn't you care at all?'

'Not in that way,' Rachel said firmly. 'And I did not make use of you, Alice. I believed we were friends.'

'Friends!'

Rachel walked to the door. 'I regret everything, Alice. I shall be leaving in the morning.'

She turned and looked at her. For a moment, she feared that Alice would plead with her to stay. Then she saw a cold, determined expression cross Alice's face.

'Yes,' Alice said. 'It would be better.'

Chapter 14

Rachel held Bertha's arm lightly as they walked along the embankment, followed by the nursemaid with the perambulator. Bertha turned every few minutes to look down happily at the baby and then to admonish the nursemaid.

'Don't jolt the perambulator, Jenny. Try to wheel it smoothly.'

'Yes, ma'am.'

'And please ensure that baby is wrapped properly. There is a breeze blowing in from the sea.'

'Yes, ma'am.'

Bertha turned to Rachel. 'I am afraid I cannot trust her to take the child out alone.'

'Oh, Bertha. You are too concerned. I am sure Jenny will attend to him.'

Bertha smiled. 'Ah, you don't know how it feels to be a mother. It is such a responsibility.'

'Yes.' Rachel looked out across the sea. No, she thought, she had never been a mother. All she had had was a fleeting glimpse into that experience. 'Bertha, I have to return to London soon. I have been here for a week, you know.'

'Yes, of course, you have your work, but it has been such a delight to have you here.' Bertha smiled. 'Perhaps you will return here one day, to live.'

Rachel smiled back. 'Yes, perhaps I will.'

'Oh, do you mean it, Rachel? Why don't you? You could work here, you know.'

'I think not, Bertha. Unless I could think of some acceptable occupation.'

'Well, perhaps you will marry your barrister and then you can both visit and I can visit you.'

'No. I have already decided about that. It is not possible for me to marry him.'

Bertha shook her head in disappointment. 'Would you visit Papa before you go?'

'Do you think he would wish that, Bertha?'

'Yes, I believe so. When he knew that you were visiting me, he made a strange remark.'

'Yes?'

'He said that perhaps loyalty was more important than morality. Can you imagine Papa saying such a thing?'

'No, I can't.'

'What do you think he meant?'

'I cannot imagine.'

She hesitated. She longed to ask Bertha what had happened when she had left in disgrace. Had Mr Damarell pursued his determination to find out the identity of the culprit?

'When he discovered you'd gone, he said your name was never to be mentioned in his presence again.' Bertha looked at her uncertainly.

Rachel blushed. 'Anything else?'

'Well, nothing was said, but I think he blamed Richard for your disgrace. Richard left soon after you did and went to Dartmouth.'

'Richard! How could he have thought such a thing?' Had Richard told his father about the money he had given her?

'Rachel, who—?'

'It wasn't Richard, Bertha,'

'I know,' Bertha said slowly.

Rachel looked at her. Did she know? 'It is all past and forgotten, Bertha.'

'Yes. But did the baby—?'

Rachel did not reply.

'It must have been awful for you. But I just can't imagine anyone doing . . . that . . . for pleasure. It seems so perverse.'

Rachel smiled sadly. 'It seems so now,' adding, 'Bertha, whatever you . . . suspect . . . you have never mentioned this to anyone else?'

'Rachel! Of course not. Oh, you don't know how I felt, Rachel. I knew you weren't to blame but I feared Papa's anger if I dared to suggest—'

'Bertha, let us not discuss it. It is long ago. I have no more regrets.' They walked in silence for a few minutes.

Bertha turned to speak to Jenny. 'I think we will return now. Jacob may catch a cold with this nasty breeze. I am going into Kingsbridge tomorrow, Rachel, to visit Mrs Foster. I have promised that I will accompany her on our regular call upon the workhouse. Perhaps you would come. You could see how the Poor Law is administered in Kingsbridge now.'

'I went there in the past with Aunt Maria. But I will come if you like and then I must return on the following day to London.' Then she added suddenly, 'Why did you call the baby Jacob?'

Bertha looked at her with uncharacteristic directness. 'I have sympathy for Jacob as well,' she said slowly.

As they walked up the path to the vicarage, Rachel remembered all those visits she had made in the past to hospitals, the homes of the poor, the sick and elderly.

Mrs Foster greeted her cheerfully. 'I was so pleased you received my letter and that you were able to come to your aunt, Rachel. I saw you at the funeral, though I should scarcely have known you. I believe you are engaged in many charitable pursuits in the capital.'

'Yes, I am. But I am more concerned with reform than charity.'

Mrs Foster smiled, turning to Bertha. 'And how is your father, Bertha? I am sure Thomas and James are a great support for him.'

'He is well looked after, I think. Mrs Greeve has been housekeeping for us for so long that she is familiar with all his needs. And we are fortunate in having servants who appear to be dedicated to their vocations.'

'Now,' Mrs Foster rang the bell and a maid brought her coat. 'It will be only a brief visit to the workhouse, but I should particularly like you to see the vast improvements we have made over the past few years, Rachel.'

As their gig went slowly up Fore Street, Rachel looked down the alleys and the cobbled side streets at the small, terraced houses. Overalled women were still carrying buckets from the pump at the end of the alleys as they had in her childhood, barefoot children were still standing on corners, old men were sitting on their doorsteps, smoking pipes. They had to wait while a rag and bone cart collected an old iron bedstead through the upstairs window of a house beyond the Shambles. Boys were coming out of St Crispins School and as they passed through the gates at the top of the hill, Rachel could see the workhouse on the hill beyond.

It was the fear of being sent to this place which had made her escape to London and she felt a sense of gloom coming over her as they went up the path.

'There are many more children here than I remember,' she observed to Mrs Foster.

'Well, of course, with the new government regulations, we now receive people from all over the area. I fear that of late there seem to have been more illegitimate births. Also, because of the impossibility of supporting their offspring, some young women simply abandon their babies. In the past weeks, we have had three such events. An almost new-born child was left on the steps of St Thomas's and another discovered by the Shambles.'

'Can you imagine,' Bertha said in horror. 'The idea of leaving a baby. Such women must be heinous.'

Rachel looked at Bertha's expression. Had it never occurred to Bertha that Rachel might have done the same? Yet when confronted with the truth of a situation, Bertha's sympathy was more acute than her criticism. Was she merely repeating attitudes she had learnt in childhood which she did not really believe?

'Perhaps you cannot imagine the lives of these women,' Rachel said. 'Many of them are desperate, deserted, with no one to turn to.'

Bertha glanced at her thoughtfully but she did not reply.

They were led through the crowded rooms by the manager of the home, a fat, unkempt woman who constantly admonished the inmates to sit or stand up straight. Old men mingled with young girls; middle-aged women sat around in small groups, a few of them sat alone, looking through the barred windows.

'I am afraid they soon lapse into idleness if they are not supervised,' Mrs Foster remarked. 'But we cannot afford sufficient staff to oversee them all the time.'

One room housed half a dozen young children of about three or four years of age. They all looked at the visitors with wide eyes, but when Rachel spoke to them, they did not reply.

'These little creatures have no one in the world, and they are all a great burden on the parish. However, even with our limited resources, we have managed to have this room white-washed and cots provided for all of them.'

'And what of the young women in this room?' Rachel asked as they passed into the next area. 'How about that girl over there?' Rachel nodded at a girl standing by the window. She was tall and thin, and the Union uniform hung on her loosely.

'She was a disreputable creature, I am afraid. She's here because she couldn't support her child. Now the child's died.'

In spite of her previous aversion to the place, it was these words which really disturbed Rachel. She felt an infinite sympathy for the girl, a wish to help her, to get her out of here.

'Surely she could be found some employment.'

Mrs Foster pursed her lips. 'There's only one kind of employment she's interested in. I'm afraid she can't stay here because basically we can only house those who are unable to work. And no respectable household would care to employ her.'

'In London, we are endeavouring to open homes for girls like her. We try to convert them from their way of life.'

Mrs Foster smiled. 'That is not a simple task. My dear husband preaches about moral values from the pulpit every week, but the persons most in need of his advice are never present. Perhaps you would like to transfer your efforts to Kingsbridge, Rachel. We are certainly in need of help.'

Rachel shook her head. Mrs Foster displayed that strange, ambivalent combination of moral disapproval and a determination to do good for these people. At best, the vast army of charitable women adopted a proprietary air of superiority; at worst, they spoke with barely concealed contempt.

On impulse, Rachel said, 'Yes. Perhaps I will, Mrs Foster.'

'Are you serious, Rachel? Would it be possible? My dear husband would be only too pleased to assist you.'

'I would not wish to be connected with any religious body,' Rachel said decisively as they walked on. 'But it occurs to me that I might open a home for destitute children and also for girls like the one we saw just now.'

Rachel heard her own words as though they were being spoken by someone else. What was she saying? Instantly, she knew she meant what she was saying. A deeper logic was operating in her mind, telling her that this was what she needed to do. It wasn't a sense of home-coming, nor of duty towards her relatives, nor love of this place. It seemed to her to be the only way to find her identity. Her life in London, although she enjoyed it, was something which had been directed by others; her life in Kingsbridge as a child, as an adolescent, had inevitably been chosen by others. What she wanted was to initiate something herself. She wanted to bring joy into people's lives. That poor girl who had lost her baby – she did not need moral judgments; she needed help to live a happy life, to enjoy her existence.

'I wonder if it would be possible for me to find a house here which might be converted into a home for young children,' she mused aloud.

'Rachel, you do mean it, don't you? Yes, of course. My husband will make enquiries for you.'

Rachel smiled. 'It's all right, Mrs Foster, I can make enquiries myself. I have had plenty of experience.'

'Yes, I forget that.'

'What about London,' Bertha asked. 'Do you not live with your friend Alice?'

'I had already arranged to move from there and find my own accommodation. It would be sensible for me to settle here now.'

'I'm so glad,' Bertha said delightedly. 'You can stay with George and me until then.'

Rachel hesitated, anticipating that George would not wish to be connected with such a project. Yet when they discussed it with him that night, she found a practical mind behind his pompous manner. She realised that she had learned to handle her own income, but she still had to learn the details of renting properties and employing staff.

'Now, have you sufficient capital to set up such a house in the first place?' George asked solemnly, after running through likely costs and expenses.

'Yes, I have saved much of my income. My intention is to approach various persons I know in London who are willing to finance such projects. I shall, of course, concentrate on getting donations locally and I hope to experience no difficulty getting voluntary help from the ladies in this area. They have always been devoted to good works.'

Two months later, aided by George's advice, Rachel was installed in a suitable house just outside Kingsbridge with ten bedrooms, three or four public rooms and a large garden. She had taken occupancy for two years.

Rachel's expectations were not realised immediately. She visited the Reverend Foster and his wife, who listened to her plans with enthusiasm. To begin with, she would accommodate six homeless or orphaned children and would solicit donations from local benefactors to pay for the necessary staff. Mrs Foster invited her to attend her next dinner party, where Rachel could tell the guests of her plans and ask for their help.

As Rachel walked along the streets of Kingsbridge she realised that she was being observed with suspicion. She knew that she would have to leave her card at the homes of these ladies if she wished to re-establish their acquaintance. All the people she had visited in the past, whose dinners and balls she had attended, bowed to her from their carriages or acknowledged her coolly in the street. However, they showed no enthusiasm to enter into conversation or make any personal contact.

Walking along the quay towards her house, she felt a pang of anxiety. Supposing it didn't work; supposing no one would subscribe to her children's home. Her money would not last beyond the two years and she no longer had an income. Well, it would work. She had made her decision to come here; this was what she wanted and somehow she would make it succeed. These people prided themselves on their public spirit; she must persuade them to help her.

She met some of them at her first dinner party at Mrs Foster's. Mrs Hyamson was there with one of her sons, who was now affianced to a young lady from Torquay; Mr Roach had passed on but Mrs Roach still entertained the guests with her melodies. Mr Markham, the dentist, and his wife were accompanied by a daughter whom Rachel had not met previously; she had been at a finishing school in Italy and now gave an entertaining account of her travels. Mrs Foster had invited the farmer, Rodney Parrish, presuming that he might like to renew his friendship with Rachel, but he had been forced to decline the invitation due to pressure of work. However, his sister Valerie attended, and seemed pleased to see her.

'I think my brother was shy about meeting you again,' she confided to Rachel.

'How could that be? It is a long time ago.'

'Perhaps you would care to come for afternoon tea?'

'That would be delightful, but I am busily engaged at the moment in arranging a new home for destitute children.'

'I had heard something of it. Do explain to me.'

'In London, I was engaged in similar projects. It seemed to me there was some need in these parts for such a place.'

Rachel glanced around her. She realised that silence had fallen and that everyone was listening to her conversation with Valerie.

'Have you now come to reside permanently?' Mrs Markham enquired. She slightly emphasised the word 'now' as though Rachel's earlier departure reflected upon her stability.

'I noticed that there is need here for provision for unwanted children. In fact, I have observed that there is much poverty amongst the labourers and farm workers and their families.' Rachel spoke in a casual tone, as though it were an accepted view.

'Indeed!' Mrs Markham looked disapproving. 'I believe the citizens of these parts pride themselves on the progress we have made.'

Rachel maintained an unemphatic voice. 'I do not think the workhouse is a suitable place for young children.'

Mrs Roach interrupted, frowning, 'Many of the ladies in this town spend some time visiting that place. I think we all do as much as we can.'

'I'm sure Rachel means no criticism,' Mrs Foster said hastily. 'She merely desires to help.'

'You have to remember,' Mr Markham observed, 'the upkeep of the place falls upon the people of Devon. These destitutes cannot expect to live in a palace.'

Philip Waldorf, the accountant she remembered from the past, observed that there would be no destitute children if mothers were forced to care for their children and not abandon them. 'In many cases,' he said, 'the county gaol is a more suitable place for them.'

'I scarcely think so,' Rachel said coldly. She realised that she could not pretend to adhere to their views; it was only persistence in her own beliefs that might win their support. 'How can these women be expected to support their children?'

'Perhaps you are unaware, Rachel, that these children were born out of wedlock. They have no one but themselves to blame.'

'And what of the fathers? I believe that many of these young girls have been seduced by the masters of the households in which they are employed. Or by their sons.'

Mrs Markham blushed indignantly. 'I scarcely think this is a conversation suitable for the dinner table. Perhaps London habits are somewhat different from those pertaining in these parts.'

'I am sure Rachel means no disrespect,' Mrs Foster looked anxious. 'I know that she is concerned only to protect the innocent children who are the result of such disasters.'

'Then I think if Rachel wants the support of the good ladies of this neighbourhood, she would be well advised to keep her liberal opinions to herself.'

'Mrs Foster is correct,' Rachel said quietly. 'The house I have acquired is to be used as a home for abandoned children, or those whose mothers cannot support them. I had hoped that I might ask for some kind of donations from the inhabitants of Kingsbridge and the surrounding districts. Such private establishments will, after all, reduce the burden on the rate-payer.'

'Well, you no doubt mean well, Rachel,' Mrs Roach said coolly. 'I am sure, when we can see the effectiveness of your efforts, we shall be willing to give some assistance.'

Rachel realised that raising money in this community would not be easy. She remembered that although the ladies had been generous in allowing their cooks to make cakes for the poor, and their gardeners to contribute surplus flowers and vegetables for harvest festivals, there had been little financial aid given to the destitute. In London, in contrast, large numbers of rich and influential people were aware that a submerged population was a disadvantage not only to themselves but to the whole community.

The next day she called on the tradesmen in Kingsbridge and Dodbrooke to tell them about her plans and managed to extract promises of help from some of them. She remembered how she and

Sophie had been permitted to walk down into Kingsbridge during their last year at the Establishment. They would buy sweetmeats and confections, and the shop-owners would ask them cheerfully about their progress. Rachel realised that the shop-keepers were remembering that young girl who had attended the Establishment, and then left precipitately. Confronted with her anew, they viewed her with a combination of suspicion and awe. Aunt Maria had taught her to be indifferent to the views of tradesmen and such persons, but Rachel knew she needed to obtain their approval.

She had engaged the services of a cook and housekeeper and, in the afternoon, she went with Mrs Foster to the workhouse to collect the six young children.

'I suggest we also take three of the young girls. They can train to be maids at the house and learn to look after the children.'

Mrs Foster looked doubtful. 'You know of their reputations, Rachel. And two of them do not come from Kingsbridge, so we know nothing of their backgrounds.'

'Then I must engage them on trust,' Rachel said smiling. She spoke to the three girls and asked their names. They all looked at her suspiciously as they replied.

'Very well. Edith, Dora and Elsie. I propose to offer you a situation as maids in a house I have acquired. You will be required to attend to the six babies I am taking in.'

They all looked at her doubtfully. They had never been confronted with such a suggestion. It had always been their job to seek employment through the offices of some benevolent person.

'What for?' one of them asked, her tone was almost belligerent.

'Speak to Miss Cavendish with courtesy,' Mrs Foster said sharply.

'It is to enable you to have respectable employment,' Rachel said. 'As you are fit individuals, you would not be permitted to remain in this place in any case.'

'Do you mean we get a wage?'

'Yes. I will also provide you with uniform and a set of clothes. And, of course, your board.'

Edith nodded towards the young children. 'One of them babies is mine.'

'Oh?' Rachel hesitated. 'Well, you will be able to care for it yourself then, won't you?'

'And still get a wage?'

'That is for Miss Cavendish to decide,' Mrs Foster said sharply. 'And remember, any misbehaviour will result in instant dismissal.'

They followed Rachel and Mrs Foster in silence. Rachel remembered her own doubts when Josephine Robertson and Jonathon Bryant had come to collect her in Brussels, her suspicion of their good intentions.

Rachel noticed that as soon as they entered the house, their truculent behaviour changed to compliance. They were installed in small bedrooms at the top of the house, and then Rachel gave them instructions about their duties.

'The children will be your main concern; there will be other persons to perform most of the household duties. You will eat in the kitchen with the servants, but the children will take their meals in the nursery. The housekeeper will show you how to bath and attend to them.' Then she added quietly, 'I am desirous of expanding this facility in the future. It is therefore important that this is seen to be a well-run establishment. I rely upon you all to behave with propriety.'

She looked at them. They were all thin and unkempt; Edith's hair was tied back with string and Dora's overall was dirty, with a large hole in the centre.

'First of all, go and have a bath. You can take hot water up to your rooms. And wash your hair. Then I will bring clothes for you to change into.'

They all muttered 'Thank you, ma'am,' as they walked from the room.

Rachel breathed a sigh of relief. At least she could probably rely upon them to carry out her wishes; they would not want to leave a place where they were treated properly. To begin with, she would not need to pay them a great deal and she would have to constantly review her financial situation.

The next day, Rachel made calls upon some of the larger houses on the way to Salcombe. She was received graciously, with expressions of interest in her activities.

One lady, a Mrs Sinclair, encouraged her to discuss her future plans. Mrs Sinclair was tall and wide, with steel-grey hair and an arrogant expression on her rosy-cheeked face. She revealed she had heard that some of the staff of Rachel's home consisted of fallen women. Did Rachel think that such persons should be in the charge of young, innocent children?

'I believe that their situation was caused by circumstances,' Rachel said patiently. She was beginning to find it easier to maintain an even and impartial tone while still persisting in stating her beliefs.

'I can conceive of no circumstances which would necessitate such wanton behaviour.'

'They will be well-supervised, madam.'

'It seems to me there are too many such persons coming into this area. And what are your future intentions? Do you mean to extend your activities?'

'In the future I intend to open a house for prostitutes,' Rachel replied.

'Indeed! I see you have brought somewhat advanced opinions down from the city. I scarcely think they will be well-received here.'

'Perhaps not,' Rachel said politely. 'But I do not believe in condemning people to destitution. I think all persons are worthy of being offered the chance to live a better life.'

'Indeed, that may be so. But perhaps a little hard labour would be a more appropriate way of showing them the error of their ways.'

Rachel rose and placed her teacup on the table, saying, 'Thank you for receiving me, madam. I hope you may find it possible to help the project in some way.'

As she walked from the house, Rachel smiled pleasantly at Mrs Sinclair. She must let these people see that she was confident about her own intentions. She knew that at first her efforts would no doubt not be viewed in a charitable light. The ladies of Kingsbridge were more likely to feel resentful of her arrogance in coming here than appreciative of her efforts.

A few days later, she called on Mr Damarell. She had visited Mill House only once since her arrival, to inform them of her plans. James had been sympathetic and offered to help. He would give music lessons to the children.

Rachel had said, 'Most of them are too young, only babies really, but two of them are three or four years of age. Perhaps they would benefit.'

True to his word, James had been the first caller at the home and played the piano for the children, while Elsie showed the two eldest children how to dance a jig.

Rachel looked closely at Mr Damarell. He seemed to have aged suddenly since Aunt Maria's death; there were dark rings under his eyes and a tired expression on his face. However he said with his usual belligerence, 'I have not seen you or any of your staff at the chapel on Sundays. I presume they attend the established church.'

Rachel blushed. She had forgotten all about the Sunday ritual. Her house was just outside Kingsbridge, up a long drive, so she could not see the road. She imagined the family groups walking past, commenting on her and her charges, going on down to the town, along Fore Street and Church Street to the churches and chapels, then remarking upon her absence from the congregations of ladies and gentlemen and neatly dressed children.

Of course, she should have thought of it; what support could she expect from the inhabitants if she did not conform to the essential church-going requirement.

'I have been much employed since I arrived,' Rachel said apologetically. 'But of course I and my staff will be attending from now on. And the children also, when they are old enough.'

Mr Damarell nodded curtly. 'I am glad to hear it.'

'I have been attempting to elicit the help of any ladies in Dodbrooke and Kingsbridge who have a little time to spare. At the moment, I have only three young girls working for me. It is a large financial commitment.'

'That would have been obvious to any gentleman experienced in such matters. Ladies cannot be expected to understand the problems of business,' Mr Damarell said shortly.

Rachel forced herself to continue. 'I am also seeking donations from persons who would be interested in supporting my work.'

Mr Damarell pursed his lips. 'In the present economic climate, the people in this area are becoming wary of the constant demands for contributions to what are frequently less than worthy causes.'

'Surely young children must be worthy.'

'If one is too liberal, it may only encourage vice and loose living amongst those who create the situation. It might appear that they are being rewarded for their sins, that any responsibility they may have had has been swept aside.'

'That is for you to decide,' Rachel said quietly. She turned to the door, feeling despondent.

Mr Damarell added suddenly, 'I recognise your good intentions, Rachel. And of course I realise that such work is commendable, and probably desirable in view of the fact that you are unlikely to be able to marry.'

She turned indignantly. 'I am not engaged in this work as a substitute for marriage.'

Mr Damarell looked at her reflectively. 'No. Perhaps not.' Then he added, 'I will see what I can do.'

She felt she almost hated him as she walked down the steps. Why had he mentioned marriage? Was he trying to diminish her? Yet what he said was true. She would probably never marry, even if she wished to. She could never tell anyone of her past because, if she did, no one would marry her. She returned with a renewed determination to her children. This venture must succeed.

When she arrived at the chapel that Sunday, accompanied by Elsie and Dora and the cook, to her astonishment she saw a notice pinned in the porch, asking for voluntary helpers for the new children's home. Volunteers were requested to apply either to Miss Rachel Cavendish at the home, or to Arthur Damarell at Mill House.

Rachel listened to Mr Damarell's sermon without hearing his words. She tried to understand what had precipitated his action; was he at last beginning to accept her? She thanked him briefly as she left the chapel with the children, but Mr Damarell only nodded solemnly and said quietly, 'I am sure you will not betray my trust this time.'

Rachel sighed. She had almost begun to feel sympathy for him because his natural feelings, any generosity he might exhibit, were always cancelled by his rigid beliefs. It was like a shutter coming down on a window just as the first rays of sun shone through.

The next afternoon two young ladies arrived, bringing fruit and sweetmeats and offering to take the children for an Easter outing. Then Valerie appeared, with a small donation from Rodney Parrish, and an offer to come herself once a week to give the three girls a day off from their duties.

As the weeks passed, Rachel found that the hostility she had first experienced began to change to tolerance. The shop-keepers gave her sweets for the children, the draper gave her remnants to be made up into curtains and bedcovers, while his wife offered to run up clothes for the children. When the doctor visited the children, he demanded no fees but gave Rachel advice on medical matters. She began to extend her activities to visiting the poor, and decided that in the future she would try to exert her influence in securing better housing for farm labourers and paupers – a controversial issue in those parts. That project would have to be put aside until she was certain that her financial problems were solved.

One evening, Rachel wrote to the *Kingsbridge Gazette* enclosing an advertisement asking for financial help for her home, and for the projected new one she hoped to open for what she called 'unfortunate young women'.

A few days later, she received a contribution from Rodney Parrish, and an unexpected one from Mr Damarell, with a brief note, 'In recognition of the humble progress you have made since you first came to this place.'

Rachel smiled to herself. She finally felt indifferent to his comments. He was unintentionally helping her to remove that sense of rejection which the past had bequeathed her. One day, she would be able to talk about it. Now, she only wanted to forget.

Rachel looked through the drawing-room window at the children, playing on the lawn with Dora and Edith. Elsie was planting some flowers with Valerie and another volunteer.

She watched the two older children. David must be about four, the age her own son would have been by now. Somehow, the pain of that memory had receded since she had come here.

She smiled as Mrs Blake came into the room with a letter. 'Just delivered, ma'am. And the builder would like to discuss the repairs to the roof.'

'Ah, show him in.' Rachel smiled. 'I am afraid we may have to delay any more financial commitments.'

As Mrs Blake went out, Rachel opened the letter. It bore a Dartmouth postmark.

Dear Rachel,
I happened to see your advertisement in the *Kingsbridge Gazette* today. A number of persons have informed me of the work you are doing in Kingsbridge and environs.

It is with pleasure that I am able to send the enclosed contribution.
Yours sincerely,
Richard.

Rachel looked at the cheque in disbelief. It was for £200. She had not
seen Richard since her return to Kingsbridge. Bertha and his brothers
visited him occasionally, but he never came near the mill or had any
contact with his father.

When the builder walked in, Rachel smiled cheerfully. 'Good
morning, sir. Perhaps we can discuss what will be necessary.'

Mrs Blake looked astonished.

'We have received another donation,' Rachel explained happily.

That evening she wrote a note of thanks to Richard, suggesting that
he visit the home to look at her work for himself. There were now ten
children to be provided for; he could see the care and protection they
were receiving.

Richard's reply was formal.

Dear Rachel,
I must thank you for your kind invitation. Owing to my many
commitments, I do not come frequently to Kingsbridge. But
should I be in the vicinity, I shall be pleased to call upon you. I fear
it must be without prior notice, as my movements are much
dictated by my duties.
Yours sincerely,
Richard.

Rachel smiled. Richard's seriousness seemed to shine out from the
communication. It was as though he had sent her a photograph. She
remembered his remonstrations when they were younger, his
protests about her behaviour with other young men. At the time, she
had thought that it was because of a secret attachment he had for her,
but now she saw that perhaps it was only his idea of what was correct.
Although he was so unlike his father, and there was this apparently
bitter rift between them, perhaps he had inherited the severe moral
codes of Mr Damarell.

The very next afternoon Rachel saw a tall, erect figure in a smart
brown suit, with curly brown hair, emerging from a gig. It was

Richard. He spoke to one of the voluntary helpers in the garden and then she watched him climb the steps.

Elsie was opening the front door as Rachel walked along the hall.

'It's all right, Elsie.' She walked towards him. 'Good day, Richard. You have arrived sooner than I expected.'

Richard stood in the doorway, looking at her in disbelief. His expression was so fixed that for a moment she thought his mind must be somewhere else, as though he had suddenly remembered an urgent duty he had neglected.

'What is it, Richard?' she asked uncertainly.

He came towards her slowly as Elsie closed the door. She had forgotten how like Jacob he was; it could almost have been Richard in the photo Jacob had sent. He seemed to be the serious version of that lively face.

'Rachel, you look so different.' He frowned and took her hand in bewilderment. She knew that he was remembering the last time he had seen her, the lost, frightened little creature she had been, clutching her valise and her bag of money as she vanished in the cold morning light.

'That seems to be the general impression. But it has been nearly four years. It is a long time.'

'I should scarcely have known you.'

Rachel smiled. 'I hope I meet with your approval.'

Richard relaxed slightly as he followed her into the drawing-room. He gazed at her as though he could still not reconcile the woman before him with his memory of the girl who had left years before.

Rachel had been receiving callers and was wearing a green silk gown and her hair was tied back with a dark green ribbon. Around her neck she wore a gold coil necklace which Alice had given her.

'I am delighted to see you, Richard,' she said, putting a hand to her head and adjusting her combs. 'But you look at me with some doubt.'

Richard blushed. 'I am pleased that you look so well, Rachel. You present such an air of confidence.' He fell silent again as though he was still quite overwhelmed.

Rachel laughed. 'That is not what I always feel. I understand that you have prospered also.'

'Yes.' Richard cleared his throat. 'I have a fishing fleet at

Dartmouth. It has been a successful venture. I am in the process of negotiating the purchase of a small shipyard. It is an opportune moment for such an enterprise.'

'But no wife, I understand?'

Richard blushed but he merely said, 'No.' He added, 'And you, Rachel?'

Rachel grinned. 'No. I have not married. But then,' she added coolly, 'perhaps that is to be expected.'

'Rachel, I deeply regretted what happened.'

Rachel shrugged. 'It is of no importance now. Let us talk of more immediate matters. Come, I will show you the house and you may meet the children, if you wish.'

He followed her through the sparsely-furnished bedrooms and the public rooms while she explained how the place was run. She had been teaching the older children to read, but soon it would be necessary to employ a governess, there were so many other matters to attend to.

'Surely they will attend the board school when they are old enough?'

'Probably, but it is important to give them a good start. Particularly the girls. Their education is so often neglected.' She thought of the three girls she had rescued from the workhouse. They could scarcely read until they began to take lessons from her.

'You must remember the class from which they come. Perhaps too much education would be unsuitable.'

'No.' Rachel said firmly. 'I do not believe in class nor in the inferior education of women.'

'I have heard of your views from some of the young ladies who visit here. It seems that some of them are much enamoured of your opinions.'

'I am delighted to hear it. I would have thought you would agree with such things, Richard. As young people, we spent much time in the library, discussing the affairs of the world. You introduced me to literature and to the theories of Darwin.' She felt a surge of gratitude towards him; Richard had been the only male in her childhood who had treated her as an equal.

Richard nodded. 'Yes, I admire what you are doing, Rachel. But I think ladies cannot afford to be too extreme. A gradual liberalisation of society is what one might desire, to improve the lot of the lower classes.'

She felt herself reacting to his words, but there was no point in arguing with him. Richard's caution did not apply only to females; it summed up his whole serious view of life.

'Come, let us talk to the children.' She led him to the garden and then afterwards they had tea alone in the conservatory.

At length Richard relaxed and seemed to accept the new woman before him, but Rachel wondered if they would ever return to their old, easy childhood relationship.

'How do you manage with no income, Rachel?' Richard was looking at her thoughtfully.

'I acquired an income in London when I was the secretary of a committee devoted to reforms of various kinds. It was sufficient for me to save some money, which I have invested in this place.'

For the first time, Richard smiled. 'You always had much determination, Rachel. I suppose you are one of these new women.'

Rachel laughed. 'If so, it is very agreeable.'

'What became of your friend Sophie?'

Rachel's face clouded. 'We lost touch with each other for some time. She is now in Egypt and I have recently had a letter. I hope she may visit me when she comes to England.'

'And is she also a new woman?'

'She always said she would not marry but now she tells me she is engaged to be married to a doctor. I suppose we all had strange notions when we were young.' Rachel smiled at Richard enigmatically.

Richard stood up, looking at her thoughtfully. 'I must leave now. I would like to help as much as I can, Rachel. Perhaps I could come again in the near future.'

'Oh, you will always be welcome, Richard. And thank you again for your generosity. I can tell you that it will go to repairing the roof.'

A thought came into her mind. She knew that she was about to say something which should be left unsaid, but some deeper instinct impelled her. It was as though she had to remind him that the woman before him was the same creature whom he had helped long ago. She would not accept the patronage accorded to a reformed character.

'It occurs to me, Richard, that I am also indebted to you for another fifty pounds.'

Richard's face reddened. He said roughly, 'Rachel, how could you refer to such a matter. You owe me nothing.'

'I would not want your help now because you felt sorry for me, Richard.'

Richard frowned. 'I do not understand what you mean, Rachel. It is not a question of feeling sorry. I admire you, Rachel.'

Rachel smiled. 'Thank you.'

She walked with him to the door and watched him disappear down the steps to the lane. He turned and waved briefly. Rachel returned to the children, feeling a warm glow of happiness. It would be pleasant if Richard visited sometimes; he had always been such a dear companion, someone with whom she could discuss almost anything.

Over the next few days, she found herself eagerly awaiting the delivery of letters, hoping that he might write again.

He called a week later, bringing some books which he thought she might find useful for the children.

'They are books from my childhood. I have no further use for them.'

'You might need them for your own children one day,' Rachel said lightly.

Richard ignored her comment.

'You are an eligible young man,' she continued. 'You have a successful business, James tells me that you are an important person in the church in Dartmouth. And,' she added, smiling, 'you are most handsome. There must be many young ladies—'

'Rachel, do not mock me.'

'Mock you! Richard, I am only talking as, well, almost a relative.'

Richard said coldly, 'It is not a topic I wish to pursue.'

Rachel raised her eyebrows. It was clear that in spite of his good-will, Richard was not entirely easy with her. 'It is simply I think you would be a good husband and father,' she said coolly.

After he had gone, she began to reflect on his behaviour and attitude towards her. Beneath that cold exterior, was he still attracted to her as he had once been? Was it simply the memory of the past that would for ever prohibit him from resuming their old, intimate relationship?

She thought about her own position. She knew that she could not indefinitely sustain her work, running the children's home, opening another house for young girls, without financial help. Donations were intermittent and uncertain; the day might come when, with no income of her own, she would have to give up the home.

Her status in the community was now assured; there was much good-will towards her and her work. Yet in the end, it was money which would ensure her success. Supposing Richard were really interested in her, she would gain added status as his wife, as well as the permanent financial backing which would ensure that she could carry on.

She blushed at her own thoughts. Was she being a pragmatic woman, like so many of the young ladies who married purely to be provided with a home, status and financial rewards? No, she told herself, her chief aim was to help her children and the poor and to promote women's rights. That was not a selfish aim. In addition, she admired Richard for his determination and diligence and for his kindness to her. He had been the only one to help her when she was rejected.

It was only when he called again, one evening, that she realised her suspicions were correct. She invited him to stay for supper and he unbent and began to relax in her presence. He told her about his fishing fleet, how the enormous catches of pilchards were sent over to the Continent and about his new ship-building venture. He had received an order for a large ketch from the French government, and another for a schooner from an American firm. As well as that, there were frequent orders for fishing vessels from Dartmouth itself.

'Do you have a large house in Dartmouth, Richard?'

'It is called Gable House, a pleasant enough house in Higher Street. It is adequate for my needs, though I spend much time away from it.'

'And you have a housekeeper?'

'Naturally. I could scarcely provide for myself.'

'Perhaps I could visit it one day.'

Richard hesitated. 'That would be possible,' he said politely. 'Though I do not think you have much interest in domestic matters.'

'No. I would not care to be a mere housewife,' Rachel agreed. 'But I would enjoy visiting you.'

'As a matter of fact, I have come with the purpose of inviting you to a social function in Dartmouth. It is to celebrate the Golden Wedding of the mayor.'

Rachel looked away, concealing her astonishment. Was it simply that she was a suitable partner for an unattached bachelor or did his motives go beyond that?

'That would be agreeable,' she said, 'though the journey to Dartmouth presents some difficulty.'

'I will send a carriage. It is for next Tuesday evening.'

The following week, a coachman took her in the carriage to the Assembly Hall where Richard awaited her on the steps. He looked with approval at her silver chiffon gown and pale blue velvet cape and her auburn hair arranged on the top of her head in a bouffant. The mayor in his robes and chains and the bejewelled mayoress, resplendent in a gold lamé gown, stood at the top of the carpeted staircase, receiving their guests as they were announced. All the notables of Dartmouth appeared to be present and Rachel quietly observed their looks of interest and curiosity at Richard's new-found companion. Few people in that town would have heard of a woman from Kingsbridge and her children's home.

As Rachel gazed around at the opulent-looking gathering, she recognised that this was a group of people who liked to parade their wealth, the comfortable and successful inhabitants of a prosperous little town. If she could capture the interest of these people, she might receive financial help of a substantial kind.

Even as she thought this, she saw Richard watching her across the table. There was a strange kind of pride in his expression and he smiled at her as she talked politely to the man on her left. She realised that he was, perhaps unconsciously, assessing her acceptability in polite society. It seemed an extraordinary thing, but he clearly feared that she might at any moment lapse into what he saw as the wild behaviour of her adolescence. Or, even worse, did he fear that she might suddenly succumb to the temptations of the flesh, as he felt she had done in the past? And did he suspect or even know about Jacob? Was he trying to persuade himself to forget those episodes in her life?

She knew she could not speak about her activities tonight. To introduce the topic of illegitimate babies or fallen women or the sufferings of a disadvantaged poor would provoke opinions from these worthy citizens against which she would have to argue. She would be seen as one of those undesirable new women, who roused even more suspicion and disapproval in these parts than they did in the city.

When she looked at him again, he was talking to an elderly lady on his left but he felt her eyes on him and glanced up. She looked into his eyes. Her studied gaze had never had any effect on Richard in the past, but now he blushed and for one moment he looked back at her. She knew then that Richard was in love with her.

After the dinner, they all went to the ballroom where Rachel behaved with decorum, talking agreeably to young ladies and formally to young gentlemen, sitting with an old gentleman who had been lately widowed and assisting an old lady to her chair. The mayor requested the pleasure of a waltz with her and she was warmly praised for her graceful dancing by the mayoress. Richard was congratulated on having such a charming companion and she was invited to a dinner-party to be held the following week at the home of another ship-builder, John Bateman. When she declined, on the grounds that Kingsbridge was sixteen miles away from Dartmouth, Mrs Bateman instantly said that a carriage would be sent for her.

When Richard returned her to Kingsbridge that night, he suggested that she might like to visit his house before proceeding to the dinner to which they had been invited.

'Yes, indeed, Richard. I have a matter which I would like to discuss with you then.' She reached up and kissed him lightly on the cheek.

Richard rested a hand on her shoulder and then turned abruptly and climbed into his carriage.

That night, Rachel lay in bed, composing her story. She had decided. She would marry Richard.

When she arrived at his home the next week, Richard was awaiting her on the steps. He told the coachman he need not wait; he would bring Miss Cavendish to the dinner party himself.

Rachel entered the large, quiet house. It was simply and tastefully furnished. Unlike his childhood home, there were few knick-knacks and in place of the heavy damasks and over-stuffed settees and *chaise-longues*, the large, wide arm-chairs and pianos and settles, an air of space was created by the prettily carved wooden chairs, a simple settee by the wide marble fireplace and neat arm chairs placed apart. A large portrait of his mother hung over the mantelpiece and tall bookcases were ranged around the walls.

'It's lovely, Richard,' Rachel said in surprise. 'Did you choose all this?'

Richard smiled. 'I am glad you approve. It is suitable for a bachelor.'

'I should think it would also be suitable for a husband. I imagine few wives have such a house to enter when they marry.'

'It is not a matter which occupies my thoughts,' Richard said shortly.

'Anyhow, Richard. I wish to bring up what you may feel to be an unpleasant and unwelcome topic.'

Richard frowned.

'Sit down, Richard. I merely wish to give you a factual account of certain matters. In view of your past and present kindness to me and your consideration for me, I feel I owe it to you to tell you the truth about those events.'

'What events, Rachel?'

Rachel was silent for a moment. She must ensure that she spoke coherently, decisively. She did not wish to have to repeat the story.

'When I left Kingsbridge, long ago, assisted by the money you gave me—'

'Rachel, you do not need—'

'Richard, please hear me out. It is important that you know. When I left, you understood that I was in a certain condition.'

'It was surely for that reason that my father turned you from his home.'

'That was as you and the rest of the family thought. It was not so. I invented the story.'

'Invented! Why would you do such a monstrous thing?'

'You may remember that, at that time, I was much discontented with life in a small place like Kingsbridge. I was bored with the visiting and domestic activities, and although I was grateful to Aunt Maria and to all of you for taking me in, giving me a home, I longed for a different way of life. I suppose my childhood in Egypt had not prepared me for such a limited existence. I felt a need to do something with my life, an ambition which is scarcely acceptable in

300

women in these parts. I believed that in London, I might find opportunities for education and employment.'

'Education! But you went to an excellent establishment. It was an expensive place. You met suitable people.'

'Expensive it may have been, but I was trained merely to be a charming housewife, a delightful hostess, a lady of charity. I did not use my mind, Richard.'

Richard frowned. 'But what—'

'I saw in a newspaper the address of an organisation in London which would find me shelter and employment. Since it was meant for the homeless, I could apply for their help only if I could prove that I had nowhere to go.'

'Rachel!'

'It may seem absurd or even dishonest to you, but I knew that if I said that I was pregnant, I should be turned from your home and thus I could proceed to London and find shelter and employment. I would be free, Richard.'

'Rachel, I cannot believe what you are saying.'

'You must believe me, Richard. Please consider. How do you think I made the progress that I did in London if my story is not true? The money you gave me so generously would not have lasted for long in that city. Through the organisation, I was enabled to meet people, other women who had the same aims as I.'

Richard stood up, shaking his head. 'Rachel, what you are saying is preposterous.' Then the full implications of her words appeared to strike him. 'Do you mean that you never—'

'Never what?'

'There were never, was never . . . any man.'

'Yes. That is what I mean.'

Richard walked to the window. Rachel knew that he could not further discuss such a topic. All it meant to him was that she was not a fallen woman, had never known this terrible, immoral intimacy with a man.

'It is impossible, Rachel. I cannot believe you indulged in such duplicity.'

'I was young, Richard. I had dreams and hopes.'

'It is not for me to criticise you. But it is an incredible thing, Rachel.'

'I had a somewhat sad childhood, Richard. I think it much disturbed my mind.'

'Yes. Perhaps the family should have been more cognisant of that.'

'I do not criticise them, Richard. They did all they could.'

Rachel smiled. She knew that Richard was now looking at her as the one who had suffered; he was beginning to believe that it was all those adverse outside forces that had led not to immorality but to her duplicity. He would need time to recover from the misery he must have endured over the past years and the shock of her latest revelations. She smiled. He would also have to come to terms with the thought that if she married him, she would never be a conventional housewife, content with life at home. There would be plenty of time.

As they walked down the steps to the waiting carriage, her thoughts turned briefly to Jacob. She felt nothing. The past was gone for ever, he would never return. He was a part of those dreams and hopes of her youth of which she had just spoken to Richard. They had no relevance to her life now. Richard took her hand and helped her up into the carriage.

Chapter 15

Richard left Gable House in Higher Street as the sun began to rise and walked briskly in the direction of the shipyard. Workmen were hurrying along in front of him, fishermen were going in the opposite direction towards the embankment and along Fairfax towards the cove, housewives were bustling in and out of the shops along Duke Street and around the Butterwalk. It was a brilliant September morning – 'a real spring in autumn' old Mrs Charles called to him from her sausage shop – and instead of going down Clarence Street, he turned along Mayors Avenue to the embankment and then walked more slowly towards Sandquay Road.

He stopped and looked out across the harbour, filled with fishing boats, and beyond to the river curving up towards Dittisham. Later in the morning, he was to meet two businessmen from Exeter who had commissioned a sea-going yacht; he had to ensure that the vessel was ready before they arrived. For the first time in his life, he found it impossible to concentrate on business matters.

After Rachel's revelations, he had been awake all night, trying to readjust his thoughts to this new situation. For nearly four years, he had carried with him the knowledge of her disgrace. He had constantly blocked out the vision of her in another man's arms, of the acts she must have performed. When she left, he had spent unhappy days and nights going through all the men of her acquaintance, trying to recollect the dinners and balls and excursions on which she had gone. He had briefly suspected Rodney Parrish, but Rodney had been so perplexed and disturbed by her disappearance, that Richard was convinced it was not he. Only Jacob had had the opportunity to spend time alone with her, but Jacob had not returned for nearly two years, and when he did he had seemed so little concerned with her departure that Richard had begun to doubt even Jacob's guilt. Surely he would have shown more concern if he had had such a relationship with her.

As time passed, the pain he had felt changed gradually to resignation. It had happened, she had gone and the love he felt for her was something he must accept. He had tried to hate her, forget her, knowing in the end that it was impossible.

Now, suddenly, his world had been shaken. What Rachel had told him meant that she had never been violated, never consorted with a man in that fashion. There had never been anyone, there was no guilt. He was faced instead with the memory of the lonely girl who had left in apparent disgrace on that misty morning. He wondered briefly why she had looked so ill when she left. And how about the doctor? He had confirmed that Rachel was in a certain state. But how could a doctor know such a thing? Doctors were fools, in any case. It had clearly been only supposition on his part.

In reality, she had been setting out on what appeared to her an adventure. He tried to comprehend the courage such an action must have taken. She had always been devoted to learning and the acquisition of knowledge, she had always seemed to have a restless ambition to escape from the confinements of domestic life. Richard felt relieved that at least he had been instrumental in helping her to achieve her ambition.

He imagined her arriving in that vast city, to which he had been only twice in his life. The noise and confusion, the utter isolation when she stepped from the train must have been terrifying. Then she had had to find the institution she had seen advertised, present herself there and convince them that she was homeless. Yet from that precarious beginning she had managed to create an independent life for herself.

If only Rachel had told him of her ambitions at the time, her real reason for leaving. Then he reflected that if she had, he would certainly have persuaded her otherwise. No one in the family could have accepted a young girl going to live in London alone.

He thought of her now, of her lovely face and her thick auburn hair falling in waves down her back; he imagined her white body, the curves of her breasts. He frowned, rejecting such intimate thoughts.

But those thoughts would not be wrong if he could marry her. He could never have considered that possibility if she had been defiled as he had thought. Ever since she had returned, he had been in a frenzy of longing for her, knowing all the time that it could never be fulfilled. Now it was different.

He began to worry that perhaps she might not consider him, in any case. Since her return to Kingsbridge, Rachel had shown no interest in any male companions. She appeared to fulfil her social engagements purely for the purpose of arousing interest in her children's home, and the one she was now opening for older homeless girls. She seemed to have lost interest in the balls and dances she had once enjoyed. He remembered his feelings of anger and jealousy in the past, as he watched her behaving in what he considered a frivolous fashion. It occurred to him that there must be young men in Kingsbridge who might wish to marry her. None of them had known of her apparent past, as he had done. He realised, however, that young men would be wary of a woman such as Rachel, however attractive. She was not merely performing charitable acts like the other young women in Kingsbridge. For her, it seemed more of a crusade. She must have made it clear that she would not be content to remain at home, dutifully awaiting the return of her husband each evening.

He drew his watch from his breast pocket and began to hurry along to the yard. Ever since Rachel had returned, she had constantly invaded his thoughts, but he had never allowed it to interfere with his work. It was only now that the problem appeared to be settled, that he realised the state of anxiety in which he had been living. Tomorrow was Sunday. He would call in at St Saviours this evening, to say he would be unable to act as a sidesman at the morning service. He would go to Kingsbridge and tell Rachel of his feelings; he must know her answer.

Early the next morning, he rode up beyond Jawbones Hill in his carriage and headed along the Kingsbridge road. He looked down over Warfleet Creek and St Petrox and beyond to the open sea. In the distance he could see the sails of fishing boats, many of which belonged to his fleet. The catches had not been so good here this year and many fishermen had gone for the season to the fishing grounds off the east coast. Yet they always returned; it was rare for Devon fishermen to leave their homes. He found himself wondering why Rachel had returned to Kingsbridge. She belonged to London, in a way. She had a sophistication which did not fit in with the mores of this society.

He reached her home in Kingsbridge as the congregations were disgorging from the church and chapels. He looked eagerly to see if she were among them. Then he noticed Elsie and Dora walking along the road.

He waved to them and stopped. 'I will give you a lift home,' he said affably, and the two girls grinned and climbed into the carriage beside him.

'And is your mistress not with you today?'

'No, sir. She's not here.'

'Why not?' he said sharply. 'Where has she gone?'

'Please, sir,' Dora said, mistaking his concern. 'We have only been to church, as she instructed. And Mrs Blake is in charge of the household.'

'Yes, of course.' Richard blushed. 'I was unaware of her absence. Is she on business?'

'Yes, sir. She's gone to London.'

Richard felt a pang of disappointment. In his mind, he had imagined that by the time he left Kingsbridge later today, everything would be settled.

'For how long?'

'Oh, we don't know, sir,' Elsie said doubtfully. 'I expect Mrs Blake can inform you.'

Edith and Mrs Blake were playing with the children on the lawn when they arrived.

'Good day, sir.' Mrs Blake walked towards him. 'May I offer you some refreshment?'

'That is very civil, Mrs Blake. But don't let me interrupt you.'

He picked one of the children up in his arms. The boy giggled and smiled up at him. For a brief moment, he considered the idea of fatherhood for the first time. Would Rachel like the prospect of children of her own?

'What's your name, then?'

'David.' The child pointed to Edith. 'That's my Mama.'

Richard turned and looked at Edith who was smiling cheerfully at the child. 'Is it, David? I didn't know that.'

'Yes,' Edith said. 'I am fortunate to be able to live here with Miss Cavendish.'

'Yes.' Richard controlled the disapproval he felt. It had not occurred to him that these girls were probably all fallen women. Of course, that would mean nothing to Rachel. She constantly defended such women. This was clearly what she intended in setting up another home for young girls. In the back of his mind, there was a moment of doubt. If he married her, he would have to accept her views on such matters. In fact, Rachel would expect him not only to accept, but also to support her activities.

He followed Mrs Blake into the house. 'I understand Miss Cavendish is not here.'

'No, sir. She's gone to London.'

'Did she say for how long?'

'No, sir.'

'No? But how about the home, the children?'

'Oh, they'll be all right, sir. She'll be returning as soon as she can. But you see, sir, she didn't know how long the trial would last.'

'The trial? What trial, Mrs Blake?'

Mrs Blake rose to her full height. Richard saw that she felt that she herself was a part of the important matters with which Rachel was connected in the city.

'Well, sir, no doubt Miss Cavendish has told you about her work in relation to the procurement of children for prostitution. The trial is in connection with that.'

Richard glanced round apprehensively to ensure that none of the young girls were listening. 'Mrs Blake, I trust this is not a topic you mention in front of Edith and the others.'

'Oh,' Mrs Blake said blandly, 'Miss Cavendish considers that such matters should be discussed openly. She holds with the view that unless young ladies are warned of the perils, they cannot be safe.'

'Indeed. Well, that is for your mistress to decide. She had not mentioned that she was going to the trial.'

'Oh, sir, forgive me. I almost forgot. Miss Cavendish left a note for you.' Mrs Blake went over to the mantelpiece and handed him the envelope.

Richard nodded casually as he took it and put it in his pocket.

'I am sure when she returns she will tell you all about it,' Mrs Blake added proudly.

'Indeed, Mrs Blake. That is no doubt correct. If she returns unexpectedly, kindly give her my regards.'

Richard climbed into his carriage and took the note from his pocket. There must be a reason for her sudden departure. He reminded himself also that Rachel was not obliged to tell him of her movements. Yet, she must know what his feelings were, otherwise she would surely not have told him of those past private events.

Rachel's brief note explained that the trial had been put forward and, as she had promised to be present, she had been compelled to leave immediately. She hoped he would not find her inconsiderate in failing to inform him, but it had been impossible. As the trial should be brief, she did not anticipate that she would be absent for more than a few days. She would miss his companionship.

Richard rode slowly back to Dartmouth. It was a warm autumn day and he stopped at the top of the hill which led down into Dartmouth and alighted from the carriage. He sat on a bench in the sunshine, trying to find some hidden message in her note. Had he appeared critical of her behaviour when she confessed to him? Or was it possible that she simply saw him as a friend? Perhaps she had no greater interest in him than that. When she returned, he would see her immediately, tell her of his love.

But the few days turned out to be two weeks. Richard bought the paper each day, becoming more and more concerned as he followed the salacious details of the proceedings of the trial at the Old Bailey.

He realised at last the reforms in which Rachel had been involved. Richard knew already from previous newspaper reports the background of the three eminent persons concerned: a Mr Bramwell Booth who was the Chief of Staff of the Salvation Army; Mr W T Stead, the Editor of the *Pall Mall Gazette*, an evening newspaper notorious for its news and articles on the patronage of brothels by well-known and influential persons, and on child prostitution. The third eminent person, Josephine Butler, was a witness in the case and had contributed to his newspaper.

It seemed that Mr Stead had known it was insufficient to present facts about the procurement of young girls. He had been to see an inspector at Scotland Yard, who had confirmed immediately that he could go to any brothel and be supplied with a child of thirteen. Mr Stead had asked whether it was true that these girls were unwilling virgins? He was told that there was not a shadow of doubt about it.

Mr Stead had taken up the matter with the Home Secretary who said that he would welcome an independent enquiry. Knowing that neither Parliament nor the general public would believe these girls were innocent, Mr Stead decided that the only way to prove his point was to procure a young girl himself.

Richard read about the absurd web of lies and deceptions which he had perpetrated. He had procured a young girl, Eliza Armstrong, taken her to a room, dosed her with chloroform, had her forcibly examined by a doctor, taken her off to Paris with a reformed prostitute, and housed her in a Salvation Army home. All done, according to the defence, for the most admirable of reasons.

These were the reformers, as they called themselves, with whom Rachel was involved in London. This was the world in which she had lived and operated.

Richard realised now that although he was satisfied about her own probity, there were other deeper matters that he should consider before thinking of marrying her. Rachel was involved in more than protecting the children in her home and the views expressed at the trial must be those which Rachel also embraced. When she talked about reform, she was speaking about changing society. What was it Mrs Blake had said? 'Miss Cavendish believes such matters should be discussed openly.'

As the days passed, Richard became increasingly aware of what marriage to Rachel would mean. Surveying the men in his yard, walking along the streets of Dartmouth to the Custom House, he felt as though he were living in a twilight world.

There was this familiar world which, although there were difficult times and good times, was essentially known and unchanging. Now there was also this other world of impending change. He recognised that he had scarcely acknowledged the tone of the reports and articles he read in the newspapers, the growing number of people like Rachel who were envisaging a different way of life, a different society. Rachel was only exceptional because she was a woman.

There was an air of discontent, of criticism of the status quo, the poor becoming more vocal as sections of the middle classes took up their cause. There was more talk about unions and strikes and better wages and conditions, and there was the growing demand by women for greater freedom. In the past, when there had been riots about poor harvests or demonstrations by a few workers here and there, everyone had always known that these were temporary, unusual events which could be controlled and dealt with, that things would settle down again. This time it was different; what had started as a stream of minor complaints by separate groups of people had gradually joined together to become an uncontrollable flood.

People in this part of the country were still living in the same ethos that he had known as a boy. Rachel and people like her intended to change all that.

But what would she do to his life? Would she bring controversy and disgrace? She had been accepted in Kingsbridge, her charitable efforts had been no bar to her admittance to polite society. Richard was proud of her achievements but even if she agreed to marry him, would he be able to accept her views?

As he rode towards Kingsbridge the day after the trial ended, Richard's fears diminished. Perhaps if they married, Rachel would forget her reforms; her thoughts would be channelled into new directions with a home and children. When he arrived at the house, Rachel had not returned.

'I have had word from Miss Cavendish that sentence has not yet been passed,' Mrs Blake told him.

'Yes, it was reported so.'

'Miss Cavendish will await the verdict. I believe she is much distraught.'

'I will call again,' Richard said slowly. 'And how are the children?' Then he added, 'You do not have any financial problems in her absence, I suppose?'

'Well, sir, I have not thought to send the bills and invoices on to her, in her present state of pre-occupation.'

'Then let me see them. There may be urgent demands.'

Mrs Blake looked doubtful. 'Well, sir, I am not sure if Miss—'

'I am sure it will be all right, Mrs Blake. Miss Cavendish informs me of such matters.' He followed Mrs Blake to the library.

'These are all the correspondences, on her desk.'

'Then just give me the bills. The envelopes are clearly marked with their trademarks.'

'Thank you, sir.'

'I will deal with them and settle the matter with Miss Cavendish on her return.'

Richard returned to Dartmouth and anxiously awaited the outcome of the trial. Rachel herself had frequently alleged that young girls – and even older ones – were being abducted and violated against their will. The reports in the papers had seemed almost obscene to Richard in the details they had printed, yet he still doubted the true intentions of this man Stead. He seemed to be a loud and opinionated bigot with less than honourable intentions.

A week later, sentences were pronounced. The reformed prostitute, Rebecca, was given six-months without hard labour while Stead himself was sentenced to three-months.

The sentence filled him with anxiety. Although the man Booth had not been on trial, Richard felt increasingly uneasy that Rachel mixed with such people. The Salvation Army probably had good intentions, but their apparent leniency towards vice and corruption, their willingness to take in fallen women, was not the way to solve the problem. They should be found useful and gainful employment. Perhaps Rachel was too trusting. She would surely be dismayed to discover the true nature of the people with whom she had been working. He felt an urgent need to protect her, to ensure that she did not place herself in such dangerous situations ever again.

It was a bleak November day as he rode out of the town towards her home on the outskirts and as he alighted from his carriage and walked up the drive, he saw Rachel standing in the drawing-room. She was wearing a pale cream gown with a brown embroidered jacket and her hair was hanging loose over her shoulders.

She saw him approaching and came to the front door to greet him.

He took her hand and followed her along the hall, saying, 'I did not know you were going.' He realised there was a note of criticism in his voice.

She looked surprise at his tone of voice. 'I am afraid my mind has been filled with the proceedings in London.'

'Yes. I regret the outcome of the trial, Rachel, though I feared that perhaps that man was not to be trusted.'

Rachel looked at him in astonishment. 'What do you mean, Richard? He is a most honourable man. It is a monstrous outcome.'

'But Rachel, it was the verdict of a jury. They believed the man to be guilty.'

'A jury! It was the biassed summing up of the judge which decided their minds. The establishment have no wish to admit that child prostitution exists. Too many of the men benefit from it themselves.'

'Rachel! That is a slanderous remark.'

'The truth often is, Richard. I have seen it with my own eyes. There is much evidence of foul practices if you work in the slums of London as I have done.'

'Rachel, I had not come to discuss these distressing topics.'

'Forgive me. I am tired and distraught with all the events. Perhaps you do not realise how devoted I am to the causes for which Alice and I worked.'

'Yes, I do, Rachel.' He added quietly, 'And how is Alice?'

Rachel frowned. 'I did not see her on this occasion. I stayed with Josephine Robertson.'

'Oh, I understood—'

'Alice and I had a difference of opinion some time ago. I had already left her place when I came to Kingsbridge.'

'Oh. You did not mention that.'

'It is a tedious matter,' Rachel said dismissively. 'But come, let us go in by the fire.'

Richard felt as though the situation was sliding away from him. He had intended to tell her of his love, to ask her to marry him and then to determine with her the extent to which her activities should continue. He had the impression that Rachel had anticipated the event; there was something evasive in her manner. Did she not wish to hear his words?

When they were standing opposite each other by the blazing log fire, he took her hands in his and said abruptly, 'Rachel, I came to ask you to marry me.'

At that moment, Edith came in with a basket of logs.

'Good afternoon, Edith.' Richard released Rachel's hands. He adhered to the custom in Rachel's household that servants were all greeted and addressed in the same way as members of the family or other visitors.

'Good afternoon, sir.'

'Richard,' Rachel said. 'Will you be staying for dinner?'

'If I may.'

'Then tell Mrs Blake, Edith, that Mr Damarell will be here.'

As Edith walked from the room, Richard looked anxiously at Rachel. He had a sudden fear that she would not even consider marriage to him.

'I am flattered by your feelings towards me, Richard. But I do not know if I can accept your proposal,' Rachel answered, sighing.

His heart leapt. At least, she had not given an outright rejection. 'Rachel, I merely ask you to consider it,' he continued eagerly.

Rachel smiled again. 'Yes, I am doing so. But I think you do not share my enthusiasm for reform. You are not much concerned with those matters which occupy me.'

'I have thought about nothing else since you left, Rachel. We have very different views, I know, but they do not affect the state of marriage.'

'Indeed they do, Richard. I would not be prepared to forego my various activities.'

'There would be no need, Rachel. You could still attend to your children's home.'

'But would you be willing for me to continue what I look upon as a career? I must still frequently go to London when the need arises.'

'Surely your main interests are now here?'

'Yes, they are, but as you know I propose shortly to open a home for pregnant and abandoned girls. And I have become a member of what is known as the Men and Women's Club, whose purpose is to agitate for genuine equality for women in all spheres. Could you support such ventures?'

Richard controlled the feelings of apprehension which came over him. At the moment, none of those outside things mattered. It seemed so long, those years of wanting her, of living in a secret world of dreams where she had not been a fallen woman but the pure, innocent girl he had first known. Then when she had returned, there had been the agony of being so near to her, yet forever apart. And then her revelation that what had appeared to have happened in the past had not in fact occurred and the joy he had felt that perhaps his love need not for ever be frustrated.

'Rachel,' he repeated. 'I love you most sincerely. I would do all that I could to make you happy.'

'Yes, Richard, I know. I have much admiration for you. For your industry and honesty and for the progress you have made. And I know you are much respected in Kingsbridge and Dartmouth. Also, you have always been very kind to me, sometimes I suspect against the dictates of your own conscience.'

'I love you,' Richard said simply.

Rachel stood up. He watched the firelight playing on her hair as she said, 'Perhaps I don't know what love is. I have a great regard for you.'

'I think women do not have the same feelings as men. It is not to be expected. But would you be content to be with me? I would be a good husband to you, Rachel.'

There was a fleeting expression on her face of doubt almost, he thought, of misery. For a second, he had the impression that she was about to tell him some distressing piece of information. Then she smiled.

'Richard, I know you are a good person. Yes, I will marry you.'

Richard flung his arms around her and, as she looked at him, he kissed her eagerly. She did not respond but seemed embarrassed by his embrace and stepped back slightly. It was a simple gesture but one which filled him with greater joy. Only some inexperienced, innocent girl would behave in such a fashion. He now knew that she had never known the embraces of other men.

'Rachel, dear, I have waited so long,' he said apologetically.

'I hope you will be happy with me, Richard. But we shall have a great deal to arrange. I shall have to organise proceedings about this home and the other one I am opening. Perhaps I will maintain these and open a new place in Dartmouth.'

Richard hesitated. He realised he had not made any pronouncements relating to her career, as he had intended to do. In fact, he had agreed to it continuing. He also realised he would not be able to be a passive observer, for Rachel would demand, at the very least, complete support.

'Will you be able to manage all that and our home as well?'

Rachel laughed. 'With ease,' she said. 'I am accustomed to many commitments.'

314

'Rachel, I am so proud of you and all your endeavours.'

As he said goodbye to her that night, he took her in his arms and kissed her gently. 'I will not startle you again,' he said smiling.

Rachel looked into his eyes. 'No, you don't startle me, Richard. I only fear that I may startle you.'

As he walked along under a starlit sky, he thought of her innocent expression as she watched him depart. In spite of her assurances, he felt that she, that all women, were vulnerable. The world was a harsh place; they needed protection. Reflecting upon her naïvety, another thought began to trouble him. Deep in his mind lay the feeling of guilt that he had carried with him ever since Rachel had returned. That past, shameful act of his had never mattered while he had been free and independent, for there was no one whom it could concern. Now he began to re-live the time when, after watching Rachel vanish into the cold morning light to go to London, the Damarell household had been plunged into recrimination and acrimony.

His father had accused them all in turn first of knowing where she had gone, then of being the cause of her disgrace. His wish to find her was precipitated by the fear that she would bring further shame upon the household.

Finally, Richard had walked out and gone to Dartmouth. Established there in a lodging house in Smith Street, he had got a job as a fisherman. He spent his idle hours wandering around the streets at night, lonely and unhappy, wondering about Rachel.

One evening, a girl had spoken to him on a street corner. She was fair-haired and pretty and she asked him to come back to her room. In his desperation, he had agreed. Even now he blushed at his behaviour. He knew perfectly well what he was doing; he could not salve his conscience by pleading ignorance. Once in her dingy little room, which seemed to possess only a bed and table and two chairs, she gave him harsh cider which seemed to burn into his brain, followed by brandy. He had watched her undress and then he had suddenly torn off his clothes and plunged on the bed with her. All his agony had found release in that wild, passionate union. She had laughed and responded in the way that he had heard those sort of women do, and as he walked back to Smith Street, his guilt was compounded by the knowledge that he had enjoyed it – he only wished that it had been Rachel.

315

Even worse, he had returned on three further occasions to the girl, and had indulged in behaviour the memory of which seared into his soul – and all the time he had visualised it was Rachel. Despairing at his own culpability, he had turned to the redemption of religion and joined St Saviour's Church, determined to channel his energies into working for their Christian endeavours. He knew now that his father had been right about the temptations of the flesh. He had to keep the terrible secret of those nights for ever. It happened to many men, he told himself, and a young, unmarried man should not feel any guilt. Perhaps even Rachel, with her liberal views, would know that such things occurred. Yet whatever happened, he could never tell her, for in a way, he felt as though he had violated Rachel already. Rachel, with her honesty and her desire to help the world, was above that kind of behaviour.

Chapter 16

Rachel blinked her eyes against the brilliant spring sunshine which flooded the conservatory. She looked round with appreciation at the palms and fig plants, the bowls of hyacinths and primulas arranged along the wide window sills. It was a long, glass extension to the house, built mainly to give Elsie an opportunity to expand her interest in plant growing. Elsie had proved not to be very adept in her care of children; she loved the open air, and spent much of her time in the garden, attending to the flower-beds. Rachel had suggested that she should extend her activities to indoor plants, and that perhaps in the future she might open a small florists's shop in Kingsbridge. Elsie was already growing enough plants to sell at the bazaars and church fêtes, the proceeds being divided between Elsie and the Home.

Rachel picked up *The Times* and glanced briefly at the front page. It was filled with articles and reports on the debate about Home Rule for Ireland. The Home Rule Bill was to be presented to the House shortly. If it failed, Gladstone would resign and they would be faced with another Conservative government. She shook her head. That probably meant that the Contagious Diseases Bill would fail yet again, and all of the other reforming Bills, too.

She put the paper down, her mind flitting across the causes that absorbed her: free education, housing, equality for women. She stood up and looked out on the garden, where Dora was attending to some of the children. David, Edith's child, was climbing an apple tree. He was the little boy who was the same age as her own would have been. She frequently found herself watching him; he was pale and fair-haired, totally unlike, she supposed, how her child would have looked. Yet he aroused feelings of longing in her that none of the other children excited.

She touched the fronds of the ferns hanging from a basket above her. Elsie must take some of these hanging baskets to the workhouse and enquire about the young girl whose illegitimate baby had just died. When she was well enough, she would come here to live. She was aware of a vague feeling of apprehension. Now that she had agreed to marry Richard, she frequently had these moments of doubt, fearing that Richard might suddenly express disapproval of her activities. So far, she had seen no sign that he intended to interfere.

Rachel glanced in the long mirror and adjusted her combs, straightening the wide collar of her dark green gown. Richard had said how beautiful she looked in this gown; how it matched the colour of her hair and her grey eyes. She smiled. He had become quite vocal since their engagement.

As she turned to leave the conservatory, Dora came in.

'Dora, I am just going to see the Girls' Home.'

'Yes, ma'am. There's a Mr Damarell to see you.'

Rachel laughed. 'Well, show him in.'

Dora went out. What did the girl mean, 'a Mr Damarell'. Surely she'd seen Richard often enough?

Then the door opened. Rachel looked in silence. It was Jacob. He stood in the doorway in his Guards' uniform of red jacket and dark blue trousers, his black hair curling down beneath his pcaked hat.

In the few seconds before he spoke, three impressions flashed through her mind. Firstly, he was much more handsome than she had remembered, and she could only look at the curving red lips and his dark eyes as though she were hypnotised. Then memories of the past flooded through her and she felt naked before him, as though she was in his power again, standing on the hill at Bolt Tail with the wind blowing wildly around them. And then she was asking herself how the small, endless series of actions and words and activities that made up one's life correlated with those few vital, never-to-be-forgotten experiences, events that changed one's whole life. Over-riding all those impressions was a sense of foreboding, an unexpected distaste.

Jacob was looking at her with a perplexed expression. He quickly recovered and laughingly came towards her. 'My goodness, Rachel. You are certainly a beauty.'

Rachel took his hand coolly. 'Hallo, Jacob. This is an unexpected visit.'

'Yes, I did not expect to be here myself. I have only just arrived. Well.' He lightly held her chin up, looking into her face. Rachel moved away from him.

'I understood you were in Afghanistan. Are you now on leave?'

'Yes, for a couple of months. Then I go to the Sudan. They're still clearing up the mess after the Gordon débâcle.'

'Jacob, it is a pleasure to see you safe and well. But unfortunately I have a prior engagement. Perhaps you will be able to visit at some later time.'

Jacob blushed. He seemed to be speechless at her indifference.

Rachel added pleasantly, 'Richard did not mention your return.'

There was a slight smile on Jacob's face when he said, 'I haven't seen him yet, but Bertha has informed me of your impending marriage.'

'Yes.' Rachel's voice was flat. She had a violent fear that Jacob would devastate her life once again. 'In the summer.'

Jacob frowned suddenly. 'You did not reply to my letters, Rachel,' he said abruptly.

Rachel said quickly, 'I didn't receive them until years later. I had left Kingsbridge.'

A provocative expression came over his face. 'You didn't wait then.'

Rachel felt as though she had been physically struck by his cool insolence. She tried to speak casually. 'That is all long ago, Jacob. I was just a foolish child.' She moved away abruptly.

'No doubt. Though you did not behave so.' There was an aggressive note in Jacob's voice. 'And does Richard know of your past little indiscretions?'

Rachel blushed. 'No, of course not.' She cleared her throat, trying to hide her agitation. 'We have not met for over four years, Jacob, nor corresponded. I am sure the past means no more to you than it does to me.'

'Be assured, Rachel, that I have no feelings for you of any kind. I am merely concerned that my dear brother may be deceived,' Jacob sneered.

Rachel felt a cold, vindictive anger. She looked at him contemptuously. 'And what would your dear father think if he knew the truth?' She saw Jacob's astonished expression, his look of anxiety. 'Perhaps you would leave now. I am pleased that you are well, Jacob.'

She walked across the conservatory, through the door and on down the drive without glancing back. Her abrupt departure was meant to signal a confidence she was far from feeling. It was the strength of her emotions which disturbed her, because they were not what she had expected. Jacob's words had filled her with a sudden fear that she might lose Richard. She knew that she appreciated Richard's support and was happy in his company, but her decision to marry him had been prompted by her need for an assured income. It was only now, with that veiled threat from Jacob, that she recognised her real feelings: it was Richard himself she feared to lose, not his income or support. Looking at Jacob, seeing that vision of the past, she had seen how important Richard had become to her.

When Richard came that evening, she greeted him eagerly.

Richard kissed her, the formal, restrained kiss that she had come to welcome. It made no demands on her, only gave her a sense of safety.

'Jacob visited me this morning,' she said casually.

Rachel noticed an expression of doubt flit across his face. 'Yes. I believe Bertha told him of our engagement. He told her he would call upon you.'

'He looks well,' Rachel observed.

Richard nodded thoughtfully. 'Jacob is always well. Few things in life trouble him.'

'Then he is fortunate.'

Richard said slowly, 'He has expressed a wish to be my best man. Would that meet with your approval, Rachel?'

Rachel frowned. 'I had thought that James would perform that function.'

'Yes. That would be the proper course. I will tell Jacob. He will, however, be a guest at the wedding.'

'Yes. Of course.'

Rachel glanced at Richard's serious expression. Was there any suspicion in his mind? He knew that at one time Jacob had held some attraction for her. It was scarcely possible that Richard, in love with her himself, had failed to notice her infatuation with Jacob.

'Jacob took me on some interesting excursions when I was a young girl,' she said casually. 'In those days I found him an agreeable companion , though,' she added thoughtfully, 'he was never as kind and helpful as James.'

Richard awkwardly put an arm around her. 'I feel honoured that you chose me, Rachel.'

'Richard, I wish very much to be married to you,' Rachel answered calmly.

He looked at her solemnly. She had a feeling that he was considering asking her about her past feelings for Jacob. Perhaps he would always wonder about that.

'Three months seems a long time,' he replied.

'Richard, I have been thinking of your father.' Richard looked suspicious. 'I know that you had some kind of disagreement.'

'That is long ago,' he said shortly.

'For that reason, would it not be possible to make your peace with him. He would surely wish to come to the wedding. He is an old man, Richard.'

Richard turned away. 'I cannot imagine his wishes in that respect.'

Rachel hesitated, then she said firmly, 'Richard, I think I know the cause of your disagreement. Now that we . . . know the truth of that matter, his past errors cannot be important.'

'Perhaps you are right, Rachel. Perhaps you are more generous-spirited than I am.'

'I'll go and see him, Richard. I don't think he bears me any animosity now. In fact, he has endeavoured to help with the home.'

'Indeed?' Richard looked surprised. He paused. 'You are right, Rachel. But it is not for you to go. I will go myself.'

He returned later that evening. There was a slight smile on his face as he said, 'Well, Papa has agreed to re-admit me to the family circle.'

Rachel laughed. 'You must not be too submissive with him. I think I have learnt how to deal with him, you know.'

'Yes. He spoke of you and your efforts with some approval. It was strange to observe a certain mellowness in him.'

Rachel experienced a sense of relief. Mr Damarell almost represented a kind of security to her now. If he were present at the wedding, if Richard was now re-installed in his paternal affections, perhaps Jacob would be less inclined to cause any trouble. But surely Jacob's threat was simply the result of injured pride; surely he would not carry it out.

James came the next day to give his music lessons to the children. He informed Rachel that Jacob and Mr Damarell had gone on an excursion to Plymouth.

'I believe Jacob has asked Richard if he can be his best man.'

'I thought that task would fall to you, James. Though of course, the decision must rest with Richard.'

'Yes, and I have indicated to Richard that he must do as he thinks desirable. After all, we see little of Jacob. He has little opportunity to share in family functions.'

'You are always so accommodating, James, but I think Jacob will not insist.'

As she walked up Fore Street to visit the Girls' Home, Rachel tried to dismiss her fears about the wedding. She could not bear to think of Jacob standing by Richard's side at the altar. Surely he would not persist in such a vengeful intention?

The next day she received a letter. It was short and uncompromising.

Dear Rachel,

I am writing to apologise for my behaviour when I visited you on Wednesday. You were correct to dismiss me. I can understand that you would never wish to see me again. I merely ask you to forgive me. Pray, let us remain friends.

Jacob.

She tore the letter into pieces, her fingers trembling. Would he persist in reminding her of his presence? It was almost like blackmail. She tried to put him from her mind but two days later, another letter arrived.

Recognising his handwriting, she almost tore it up unopened but fear made her read it.

Dear Rachel,

I had hoped for a reply. But common sense tells me that you are not the sort of person lightly to change your mind. Yet it has become of painful importance to me that I should not leave here without your forgiveness. In view of our past friendship, I beg you to reply. You have roused in me an unaccountable feeling of guilt. I wish only for a word.

Jacob.

Rachel re-read the note. Supposing he continued to write in this manner; supposing Richard should find out? Was it possible that, in the end, Jacob would tell him? Was he so overcome with injured pride that he would do that? Did he feel that he could finally get his revenge on Richard for his own childhood resentments?

If only she could tell Richard, if only it were not necessary to conceal the truth. Yet she knew it would never be possible. It occurred to her that it might be better for her to reveal it to Richard than leave it to Jacob. No. There was nothing she could do but wait.

At the request of Josephine Robertson, she had arranged to go to London to celebrate the repeal of the Contagious Diseases Act. There was also an important conference to attend about housing and afterwards they were to see *The Mikado*. Sitting in the hall, listening to the speeches and arguments about housing for the poor, Rachel could think only of the impending disaster that she feared awaited her at home. Yet when she returned to Kingsbridge, there were no more letters and Bertha informed her that Jacob had gone away to see friends.

A week later, Rachel was sitting in her drawing-room, writing the speech she was to make about seeking donations for her children's homes, when Jacob walked in unannounced. Rachel sprang up.

'Do not blame your maids for not announcing me, Rachel. I came in through the conservatory.'

'Indeed. It scarcely seems necessary to behave so.'

'I thought you might not see me.'

'Then you are correct about that.' She looked at his handsome face. There was an expression of anxiety on it which she had never seen before.

'Rachel, I must talk to you.'

'Then please say what is on your mind and depart.'

'Rachel, in six weeks' time, I must go to the Sudan.'

'Yes. I believe James mentioned it to me.'

323

'Rachel, how can you be so indifferent after what happened between us?'

Rachel glanced anxiously through the window. She was expecting Richard at any moment. What would he deduce if he found Jacob here again?

'Jacob,' she said coldly, 'if you have any regard for me, you will never mention this matter again. Please leave now.'

Jacob looked at her stubbornly. 'The other day, Bertha said something which made me suspicious.'

Rachel frowned. Bertha would never reveal their private conversations; he was simply trying to confuse her. She did not reply.

'I was trying to ask her once again why you had left and she said perhaps I should know better than anyone.'

'I do not understand her words,' Rachel said distantly.

'Rachel, you do. You must. Rachel, it cannot be what I fear, can it?'

Rachel looked at his perplexed face. She knew that she could deny it, invent a story and dismiss his fears for ever; or she could tell him the whole distasteful sequence of events. Perhaps that was what she needed to do; she realised she had never told anyone, never shared the grief she had felt. Perhaps even the need to return to Kingsbridge had been bound up with that sense of loss. Perhaps if she told him, it would absolve them both from the past. Perhaps then he would leave her in peace.

She looked at him distantly. Her voice was cold and remote as she said, 'I do not wish there to be any recriminations, Jacob, in regard to what I say.'

'Recriminations against you?'

'No, Jacob, not me. But you might feel adversely towards others.'

'Rachel, I only want to know my responsibility in it. I must know.'

'It is all long past, Jacob. I have no wish to think of it. But perhaps it would be more surely buried if I spoke of it. I have never told anyone the whole truth. When you left, I found I was pregnant. I didn't know what was wrong with me. I didn't even know how women got pregnant. I thought I had a stomach disease.'

'Oh, Rachel.' Jacob spoke in a pained voice as his own culpability struck him.

'Aunt Maria took me to a doctor, who quickly diagnosed the truth.

As a result, your father evicted me from the house.'

'Evicted! What do you mean, Rachel?'

'I was to go to the workhouse.'

'Workhouse! How could he do such a thing?' he said indignantly.

'Jacob, I see now that his conduct was inevitable. You know yourself that he could not bring such shame upon his own household.'

'What of the others? Mama and James and everyone?'

'They were kind, Jacob, but of course they could not interfere.'

'And then?' Jacob appeared to ask the question reluctantly, as though he did not wish to know the answer.

'Richard gave me the money to escape.'

'Richard!' Jacob frowned. Then he said slowly, 'Did he know that I was responsible?'

'No,' Rachel said. 'No one knew.'

'Rachel, do you mean—?'

'I mean nothing, except that no one knew.'

Jacob stood up and walked to the window and then he came back and sat down again.

'You have no need to look so overwhelmed. I have long since recovered from the experience.'

Jacob said quietly, 'And then, Rachel?'

Rachel spoke in a matter-of-fact tone. 'I went to London and took a room in a boarding-house. When Richard's money ran out I was reduced to living in the Rookeries off Leicester Square.'

'Rookeries?'

'You may be unacquainted with their existence. They are similar to those off the Whitechapel Road and Waterloo. Slums, Jacob. Your child was born in a room with bare boards and a chair. I lay on a sack, bloodstained by previous occupants.'

Jacob's face was white.

Rachel felt a cold determination inside her. Now that she had begun, she would tell him everything. It was as though she were absolving their joint responsibility.

'It was a boy. It did not live. It was delivered by a woman from the room downstairs, smelling of alcohol and filth.' Rachel went on speaking evenly. 'I took the child and left it on the steps of a church, wrapped in my petticoat.' Her voice trembled. 'That was the hardest part. Inside me, perhaps I still mourn.'

Jacob was standing at the window with his back to her. She sighed. Now she had spoken the words, she felt a sense of relief. It was the truth. Her grief had been only for that lost child.

Jacob turned suddenly. 'Did you not care for me, Rachel?'

Rachel felt a calmness come over her as she said truthfully, 'I thought I did, but I see you treated me as a mere plaything, something to be enjoyed and forgotten. Now I have no feelings.'

'Do not condemn me, Rachel.'

'I do not condemn you. I have told you this for my own peace of mind as much as yours. It is almost a burial service. The past is dead.'

'But Richard. What of Richard?'

'That is of no concern to you. Richard is an admirable person. He has been loyal and honest and supports me in my reforming activities, even though I feel he does not always agree with them.'

Jacob said slowly, 'If he knew the truth, perhaps he would not marry you.'

'No man could, Jacob.' Rachel looked at him indifferently. 'But I have no fear of your threats.'

She saw Richard walking up the drive. He smiled and waved when he saw her, then she watched the smile fade as he spotted Jacob. Rachel glanced coolly at Jacob. He was watching Richard with an expression of curiosity on his face. At that moment, she knew her words were true. There was nothing that Jacob could do that would change her love for Richard; whatever happened, he could never take that away.

Richard came in and nodded briefly at Jacob.

'I thought you would be earlier,' Rachel said.

'I was delayed at the yard. Hallo, Jacob.'

'Rachel has been extolling your virtues,' Jacob said lightly. He smiled. 'I begin to see you in a new light.'

An expression of irritation crossed Richard's face.

'Jacob came to express his regrets that he will not be at the wedding. He must depart in six weeks' time,' Rachel said smoothly.

'Yes. Father mentioned it. It is a pity,' Richard replied.

Jacob glanced briefly at Rachel. 'It is how my life goes,' he said. 'But I will leave you two love birds in peace.'

He came over and kissed Rachel lightly on the cheek and then took

Richard's hand. 'I hope you will both be happy, Richard.'

Rachel saw the doubt vanish from Richard's face. He sounded almost apologetic as he said, 'Thank you, Jacob. I am sorry you won't be at the wedding.'

As they watched him walk slowly away down the drive, Rachel felt a surge of anxiety. The confidence she had managed to express when Jacob was there was overshadowed by the reality of what he could do. She could not face the thought of losing Richard.

Two days later, as she had half-feared, a letter arrived. The contents were more disturbing than their meeting had been. She had spent the past two days alternating between hope and despair. Her intention to close the past for ever was vitiated by the thought that she had somehow created a distasteful new bond between them. She now shared with Jacob a secret she had revealed to no one else.

She read.

Rachel dear,
This letter is not intended to be a journal of my petty sufferings. It is a letter addressed to your feelings, Rachel. Ever since I returned, I have realised that I never admitted my true feelings towards you. It was only when I saw you again that I realised that I love you, Rachel. I want to be with you for ever. You are, of course, betrothed to Richard, but I feel you do not love him as once you did me. Surely I have the first right to your affections? I was the choice of your heart. Could it not be so still? Believe me, Rachel, I am a changed man. My life will be spent only in caring for you. If you would agree, you could come with me to Egypt, which you so loved. We could have a residence in Cairo, and when my tour in the Sudan is finished, I can leave the Army and obtain some situation with the Embassy. As you can see, I have thought much about it all. If I undertake to tell Richard the truth of our association, I imagine he will not wish to interfere.
Rachel, will you marry me?
Yours for ever,
Jacob.

Rachel opened her mouth to breathe in air, as though she were about to choke. She stumbled upstairs to her bedroom, trying to control the anger and fear which threatened to overcome her. She was speechless, unable to formulate any coherent thoughts from the feelings of indignation at Jacob's self-absorption, his treachery towards Richard and arrogance. Jacob had no concern for Richard's feelings, no perception of what it might do to him. He did not consider for an instant that Richard had always remained true to her, even against his own conscience.

Then the fear re-asserted itself. What would Jacob do next? If only she could tell Richard, if only she could share the past with him. Jacob could destroy so much. Supposing she had to leave. She thought of the children in her Home, of the girls who relied on her, who would carry on if she left? And what of the plans forming in her mind about what she would do when she moved with Richard to Dartmouth? She told herself that her fears were extravagant. Even if Richard did not marry her, she would carry on with her work. Yet how could she continue to live here if Richard did not want her?

She tore the letter up. If only he would go away, leave, never to return. Rachel waited, knowing that he would come again and she would have to receive him. When, two days later, she saw him walking slowly up the drive, she watched in silence. There was a different expression on his face. He had come to some decision.

'I am not here to disturb you, Rachel. I won't trouble you again,' Jacob greeted her.

Rachel looked at him suspiciously. 'I hope not, Jacob. In that case, why have you come?'

'I know your answer, Rachel. You do not love me.'

Rachel shook her head. She answered him reluctantly. She must convince him, persuade him to go for ever. 'No, Jacob, I don't. It was simply a youthful dream that you must forget.'

Jacob walked to the window. 'I wish I could,' he said, 'but I know now that I can never forget you, Rachel.'

'Jacob, I shall not forget our past friendship. But that is the past.'

He looked at her with sudden resentment. 'You cannot dismiss me so easily, Rachel. How can you have forgotten?'

Rachel felt a sudden surge of anger. 'How dare you harass me in this fashion. It is contemptible after what has happened. I wish I might never see you again.'

Jacob looked for a moment as though he would strike her, then he shook his head and turned abruptly towards the door. 'I had to come to hear the words from your own lips.' He turned back suddenly and said in a pained voice, 'Rachel, I wish you every happiness with Richard.'

And then he was gone.

Rachel watched Jacob disappear down the drive. She walked firmly to her study and began to read her correspondence. Was it true? Had he really finally accepted it? She feared that he would return again but, as the hours passed, she began to feel renewed confidence. The following afternoon, she heard footsteps coming along the drive. She did not look, but her heart pounded as she waited for Elsie to announce him.

When she turned, it was Richard who walked in. He smiled and kissed her on the forehead, saying, 'You look anxious, dear. Is there some problem?'

'No, Richard. I was absorbed. How is the ship going?'

'It is to be launched in three days' time. That is the purpose of my call. I thought you might like to be present.'

'Yes, indeed.' Rachel smiled. 'It will give me an opportunity to inspect the house I am taking over for the children.'

'I have already contacted the owner. And I have had representations from the vicar about two young girls you might wish to employ there.' Richard smiled. 'I believe they are in need of some protection.'

'Good.'

'Oh and one other thing. Jacob had a communication today to say that he will be leaving earlier than expected. He is to join the ship and his regiment at Plymouth in a month.'

Rachel controlled the feeling of joy which overcame her. 'That is a pity,' she said expressionlessly.

'I expect it was a pleasure for you to see him again,' Richard said uncertainly.

Rachel managed to smile casually. 'Yes, it was. But I suppose we have less in common than we once had.'

'I suggested we should accompany him to the port. Papa would wish to go. I think, of late, Papa has been more aware of his advancing years and regrets every departure of Jacob's.'

'Yes, of course.'

* * *

Although it was summer, it was a cold and blustery day when they travelled to Plymouth. She remembered the last time, when she had waved to him disconsolately, believing that he would return to her. Now there would be no waiting, no return. Jacob stood in his uniform, talking to Mr Damarell, pointing out his fellow officers as they passed. He had been cheerful and talkative during the journey, laughing and joking in his usual fashion. When he spoke to Rachel, he had betrayed none of the feelings which he had expressed only a few days before. Rachel held Richard's arm as they stood at the quayside. Then James called Richard over to look at a notice on a board.

Jacob came over to Rachel and smiled down at her. She looked into his eyes expressionlessly. 'Rachel, it's not too late,' he said softly, a smile still on his lips, as though he were speaking of some casual matter. 'I can simply take your hand and lead you on to the ship with me. No one will stop us. And we can sail away into the sunset.'

'Jacob,' Rachel said in a low voice. 'It was only a dream. You will forget me.'

He looked at her solemnly and said, 'It is not the end, Rachel.'

He turned away, smiling again at his father, and then he was shaking hands with him and his brothers. As he turned to kiss Rachel goodbye, a violent gust of wind engulfed them and he held her momentarily in his arms to support her. Then he was walking away, up the gang plank.

Richard came and put an arm around her shoulders and she watched as the ship moved slowly away, with Jacob standing on the deck, his eyes on her until she could see him no longer.

Chapter 17

Rachel looked round impatiently at the confusion that greeted her as she entered the dining-room. Bertha and Aunt Bessie were busily cutting small strips of cake and passing them through her platinum wedding ring. Then they wrapped them in tiny pieces of decorated paper and fastened them with pieces of ribbon. Tomorrow they would be given to young unmarried guests at the wedding.

Aunt Alice and Aunt Emmie were examining the latest gifts to arrive – a harp from Uncle John Thomas and Aunt Edith of Brixham and a large porcelain vase from Aunt Julia in Kingsbridge.

'Ah, Rachel, there you are.' Aunt Bessie greeted her. 'Now, have you got your trousseau laid out upstairs? The visitors will all want to see it this afternoon, you know.'

Rachel concealed a sigh as she answered. 'Yes, they are all prepared in one of the bedrooms. Perhaps you would be good enough to show them. I have to go to the Home to make final arrangements for the children.'

Aunt Alice looked doubtful. 'Are you sure it is wise, dear, for all of them to come to the reception. Will the helpers be able to cope with them?'

'Yes. They are quite accustomed to it. And Edith and Dora and Elsie will be in charge,' Rachel said firmly.

'Well,' Aunt Alice retorted. 'It is your decision, of course. Does Richard know of their being invited?'

'Of course he does. It was his suggestion. The two eldest girls are to be bridesmaids, remember.'

'Indeed. You are fortunate to be marrying such an accommodating husband.'

'If Richard returns before me, could you tell him that I have gone to the Home and will be back later.'

Rachel glanced into the drawing-room as she left. The servants were busy with the final arrangements of flowers and decorations, supervised by Elsie.

'It is very impressive, Elsie,' Rachel said as she glanced around at the giant bouquets and vast urns of flowers. 'When it is over, perhaps you would arrange for them all to be sent to the workhouse.'

Rachel walked out of the front door, breathing in the warm July air. She looked out across the hill, over the steep layers of the roofs of houses, dipping down to Bayards Cove and the harbour. It was much more beautiful here than in Kingsbridge, she reflected. It would be a pleasant place in which to live and there were more attractive houses here in which she might open a school.

For the last week, she had been installed in Richard's home after giving up her house in Kingsbridge and transferring the children to a new Home in Dartmouth. Bertha had come to stay with her two-year-old, Jacob. Rachel smiled to herself. It would have been unthinkable for her to remain alone in the house with Richard and the servants before her marriage.

She walked down the hill to the Home which lay beyond Victoria Road and up the hill on the other side. The unexpected vistas of the sea and the harbour and undulating hills gave her constant pleasure here. Perhaps one of these large houses would be suitable; it would be convenient to be near the Children's Home.

As the children came running towards her, she felt a sense of peace. Whenever she saw them, she knew that her decision to return to Devon had been right. And it was here, too, that she had discovered her feelings for Richard. It seemed to her now that she had always cared for him. Her infatuation with Jacob seemed now to have been an incomprehensible aberration. One day, she would look back on it with indifference. Now, she only felt an infinite thankfulness that he had gone. It was more than love that she felt for Richard, she also felt a growing respect for him. She knew that, in his heart, he would have preferred her to be like other women: content with her home and doing small charitable works in her spare time. He no doubt realised that she would always be wanting to do more, that she was likely to extend her activities into more controversial areas. She occasionally saw him look uneasy when she criticised conventional society or the invidious position of women, and yet he was willing to consider her views while maintaining his own beliefs.

Dora and Edith showed her the dresses which had been made for the girls and the sailor suits which the boys were to wear. Rachel smiled as the children paraded proudly in the drawing-room.

'I'll see you all at the reception,' she said as she left. It had been agreed that the church service might make too many demands on their powers of restraint.

Early next morning, Bertha came into her bedroom, saying, 'Now, you must have your breakfast in your room, Rachel. Richard is downstairs and it would be unlucky for the bride to see the groom before the wedding.'

'Oh, Bertha. I do not hold with such superstitions.'

Bertha rolled her dark eyes. 'Perhaps not. But Richard may think otherwise, you know.'

Rachel laughed. 'I haven't discussed it with him.'

'And you will have no opportunity to do so. Here.'

Bertha nodded as one of the servants brought in a tray. 'Good morning, Jenny. Please place it on the table. And then get the water ready for Miss Cavendish's bath. I'll go and dress Jacob and myself, Rachel, and then I'll come back and help you with your dress.'

As Rachel sat in the bath, contemplating the trousseau which had been laid out on her bed, she experienced a final spasm of doubt. These were her last moments of real freedom; from now on there would always be Richard to consider, Richard to convince. Then she reflected that she was also entering a situation of greater freedom. As a married woman, she would have a different status; no woman could be unaware that a spinster was treated as an inferior being, however emancipated and successful she might be. She would also be financially secure for the first time since before her parents died.

Bertha returned and helped her into her camisole and petticoats and then pulled the white moiré antique crinoline wedding dress over her head. The skirt was richly embroidered with white silk stitching and the deep neckline was bound around with white velvet.

'Oh, it's lovely, Rachel. You look wonderful,' she exclaimed. She combed Rachel's long hair, coiled it in plaits and bound it round her head, fixing it with silver combs. Next she placed the orange blossom on Rachel's head and arranged the long veil down her back and across her face.

Rachel put on the pearl necklace which Richard had given her as one of her wedding presents and looked at herself in the long mirror. 'Oh, it's beautiful, isn't it, Bertha?' she said, contentedly.

'It's your nice, neat figure and your tiny waist. I wish I were like you, Rachel.' Bertha looked at her enviously.

'Don't be silly, Bertha. You have lovely black hair and many people think that a plump figure is more attractive.'

Rachel watched from her bedroom window as Bertha and her family left for the chapel. Then the servants followed in another carriage. She went downstairs, where Mr Damarell awaited her. When he had offered to give her away, she had felt a fleeting reluctance, unable totally to forget his past actions. Then she reflected that it would cement the renewed contact between Richard and his father. It was a small gesture on her part, after all.

He smiled at her now as he helped her into the carriage and then climbed in slowly beside her. 'I am pleased to be doing this, Rachel,' he said as they rode along.

'And I am pleased to be marrying Richard.'

As she stood at the top of the aisle and saw Richard at the altar in his black frock-coat and grey striped trousers, she felt a surge of warmth towards him. At that moment, she felt she would give up all her plans for homes and schools if he wished it. He turned and looked at her as she walked towards him, followed by her six bridesmaids. She smiled at him, he saw the expression in her eyes and took her hand as the organ began to play.

Then the vicar was placing the platinum ring on her finger, she was walking down the aisle to the triumphal tune of the Wedding March and they were standing in the sunshine, posing for the wedding photographs.

The Wedding Breakfast was held in the Castle Hotel and was followed by an evening ball. Tomorrow, they were to go on their wedding tour of Cornwall. Aunt Bessie had informed Richard that Norway was now a desirable place to go for wedding tours, but Rachel had been reluctant to leave the children for a fortnight and Richard had appeared unenthusiastic about foreign travel.

At midnight, Richard proposed that they should leave and return

334

to the house. They had an early start in the morning. The guests lined up on the steps of the hotel to wish them happiness.

Mr Damarell awkwardly put an arm around her. 'You are welcome as a daughter-in-law, Rachel. I am sure now your only purpose is to do good in the world.'

Rachel smiled. Since Aunt Maria's death, he had not exactly abandoned his critical attitudes but had toned them down. In his solitude, he had found it necessary to be more tolerant of other people. She kissed James and Thomas and Felicity and then climbed into the carriage which would take them the short journey to their home.

Richard put his arm around her. 'You must be tired, Rachel. It has been an exhausting day.'

'No. I'm all right. But it will be nice to have a little quiet.'

When they got back to the house, Rachel went up to the large bedroom while Richard remained downstairs.

Jenny came and took her wedding dress to hang in the closet and she let down her hair and put on her new white chiffon night-dress. She sat looking through the window at the dark shadows of the hills, listening to the distant call of an owl. Glancing at the wide, white-covered bed, she was struck by the strangeness of sharing it with another person. From now on, she would never be alone; Richard would always be there. Memories of her childhood, of those first nights when her parents has gone and left her in England, came into her mind. The loneliness of those hours. She put the thought from her mind and when Richard came up, she watched him as he stood with his back towards her, removing his black jacket and his striped trousers. He pulled on his night-shirt and then turned and smiled at her.

There was an embarrassed expression on his face as he climbed into bed. 'Rachel,' he whispered, 'this is the fulfilment of all my dreams.'

For a moment, she felt her body go rigid; for a second, her thoughts went to Jacob, to their last night together. Then she put her arms around Richard and lay still as his hands moved over her body. She felt as though she were an observer, as though her body were here but her spirit was outside, watching her. He was kissing her, touching her, lying on her but she did not move. Finally, he lay still, and she breathed deeply and kissed him on the forehead.

'Now you are my wife,' he murmured.

Richard put an arm around her and held her close to him. She looked at him as he slept with a feeling of guilt that she had felt none of the wild passion she had once known. It was as though her body were sleeping, still drugged by the past . . .

The next day, they went to Newquay to a hotel high on the cliffs overlooking the stormy sea. The July sunshine had changed to rain but Rachel felt a strange kind of happiness. Richard was concerned only with her wishes; they walked by the sea, explored the busy little harbour, Richard talked to the fishermen and told Rachel about the tides and winds and made plans with her for her new school. Each night as he made love to her, she lay passive and still in his arms. It seemed to her that this was what Richard expected. She thought of the women's books she had read, which said that ladies did not show any interest in or discuss these matters. Then she remembered her conversations with Alice and her other associates in London. Sex had been a matter for discussion not an undesirable mystery. One day, she would be able to talk with Richard in the same way.

When they returned to Dartmouth, she inspected the large house she had seen near the Children's Home with Richard.

'I want it to be a rural school for women who have had no education,' she said, looking round.

'It may be difficult to get recruits,' Richard said doubtfully. 'They are more concerned with working in the fields or doing home-work than learning.'

'Well, I shall visit them to try and persuade them.'

Richard smiled. 'You won't be popular with their husbands, Rachel. And indeed, I don't know whether I agree.'

'Richard! How can you say that? You made so much effort to educate yourself in various matters, long after you left school.'

'But what is the point of education for them, Rachel? They don't need it.'

'Richard, I believe that education gives people a better life. Half the poor people here can't even read. They have no opportunities.'

'Well, I am willing enough to support you, Rachel. But I fear you will have little success.'

Rachel began to go round Dartmouth, calling on women in their tiny cottages, suggesting that if they were employed during the day, they could come to the school in the evenings. If they could read and write, they would increase their chances of finding better employment. They listened to her politely but pointed out that they worked in the evenings, and at night as well as during the day. She visited one- and two-roomed tenements which often housed ten or twelve people. She saw, as Richard had told her, that even the children could not attend school. They were employed carting fish, cleaning the streets, running errands, selling newspapers.

'I find these people very unresponsive,' Rachel observed one evening.

Richard sighed, a look of exasperation on his face. 'Rachel, you cannot expect to come and re-order this community. You will not succeed.'

A few days later, Rachel approached the topic again. 'Richard, I have another idea.'

Richard looked apprehensive.

'Going around Dartmouth, I have realised how much unemployment there is in this town. It is like London on a smaller scale.'

'Times are difficult, Rachel. There has been a great fall in agricultural prices; many farmers are finding it difficult to survive themselves. But what was your idea, Rachel?'

'I thought the house we have leased could become a workshop for the unemployed, both men and women. I could acquire instructors to train people in new trades.'

'And how will you pay the salaries?'

'I will go to London, Richard. I know a number of sympathetic people. We might be able to get some government assistance or I could speak to people in the Men's and Women's Club.'

'Perhaps it is possible,' Richard said reluctantly.

'I'll go tomorrow.'

Richard nodded slowly. 'Very well. But I hope you will not be absent for long.'

'No. Of course.' She kissed him lightly on the cheek. 'You are very good, Richard.' For a second, she looked at him doubtfully. Was he beginning to tire of hearing about her plans? Yet he had known of her intentions when he married her, he had said he would not try to limit her activities.

She returned from London a few days later full of enthusiasm. Her trip had been more successful than she had hoped. She had had an exhilarating few days, visiting Committees, contacting influential people, and going to the theatre in the evenings. The result was the promise of sufficient funds to equip her rural school and pay the salaries of two instructors for a year.

Richard had not returned from work and she decided to walk down to the shipyard to meet him. She saw him coming towards her as she walked past the great steel scaffolding on which men were balanced precariously, high above her. There was a continuous noise of hammering and of steam hissing from funnels and chimneys. Richard frowned as he greeted her, kissing her lightly on the forehead. He was shouting something to her but she was unable to hear, so he took her hand and led her into one of the workmen's huts and closed the shaky door, before saying, 'It's not advisable for you to come down here, Rachel. It could be dangerous.'

'But I've been here before.' Rachel was surprised at his words; why was he behaving in such a protective fashion?

'Only with me. Apart from that, it is not an appropriate place for ladies to be.'

'Oh, Richard. What is wrong with my coming here? I can look after myself.'

'Nevertheless.'

She looked at his irritated expression. He was clearly aware of all his workmen, of the comments he anticipated them making about her.

'I only came to tell you about my visit.' She felt disappointed that he had not enquired about it.

Richard smiled reluctantly. 'Yes, of course. It is only my concern for you. Come, I will walk home with you.'

He did not greet the news of her success with the enthusiasm which she was feeling. 'I trust it will not mean that you will be personally involved in this establishment. Many of these unemployed people are rough and uncouth.'

Rachel took a deep breath. 'Yes, it does mean that, Richard. The two instructors will be concerned with teaching new skills and occupations. I shall be teaching reading and writing.'

'I do not like it, Rachel.'

Rachel frowned. She had feared that for Richard there was a point beyond which she should not go in her activities. For her, it was a matter of principle that she should be free to follow her instincts, to do whatever she thought was necessary. 'I am sorry, Richard. It is important for these people. It is my duty to do what I believe to be right.'

'But how about your duty to me?'

Rachel frowned. It was the first time that Richard had said such a thing. Would he try to dictate to her? Did he still adhere to that old view of the married woman's place, when he had appeared to agree with her attitudes? 'Richard, it in no way confronts you. My duty to you as a wife is in no way diminished.'

Richard hesitated. 'Rachel, it is my own position which makes the matter difficult. I am a well-known member of this community, I have a certain standing. It does not appear seemly that you should be involved in this fashion.'

They had reached the gate of their home. As Rachel opened it, she turned, leaning on the bars and said quietly, 'Richard, when you married me you knew what I was, what my intentions were. You said you would never interfere.'

Richard followed her along the drive in silence.

'Remember Richard, I am a married woman. These men will treat me with respect.'

Richard pursed his lips. 'Very well,' he said. 'But I wish your maid to accompany you always when you are engaged in activities at that place.'

'Yes,' Rachel said lightly. 'I will do that.' She realised that if she was to implement the plans which were evolving in her head, she would have to be more circumspect, perhaps more secretive. Yet conflicting with her determination was the consciousness of Richard's forbearance. She was asking so much of him. Born and bred in this tightly-knit community, he had little appreciation of the changing world she had lived in. She felt a glow of affection, thinking of his generosity.

Within a few months, a dozen men were installed in the new workshop. She found that, contrary to what she had read in the papers, the unemployed had no desire to live on charity. Their main concern was to find a place in the world, to provide a home and livelihood for their wives and children. They were being trained as bricklayers and carpenters and stone-masons and, as the months passed, they began to speak of setting up on their own account.

She wrote a report for the Plymouth and Exeter newspapers and formed a committee of people who were interested in extending the project throughout the county. There were also critical letters in the papers, alleging that too much was being done already for men who had no desire to work, and who were simply exploiting the generosity and goodwill of people like herself. It was suggested that she was creating a dangerous precedent, giving the indolent poor ideas above their station. Rachel read the comments with impatience. She had become accustomed to reading such opinions in the London papers, though those attacks had always been more vitriolic and abusive.

In spite of her involvement with their welfare, she was becoming concerned with another problem. Visiting the children each day, she became more and more aware of her wish to have a child of her own. Before her marriage, she had crushed the longing that arose in her whenever she thought of the little creature she had held in her arms so briefly. She had not realised that, now that she was married, the longing would become almost an obsession. Talking and playing with the children, she wondered why it was that she had not become pregnant. Had something dreadful happened to her long ago, so that she could never conceive again?

One evening, Rachel watched Richard as they sat in the drawing-room before dinner. Was it possible that Richard had no real desire for children and that he was the cause of her failure?

Richard was reading the newspaper. She leaned over and touched his hand. He looked up and smiled. 'What is it, dear?'

'Would you like to have children, Richard?'

Richard looked surprised. 'But of course I would. Nothing would give me greater happiness.'

'It is strange that I have not—'

'Dear Rachel, we have been married only about nine months. I am sure it must happen.'

'Bertha is expecting again, and Felicity tells me that she also is hopeful of that event.'

340

'I wonder if you do not overdo all your activities, Rachel. Perhaps if you had a less demanding life—'

'Richard, I am not tired. I have so much energy.'

'Then let us not be concerned, my love. I am sure that in time, we shall be blessed.'

As the months passed, Rachel became more and more impatient. Was her failure really due to her early experience of childbirth? Had her body been so damaged that she would never bear another child? Then it occurred to her that perhaps it was her passive behaviour which made it impossible. Perhaps if she behaved as she had done with Jacob, it would be different.

That night, as she awaited the nightly assault, she suddenly became alive, flinging her arms around Richard and kissing him violently. Momentarily, she felt his body stiffen and move away from her. Then he tore off her night-dress and abandoned himself to the wild excitement that she had once shared with Jacob.

The next morning, Richard seemed to look at her with curiosity, as though he could not believe what had happened. She did not attempt to explain her actions; her hopes and intentions were beyond explanation.

That brief encounter had another effect, for she felt that it had resurrected her feelings, that she could at last relax in Richard's arms, respond to his embraces. Richard also seemed to feel a new tenderness towards her. But as the months passed again, she became obsessed with the longing for a child. She spoke of it constantly to Richard and when Bertha's second child was born, she went to stay with her for a week, to care for the child.

One evening as Richard was reading *The Times*, he suddenly exclaimed abruptly, 'Good heavens, Rachel. There is information here about Jacob.'

Rachel looked up from her book, a cold feeling running down her back 'Yes?' She spoke calmly.

'He's in this list. Been awarded the MC. Bravery in action.'

Rachel frowned. Did it mean that he would be returning to England? Was she to be haunted by him for ever? 'I am pleased,' she said foolishly. 'I am sure your father will be proud.'

'Yes.' Richard looked at her thoughtfully. She wondered what he

341

was thinking. She could never rid herself of the fear that one day Richard would guess her secret.

'Of course, I am concerned for Jacob,' she added casually. 'He was a part of my childhood, as you all were.'

Richard smiled but he looked puzzled at her further comment. 'Yes, dear, of course you are.' He stroked her cheek lightly. 'But that was long ago, wasn't it?'

'Yes, Richard, it was,' Rachel said fervently.

Chapter 18

Richard walked briskly down Victoria Road, past the Butterwalk and along the embankment to the shipyard. It was a bright May day, but as he saw the usual dozen or so men hanging around outside the yard, he felt a sense of depression.

'No,' he said quietly, 'No work today,' and he passed through his gates into the yard.

At one time, there had been only one or two standing there, but the numbers seemed to be increasing and he knew that they were likely to increase further. Times were getting more and more difficult; the competition from abroad was affecting not only ship-building but the mining and cloth industries as well. Ever since he had married Rachel, she had made him more and more aware of the effects of unemployment on these people.

However, his real anxiety lay with Rachel herself. After almost two years of marriage, they were still waiting for a child. Although it would have pleased him to be a father, he knew that he did not have Rachel's desperate need. Women were different. In spite of all her talk about careers and equality, having a baby seemed to be the most important thing in the world to her. Richard sighed as a foreman came into the shed.

'Morning, Mr Damarell.'

'Good morning, Matthew.'

'There's some scaffolding needs repairing, up on Block C. I'll have to take some men out of the engine room.'

'Have we got work for any of them?' Richard nodded towards the men bunched together round the gates.

'Well, sir, I suppose if we used them, I needn't move the others.'

'All right. Just take them on day rate.'

Richard turned to his table of plans as the man went out. He sat down and picked up the papers but his thoughts returned to Rachel. If only they had a child, perhaps she would be more contented. He had a feeling that she was becoming more and more involved in her reforming activities – as he called them in his mind – because of her dissatisfaction with her married life. He had watched the wistful expression on her face as she talked to the children in the Home. Then he thought about his father and Aunt Bessie and all the others. They commented frequently on the fact he and Rachel were still childless; it was unnatural, Aunt Emmie once remarked. Aunt Bessie suggested that Rachel should rest more, spend more time at home where women belonged. Even his father seemed disappointed that Rachel had not given him a grandson.

Their opinions were of no importance. It was Rachel that mattered, their marriage. He hated to see her unhappy when he appeared unable to remedy the cause. Was there some physical reason why she had not conceived? Could it be connected with those visits he had once made to that girl down in Smith Street? Had he contracted some disease that had removed the possibility of fatherhood? He stood up. Tonight, he would speak to Rachel, insist that she must live a more moderate life, restrict her activities. That must be the reason.

That evening, he smiled at her across the dinner table. 'Rachel, dear, it has occurred to me that we do little entertaining.'

Rachel looked surprised. 'I did not think you enjoyed such activities. We have members of the family here when possible.'

'Oh, I know James and Thomas and the aunts visit from time to time. But at one time, in your youth, you much enjoyed dances and balls.'

Rachel laughed. 'Oh, Richard. That was long ago. I have more serious interests nowadays.'

'Yes, I know. But perhaps it would be better for your health. Perhaps these activities cause you anxiety.'

'Well, yes, but it is the reasons which cause me anxiety rather than the activities. In fact, I had an interesting letter today which I must show you.'

She went to her study and returned with the document. 'It is something I must attend to. It is most encouraging, Richard.

These women are at last beginning to have some confidence in me.'
Richard read the letter slowly, deciphering the spelling.

Dear Mrs Damrel,
We no you have the poor ome for childrn but ow about us muthers
with too meny to feed. My usband dont bring ome enuff to feed us
with an I work in the feelds. Why dont I get payd the same as im? I
work 12 ours a day and ave to walk 5 miles. We ave 7 mouths too
feed. Now the farmer cut me pay. I respecfly ask your advise. This
is confidenshal.
Mary Butcher.

Richard looked at Rachel. She was wearing a pale blue gown and her
hair was tied back with a velvet ribbon.

'You were wearing a gown like that when I asked you to marry me,'
Richard said suddenly.

Rachel smiled vaguely but she went on, 'I shall visit her, Richard.'

'What? Oh, yes.' He blushed at his words, at her apparent
indifference. 'No,' he added, 'perhaps that would not be a good idea.'

'Why ever not?'

'Rachel, the farmers are having a difficult time. No doubt they are
paying the wages they can afford.'

He saw Rachel's expression harden. 'Perhaps,' she said coldly.
Then she added inconsequentially, 'Well, if you wish to have some
guests for dinner I can arrange it,' and she stood up and kissed him
lightly on the forehead.

Richard smiled. Perhaps it would be better if he were more firm.
Perhaps he could divert her attention away from reform by suggesting
specific things himself. As she did not mention the letter again, he felt
convinced that this was the best thing for him to do. A week later he
received a letter from another source.

It came from a gentleman farmer who lived up on the hills beyond
Dartmouth.

Dear Sir,
It is my painful duty to write to you upon a most obnoxious matter.
I have in my employ women who work in my fields, women who
have been so employed by me for some years. This week, they

presented me with a document stating they had decided to form a Union to protect themselves from exploitation. They have made demands that their hours of work be reduced and their rates of pay made equal to that of men. When I demanded to know where these absurd ideas emanated from, they informed me that they knew they were within their rights, because Mrs Damarell your good wife – had told them so.

I know that Mrs Damarell is involved in good works, but am convinced that she would not be party to such impudence and deceit as exemplified by these women. I fear that perhaps in conversation with them, she has not appreciated the depth of their ignorance and that they have been given the wrong impression. It is always dangerous to treat the lower classes as mental equals.

However, it is my duty to protect myself and other farmers who might find themselves in a similar situation and I must request you to explain to your dear wife that employees must not be encouraged to make demands of this nature. I should of course have sacked the lot of them on the spot were it not for the fact that I have never had such trouble before and that to find a dozen or so replacements would have placed me in a tiresome and inconvenient position.

I trust I may rely upon your instant action.

Yours dutifully,

Robert Carter

Richard read the letter with incredulity. He got up from the breakfast table, walked to the door and called up the stairs.

Rachel had already gone up to get her cloak to go to the workshop. There were now twenty unemployed men there and she had managed to get another year's grant through some Select Committee in London. She came down as Richard called.

'Rachel, what is this?' He looked at her angrily.

Rachel took the letter and read it expressionlessly. 'What arrogance,' she said indignantly. 'Does this man really think he has the right to treat women in this way?'

'Rachel, is it true what they say?'

'Yes, it is.' She looked at him belligerently. She must have ignored his request the other day.

'But what happened?'

'We had a meeting. I went to their homes, Richard. They live in absolute hovels. They must walk to work in their ragged clothes, their children are half-starved, and they are paid about sixpence a day. Why should men be paid more?'

'Because they do heavier work. They are more skilled.'

Rachel looked at him contemptuously. 'I don't believe it. And in any case, they are still devoting as many hours. It is their time which is important, not what they do.'

'Women are always paid less,' Richard said impatiently. 'Such matters are nothing to do with you, Rachel.'

She turned on him angrily. 'It has everything to do with me and everyone else. I thought you believed in the protection of women.'

'That's quite different.' Richard took the letter from her. 'Rachel,' he said decisively. 'I have felt recently that your activities are going beyond the bounds of all reason. I wish you to restrict your future projects to the Children's Homes and to this rural workshop. I cannot have you involved in any kind of trouble-making.'

'Trouble-making! Is that how you see it?'

Richard realised that she was on the verge of tears. He did not want this argument, all he wanted was to be happy with her. Yet he could not evade the issue. 'Yes, Rachel. I do.'

Rachel sighed deeply. Then she said quietly, 'Very well, Richard.' He put an arm around her. 'Can you not be content with what you are doing, without getting involved in this kind of thing?'

Rachel glanced across at the grandfather clock. A look of impatience flashed across her face. Then she appeared to concede. 'Richard, I do not wish to disturb you. We will discuss it some other time. Let us walk down the road together.' She smiled, a look of apprehension on her face. 'I am going to Exeter today.'

'Exeter! You have not mentioned it.'

'It is nothing, just a meeting,' she said dismissively.

'Not in connection with this matter?' Richard waved the letter in his hand.

'No, of course not, Richard. Just a discussion.'

'Well, we'll talk about it this evening.' He walked with her to the inn where she would get the coach to Exeter. She waved to him as he turned and walked towards the shipyard.

* * *

She had not returned that evening and he walked down to the quay and waited for the coach to arrive. Rachel was not there. Richard had a feeling of panic. She never stayed away for the night unless she went to London. What could have happened? He went home, supposing that she might have come in someone else's carriage. Some of the farmers and gentry still chose to use a carriage in preference to the discomforts of the stage-coach or horse-bus.

He waited anxiously as darkness fell. Then he heard footsteps coming up the drive and Elsie came in and announced that the constable wanted to speak with him.

Richard went out hastily.

The man removed his helmet. 'I'm sorry to bother you, sir. I've had a message from Exeter,' he said.

'Yes?' Richard felt his heart beating violently.

'A bit of trouble, sir. It seems your good wife, Mrs Damarell, got mixed up in some sort of brawl.'

'Brawl, Constable. What are you talking about?'

The constable hesitated and said hastily, 'Of course, sir. It's nothing to do with your wife. I mean it's not her fault. But there's been a strike at a factory there. I've heard it was the girls, there, sir. It appears they had a demonstration there today and there were scuffles with the police.'

'But, my wife—'

The constable looked even more embarrassed. 'Well, sir, she's in Exeter Gaol, sir. Course, I told the Chief there must be some mistake, sir. I know Mrs Damarell does all this work for the unfortunates in our society and somehow she must have got caught up.'

'Caught up, indeed.' Richard said shortly. He was shaking with anger. 'I'll go up there immediately and sort the matter out. Someone is going to suffer for this impudence.'

'Well, sir, I'm sorry. I'm sure its a mistake.'

'People don't make mistakes like that and get away with it.'

Richard called the coachman to get the carriage and horses out and then commanded him to go as fast as he could. He knew that his anger was really directed against Rachel. What had she done? She had lied to him that morning. She had known where she was going – she

348

had not only deceived him, she was now bringing disgrace on him. They rushed through the countryside, up the steep hills and along the dark lanes but it was after midnight before they reached Exeter.

Richard went immediately to the gates of the gaol and demanded admittance. The keeper took his name and bade him wait in the lodge at the entrance while he went to speak to the gaoler. His temper now at breaking point, Richard walked up and down the barred room and then the keeper returned and escorted him through the yard to a room on the first floor.

There was a stench of human bodies as they walked along the passages. He peered into the dark, barred cells, each one containing half a dozen people, men and women mixed together. There appeared to be no beds, only straw palliases on the floors. His anger and disgust increased at the thought that Rachel would be equated with such people.

The gaoler greeted him politely.

'I believe you have my wife here,' Richard growled at him. 'How dare you bring her to a place like this.'

The gaoler frowned. 'It is not my responsibility, sir. She was brought here by the police.'

'On what grounds?'

'It is alleged she was one of the ring-leaders, sir.'

'Ring-leaders of what?'

'These factory-girls, sir. They marched through the city with banners, shouting abuse about their employers. Then they confronted the police. They refused to move on, sir.'

'There is no law against marching on a demonstration.'

'Well, sir. There was incitement to riot, I understand.'

Richard began to advance towards the gaoler. 'Take me to my wife immediately. I will remove her from here.'

The gaoler hesitated. 'Well, sir. I must ask you to sign a document that you will ensure that she causes no further breach of the peace.'

'How dare you speak to me in that fashion. Do you not realise I am an influential person in Dartmouth. You will suffer for this.'

'Sir, I am merely doing my job. Pray, if you will simply sign it, I can accede to your request.'

Richard hesitated. Would he, by signing the document, be

admitting her guilt? Would it be looked upon as some kind of confession?

'Very well,' he said. 'But this is not the last you will hear about this matter.'

Richard followed the gaoler along a passage to a cell. He opened the door. Rachel was sitting on a bench, surrounded by half a dozen dishevelled-looking girls all talking quietly. As he walked towards her, Rachel stood up. There was a defiant expression on her face.

'Rachel, are you all right?'

'Yes, I am, but it is monstrous to be treated in this way. The police behaved like hooligans. We did nothing harmful. I shall see that they are prosecuted.'

'Rachel, let us not discuss it now. I shall take the matter further with the appropriate officials.'

'This will be brought up in Parliament,' Rachel shouted. 'You see, I told you how women are treated.'

Richard glanced at the gaoler. 'Rachel.' He spoke sharply. 'We will deal with it later. Come.'

Rachel glared at the gaoler. 'Can we all go then?'

Richard hesitated. 'I have no authority to take them with us.' He looked at the anxious faces around him.

'I cannot leave them,' Rachel said firmly. 'They have no one to speak for them.'

'Rachel—' Richard's voice trailed into silence. He turned to the gaoler. 'Can these ladies be released also?'

'Well, sir. Only if you can undertake the same guarantee on their behalf.'

Richard looked at Rachel's determined expression and the drawn faces of the women. 'Very well,' he said curtly.

Rachel nodded abruptly. 'Come girls. We can go,' she said and the girls followed her along the passage.

At the gates Richard looked at them doubtfully.

'Thank you, sir,' one of them said. 'We didn't do anything wrong, sir.'

'I'll visit you again,' Rachel said. 'Get off home now.'

Richard stood by her side as they walked off down the street and then he climbed into the carriage behind her.

'Now,' he said sharply. 'What happened?'

He saw a look of satisfaction on Rachel's face as she explained. 'They are on strike for equal pay with men. We marched through Exeter. The police snatched a banner I was carrying.' Rachel laughed. 'I kicked one of them.'

'Rachel, how can you behave in such a way? It does nothing for the cause you allege you fight for.'

Rachel shrugged her shoulders. 'They are savages, Richard. All men are afraid of women getting any kind of justice.'

'That is absolute nonsense. They are simply doing their jobs. And why did you not tell me this morning where you were going? You said it was a meeting, a discussion.'

Rachel laughed again. 'It was, it just turned out differently from what I expected.'

'This kind of behaviour must cease, Rachel. I will not have you disturbing our lives in this fashion. You are becoming too extreme.'

He saw her grey eyes contemplating him coldly before she spoke. 'Richard, you are not interested in me and my beliefs. You only care about the way that I affect your life.'

He felt a deep longing for everything to be different, for Rachel not to be attached to all these new ideas, for them to have a child. He could not countenance this behaviour. 'Rachel,' he said angrily. 'I only care about you. But you are doing nothing for our marriage.'

'How dare you speak like that! You simply try to imprison me.'

'Imprison you! I have just come to release you.'

Rachel was silent for a moment. 'Well, I'm grateful for your help with the girls. But I will not give up. These things are important to me.'

When they reached home, she went straight upstairs but Richard sat in the drawing-room, drinking a cup of cocoa. Perhaps he should try to involve her more in the affairs of St Saviours. She rarely went to church with him now, she was always involved with the children at the Home, or installing another girl in the house she ran for women rescued from the workhouse.

The next day, his intention to visit the police authorities in Exeter to make a protest was vitiated by events nearer at home. A messenger arrived at the shipyard from Kingsbridge to say that his father was critically ill. He had been suffering from influenza which had developed into pneumonia.

351

He immediately went to the Children's Home but Rachel was not there. He returned to the house but she had left a message to say that she was visiting. Richard breathed a sigh of relief; the fact that she had decided to make calls, as other ladies did, must mean that she had been persuaded to return to more normal activities.

He could not wait. He asked Mrs Blake to inform Rachel that he had gone to Kingsbridge to visit his father and then went along to the Butter Walk to get the horse-bus.

He was surprised to find that James and Thomas, with his wife, were already at Mill House with Aunt Bessie and Emmie. There was the familiar air of impending death about the house. Curtains were drawn, the servants were even more silent than usual, and conversations were conducted in an exaggerated whisper.

'Is he very ill?' Richard asked.

Aunt Bessie nodded in her usual dramatic fashion. 'You had better go to him. He was asking about you.'

Richard climbed the wide staircase, accompanied by James.

'The doctor came and gave him an enema but it seems to have caused little improvement.'

As they entered the room, the doctor came over to them. 'He's asleep at the moment. Perhaps it would be better to leave him. Come up later.'

Richard and James retreated.

'I fear there may be complications,' the doctor went on as he followed them. 'Of course, he's seventy-one. A good old age, you know.'

Richard nodded. He knew that this was the doctor's way of saying there was little hope of recovery.

Aunt Emmie supervised the preparation of lunch.

'I cannot stay,' Richard said. 'I will wait until father is awake and then I must return to Dartmouth.'

'Perhaps you can return tomorrow with Rachel,' Aunt Bessie suggested. 'I know he would wish to see her.'

'Perhaps,' Richard said doubtfully.

He had never recovered from his first experience of death when he was a child. At every funeral, he was always re-living that of his mother; every death re-awakened that old pain.

352

But the death of his father was destined to be as sudden as that of his mother. The doctor had returned to the sickroom and came down almost immediately, saying apologetically, 'I am afraid you are too late, Richard. Your dear father has passed on. He knew nothing. He did not suffer any pain.'

The ladies burst into tears and followed the men up the stairs. They all stood in silence, contemplating the stern face with the white beard trailing across the sheets. Then they crept from the room and down the stairs.

'Now,' Aunt Bessie said. 'Would you all like me to attend to the domestic arrangements?'

Richard listened to the busy conversation which now ensued between the ladies. Thomas's wife Felicity agreed to attend to the flowers, Aunt Emmie would deal with the funeral supper, James and Thomas would arrange for the carriages and organise the service.

'I'll deal with all the cards and invitations,' Aunt Bessie concluded.

'I can remain here for the rest of today,' Richard said, 'I'll attend to the Registrar and any other official requirements.'

After going down into Kingsbridge to register the death and visit the undertaker, he went upstairs alone to his father's room. Looking down at the old man, his thoughts returned to Rachel. He had thought that men knew little about women, but did one ever really know anything about anyone? What had he known of his father? What were the real thoughts that had gone on in that venerable head? His father had appeared to be a clear, definite personality. Consistent, opinionated, harsh, even. Yet how had he felt inside himself? Had he seen himself like that?

It was almost midnight once again when he returned to Dartmouth. He had taken his father's carriage with the intention of returning to Kingsbridge the next day with Rachel. As he drove along the embankment and up Crowther's Hill, he saw smoke rising above him. He frowned anxiously. Was it his house? He whipped the horses into a gallop and turned into the drive. A crowd of people surrounded the house and, before them, he saw the fire-carriage. There was a pall of smoke coming from a window on the ground floor but the remainder of the house seemed to be unaffected.

He sprang from the carriage and dashed up to the firemen. 'What is it? What's happened?' People were pushing past them, throwing buckets of water through the open window as he stood there, confused.

'It's under control, sir,' one of the fireman said. 'Fire started in the downstairs. A real conflagration when we arrived. We controlled it,' he said proudly.

'Yes,' Richard said impatiently. 'Where is my wife?' He rushed into the house. A smell of burning greeted him. He peered into the drawing-room. Most of the furniture was demolished. The walls were black, the curtains hung in black strips from the windows.

'It's out now,' Richard shouted. 'Tell them to stop throwing water.' He looked at the pools of brown water floating across the carpet.

'Wanted to make sure,' the fireman said.

'Where is Mrs Damarell?' Richard repeated. He looked into the dining-room. Then he saw Rachel coming down the stairs. 'Rachel, are you all right?' He looked at her pale face and dishevelled hair.

She hurried towards him. 'Richard,' she said anxiously. 'I saw them. It was deliberate.'

'What do you mean?'

Rachel pointed angrily towards the windows. 'I was standing in the drawing-room and I saw three men in the shadows. I went over to the window to see what they wanted.'

'Why didn't you call the maids?' Richard remonstrated.

'How could I? It all just happened. I opened the window and one of them threw a lighted flare in. I ran back and then they threw more in. They could have killed me, Richard.'

Richard strode back into the hall. 'Who started this?' he demanded.

A fireman looked at him blankly. 'We don't know, sir. There was no one here when we arrived.'.

'We'll have to find out more about this.'

Suddenly, Rachel burst into tears. Richard put an arm around her. 'Come. It's all right.' He had not seen her cry since she was a child; even when she had left, long ago, for London. 'Let's go into the library. Here, sit down.' He called for Elsie to make her a hot drink of rum and lemon and asked, 'Did you see who it was, Rachel? I will call the police.'

Rachel hesitated. 'Yes, I know,' she said slowly. 'But we can't report them.'

'What do you mean?' Richard looked at her in disbelieve. 'Of course we'll report them. They'll go to gaol for this.'

'No,' she said.

'Rachel,' he said in irritation. 'This isn't a case of defending the poor and deprived. These are dangerous men.' He watched Rachel as she stood up and walked round the room.

'They wanted to stop me.'

'Stop what, Rachel?'

'This afternoon, when I went visiting, I called on Victoria Blandish. She had agreed that we should have a meeting in her house of some of the women who wrote to me.'

'Rachel, what was the meeting about? We agreed that you should not involve yourself in such matters any more.'

Rachel tossed her head. 'We didn't agree. You decided.'

'Rachel, you lied to me. What was the meeting for?'

Rachel shrugged her shoulders. 'I simply told them a few facts about contraception.'

'Contraception!' Richard looked at her in horror. 'Rachel, women have been imprisoned for publishing information about such things.'

'If women continue to have more babies than they can support, they can never have better lives.'

'Rachel, that is for their husbands to decide.'

'No. It isn't. Their husbands treat them as mere objects to satisfy their desires.'

A feeling of despair washed over Richard. Rachel was becoming more and more impossible; their whole lives were being disrupted by her obstinacy. Richard tried to control his voice.

'Rachel, you have gone too far. All these activities must cease forthwith.'

Rachel looked at him distantly, as though his words had no meaning. 'Anyhow, I cannot inform the police. These men would probably then take it out on their wives.'

'I shall decide about that, Rachel. In the meantime, you will confine yourself to visiting the children and the girls and your lessons at the training school.'

'No. I shall not. Tomorrow, I am going to London. The new Act to prevent cruelty to children is to be debated in the House of Commons. I have arranged to go. I intend to be there.'

'Very well. You may carry out that final engagement. After that, you will confine yourself to what I have said.'

Rachel turned away in silence.

'I have some other news to tell you, Rachel.' Richard paused. 'I went to Kingsbridge because father was ill. He died this afternoon.'

Rachel turned white. 'Oh, no, Richard. Why didn't you tell me. Oh, Richard. I'm so sorry.' She came and put a hand on his arm but he brushed her aside.

'I am going again tomorrow to assist with the arrangements. I had thought that you would come, but in view of your other plans, presumably that will not be possible. I will ensure that Joseph, the coachman, and the gardener remain here to see that nothing untoward occurs. I shall return before dark.'

The next day, he walked with Rachel down to the coach. She talked to him with a quiet civility which concealed her real feelings. But what was she thinking? Did she intend to continue her provocative behaviour? She was being totally unreasonable. Every argument they had seemed to take them further and further apart. If only they could have a child, surely all their problems would be solved?

Richard felt an emptiness inside him as he walked up his father's drive. He imagined the tall figure of his father standing on the steps of the conservatory; he seemed to have been standing there for ever. As he approached the house, he saw another figure standing on the top of the steps. He frowned. It looked half-familiar yet there was something strange. Was it? Could it be? Then he knew that it was.

'Jacob,' he said in astonishment. He looked at the handsome face and tall figure. 'How did you get here so speedily?'

Jacob took his hand, smiling. 'Hello, Richard. It was only chance that I came on leave. I did not expect to come upon this misfortune.'

'You look pretty rough, Jacob. Have you been ill?'

'I was wounded in a skirmish,' Jacob said casually. 'I have come on an extended period of convalescence.' Richard held his arm lightly. 'Let us go in, Jacob.' He opened the door and followed Jacob into the conservatory.

'I'll soon recover,' Jacob said smiling again. 'It's only my leg.'

Richard sighed. He had a strange, superstitious feeling that all the recent events, Rachel being in Exeter gaol, the attack on the house, the deterioration in his marriage, their longing for a child, his father's death, Jacob's arrival, were going to culminate in some impending tragedy.

'And how is lovely Rachel?' Jacob asked slowly.

Richard saw that there was a look of pain on Jacob's face.

Chapter 19

Rachel did not turn as the pall bearers came slowly down the aisle, carrying the coffin. She stood between Bertha and Felicity, their faces hidden by their black veils. The coffin was followed by the four brothers. Richard looked straight ahead but James gave her a brief smile. Behind them came Thomas, looking uncomfortable in his tight black jacket. Then, beside him, she saw Jacob. A tremor of anxiety went through her when she saw his gaunt face. What had happened to him? Richard had told her that Jacob had been wounded, but he had said that his condition had improved. The shock of knowing that he had returned, the fears that were re-awakened in her, had plunged her into a turmoil even more violent than she had felt when he left. The fact that he had been wounded did not diminish his capacity to cause her distress.

'Sit down if you feel too distraught,' Bertha whispered.

'Funerals disturb me,' Rachel whispered back. She sat down and drew her veil lower across her face.

Listening to the solemn opening prayers of the vicar, she thought again of the loss of her own parents and little Charlotte at sea. There had been no funeral for them, they had vanished from her life without any tangible proof of their existence, but that terrible event had changed her life. Is every death also a beginning, she wondered? Was this to be another beginning, was everything to start all over again, was history to repeat itself? She heard little of the service, waiting for the four men to turn and follow the coffin from the church. As they passed, she glanced up for one moment, watching Jacob's rather bowed figure, but she did not look at his face.

It was only when they reached the house and the four brothers stood at the top of the steps, receiving the mourners for the funeral reception, that they came face to face. His dark eyes looked into hers and she formally touched his cheek with her lips.

'Hallo, Rachel. I am sorry to meet you in these circumstances,' and he turned to Felicity who was following behind her.

Rachel went on through the conservatory and down the hall into the drawing-room. Richard sat by her side at the reception but Jacob was far away down the table. Now that her hat and veil were removed, she did not dare to look at him, anticipating that the feeling of dread he had aroused in her must be evident to everyone.

'Jacob looks much worse than you had intimated,' she remarked to Richard.

'He was badly wounded, Rachel, but I did not wish to give you the impression that he was desperately ill. He already looks better than when he arrived.'

Rachel shook her head. 'He looks as though real recovery may never be possible.'

'Don't worry, Rachel,' Bertha interposed cheerfully, 'You remember what Jacob was like as a child. Full of resilience.'

'I never knew him then,' Rachel said. 'I only met him when he was quite a young man.'

She saw Richard looking at her reflectively.

'How did it happen, Richard?'

'He was wounded in a battle on the North-West Frontier. Lost a lot of blood. Then he contracted malaria.'

Richard turned away abruptly to talk to James, as though he wished to end the conversation. She realised that he had told her almost nothing about Jacob's injury, had almost given the impression that he was merely here on a vacation. Once again, she wondered if Richard had any suspicions about her feelings for Jacob. Did their recent disagreements, and his discovery of her deception, make him suspect that her story about going to London had also been a lie?

At last, she permitted herself to look across to Jacob. Their eyes met, but she looked at him as though without recognition. Then she turned away. She felt Richard's eyes on her and smiled at him. If only he could accept her as she was. If only their disagreements could end. Was he concerned for her welfare or was it merely his male attitude of superiority? She longed at that moment to take him in her arms and tell him of her love for him. Perhaps he had never been certain of that, perhaps she had never revealed her true feelings.

She did not look at Jacob again and followed Richard as the family all went from the dining-room, to assemble in the drawing-room. James, as the eldest son, stood at the top of the table for the reading of the will.

The document was long and detailed. Somehow, Rachel reflected, the old man had managed to inject the same pious tone into his will as he had into his everyday speech.

It was expected that everything would be left to the four sons and Bertha, but one aspect of its division caused a consternation which at first left them all silent. Thomas, who now had a large foundry, had expected to inherit the mill. He had lived in Kingsbridge all his life, he was the only son, apart from Richard, capable of carrying on such a project and Richard, living in Dartmouth and with a fishing business and shipyard, could not have managed such a further commitment. Instead, Thomas had been left the house, to dispose of as he saw fit; the large capital was to be shared between Richard and James; the furniture, gold, silver and antique effects, as well as the carriage and horses went to Bertha. The clause relating to the mill, with all its implements and equipment, had been left to the end. By then, everyone anticipated the answer. Only Jacob had not yet been mentioned. James looked at the final paragraph and they all saw the expression of anxiety on his face as he absorbed its contents. His voice reflected his bewilderment as he read.

The mill I leave to my respected daughter-in-law, Rachel, the wife of my son Richard. Over the years, her behaviour and determination have earned my love and respect. In my advancing years, she has given me solace. It is my hope that the proceeds of the mill may advance her many benevolent endeavours.

James paused to allow his audience to comprehend what sounded like an impossible statement. Rachel watched Thomas's look of dismay as he heard the pronouncement. She saw Felicity's pained disappointment as she looked at her husband. Then she looked at Jacob.

There was a curious, disjointed smile on his face.

'The remainder merely deals with the duties of the executors,' James said slowly. 'Do you want all that read?'

'No. We can attend to that later,' Richard said.

361

Jacob pulled himself to his feet. He was looking at Rachel with animosity.

'Well, the old man managed to surprise us in the end,' he said, laughing. 'But I wonder if it has the approval of everyone?' He looked across at Thomas. 'Thomas?'

Thomas's round, honest face had an expression of bewilderment. 'Well, I don't know. What am I going to do with this place? Dispose of it, he says. What do you think, Felicity?'

Felicity shook her head slowly.

'Well, I don't know either.' Jacob smiled. 'It seems that our dear sister-in-law has somehow managed to influence dear Papa in her favour.'

Rachel blushed, looking round at their bewildered faces. 'I had no idea,' she said uncertainly.

She felt their eyes on her, Aunt Bessie and Emmie, Uncle Jonathon, Bertha. Then she looked at Richard. 'I wonder why,' she said slowly.

'Perhaps he wished everything to be sold,' James said doubtfully. 'The house and the mill.'

'It would certainly be of some benefit to Rachel,' Jacob said sarcastically. 'Are we certain that this will is a genuine document?'

They all looked at him in surprise.

'Jacob, what are you implying?' Richard looked at him disapprovingly.

'I imply nothing, dear brother Richard. Although you also, through your wife, appear to be benefiting somewhat injudiciously.'

Rachel said slowly, 'I do not understand why Jacob has received nothing.'

Jacob laughed humourlessly. 'No. It is a mystery. Or is it that someone made allegations about me to my father? Was I painted as some kind of criminal?'

'Jacob,' Bertha said indignantly. 'How can you speak so? Perhaps as you were absent, he forgot.'

'Bertha, please do not stretch my credulity further. There is something suspicious about this whole matter.'

Aunt Bessie said in an accusing voice, 'It seems strange to me too. I always looked upon Jacob as his father's favourite.'

'It was for my father to decide how to dispose of his property,' Richard said defensively.

Jacob looked at him with a supercilious smile. 'No doubt you approve. But I do not intend to leave the matter here.'

Rachel forced herself to address Jacob. Through Mr Damarell's unexpected generosity, she felt as though her life were closing in on her. It seemed as though her options were diminished rather than expanded by it.

'Do you have an income, Jacob?'

'No, madam, I do not. Fortunately, when I have recovered, I shall be going back to my regiment. I do not expect to remain in England.'

They all looked at him in silence. As James folded up the will, he said, 'If you are dissatisfied, Jacob, I suggest that you pursue the matter with the solicitor. He will be able to advise you on the best course to follow.'

Richard stood up.

'Yes,' he said coldly. 'I will not have any insinuations made against my wife. We all have to see him next week to discuss procedures. You can voice any objections then, Jacob. Perhaps you would arrange a meeting, James. We must leave now, Rachel. We have to get the horse-bus to Kingswear.'

'Perhaps I can visit my wealthy relatives in Dartmouth,' Jacob said provocatively. 'I must come and inspect my young brother's shipyard.'

Richard nodded briefly. 'As you wish,' he said curtly.

'I am remaining here in Kingsbridge for a few days,' Bertha said in a conversational tone, ignoring the tension around her. 'To supervise the clearing-up. Perhaps I could come over one day to see you, Rachel.'

'Yes, of course, Bertha.' Rachel smiled. 'You know you are always welcome.'

Rachel followed Richard down the steps to the carriage. She sighed as they trotted away down the drive. 'I do not understand your father's Will,' she said instantly.

'No.' Richard looked perplexed. 'I can see that Jacob would feel devastated by such a thing. If my father had such feelings for you, he might still have divided the bequests. Why did he turn on Jacob in such a way?'

Rachel shook her head although the answer was on the edge of her understanding. The blame that Mr Damarell had attached to her in the past must have been transferred to Jacob. Yet how could he have discovered Jacob's responsibility in the matter? There was no one who could have told him. Her mind turned suddenly to Aunt Maria. Had she read those three letters and then re-sealed them? Would she have told him? But if she had, why were they hidden in her drawer? Why did she secretly give them to Rachel? Rachel sighed. It was useless to speculate. She would never know the answer.

'Richard do you think it is appropriate for me to accept the mill?'

'It is not a question of appropriate, Rachel. It is a legal situation. You could of course pass it on in the future, if you so wished.'

'To Jacob?'

'I don't know, Rachel. Perhaps these are matters we must discuss with the solicitor.'

'We have a sufficient income, haven't we, with the shipyard and the fishing fleet? And we have no children to whom to leave it.'

Richard frowned. He spoke almost reluctantly, as though he must make the point. 'If you spent more time at home, we might be so blessed.'

'It has nothing to do with my being at home,' Rachel sighed with irritation.

'Then what is it to do with?'

'I don't know.' Rachel shook her head dismissively and turned to look through the window at the darkening sky. Richard went on to complain that he was still concerned at her behaviour, but now she only half heard his words. In the back of her mind was the thought that if she gave the mill to Jacob, she might ensure his silence. She would no longer feel threatened by his presence. She knew now, faced by this strange crisis, that in the end the only thing that mattered to her was Richard's happiness.

The next evening, she watched through the conservatory windows as she saw a carriage coming up the drive and Bertha alighted, followed by her husband, George.

'Hallo, dear. I've so been looking forward to this,' Bertha greeted her warmly.

Rachel smiled.

'Jacob had intended to accompany us,' Bertha chattered on. 'But he changed his mind at the last minute.'

Rachel turned, concealing the anxiety she felt. Why would he wish to come after his behaviour at the funeral? George put an arm around her and kissed her politely on the cheek.

'Hallo, Rachel. You look as well as ever.'

'Thank you. Come in. I thought Jacob felt some animosity towards me after the will was read,' Rachel said casually.

George shook his head solemnly. 'It must have been a shock, but I believe he does not really blame you, Rachel.'

'No?' Rachel said hopefully.

'No doubt he and Richard will come to some accommodation.'

Rachel smiled quietly; it would not occur to George that she might have any say in the matter.

As she talked to Bertha and George at dinner and sat with them later in the drawing-room, her thoughts were dwelling on what she would do tomorrow, when they had gone and she would be free.

But Richard proposed that they should stay a further day. 'It is so good for Rachel to have some pleasant social life,' he said, smiling at her. 'I hope that in future she will be less involved in her other activities.'

He spoke the word 'other' as though she had been connected with something undesirable.

Rachel smiled. 'Bertha and George are always welcome,' she said sincerely.

Richard had departed to the shipyard when she stood on the steps in the sun the following morning, waving goodbye to them. As the carriage disappeared round the corner of the road, she dashed upstairs and changed into her pale blue silk gown and light cashmere cape. She had made her decision. She would sell the mill and give Jacob the proceeds. She could persuade Richard that this was the only ethical thing to do. As far as Jacob was concerned, it would be on the understanding that he would never return to Kingsbridge. He would go to a solicitor and sign an undertaking to that effect.

She informed Mrs Blake that she would be out for the day attending to the children and then visiting the Girls' Home. She went across in the ferry to Kingswear and an hour later was standing on the embankment at Kingsbridge. The horse-cab trundled up Church Street and beyond Waterloo Place to Mill House.

She walked slowly up the drive. The house seemed deserted and lonely. She sat down on a garden seat, looking across the hills bathed in sunshine. Could she trust Jacob to keep to such an agreement? Would he leave her in peace? He had stated his intention to go away again. He would never settle here. Perhaps he would never settle anywhere.

Her thoughts turned to Richard. She knew she was doing this for him; in spite of their problems, she knew she must protect him for ever from her past, from Jacob's possible treachery.

Gertie opened the door and looked at her in surprise. 'Oh, Mrs Damarell. How nice to see you.'

'Hello, Gertie.' Rachel smiled. 'How are you?'

'Oh, very well, ma'am.' She looked around uncertainly. 'I'm afraid Mr James and Mr Thomas are at work.'

'Yes, of course. Is Mr Jacob not here?'

Gertie looked taken aback, as though she had forgotten about him. 'Oh, of course. Mr Jacob. No, ma'am. He's gone up to the mill.'

'Oh, has he?' Rachel hesitated. Of course, Gertie would know nothing about the will and the disposal of the property. At least, officially.

'Well,' Rachel said casually, 'perhaps I could have a cup of tea and I will call again another day when I am in the vicinity.'

'Oh, yes, ma'am.'

Gertie brought the tea, followed by Maggie and Lizzie, who had been informed of Rachel's arrival. She knew she had formed a bond with these girls in childhood; it was almost, she thought, a friendship. She considered telling them that her visit must be kept a secret, that she did not want it mentioned. However, some deeper instinct told her that she could not indulge in such behaviour with servants.

'Shall I ask Joseph to call a horse-cab, ma'am?' Gertie asked as she prepared to leave.

'No, Gertie. It is a lovely day. I shall walk to the coach station.'

They watched her walk down the drive and when she knew she was out of sight, she turned up the hill towards the mill. As she left the houses behind and turned into the country lane, she felt a sense of foreboding. What was Jacob doing at the mill? Had he really wanted it? How was that possible? He had, after all, left it so long ago.

She walked slowly between the tall hedges. The heat cast a haze over the hills, the smell of wild flowers and thyme surrounded her. The sun pervaded everything. It was a golden day. She saw the mill in the distance. Her heart began to beat faster. She noticed a few men in the distance, hauling large sacks of grain. She had forgotten about them. Of course, the mill was still working. Thomas had told her the foreman was in charge and reported to him each day. She stood still, looking. Was Jacob there?

The men disappeared from sight as she rounded a corner in the lane. Then the lane straightened out again and Jacob was walking slowly towards her, his eyes on the ground. Seeing him, the solitary figure against the background of the mill and the rising hills and the great expanse of the sky, she was aware only of his frailty. He was still like a child, wanting to be noticed, wanting to be loved; a child unable to reach adulthood and accept any responsibility. Like a child, he was also dependent and she knew from her own experience that his father's rejection must be proving impossible for Jacob to accept.

He looked up suddenly and saw her. She stopped.

'Hallo, Jacob.'

He came slowly towards her.

'I wish to talk to you.'

There was a cold, distant look in his eyes. 'Sit here,' he said abruptly, pointing to a bench in front of the hedge. 'My leg is troublesome in the heat.'

Rachel sat down at the end of the seat.

'We used to play here when we were children,' Jacob said inconsequentially. 'This was a ship and I was always the captain.'

'Jacob, I wish to make a proposition.'

'Indeed. That is a pleasant prospect.' A smile hovered around Jacob's lips.

Rachel ignored his remark. 'Jacob, I am willing to pass the proceeds of the mill to you if you will give me a certain guarantee.'

Jacob slowly turned his head and looked at her assessingly. He nodded thoughtfully, as though he were trying to make some sense of her remark.

'And what might that be?' he asked quietly.

'That you will never return to Kingsbridge.'

He paused. 'Not even for a funeral?' he asked sarcastically.

Rachel blushed. 'Well, that might be an exception.'

'And why, may I ask, do you have this aversion to my presence here?'

Rachel frowned. She had intended to be aloof and remote, but her fears about his return had been with her for so long, her anxiety so excessive, that she could not prevaricate.

'You know quite well why, Jacob. I am afraid you may say something which would destroy my marriage.'

'Well! Last time we spoke, you expressed the view that you feared nothing that I could do. What has happened to change that?'

'Nothing has happened. But I think you have some malicious intent towards me.'

Jacob was silent. He looked thoughtfully into the distance and then back at Rachel. 'Well,' he finally said, speaking carefully as though he found it difficult to contain his feelings. 'You do seem to have forgotten that last meeting. Do you not remember my final words?'

'You hoped Richard and I would be happy.'

'Ah, you do recall.'

'Jacob,' Rachel suddenly spoke urgently. 'I could not allow Richard to be hurt.'

Jacob raised his eyebrows. 'And why should he be, Rachel?' He spoke in the same urgent tone which she had used. 'I have no wish to come between you. Have I said or done anything to imply that?'

'No. Not this time. But in the past.'

'The past, the present, of what interest is that to you?' He spoke with a cutting emphasis.

Rachel looked at him with a confused expression. What did he mean? 'Then you will not cause trouble—'

He turned on her angrily. 'I, cause trouble? And what have you done to me, Rachel? What have you done to my life?'

She stood up, fearing that he would strike her. 'I regret the business about the mill but I have offered—'

'The mill? It has nothing to do with the mill. Don't you know what's wrong with you?' he went on bitterly. 'You don't fear me. It's your own deception that worries you. You're the one who deceived Richard, not me. You only fear me because I could reveal your dishonesty, not mine. And now you think you can buy me off with a nice little present of the mill. Well, I don't want it. You can keep it. And you can go on blaming me for your own guilt.'

Rachel stared at him for a moment. It was as though he had removed a barrier from her mind and there, beneath her fear and animosity, lay the truth. Jacob was not responsible for her anxiety. In fact, it was nothing to do with him. It was herself she feared. She shuddered.

Their eyes met.

'Yes. You are right.' Then she added, 'I do not blame you, Jacob.'

The animosity had gone from his voice as he said, 'We make our own decisions, Rachel.'

Rachel turned abruptly and began to walk quickly down the lane. As soon as she rounded the corner, she began to run until she reached Fore Street. She hurried on down the hill and threw herself into the horse-bus just as it was leaving.

Jacob's words turned in her mind. It was her own guilt that disturbed her peace of mind. There was her answer. She realised too late that she had taken the wrong horse-bus, one which went around the villages before reaching Kingsbridge. When she reached Dartmouth it was already dusk and she hurried along the almost deserted streets. She had told Mrs Blake that she was going to the Girls' Home but Richard would be worried after recent events.

When she arrived at the house, Mrs Blake came to the door. 'Oh, ma'am, we've been waiting for you.'

'Why? What's happened, Mrs Blake?'

'There was a message from Mr James in Kingsbridge.'

'James?' Rachel frowned, trying to collect her thoughts.

'There was an accident at the mill. It was Mr Jacob, miss.'

Rachel felt her body tense. 'Yes?'

'He's been taken to the hospital in Kingsbridge. Mr Damarell has gone over, ma'am.'

'Mrs Blake, what happened?'

'He said it was something to do with the machinery. Something crashed down on Mr Jacob. Mr James didn't know why he was there.'

'Was it serious, Mrs Blake?' Rachel closed her eyes.

She heard Mrs Blake's voice as though from a distance. 'Yes, ma'am. Mr Damarell said I was to tell you without frightening you.'

'Yes?'

'It seems he was crushed, ma'am, and by the time they got to him, it was too late to do anything.'

369

Rachel tugged at the neck of her gown. 'It's so hot in here, Mrs Blake.'

'Here, ma'am. Let me have your coat. Come and sit down, ma'am.' She took Rachel's arm and led her into the drawing-room. 'There. I'll go and get you a nice hot drink. It will make you sleep.'

'I'm so hot, Mrs Blake.'

'I expect that's just the shock. You just wait here.'

When she was gone, Rachel began to shiver. She did not try to formulate any thoughts; it was as though the future was waiting for her. She felt as though the events of the past few days had laid her life bare. It was too late now. She knew now what she had to do.

Mrs Blake returned almost immediately, saying, 'Here you are, my dear. Drink this. Then you must get to bed.'

'No, Mrs Blake. I'll wait for Richard to come back.'

'Mr Damarell said for you not to wait for him, ma'am.'

Rachel smiled bleakly. 'It's all right, Mrs Blake. Put a light to the fire. I feel chilly now. I'll just wait for a while.'

'Very well, ma'am,' Mrs Blake said reluctantly. 'Call if you need me.'

Rachel watched the flames slowly circling round the logs. She settled down to await Richard's return.

Chapter 20

Rachel was awakened by a cold hand on her cheek.
'What are you doing here, Rachel?'

She looked into Richard's tired eyes. 'I was waiting for you. What time is it?'

'Five o'clock. It's almost light. You should have gone to bed.'

There was an expression of gratitude on his face that she had waited for him. Momentarily she felt the burden of the decision she had made. There was no going back. It had to be done.

'I was too upset and worried about you. How did it happen, Richard?'

He shook his head but did not reply to her question. 'I went to the hospital with James. Then to the coroner. There has to be an inquest, of course.'

'Oh, I hadn't thought.'

Richard hesitated. 'James and I went up to the mill.'

'Yes?'

'I don't see how it was an accident, Rachel.'

Rachel frowned uncomprehendingly. 'What do you mean?'

'He was lying on the ground beneath the tower.'

'But Mrs Blake said he had been . . . crushed.' Rachel closed her mind to the spectacle of some gigantic piece of machinery falling on him.

'That was the incoherent message I got. But I think that was just some kind of speculation amongst the workmen.'

'Then what—?'

'I think he must have fallen.'

'Fallen, Richard? But how?'

'If he went up to the tower and leaned over, he could have over-balanced. It's a stone staircase to get up there, but the

371

stairs are inside, so he couldn't have fallen from those.'

Rachel tried to imagine the tower. 'But there's quite a high wall round the edge, isn't there?'

'Three feet.'

'Do you think he got giddy or something?'

Richard shook his head uncertainly.

'But why would he go up there, Richard?'

Richard said slowly, 'There isn't an answer, Rachel. I suppose there won't be.'

'Richard, you don't think—'

'I don't know, Rachel. I can't believe that Jacob would take his own life.' Then he turned to her suddenly. 'What do you think, Rachel?'

She looked at him in astonishment. 'Me? How can I know, Richard? Perhaps he was upset about your father.'

Richard nodded vaguely. 'You need some sleep,' he said suddenly.

'And you, Richard. There'll be time to think about this.'

He followed her up the stairs. Why had he asked that question; was there still, even now, some doubt in his mind about her feelings for Jacob? Had someone seen her with Jacob this afternoon?

Anyhow, she would now have to wait until the Inquest was over to carry out her decision. When that was done, she would have to leave Kingsbridge for ever. It was impossible to place Richard in that situation at this moment. Richard had enough to deal with.

The Inquest took place three days later in the large first floor room of the Castle Hotel. The coroner sat on the dais before them and when he recognised Rachel, he nodded gravely. She imagined that she saw an expression of suspicion on his face, an inherent disapproval.

It was a hot afternoon, and the sun blazed through the windows on the packed hall. She could hear the voices of the crowd gathered outside; the circumstances of Jacob's sudden death had created the usual village gossip and speculation. James had told her that news of the will had somehow leaked out and an anonymous letter had been delivered to Mill House, alleging that Jacob's death was linked with Rachel's acquisition of the mill. She had robbed him of his birthright.

Bertha was sitting on her right, dressed in a black velvet gown and black shawl. James and Thomas sat on her left and Aunt Bessie and other relatives sat further along the row behind her.

The coroner was a thin grey-haired man with two teeth missing in the front. He had a habit of stretching his lips, not in a smile, but as though to test the resilience of his flesh, so that the two gaps made him look like some heinous Frankenstein. He appeared to be heavily impressed with the importance and responsibility of the task ahead. His voice was slow and flat like an untuned piano.

'The business of this enquiry is to ascertain the circumstances under which the deceased, Jacob Damarell, an officer in Her Majesty's Guards, met his death on Thursday 25 July last. We are concerned to establish the facts and you' – his eyes turned to the row of fourteen men and women seated in two rows on his right – 'members of the jury, must listen to the evidence of the witnesses and make your judgment of those facts.'

Rachel unbuttoned her gown at the neck. The air was becoming suffocating. Someone asked if the windows could be opened, but the coroner said that the noise of the crowd outside, plus the distraction of carriages and boats' sirens, might impede the ability of the jury to hear clearly or to concentrate. The windows must remain closed.

Mr Ralph Palfreman was the first witness to be called. He was the official doctor who had examined the deceased after death. The coroner asked Mr Palfreman to give his findings.

'The deceased had a severe wound on the back of the head. His skull had been cracked and he had multiple injuries to his spine.'

'In your opinion, was this the cause of death?'

'There is no doubt about it.'

'Did you form an opinion as to what had occurred?'

'Death was consistent with someone falling from a great height.'

'Have you any evidence as to whether this was an accident or a deliberate action on the deceased's part?'

Mr Palfreman frowned. 'It is impossible to say. The speed of descent will be the same whether someone jumps or falls. The force of impact will also be the same.'

'There is no question in your mind that the deceased could have been pushed.'

Mr Palfreman shrugged. 'Of course, he could have been. But in my opinion that would be unjustifiable speculation.'

'Did you form any opinion as to what, if the deceased fell, could have caused such an event?'

'It is possible that he fainted. The discomfort from his leg could cause such a result, I suppose.'

'Suppose, Mr Palfreman?'

'Yes. It could happen.'

'If an individual falls suddenly in a faint, would you expect him to fall over a three foot wall?'

'It depends upon the position in which he was standing.' Mr Palfreman hesitated then he added reluctantly. 'He would probably be more likely to fall backwards.'

'Thank you, Mr Palfreman.'

The coroner then called the solicitor whom Richard had engaged to attend the inquest.

'Do you have any questions, Mr Barnden?'

Mr Barnden was a tall, thin man with a monocle and a quiet voice.

'Mr Palfreman, were you previously acquainted with the deceased?'

'No. I am not a local doctor.'

'Were you aware that he was already a sick and ailing man?'

'No, sir. I was not.'

'Did you not know that he had been severely wounded in Afghanistan and it was feared by his relatives that it might still prove fatal.'

'I knew that he had an impaired leg.'

'Could not that have caused him to stumble and fall from the tower?'

'It could have done.'

'If you had realised that this man was in a considerable amount of pain, that he had been already weakened by the past loss of blood, that he suffered from some kind of malarial sickness, would that have led you to conclude that he might have fainted?'

'It is more likely than if he had been well.'

'Would not his appearance have given you cause for concern and suggested to you that such might be the case?'

'When I saw the deceased, the injuries he had received would have been sufficient to give him a haggard appearance, which is what I observed.'

'And there was no other evidence which suggested he had suffered the injuries from anything other than the fall?'

'No, there was not.'

'Regarding the suggestion that he could have been pushed, was there any evidence of a struggle?'

'Not that I could see. There was no evidence to suggest a struggle of any kind.'

'Thank you, Mr Palfreman.'

Rachel looked anxiously at Richard. Why were they asking all these questions? Richard smiled at her comfortingly.

'Don't be upset, Rachel,' he whispered. 'They have to ask these questions to establish the cause of death. It's a legal formality.'

The coroner called the next witness. This was the workman who had found Jacob.

'Mr Dodds, may I have your account of the events of the afternoon of Thursday 25 July.'

The workman related how he had walked round the side of the mill and come upon Mr Damarell's body. He had heard and seen nothing previously. After sending an urgent message into Kingsbridge to get a doctor and the ambulance he went back to Mr Damarell. Yes, he knew that Mr Damarell was already dead. He saw that the door leading up to the tower was open.

'Had you seen anyone else in the vicinity of the mill that day?'

It was only at that moment that Rachel realised the implications of the questions. If it were known that she had been with him, she could be thought responsible for his suicide. It could even be suggested that she had caused his death. Rachel clenched her hands together to control her panic. Surely, no one had seen them. She had told Gertie that she was going straight back to Dartmouth.

'Are you all right, Rachel?' Richard asked anxiously, noticing her expression.

She nodded.

'Would you like to leave? Does it distress you?'

'Yes. But no, I'll stay.'

She looked at the workman. What had been his reply to the coroner's question?

'I saw him walk off down the lane,' the workman was saying. 'And then he came back again about half an hour later.'

'He was alone?'

'Yes, sir.'

'Did he speak to you?'

'He said something about the heat, sir. I asked him if he'd like a cup of tea, but he said something about he was leaving soon. He didn't need anything.'

'Did he seem quite composed, Mr Dodds?'

'Yes, sir. Mr Damarell was always cheerful. But he seemed a bit tired with the heat. I thought it was his leg giving him trouble.'

'Did you see where he went?'

'No, sir. I went on to the yard. I thought he'd gone. I didn't see him again until I found him.'

The coroner nodded. 'Thank you, Mr Dodds.'

James then gave a brief submission that he had gone with the ambulance to the mill and escorted his dead brother to the hospital. He confirmed that Jacob had seemed his normal self when James left for work that morning. Yes, he had an equable and cheerful temperament. No, he thought it more than improbable that his brother would have taken his own life.

No more witnesses were called and after a brief consideration, the jury returned a verdict of death by misadventure. The coroner expressed his sympathy for the relatives of the deceased and they left the hotel in a silent procession.

As they climbed into their carriage, Rachel had a picture of Jacob, standing on the tower. Had he committed suicide? Was it her fault? He had said his leg was troubling him, he had looked ill ever since he returned, surely it was an accident. She glanced at Richard, looking pale and exhausted beside her. He smiled briefly.

'It's over now, Rachel.'

'Yes.'

She took his hand, longing to comfort him. Their arguments and disagreements about her activities, the frustrations she had felt, now seemed to have no relevance. She felt only admiration and gratitude for all he had tried to do for her. She remembered again how he had helped her after Jacob had gone away, how he had given her the money to go to London; how he had accepted her story when she returned. How he had supported her just because he loved her. It was only now, when she knew that soon she would be leaving, that she knew how important he was to her. Would he realise that she was telling him the truth after all this time because she loved him? He would never know how much she cared. She saw that her revelation would simply convince him that it was Jacob she had loved. He could never accept what had happened, in any case.

Rachel walked with him along the garden path. It was now. She had decided. She could feel the beating of her heart as she climbed the steps. The house was silent and deserted except for the servants. None of the relatives had returned with them.

Mrs Blake brought a tray of tea. Richard stood by the fireplace, his elbow resting on the marble mantelpiece. Rachel hesitated. In the back of her mind was the realisation that, now that Jacob was gone, there was no need for her to tell Richard at all. She knew with a sense of shame that she had been aware of this fact from the moment of Jacob's death. Was there any need, any point, in resurrecting the past? Suddenly, another thought came into her mind. What she intended to do was not for Richard's sake but for her own. With Jacob's death, the fear of betrayal had been removed. Only the guilt remained. By telling Richard the truth, she would absolve her feeling of guilt by passing the burden to him. It was Richard who would suffer, not her.

If she really loved him, all that mattered was Richard's happiness, their life together. She walked over to him.

'Dear Richard, you look exhausted.'

Richard put an arm around her, saying, 'Jacob's death has made me realise how uncertain life is, Rachel.'

'There are a few certainties, Richard.'

'Perhaps at the moment there seem to be very few.'

Rachel smiled at him. 'Well, there is one, Richard. I know that you are the most important thing in my life.'

'I could not live without you, Rachel.' Richard looked into her eyes.

Rachel looked at him doubtfully. Why had he said that? Had he somehow been aware of her intention to leave?

Her fingers caressed his face.

'There would be nowhere to go without you, Richard.'

Richard stroked her hair, seeming to hesitate. Then he said slowly, 'Was there ever somewhere else for you, Rachel?'

She looked at him intently. 'No, Richard. There was only you.'

There was a strange, quiet expression on his face, as though he was suddenly at peace with himself.

Rachel smiled as he drew her towards him.